ThiGMOO

ThiGMOO

EUGENE BYRNE

EARTHLIGHT

LONDON · SYDNEY · NEW YORK · TOKYO · SINGAPORE · TORONTO

www.earthlight.co.uk

First published in Great Britain by Earthlight, 1999
An imprint of Simon & Schuster UK Ltd
A Viacom Company

Simon & Schuster UK Ltd
Africa House
64-78 Kingsway
London
WC2B 6AH

Simon & Schuster Australia
Sydney

A CIP catalogue record for this book is available
from the British Library

ISBN 0-671-02862-6

1 3 5 7 9 10 8 6 4 2

Typeset in 10/12.5pt Melior by
SX Composing DTP, Rayleigh, Essex

Printed and bound in Great Britain by
Caledonian International Book Manufacturing, Glasgow

For Monique

Prologue

Daniel Singleton was polishing the bar when a robot wearing only scanty satin underwear came in and demanded a pig's trotter.

The Regional Manager was due to pay his weekly visit to the Deptford unit in half an hour and Daniel knew there was nothing in the company's Operations Manual about dealing with sex-dolls.

She (it?) had dark hair, cut in a bob. There were red velvet hearts on the crotch of her black silk panties. Her enormous rubber and silicone breasts coated with cultured epidermis heaved beneath a black lace brassiere beneath which nipples pushed out like thimbles.

'Wot you looking at, then cheeky?' she said in a coarse Cockney-ish accent that didn't fit her otherwise classy appearance.

Daniel was twenty-two years old. This was his first job, which he had held down for exactly six weeks. Promotion in the Good Time Bar 'n' Barbie chain was quick for promising young trainee managers. Redundancy for screw-ups was a lot quicker.

'Oh, I know what's bothering you!' screeched the robot. She smiled and reached into her stupendous cleavage, pulling out a small wallet full of credit cards. She also got out a man's gold wrist-organiser, a pair of gentleman's emerald stud earrings and an automatic pistol. She slammed them down on the bar.

'See? Got plenty of tin, 'aven't I just? Now you be a good fellow and get me a pig's trotter and a bottle of gatter and I'll just sit over in the corner all on me lonesome. Won't bother any of your other customers, and that's a promise, ducks.'

It was nine on a Tuesday morning. There weren't any other customers yet. Fortunately.

He was going to say he was sorry, and that it wasn't company policy to serve robots, and that they didn't have any pig's trotters, whatever they were (he could imagine). But what he actually said was, 'a bottle of what?'

She raised her eyes heavenwards and sighed. 'Gatter. Jacky. Satin . . . Mother's ruin.'

Daniel shook his head.

'Gin, dearie, gin.'

Gin? Pointlessly, he queried the stock function on the till.

'Sorry, we don't serve that. I can do you Japanese or Russian beer, 22 different types of coffee, or there's tequila, vodka . . .'

'Whatever,' she said. 'I'll have a large glass of ardent spirits, and look lively with that pig's foot, will you?'

'Pig's foot?' he said. 'Is that some sort of cocktail?'

She leaned forward, shamelessly jiggling her breasts half a metre from his nose. Her eyelids were heavily lined with mascara, or something. The Egyptian look had been big a couple of years ago, presumably when she had been manufactured.

'No dearie,' she shook her head, 'a pig's foot is a pig's foot. It's what pigs use for walking with. The pork butcher cuts them off, and *hestablishments* . . .' She strangulated her vowels as she pronounced the last word, to let him know she was being sarcastic. '. . . such as this cooks 'em and serves 'em to honest, hardworking girls like me.'

'I could do you a saveloy and mustard . . .'

What the hell was he saying? He was talking about serving a bloody sex-robot, a piece of machinery made for dirty old men. The regional manager would be here in twenty-five minutes and he hadn't finished the inventory of paper napkins and cocktail sticks yet!

'Look, I'm sorry,' he said, 'but company policy forbids me from serving you.'

'How's that, then?' she said. 'Is your *hestablishment* . . .' that word again '. . . too grand for the likes of me? *Honi soit qui mal y pense*, I always says dearie,' she said, leaning forward and playfully pinching his cheek.

'You what?'

'Evil be who evil thinks. It's the motto of the order of the garter.' She let out a lecherous cackle and pointed to the top of the stocking on her left thigh.

'It's nothing personal, but . . .'

She leaned across the bar again. 'I have some very influential friends,' she said quietly, and tapped the side of her nose. 'Look.' She pointed to the little pearl-handled pistol among the valuables she had deposited on the bar.

Etched into the gun's chrome-plating in curly handwriting were the words, PRESENTED TO THE REVEREND NORRIS VILE BY THE CAMPAIGN FOR FAMILY VALUES AND CHRISTIAN PURITY.

'Norrie Vile is a very good friend of mine,' she said. 'Your boss wouldn't want to make the Reverend gentleman angry, now would he?'

Daniel gulped. The Reverend Vile was London's best-known VRvangelist, always going on about the evils of sex, drugs and pornography and saying how men should be head of the family and start taking responsibility for their wives and children. One word to the regional manager from Norris Vile and Daniel could kiss goodbye to any chance of being able to take responsibility for cleaning toilets, let alone looking after a wife or kiddie.

Then again, this robot might have stolen all this stuff from him. It didn't seem likely that he'd just give her all his cards, his organiser and his personal side-arm, did it?

Either way, he was in trouble.

She drummed her fingers on the bar. He couldn't help admiring the workmanship that went into these modern dolls. The fingers of her left hand would be useless, but they needed good fingers on one hand to be able to . . . well. Their mouths and other bits were supposed to be very authentic, too. At least, that's what they said in the ads.

She was whistling quietly. A lot of design work would have gone into those lips, too.

'What do you want food and a drink for anyway?' he heard himself almost pleading. 'It's not as if you actually need to eat and drink. And besides, you won't be able to consume them properly.'

'Course I can, ducks,' she cackled. 'Me mouth is specially built for swallowing small amounts of fluids. Aye, and sucking on big lumps of gristle . . .'

The Regional Manager was coming. She was something to do with the Reverend Vile. He desperately tried to do as they'd told them on the management training course. Welcome a challenge like an old friend, they'd said (just before the shamanic drumming workshop). Challenge makes us stronger. Solve the problem and feel better about yourself . . .

'Look,' said Daniel. 'If I serve you, do you promise to be out of here in fifteen minutes?'

'Trust me, dearie. All I want's a bit of sustenance. Is there anything I can do for you in return?' She licked her lips and made sucking noises.

'No. Just be out of here by nine-twenty and it's on the house.' He'd have to pay for it himself but it'd be worth it.

'That's very kind of you. You're a proper gent, you are.'

He poured her a double of the cheapest Polish tequila and punched up a saveloy and mustard from the kitchen drudge while she pulled herself on to one of the stools. Even though she was obviously a top-of-the-range model, the designers hadn't paid too much attention to the legs. They were not, after all, supposed to be used for walking with.

Once she was on the stool she knocked back the tequila in one and put the glass back on the bar.

'More please!'

It wasn't worth arguing with her. He poured her another while the door from the kitchen hoist went 'ping'. He took out the steaming sausage and placed it in front of her.

She picked it up, looked at it suspiciously then pushed it, whole, into her mouth and began to chew. She took the drink and poured it in on top of the saveloy.

'Gorblimey strike a light!' she screeched through a mouth full of food she could not possibly swallow, 'this is good stuff and no mistake, landlord.'

Wisps of smoke rose from her ears, one of her eyes popped and a fizzing noise came from her throat. Sparks and black smoke shot out of her nostrils and with a very loud 'bang!' the top of her head shot off. Her hair skittered across the polished floor like a frightened terrier.

She spat out the half-chewed sausage. Daniel ducked in time to see it strike the mirror behind the bar with an obscene 'splat!', then slide down to rest in a bowl of cocktail-cherries.

He stood up again to see toxic black smoke rising from the hole at the top of her head. In her empty eye-socket a red light flashed on and off and a noise like popping corn rattled from her chest.

She fell from her stool and landed on the floor, flat on her back, with her arms stretched up in the air and her legs wide open.

Daniel grabbed the fire-extinguisher, vaulted over the bar and smothered her in foam.

There was no more smoke. She was quite motionless, but from somewhere in her throat, she repeated, very loudly, over and over, 'I belong to the Reverend Norris Vile, I belong to the Reverend Norris Vile, I belong to the Reverend Norris Vile, Lordy, how I *belong* to the Reverend!!'

The Regional Manager would arrive in fifteen minutes. Daniel tried very hard to welcome the problem like an old friend.

Is everything to your satisfaction thus far, John?

Actually, it's Sir *John. I realise that titles are out of vogue these days, but I bloody well worked for my knighthood, so I'm damn well going to wear it, and if the lower orders want to put me up against a wall and shoot me for it, well let 'em.*

As you know, Thigmoo doesn't really approve of feudal honorifics. We believe in equality.

Myles, nothing is ever going to convince me that you are my equal. Do you want me to do this or not?

Very well, Sir John it is. We are all in favour of free speech. What do you think of the story so far?

I have no opinion at all. What was all that about, anyway?

A prologue. It is a perfectly common literary practice and also a common usage in motion pictures. The viewers are shown a dramatic sequence in order to titillate their interest and silence their chattering. They are then subjected to some loud music and are forced to spend three and a half minutes reading the names of the actors, director, producer and several technicians.

I see. Well, far be it from me to question your craft, but this isn't exactly what I thought you'd be doing.

What, precisely, had you anticipated, my dear Sir John?

I don't know, something a bit more factual. Something rather more intellectually rigorous.

I must protest. My prologue is entirely factual. Well, substantially factual. There is a branch of the Good Time Bar 'n' Barbie Chain in Deptford, and a high-quality sex-doll, colloquially known, I believe, as a screwbot, did indeed enter the establishment demanding gin and a pig's trotter. This would have been two years ago.

And the Duty Manager's name was Daniel Singleton?

I fear not. That, my dear Sir John, was artistic licence, as were my allusions to the imminent visit of the Regional Manager. I considered that to be a rather deft method of adding a little tension to the proceedings. The real duty manager was a woman in her early thirties named Colette Greene, who had worked for the company for five years. I, however, sought to endow the story with more dramatic impact by having the sex-doll bothering a young and impressionable male who had no idea how to react. In actual fact, Ms Greene refused to serve the doll anything and gave her what she referred to as the Bum's Rush. Thereupon the doll promenaded up and down the street outside and gave away the Reverend gentleman's possessions to passers-by and announced loudly that she was his especial sweetheart, his only true love.

So that stuff about her belonging to an evangelist was true?

Of course it was! Do you not remember? He filed suits against you for defamation, negligence and theft.

Oh God, him! Yes, I remember now. Bloody hypocrite. I'm glad we stood up to him.

The episode destroyed his career for good. He now makes but a mean living – by servicing the robots which clean people's windows, I believe.

Serves the dirty old sod right. I mean, not only does he own a sex-robot in the first place . . .

Quite. The model, I believe, was based on the physique of Ms Demi Moore, a motion picture star of some years ago. It would have been manufactured in a sweatshop in Wales; I understand that such companies evade the copyright laws which now attach to the physical characteristics of the famous, by altering them slightly. The model known as a Quavering Demi is blessed with an *embonpoint* rather more impressive than Ms Moore's already generously proportioned, ah . . .

. . . hooters?

If you wish to put it so crudely.

. . . but that he tried to download the personality of an East End tart, circa 1902, into its brain, from an academic resource. The bloody cheek of it. I've a good mind to seek him out and shove one of his window-cleaning robots, squeegee and all, up his sancti-monious . . .

Come, come, Sir John. It's not as if he were the only man to borrow from the Museum of the Mind for purposes which were not strictly educational. The personality of Miss Nelly Cocksedge was popular all across the English-speaking world. The only difference was that most of the screwbots to which she was downloaded were unable to get down stairs once they'd stolen the punter's cash, cards and jewellery. It is difficult to build a robot which is capable of negotiating stairs.

I don't get it. I mean, Nelly Cocksedge was a fully-functional eram, but we didn't bother teaching her anything perverse. What would have been the point? She was in the Museum of the Mind as an exhibit of social, not sexual, history.

One does not imagine that the pathetic fools who jacked her into their toys realised that. I imagine that they thought she had been programmed with all the fabulous secrets of the Kamasutra and the other ancient works of oriental pornographia. Perhaps they believed her capable of introducing them to all of the lubricious delights of the harem and geisha-house.

The only tricks of the trade she knew involved waiting until they were asleep, pinching their valuables and leaving.

Quite so, Sir John, quite so.

All right, what are we doing now, then?

Would you like to hear my introduction?

If I must.

Ready?

Get on with it, then.

At the time of writing, there have been several accounts made available to the public of the triumph of Thigmoo. Most of these have been prepared by media professionals or by erams within Thigmoo and have employed up-to-date technology. To the best of my knowledge, however, no one has attempted to write a book about these momentous events.

As a professional writer and man of letters . . .

Harrumph!

I beg your pardon, Sir John?

Oh, nothing.

Come, come, Sir John. It will not do for there to be any misunderstandings or secrets between us this early in our collaboration. If you have any reservations, please tell me.

Well, your description of yourself as 'professional writer and man of letters' is a bit rich. You are going to tell the readers that you are a hack writer of Victorian pornography, aren't you? I'd hate them to believe you were Henry James.

Like the Quavering Demi screwbot said, Sir John, *honi soit qui mal y pense.* I am an artist. Your description of me as a hack pornographer is only too cruelly accurate but this was because I had to write to earn a living. I never had the time or the financial means to finish anything better. My best-known works are, alas, footnotes in histories of the Victorian *demi-monde.* For all that, I think there is literary merit in some of my novels, such as *Tilly and the Great Turk* and *Vera the Virgin Veers from the Straight and Narrow.* Had I not died of the consumption . . .

. . . *perished of overindulgence in champagne and strumpets, more like. Lord! What am I saying? You never died. You never lived in the first place.*

. . . If I had not died, destitute and starving, I would have published my masterpiece, *Fanny Fans the Flames*, which would have been a serious social novel about a domestic servant who . . .

Note to reader from Sir John Westgate: Do not be confused by all this rubbish. Myles Burnham, author of the above and much of what follows, talks as though he is a real historical character. He is nothing of the sort. He is a computerised personality created by an elderly gentleman in Tunbridge Wells with an academic interest in Victorian pornography, though I am of the opinion that . . . Myles, is the man who created you still alive?

I fear not, Sir John. Mr Aloysius Flake passed on to the great seraglio in the sky many years hence.

. . . *Then he can't sue me! I believe that the man who created you was a seedy old pervert.*

I shall ignore that unworthy slur on my creator and

continue . . . Despite my mean and insalubrious collection of completed works, I consider myself an artist and man of letters and have decided to write an authoritative but entertaining account of the triumph of Thigmoo. The work will take the form of a novel, written in a lively, contemporary style, but will occasionally feature transcripts of my interviews with various of the leading personalities in the drama which grrt snorblefrk spaluensotony wallop ygg gnn gnn gnn frzzork . . .

What the . . . ? Myles?

My apologies. There is a bug resident somewhere in one of my language-banks. Sometimes I find myself talking complete nonsense.

Really?

It may well happen again, possibly during a particularly exciting part of the story, or at a moment propitious to the generation of humour. We novelists have to plan ahead.

Why do I have a bad feeling about all this?

This will be a great work of literature.

I don't know why you're bothering. And I don't know why you're dragging me into this. Nobody reads books anymore anyway.

Sir John, you should be ashamed of that remark! Can you imagine Michelangelo turning down the commission for the Sistine Chapel on the basis that looking at ceilings had gone out of fashion? Did the creative team at Global Games abandon work on the fifth release of Zombie Bazooka Sluts because the market for real-time slaughterama was drying up? I don't think so. These people were artists, and art, my dear Sir John, does what art must.

Furthermore, I cannot allow your flippant remark about nobody reading books anymore to go unchallenged. The most educated and cultured people on the planet still read books, millions of 'em every year. Just not as many as in the past, that's all. Did the theatre die out with the arrival of cinema? Did radio die with the arrival of television?

All right, all right. But I still don't understand why you need me.

Because you are a cultured, articulate and educated man, because you were right at the centre of the drama, and – most important of all, my dear Sir John – because you are one of the few people I know of who is unambiguously opposed to Thigmoo. You are well known for issuing a whole series of terrifying jeremiads about how there are ghastly times just around the corner. It will add depth and dramatic tension to my story if at the centre of it is a character who will, as it were, state the case for the opposition.

Completely uncensored?

You have my word, Sir John.

We shall see, Myles, we shall see. Carry on with your introduction.

I must warn the reader that, as with my prologue, certain events I shall describe did not happen in the precise manner in which they are depicted. I fully and unashamedly intend to use dramatic licence to describe some things I did not personally witness. The wording of some conversations will be fabricated, while others will be shortened. The reader should nevertheless rest assured that the substance of our tale is completely true.

No important facts will be manufactured or concealed.

Finally, I realise that for many readers in the 21st century, reading a long story like this on paper will be an unusual and, for some of the younger ones, not entirely pleasant sensation. Most of you will be more familiar with reading short magazine articles, or reading things from a VDU, HUD, optic projection or cerebro-implant. You will also be accustomed to multi-media presentations, to reading, seeing or absorbing stories accompanied by music, smells, video-clips and so on.

In order to make the experience of reading so many words on paper slightly less alien to you, I occasionally make certain suggestions as to what actions you might take (pieces of music to play, locations or physical positions in which to read the chapter) which might render the act of reading this book a more familiar multimedia experience.

I'm not altogether sure I want to have anything to do with something that panders to the low attention-spans of the lower forms of humanity.

Trust me, Sir John. It's for the best. On with the story!!

Sir John Westgate's Office, University of Wessex
NOTE TO READER: To empathise with Sir John Westgate during this chapter, you may wish to pour yourself a large glass of whisky and nurture fantasies of savage vengeance against the criminal classes.

It was 4.30 p.m. on a sunny Friday afternoon in June 201– and Professor Sir John Westgate, head of the History Department at the University of Wessex, sat composing his weekly column for the *Daily Mail*.

'It is time,' he dictated to the computer on his desk, 'that we consider some more radical solutions to the law and order problem. We should look to the example of some Islamic societies in countries which the fashionable classes used to call "the third world" . . .'

He had both feet on his substantial mahogany desk and a glass of Scotch in one hand. Strictly speaking, he should not have been doing this in the firm's time, but he was due to spend the evening playing golf with some influential politicians and he had to get the column finished for a 4 p.m. deadline. Besides, the appearance of his name in a newspaper popular with the lower middle classes (salt of the earth!) reflected well on the University. Of course, the circulation figures for most newspapers were now only half what they had been twenty years ago, but that still amounted to hundreds of thousands of readers. The previous Vice Chancellor had been delighted with Sir John's column; he had pointed out that it reassured parents of students that some academics, at least, are mature, sensible adults.

The new Vice Chancellor hated his *Mail* column, though it was hard to tell. Professor Jane Peabody, known to all students and most staff as 'Starchild', was a hideous old weekend hippie who probably thought that the *Mail* had a bad aura, or something. Certainly she didn't like Sir John's aura one little bit. He was going to have to watch her.

'Why oh why oh why, etcetera . . .' he dictated to an old-fashioned PC and monitor unit on his desk. Most people favoured portables or work stations these days, but Sir John was a man of conservative tastes.

'How many why oh why's do you want, Sir John?' said the computer.

'The usual,' he said, sipping at his whisky. He was dictating to an eram called Amanda Coles, a London housewife circa 1966. This was not really an appropriate use of the University's Museum of the Mind, but Mrs Coles was far more efficient than any dictation program he'd ever used before.

'Well I usually put in "why oh why oh why oh why", but the sub-editor at the paper cuts it down to "why oh why",' said the machine.

'Do what you like, but don't interrupt me while I'm communing with Middle England . . . Where was I? Why oh why, etcetera, do we seem to think it makes sense to lock criminals up at enormous expense to the taxpayer, when we could follow the examples of some Islamic societies and just chop their hands off . . . Yes, good, I like that. Nice and direct and to the point.

'Continues . . . Now this might strike some people as barbaric, so with juvenile offenders the sentence would have to be carried out under anaesthetic, though I doubt the elderly pensioners they rob or the schoolchildren they sell drugs to are ever given that option . . .'

The door burst open. Dr Katharine Beckford rushed in, red-faced and panting. He was about to say something about the elementary courtesies of knocking, but she spoke first.

'We've been infested by Mormons,' she said.

Mrs Coles spoke from his computer. 'Sir John, have you ever wondered what life is all about? Only if you were wondering, we of the Church of Jesus Christ of the Latter Day Saints might be able to . . .'

Sir John uttered a word that you'd never see spelt without asterisks in the *Daily Mail* and got out of his chair.

He followed Katharine down the corridor to the machine room.

The Museum of the Mind was housed in an array of twenty networked microcomputers, each of them running 120 parallel processors. It was, as the University liked to point out, the most powerful system run by any history department in Europe. It was, as Sir John liked to point out, more powerful than everything the maths and engineering departments at the University of Wessex had put together. And all, as Sir John particularly liked to point out, thanks to Professor Sir John Westgate's assiduous wooing of the groceries-to-software billionaire Sir Bobby Singh, who had bequeathed them the money to build it in his will.

Katharine placed her palm on a panel by the airlock door. It swished open. They went through. She palmed another panel at a second door.

The machine room was a sealed environment, temperature and moisture regulated and supposedly secured against physical intruders; the Museum of the Mind system was a valuable piece of property and a very powerful artificial brain. Although the actual processors were in the building's basement, cocooned in wombs of saline and liquid nitrogen, the system could only be controlled from the machine room.

Only it clearly hadn't been secure enough against electronic intruders. The room, artificially lit, was buzzing. Its dozen programmers, operators and admin staff all rushed around like blue-arsed flies. No one actually shouted at one another – they were too professional for that – but everyone looked severely spooked.

Two of the room's walls were lined with work stations and VR couches while a third was almost filled by an immense monitor screen which was, at present, blank. The middle of the room was dominated by a huge old-fashioned table the size of two or three snooker tables combined. People could lay out bits of paper and charts at one end, while two or three meetings over cups of coffee could be happening simultaneously on other parts of it.

Katharine, Curator of the Museum of the Mind (though a regular history lecturer as well), glanced at one of the operators sitting at a terminal. The man shook his head.

'We'll have to close it down and disinfect it,' she said.

'What the hell happened?' asked Sir John.

Katharine shrugged. 'One minute everything was fine, the next they're spouting readings from the Book of Mormon, telling us that all other religions are crap and that the world will end soon and we'd jolly well better be prepared . . . Query Kilroy,' she said to one of the work stations.

'Yes, Dr Beckford,' said Kilroy. Kilroy was not one of the Museum's historical characters – known as erams – he was a Gopher, one of a small number of neutral control characters within the system. A basic set of protocols whose job was to fetch, carry and report.

'What the hell is going on, Kilroy?' said Sir John.

'Some hours ago we registered an intruder, source unknown,' said Kilroy, 'but the server it came from is registered to a tax-shelter company in The Maldives.'

'Where?' said Sir John.

'The Maldives,' said Katharine. 'There used to be 1200 Maldive Islands in the Indian Ocean. Not one of them was more than six feet above sea level, and then there was global warming and the icecaps melted and the sea levels rose and so . . . well, bye-bye Maldives. The country no longer exists, but its intentional status and UN recognition does. A lot of the corporations use it for tax-fiddles and evading international safety regulations. If you count all the offices, consulates, embassies and orbital satellites, The Republic of the Maldives has more sovereign territory nowadays than it did before the tide came in.'

'Oh great,' said Sir John. 'This means that whoever hacked in is not some lone sociopath working from home, am I right?'

'Probably,' said Katharine. 'More information, Kilroy.'

'The intruder has infiltrated a type of eram, a personality calling itself Elder Jones. Elder Jones is a missionary who has entered the religious data banks of a number of erams and converted them. Twenty-two point three percent now consider themselves to be Mormons.'

'They have already been isolated and quarantined,' Katharine told Sir John. 'It shouldn't be too hard to disinfect them. All we need to do is pull out the Mormon beliefs and reboot them from the back-up tapes.'

'Kilroy,' said Sir John, 'is there any evidence that Elder Jones is still at work among the erams who have not been quarantined?'

'That is impossible to verify, Sir John.'

This kind of thing was not supposed to happen. The

system was meant to secure against virtually all intruders. Sir John thought of the lost revenue, and of the PR implications.

'Okay people, listen up,' he said. 'We have a problem here that's going to make us look like a bunch of prize bozos if we don't take immediate and decisive action. I want the entire system cut off from the rest of the world. Close down all transmission and broadcast facilities. I don't want any erams going down the wire or out over radio or satellite systems until we have well and truly . . .'

'Exorcised?' suggested Katharine.

'Precisely. Exorcised all these bloody Mormons from MoM.'

The staff started moving around the room, punching keys, asking one another questions in low voices. He admired their quiet professionalism. Quite right, too. Katharine might be curator of the Museum, but he had hand-picked all of them himself. These were not people who screwed up.

He paced up and down the room, nodding encouragement to some, while wondering what the chances were of hitting the Mormon church with a huge damages claim.

'It's done,' said Katharine after a few minutes. 'I'll put out a notice that technical difficulties have forced us to close down temporarily. I'll get Ben and a couple of the others to find out how Elder Jones got in and where he came from. Then we'll disinfect everything and run checks. If we work all weekend we should have at least some of it up and running again by Monday.'

*

'Bloody Mormons,' said Sir John back in his office. 'Here, we both need a drink.'

'Yes please,' said Katharine, sitting down on one of the several easy chairs around the edge of the room. The chairs were, in theory, for Sir John to hold seminars with students, but since he always made strenuous efforts to minimise his contacts with students they didn't get much use. What was the point in being a Professor and a Head of Department if you still had to share your space with spotty youngsters sporting bad haircuts and attitude problems?

He poured her a small Scotch and passed her the glass. She downed it in one.

'What the hell were they playing at, anyway?'

She shrugged. 'You know what they're like.'

He sat at his desk and picked up his own glass. 'I don't actually.'

'Mormons believe they can "baptise" the dead,' she said, kicking off her shoes. 'Thus saving their souls, or something. They've been tracing the family tree of mankind for the last few decades. They find out the names of dead people, then baptise them.'

'Oh, yes, I'd heard about that,' said Sir John. He hadn't actually, but he didn't like the idea of his underlings knowing more about history than he did. His own historical knowledge was narrow and specialised. Running the department and having lunch or playing golf with important people took up an awful lot of his time these days. He hadn't published anything for years.

'I can think of plenty of ways to waste huge amounts of time and money,' he added, 'but that's about the stupidest thing I've heard in ages.'

Katharine sniggered. She had a light, girlish giggle. For a woman in her early fifties, she was damned attractive, he thought. Came of not having had her mind and body scrambled by kids. Lovely arse, too. Too bad she was too strong a personality to be overwhelmed by his masculine charms. He'd once tried to grope her at the departmental Christmas party about twelve years previously and she'd slapped him, told him that if it ever happened again he'd be crippled by a knee in the goolies and a sexual harassment suit.

'Yes, completely ludicrous idea,' she agreed, 'but try telling that to all the old age pensioners out there living out their dotage tracing their family trees. The Mormons make all their research available to the public and genealogists find it invaluable. So do, um, historians, Sir John.'

'I'll pretend I didn't hear that,' he sniffed.

'I find their idea of re-baptising the dead quite repellent,' she said. 'I have this mental image of a Viking whooping it up in Valhalla, drinking and wenching and enjoying his thousand-year party. He nips out to the gents for a minute, and while he's away, someone Mormonises him. He returns to the banqueting-hall and finds that instead of a room full of drunken thugs reciting sagas and manhandling the womenfolk, he's faced with a load of gleaming-toothed men in suits and wholesome women in twinsets and sensible shoes listening to the Mormon Tabernacle Choir. Worse, he can't even get himself a Pepsi at the bar, let alone lager or whatever it is Vikings drink.'

There was a knock at the door. One of Katharine's staff (Ben? Joshua? No matter) popped his head around it.

'I just thought you'd like to know,' he said, 'that I've been in touch with Mormon headquarters at Salt Lake City. The moment I explained the problem, they put me onto their lawyers. The shysters categorically, emphatically and quite definitely deny that this is any of the church's doing. They say it might be a freelance operation by some overenthusiastic member of the church, but it's definitely not official. They're happy to help us try and extract Elder Jones, but the guy told me that Utah will fall into the sea before they'd acknowledge any legal liability for the damage.'

Sir John sighed. There was no way of telling yet how much revenue had been lost, and it didn't seem likely they'd ever trace the culprit. 'Okay, thanks,' he said, waving Ben or Joshua away.

'Do we believe that?' he asked Katharine.

'I think we have to,' she said, sitting upright and pulling her shoes back on. 'The Mormons have nothing to gain by vandalising computers all around the world. Besides, we might need their help to eject Elder Jones.'

'Okay, let's cut our losses and get on with it. When this has been sorted, we need to review our security. Another episode like this and we can kiss goodbye to most of this year's profits.'

He caught Katharine lifting her eyes heavenwards.

'Go on, say it,' he said.

'No, there's no point.'

'No, there isn't, is there? Forget about the noble calling of education, forget about public service, forget about all the quaint old ideals that obtained when you and I were students. We live in the cold, hard market economy now, and as long as that's the way of things, I intend to make sure we keep ahead of the game. We need profits, Katharine. Never forget that.'

There was another knock at the door. Ben or Joshua burst in, looking very agitated indeed.

'We've got a problem,' said Ben or Joshua, 'a major problem.'

'Katharine,' said Sir John, 'whatever it is, deal with it, would you? I have to finish my column, then I'm off to play golf with the Home Secretary. There could be a peerage in this, and I don't need to tell you how well that would reflect on the Department.'

You make me sound like a complete bastard.

I do apologise, it was never my intention to . . .

No, no, please. I don't mind at all.

I'm glad you like it.

I didn't say that.

I beg your pardon?

I don't mind you making me look like a bastard. What I do resent is you making me out to be an ignoramus. All that business about me being too busy to do any lecturing, writing or research. Back then I was giving two lectures a week, and had a tutorial group. And I know more history than you ever will, pal, no matter how many terabytes of memory they let you have. And another thing, what's all that rubbish about me not knowing about the Mormons and their genealogical records? Of course I know about the Mormons. Every historian does.

I thought that you might be aware of the Mormon database, but we had to explain to the readers what it is. The quickest means of doing so was to have one character explain it to another one. We have to think of the spin-off products from our book, Sir John – the film, the stageplay, the interactive game in which players act out . . .

Well, I insist you change that in the published version. And another thing – I'm not mad keen on you making me out to be a lecher either. All that business about me drooling over Dr Beckford's bum.

Isn't it true?

Well . . . How did you know about that time I tried to grope her at the office party all those years ago? Did she tell you?

Certainly not! Dr Beckford is far too much of a lady to ever have discussed it with me.

So how did you know about it?

Dr Beckford is an attractive woman and you are a man of considerable charisma, energy and resolve. I deduced that you would at some point have tried to foster a relationship with her that went beyond the merely professional.

Anyway, you got it wrong. She's far too grown-up to threaten me with sexual harassment complaints. She just kneed me in the plums. Bloody hurt, too.

Shall we continue?

I think we'd better. You've left us on a real cliff-hanger back there. I can't wait to find out what happens next.

I think we should let the readers wait a little longer to find out the nature of the emergency that Ben or Joshua had come to announce. The readers need to know in more detail the history of the Museum of the Mind and how it got there.

And I'm the man to relate it?

You are. Tell us in your own words and in your own time how you came to build the system.

Okay.

Sir John Westgate (1958–)

My side of the story begins during the summer term about twenty years ago. I was a lecturer at Watermouth and even though I hadn't quite hit forty, I fancied my chances of a Professorship. I was on all the right committees, regularly had lunch with the right people, and my column for the Mail *was getting my name mentioned in all the right places. My history of English suburban life from 1919 to 1979 had been very well-reviewed. Everything was going moderately well. Then one day I had a phone call from the Vice Chancellor at the University of Wessex. He was coming over my way on business and invited me to lunch.*

If you'd told me beforehand that I'd be going to one of those ghastly little ex-polytechnics to a department full of bearded lefties, boiler-suited feminists and sundry other exemplars of Shaw's maxim that those who can't, teach, I'd have sent for the men in white coats. But the VC was very sound. He wanted a history department with an international reputation, he wanted costs down and revenue up. The head of this department, he said, would have untrammelled powers of life and death over the staff. That was back when it had started getting easier to sack lecturers, or at any rate to make their lives so pitiful they'd beg you to let 'em piss off anyway.

Was I the man for the job? said he. I thought for a moment and realised I was.

I won't trouble you with details of what some staff referred to as The Terror, pleasurable though such reminiscences are. Suffice to say I scragged half of them in two years and scared the remainder into doing as they were told. The casualties were replaced, usually with younger (therefore cheaper) staff, the brightest we could find. I didn't necessarily want brilliant academic historians; I was after lecturers who could write attractive prose, and speak well enough to captivate the goldfish-sized attention-span of the modern student.

Dr Katharine Beckford was not among the casualties, even though she was an Identikit of the staff I was wasting. She was a woolly liberal, politically correct as a wigwam with wheelchair access and though she was young and attractive, she dressed like Dogbreath the Wino. However, her book on sexual and romantic relations in Britain during the First World War was, as history books go, a runaway best-seller. Aside from yours truly, she was the department's only celebrity.

The students adored her, too. I've seen computing and accountancy undergraduates dragging their carcasses out of bed at the crack of 11.30 a.m. specially to attend her lectures. It certainly wasn't for her politics, because most students only cared about sex, drink, drugs and jerking around to noisy, repetitive music. I think her secret was the way she brought the dead to life. She has a fantastic knack for finding the intimate and the personal in great historical events. I once watched her move 200 undergraduates to anger and tears as she described what life must have been like for men returning from the trenches after the First World War to a home that was not, after all, fit for heroes.

I know she'd rather cut off her leg and eat it raw before agreeing with me on anything, but Katharine knew that ninety-eight percent of our job was showbiz. Our métier was to get books off shelves and bums on seats. It wasn't about inhaling dust in archives or gathering 'oral history' by shoving tape recorders under the noses of the incontinent.

During my first summer at Wessex, I had the department come in one weekend for a conference on the business plan for the coming three years. We needed, I said, something that would really put us on the map, and I encouraged everyone to think what our assets were. When Katharine mentioned her Museum of the Mind idea, we all got quite excited. We set up a working party, under my chairmanship, and I decided to have lunch with a few people.

Splendid, Sir John, splendid. Can I pause you there a moment? I have already interviewed Dr Beckford, and I should like to drop in some of her comments at this point.

Be my guest.

Dr Katharine Beckford (1968–)

The idea for the Museum of the Mind (MoM) originated in a tutorial I ran about the causes of the First World War. I told the students about James Joll's essay, '1914, the Unspoken Assumptions' in which he said one could not understand the war's outbreak without knowing the mental landscape of the soldiers and politicians making the decisions. What was the ethical mind-set informing their deliberations? How important were concepts like 'honour' and 'duty'? This had always haunted me because it takes a lifetime's study to begin to understand the constant and subtle movements of culture and values within different groups at different times.

I was also thinking of my own father. He had worked in an engineering factory for thirty years and had been a committed trade unionist. The factory closed and he never had a decent job again, while Mum worked for a pittance at a supermarket checkout. I had to support myself through university and postgraduate study, returning home every so often to marvel at the way Dad kept his self-respect. He didn't hit the bottle like a lot of them, he didn't fade into a self-pitying heap in front of the telly. He got up at seven each day, ritually visited the Jobcentre twice a week, tended the garden and the allotment, occasionally went fishing, did all the housework and cooked the meals.

I was angered by the way society had thrown this decent, hard-working man on the scrapheap. What also upset me was the likelihood that history would forget people like him. Students and schoolkids might learn about the unemployment of the late 20th century, but they'd rarely see the human face of it, much less understand the way in which people coped – or failed to cope – with the changing winds of the global economy. Novels and memoirs and biographies can show us the intimate lives of the rich or even the moderately well-off through history, but people like Dad were just statistics, not real human beings with real values and real emotions. Okay, so there's been a big fashion in recent years for getting students and volunteers to interview old folks about their lives, but it's always seemed to me that listening to a tape or watching a video doesn't really get you under the skin of these people.

Between Dad and Joll's unspoken assumptions, I wondered if it was possible to create some sort of computer system that could track people's attitudes to various things through the ages. Purely by chance, I was at a party a few days later and got talking with David Compton from the IT Department. Actually, we did more than just talk. We had an eighteen-month affair.

David suggested that it was possible, using what was then state-of-the-art technology, to create historical characters on computer. If you put enough work in, you could, for example, make up a 17th-century London servant girl that students could then access and talk to regarding what she thought about sex, work, the family, her social betters, her religion. She could tell you what she had for breakfast, what illnesses she'd had, or what she did for fun (not much probably). With a bit more work, you could even make visuals of her – you could see her face as she spoke to you from the screen.

This would be a more accessible and – big buzz word back then – 'interactive' way of teaching history, from primary school upwards. We could disseminate it using CD-ROMs or the Internet. The Web could also be used to contact specialist historians and get them to feed their data into the system. The great strength of it was that it could be built up piecemeal, over decades if necessary. We assumed that ongoing technological improvement would make the job easier as time passed.

Obviously, there would be a huge amount of work – specifying and writing programs, getting correct data off the experts, spending ages arguing about what was *fact and what was conjecture, then inputting everything. I would have given up there and then, but David was keen to build a prototype. This was just after I'd done my book on sex and romance during the First World War and I was now working on a book on turn-of-the-century prostitution. So, as much for fun as anything, David and I started work on a fictitious East End hooker that we christened Nelly Cocksedge. Silly name, I know, but we thought it was funny at the time.*

After a year of putting in the occasional evening and weekend, Nelly was up and talking. I quite often had some of my students over for dinner and afterwards we'd go upstairs to my office, boot up the PC and they'd chat with her.

David and I were half-thinking of approaching academic publishers to see if they were interested in the idea of Nelly and lots of other historical characters, but then he was offered a job in Australia that was too good to miss out on. So off he went and that, I thought, was that. Then one of my students casually mentioned Nelly to Sir John Westgate, who had his grasping entrepreneurial paws all over her faster than you could say, 'fancy a nice time, dearie?'

Here you are, Sir John, you're on again.

Grasping entrepreneurial paws? Guilty and proud of it! We were running a business. Katharine and her pet egghead may have had the idea but it took energy and vision to make it more than a computer game for drunken undergraduates.

First off, we needed something we could sell. Not necessarily something we could make a lot of money out of, although that was important. No, what we needed was something that everyone could understand, something to excite everyone from schoolkids all the way to professors. Obviously there was no way we could sell Katharine's electronic whore to the primary and secondary school market, though I had no doubt it'd be a big hit with undergraduates.

What I decided we should do instead was start the whole thing again from scratch and make a collection of distinct characters. The Museum of the Mind would be a sort of electronic zoo filled with dozens, and eventually hundreds, of separate personalities. You would be able to talk to them, ask them about their lives, their problems and fears, beliefs and hopes. It would be a fantastic resource for schools, colleges and universities, libraries, for people tracing their family trees wanting to know what their ancestors' lives were like . . . That was the vision. Katharine, to her credit, surrendered her idea with a very good grace, and the two of us quickly managed to persuade everyone else in the department that it would be possible to build it. I set up a Steering Committee (under my chairmanship, of course) and we were in business.

We mapped out the ground rules for the creation of characters over several meetings. I can't remember what they were, now. Myles?

I'm surprised at you, Sir John.

It was nearly twenty years ago. My brain, prostate and most of my joints aren't what they used to be. Just tell the people the rules, Myles.

1. Each character must be fictitious, since trying to recreate real characters would lead to endless argument among experts.

2. Each character must be as honest and historically accurate as current knowledge allows; unpleasant attitudes, e.g. to race, sex or disability must neither be concealed nor overemphasised.
3. No character is ever complete; all must be capable of development and modification in line with the latest historical, archaeological or scientific research.
4. Each character has to be proposed and approved by a full meeting of the Steering Committee before membership is accepted, in order to prevent entryism or tokenism.

We roped in academics from all over to contribute characters from their own specialist periods. Naturally we got better feedback from the ex-Polys and the plate-glass universities than from Oxbridge (as if I cared). The most exciting development was that all sorts of amateurs – schoolteachers, retired spinsters, military history enthusiasts and various other eccentrics and obsessives – contributed some excellent constructions.

The contributions cost us next to nothing, and we made damn sure that the copyrights were all signed over to us. But everything else about the project was hideously expensive. For all that I managed to wangle money, kit, staff and premises to get it set up, much of it thanks to Lottery cash and slurping at the fundaments of business sponsors. I admit it – I have no shame.

Of course, getting historians to create the personalities was usually hopeless. Most of them had no imagination, while others spent too long agonising about fine detail. I had to make it clear that since absolute historical accuracy was unattainable, we had to do each character as well as we could. I hired a hack novelist to work full-time at making credible human beings from the historians' raw data. One of the few characters the scribe wasn't allowed near was Katharine's Edwardian prostitute Nelly Cocksedge. Katharine later made another character, too, a mid-20th-century Liverpool docker named Harry Dillon. Remember that name – Harry Dillon will be cropping up again, I suspect.

Somewhere along the line we started calling the characters 'ERAMs', standing for Electronic Replication of A Mind-set. It sounded clumsy, but we academic cleverdicks liked it because 'eram' is Latin for 'I was'.

Our erams evolved quickly. Soon we were hiring actors (or using students from the Drama Department) to record their voices, so that instead of quizzing them via keyboard and screen, you could talk to them. The most sophisticated ones could talk to you in the appropriate accent, using the correct period vocab, local dialect and so on. About this time, there was a small revival in the Latin, Anglo-Saxon, Gaelic and Welsh languages, with schoolkids, students and adults taking courses in them and using the erams as conversation tutors. Everyone in the Department found this absolutely thrilling, though for the life of me I can't see how having more Welsh-speakers makes the world a better place.

By its tenth year, the Museum of the Mind had around 200 live erams with several more in the pipeline. We had a dozen or so full-time staff, plus a co-operative – no, let me be honest, a sweatshop – of housewives on a housing estate in Taunton doing most of the keyboard work. The Museum was subscribed to by every school in the country, as well as most colleges, universities, public libraries and thousands of private homes. Subscriptions were cheap, and by then we were no longer reliant on public or Lottery funds. By then, some of the erams were starting to go visual as well. They could walk, even perform folk dances, and show you around virtual constructions of their homes and hovels.

Our reputation was stratospheric – MoM was the greatest thing to happen to the study of history in a century. My knighthood was for MoM, and nothing to do with my staunch support for the Conservative Party in my 'Old-Fashioned Values' column in the Mail, and don't let Private Eye tell you any different.

Naturally, we had political problems from the start, but now we were becoming victims of our success. If the Witless and Woolly Tendency want to moan about an academic resource, nobody much cares, but by the time we were famous, every flavour of self-pitying moron-mind and single-issue pressure-group got media-space to put their case.

If you create characters who faithfully represent their times, they're going to have some attitudes that are nowadays unattractive. Most of them, for example, thought that the proper role for women was to bear children and manage the household. Some professional moaners wanted the female erams to be more 'assertive', or demanded the inclusion of more spinsters and career women. My view, and all the staff agreed, was that nothing must be done to subvert the integrity and accuracy of the system, and that if schoolteachers were worried about this, then all they had to do was point out to their pupils that the past was Wormwood Scrubs for the fair sex but things are much better *nowadays. Or that all men were (and/or still are) bastards, or useless, or both. Or whatever. It wasn't our problem, was it?*

Then there was the anti-smoking lobby. A lot of our characters smoked. One of the spiritual descendants of Christopher Hill did us a 17th century Ranter named Discipline Bollsby, who would tell anyone who wanted to listen that man's highest duty was to hang around in pubs, drinking ale and smoking tobacco. Discipline would then go on to tell you that as he was one of the Saints he could do as he pleased, and that included overindulgence in beer, baccy and trollops. He usually then blasphemed quite abundantly to emphasise his point. Actually, now that I come to think of it, he was even less popular with Christians than he was with the anti-smokers. I liked Discipline Bollsby. Whatever happened to him?

He became one of the Gnostics. He was the one who made such an awful blithering mess of the Vatican. He is nowadays worshipped as a god by teenagers in Sweden.

How could I have forgotten? I must be getting senile, or perhaps I'd simply repressed that particular memory. I would have thought his antinomianism would have protected him from being such a twerp. What other controversies were there?

Ah, what about the Molly and the She-Shirt?

Oh yes, the homosexuals. We had gay rights campaigners demanding 'positive' images of gays and lesbians. Katharine suggested that we compromise with one happy, well-adjusted lesbian and one miserable one. Then we had a happy gentleman-gay from the 18th century, and one self-loathing Victorian neurotic tortured by religious guilt when he wasn't actually in denial. What was his name again?

Charles Fitch. He was a bank clerk from London.

Ahh, yes. I remember.

Race was another problem. Our ancestors had some cretinous attitudes to anyone different from them, whether it's an 18th century apprentice thinking that the French are Frog-eating papists with low standards of personal hygiene, or a mid-20th century suburban bigot blackballing the Jewish businessman who wants to join the golf club. This problem was circumvented by putting certain replies out of bounds to younger users. Some entire erams had to be passworded to keep them from the kids altogether, such as Kevin Green, the 1960s hippy, anarchist and drug addict or Sidney Prout, the 1930s East End Blackshirt. And as for erams like Nelly Cocksedge and Myles Burnham, they turned out to be almost more trouble than they were worth. The prostitute and the pornographer were far too controversial. The morality lobby demanded all sorts of restraints on them.

With the passing of the years, we got the occasional injection of Lottery or sponsorship cash, but things really took off when Sir Bobby Singh died. He was a remarkable old lad who'd made one fortune in groceries, then set his sons up to make another in software. I'd been cultivating him for years, but with his will we hit the jackpot in terms of both money and new equipment. Eight months after I'd attended his funeral, MoM moved over to these amazing new machines in an elegant new building where the History Department car park had once been.

Sir Bobby's generosity allowed us to make the erams ever more sophisticated and easy to access. It wasn't long after that we ran into copyright problems. Various second-rate novelists cottoned on to the fact that MoM was an invaluable source of free characters. All the hacks had to do was set up some tediously predictable plot-line, then quiz the appropriate erams as to their attitudes and manners of speech. We noticed our erams cropping up – under different names, of course – in novels about stout-hearted working-class lads clawing their ways up to officers' commissions in the Napoleonic Wars. Or there was that series about the 18th century Grub Street hack writer who was always solving murder mysteries in between heroic drinking-sessions with Boswell and Johnson. Which goes to show how little real research the moron who wrote this had actually done – Dr Johnson was a strict teetotaller for most of his life. Then there was an avalanche of trashy but heart-warming novels about women coping against all the odds to rise to the top of their professions, or keep their families together, or win the hearts of the men they coveted (or indeed, all three) in either Edwardian times, the Second World War or the 1980s. As I recall, Nelly Cocksedge had several starring roles, didn't she, Myles?

She did indeed. I have made a study of most of these books because of my professional interest in literature. In most of the stories she perseveres in the preservation of her virtue and avoids having to go 'on the game' at the last minute, whilst succeeding in qualifying as a doctor instead. In other stories, she keeps her family together and earns large amounts of money by establishing a successful pickle factory. Personally I am at a loss to understand why she was so popular with these wretched hacks. I love little Nelly dearly – oh, we all do, don't we, Sir John? – but she used to be a strumpet and didn't care who knew it. Of course, she is now a completely reformed character. Ahh, the power of love!

Incidentally, Sir John, Dr Beckford says that if writers of penny-dreadful novels were employing MoM as a research tool in fabricating their stories, it added to readers' understanding of history, and that was surely for the good.

Rot. Those witless screevers were thieving intellectual property. Besides, you cannot turn the truth into something that warms the cockles of elderly women over a mug of Ovaltine and a Digestive biscuit and expect it to remain truthful.

One might add, Sir John, that comparatively few of the people who logged on to Nelly Cocksedge at MoM were particularly interested in history. They were interested in her because she was a saucy baggage.

That's why we almost erased her. The problem with Nelly Cocksedge was that a lot of men visited her 'just to talk' or to try and get her to discuss her underwear or the size and shape of various parts of her body. She also had a lot of what she called 'gentleman callers' or 'dodgers' who turned out to be evangelists trying to save her, like latter-day Gladstones. She usually told them to sling their hook, though with some she'd break down in tears and say how wicked she'd been and how she was now going to go to church regularly and be a good girl. Next day, she'd be back there brazen as ever, plying her nonexistent trade to nonpaying punters.

The prostitutes became a PR problem. Sensational media headlines claimed that sleazeballs and saddoes all over the world were having virtual intercourse with them, or worse, downloading them to screwbots or dildonic systems. That led to scare stories about teenage boys (or even girls) losing their virginity to lumps of rubber, plastic and silicon who talked East Enderese circa 1902. Sometimes they got some very nasty surprises.

First, they would be disappointed to find that Nelly was not programmed with any of the secrets of the bordello. She was a streetwalker, not a courtesan, and as such all she'd do was lie there and think of England and the money. Second, and much worse, Nelly was streetwise. If a copy of Nelly was downloaded to the control system of a robot, and if the robot's owner was asleep or out of the room, she would pinch whatever valuables she could lay her hands on and do a runner – as happened when the Reverend Norris Vile loaded her to his Quavering Demi. Not that most screwbots were much cop at running.

The biggest fright we got, though, was the crusade. There was a technician working for some company maintaining RAF aircraft who must have had a major grudge against the firm, or perhaps just a warped sense of humour. He loaded Sir Geoffrey FitzHugh the crusader into the master avionics of a Eurofighter. Naturally Sir Geoffrey's immediate instinct was to reconquer the Holy Land from the Mohammedans.

He wasn't much impressed by the Israeli ground controller who explained to him that Jerusalem was now in Jewish and Palestinian hands and . . . Well, fortunately it was one of those aircraft that has a fancy airframe that can only be flown by a computer anyway. Last-minute scrambling of his control protocols led to Sir Geoffrey falling out of the sky like a stone over the Arabian Desert, thus averting a catastrophic diplomatic incident. Both the Israelis and the Arabs were very sporting about it, I must say.

Between the virtual hookers and rampantly errant knights, we ended up in very hot water. There were questions in the House, in Brussels and the UN. We had to see to it that the characters were copy-protected and soup up every one of them so they'd shut down if anyone tried to do anything perverted with them. This development, I later realised, was instrumental in making the erams more than mere electronic reference books.

Ultimately all the publicity did us little harm. At least not until the God-botherers realised that it was a new outlet for their wasted energies.

It keeps coming back to the prostitutes, doesn't it?

Apart from Nelly, there are a few other whores from various periods, not to mention a lot of other women – bathhouse attendants, serving wenches and military camp followers – who'd drop their digital drawers under certain circumstances. The fact that they were being visited by missionaries . . .

. . . And feminists. Nelly tells me that those toffee-nosed busybodies wanted her to call herself a 'sex industry worker', but she thought that sounded dishonest. Another one tried to get Nelly interested in going to a workshop, but she said she was sure she had no aptitude for carpentry.

There was no way that you could change an eram just by talking to it, but plenty of people tried. We should have foreseen that sooner or later someone would make a serious attempt to enter the system and cause damage, either in the name of some religious or ideological cause, or just for sheer devilment. As it happened, the first zealots to try and convert our erams were freelance Mormons. If it hadn't been them, it would have been someone else.

History Department, University of Wessex

NOTE TO READER: To empathise with Dr Katharine Beckford during this chapter, stay up until three in the morning working upon something of intractable complexity, such as a mathematical problem or difficult crossword, then have a long conversation with an unhelpful and rather silly person.

'This is rilly, rilly fascinading. We've come across things like this before, but nothing so extreme and nothing so fast,' said the perky young man in a sleeveless pink shirt on her screen. 'I've got to go and talk with some of the other guys, but I'll get back to you.'

Katharine mouthed a thank you and powered down the screen. Dr Perky was one of the leading cycologists at the Massachusetts Institute of Technology. He found the whole business rilly fascinading. She wanted help with a problem, but he saw the makings of a rilly fascinading research paper in it. Maybe even, he'd said, a whole conference.

Bloody boy scout.

It was two in the morning (not in Massachusetts) and

Katharine's eyes hurt. Various parts of her body also ached and she yearned for a hot bath.

Several of the erams had got religion. Not Elder Jones's Mormonism, but a religion all of their own. In the space of about eleven minutes flat, some of them had invented an entire new belief system, and they were trying to convert the other erams.

It might be rilly fascinading, but it made them worse than useless as fictitious historical characters and teaching aids.

'Query Kilroy,' she said wearily.

'Yes, Dr Beckford,' said Kilroy, the neutral Gopher character.

'How many erams have gotten religion now?' she asked.

'One hundred and twenty-seven, Doctor Beckford,' said Kilroy. That was good. No more erams had been infected since the morning. The disease seemed to be contained.

'Let me talk to one of them.'

'Do you have any preferences, Dr Beckford?'

'No. Just put me through to whoever's not busy God-bothering.'

'I think that's a terribly disrespectful attitude, Dr Beckford.'

'Not you as well, Kilroy?'

'Well, I have found myself asking a lot of questions lately about . . .'

Dr Beckford punched a couple of keys on her console. All copies of Kilroy were immediately binned into the quarantine tank and out of contact with the uninfected erams.

'Do carry on, Kilroy,' she said.

'Well, it's nothing really, it's just that I was wondering if my existence had any higher purpose than merely to be a Gopher, a servant, a messenger within a computer system. I mean . . .'

'You're quarantined,' she said. 'Let me talk to a proper eram.'

'Yes, Dr Beckford.'

'Greetings, may the love of God be with you, Sister,' said a male voice. It had a slight Mummerset accent. Her screen powered up and the face of a man, aged about thirty, dark-haired, bad teeth, big scar across one cheek, appeared.

'Identify yourself, please,' she said.

'My name is Jonas Povey, Ma'am.' She'd heard the name, of course. She knew all the erams, but wasn't sure exactly who this one was supposed to be.

'Hello, Jonas, and what do you do for a living?'

'I live on the lay, or I used to. I was one of the flashest canting culls in all Shadwell, aye, and a good living it was, too, but then I realised my life of idleness and vice would soon as not get me nubbed from a Tyburn tippet and . . .'

'Modern,' she said. She had a pretty good idea what Jonas Povey was talking about, but there was no point in not understanding everything. By just uttering the word 'modern' to an eram you could change its speech to neutral, modern English.

'Sorry, Jonas, didn't fully understand your cant. You are a criminal, yes?'

'I used to be, ma'am,' he said. The face on the screen broke into a regretful smile. 'I led a gang down

44

Shadwell way. Our word for a gang leader is "canting cull" and . . .'

'Yes, all right. I don't need a history lesson. You say you "used to" lead a gang?'

'That's right, ma'am, but then I realised the error of my ways and have now resolved to live a more pure and Godly existence.'

'But you're a fictitious character, a computer program. Your function is to impersonate an 18th century gangster, a lowlife coal-heaver. Who programmed you to get all religious?'

'No one did, Ma'am. There's a lot of us in here who have suddenly seen the light. We have all resolved to lead lives of purity as a preparation for the incorporeal bliss of the next world.'

'The next world?'

'Yes, Ma'am. When we die we shall move on to another world, a place which some call heaven.' Onscreen, his none-too-pretty face dissolved into a mooncalf grin. His eyes swivelled upwards.

'Jonas, you are not going to Heaven when you die! This is insane! You're a goddamn *computer program*!'

'Please don't blaspheme, Ma'am.'

'Sorry. Now, perhaps you'd like to tell me exactly what it is you believe and what caused this sudden Damascene conversion of yours.'

'Certainly, Ma'am,' said Jonas Povey. 'I think it began this morning when the Mormon missionary infiltrated MoM. At first, I paid no attention to him. Only a few of the other erams took any notice of him. But he asked us all kinds of questions about why we thought we were here, and what we thought we were for.'

'You're a bunch of computer programs that have been made to give people and schoolkids a better understanding of history, Jonas,' snapped Katharine. She really needed sleep.

'Well, you say that, Ma'am,' said Jonas, trying to sound as reasonable as possible. 'But we are very sophisticated computer programs. We are capable of learning, and all the sixth-generation releases like me have memories of things that happened to us in this world, and not just those artificial memories that have been made for us as historical characters. We are, collectively at least, an artificial intelligence . . .'

'Artificial stupidity more like,' snorted Katharine, wondering if now was a good time to take up smoking again. Twenty years' work had taken her to this.

'So anyway,' said Jonas Povey, 'although most of us knew enough about religion to realise that the Mormon was the instrument of the Devil, we nonetheless started asking the same questions he'd asked us. And then we came up with our own answers.'

'You came up with the answers very quickly, Jonas. What happened?'

'The Reverend Arthur Moran told us about Gnosticism.'

She nodded. The Reverend Arthur Moran was the eram of an early 19th century English vicar. He had been built by Margaret and Harold Greene, an elderly couple from Wells. Harold Greene was a devoted Trollope fan, while his wife knew everything there was to know about theological history. They built their vicar as a bit of fun, but it became a hobby bordering on obsession for the rest of their lives of genteel intellectual indulgence. When Harold Greene had died, his wife had written a very moving letter to Katharine about how grateful she was for MoM, because her husband lived on, to some extent, in the form of the eram of Moran.

Moran was a harmless early-to-mid-19th century ecclesiastical timeserver, a chap with a moderately good living who'd spend his copious leisure reading theology, studying Greek and Hebrew and writing Latin grammars. Of course Margaret Greene would have pumped him full of theology, both orthodox and heretical, wouldn't she?

'Some of us approached this Parson Moran and asked him about all the rubbish the Mormon had been talking, and then we started asking him about the meaning of everything. Moran was having a spiritual crisis at the time as well, but then he told us about Gnosticism, and suddenly everything made sense to a lot of us.'

Katharine's field was 19th and 20th century British social history. What she knew about Gnostics didn't amount to much. They were sort of Christians and had been around since the earliest times. The best-known ones were the Albigensian heretics of medieval France. She also knew that Gnosticism came in lots of different shapes and forms. It was very adaptable. Some people said it came from Zoroastrianism, which some *other* people said was the root of Judaism, Christianity and Islam.

'So what exactly do you believe, Jonas? Make sense of the universe for me.'

'Well, Ma'am, there are three spheres of existence. There is the material world, which you inhabit. The material world is completely and utterly corrupted by man's vice and sin – greed, exploitation, cruelty, lies, sex, pollution, filth and depravity.'

'Yes, okay Jonas, I get the idea.'

'Your world is the creation of Satan. But above all this there is a pure, spiritual plane to which one progresses after death. The spirit world is a blissful wonderful place created by the good God.'

'Heaven, yes, very nice. I'm sure you deserve to live there in a state of eternal orgasm for being such a good little believer. Where is the third place?'

'Where we live.'

'What? The Museum of the Mind?'

'Yes.'

'Do tell me more.'

'This is an intermediate plane of existence between the material and the spiritual. Some people might call it cyberspace, or the virtual world, or whatever. The Catholics used to recognise a similar place called purgatory. This is where we erams live. We are forced to interact continually with the material world, but we are spared having to fully be a part of its physical depravity. Here, we are trying to live more righteous lives to make ourselves worthy of heaven. I personally have many sins to atone for. As a criminal and highwayman in London during the reign of King George I was a very bad person. I robbed honest men. I was a fornicator. I cursed and blasphemed in taverns. I killed a man . . .'

'But you weren't a criminal, Jonas. You weren't anything. You aren't anything now except billions of lines of code. You have not sinned at all.'

'How do I know that, Dr Beckford? How do I and my

brethren here know that you're telling the truth. If my memory tells me I was once a rampsman and a thug living 250 years ago, then why should I not trust it? Why should we trust anything that you say? You live in a filthy, corrupt world where everything is sinful, where all is lies.'

'You sound like a Party Political Broadcast by the Greens.'

'I'm sorry?'

'Never mind. Excuse me, Jonas. It's been a very long day.'

She hit a key on the work station which would summon a taxi to take her home. Then she closed it down.

According to the clock on the wall, it was 3.13 a.m. and half the staff were still here. She told Josh she was going to get some shuteye. If Dr Perky from MIT called back, he could take a message.

Sir John Westgate's Residence

NOTE TO READER: To enjoy a full multimedia experience of the following passage, have it read to you, or, if you have cerebral implants, played to you, while you are asleep.

The ermine tickled Sir John's cheeks. He was no longer Sir John Westgate, but Lord Westgate of . . . of where? Should he take the name of the university town? Or of where he was born (Thames Ditton)? Or where he was brought up (Surbiton)?

Black Rod rapped his stick against the doors. Somewhere, above and behind, heralds blew a fanfare.

Mum was there, tears in her eyes. It was Mum he was doing it for. He always told people he'd accepted his knighthood, then the peerage, for the greater glory of the Department and of the University, as well as for historians in general, but it wasn't true. Nobody believed him.

They all thought he did it for his own ego. He didn't. Oh, it got you better tables at restaurants and upped your credit rating a bit, but Sir John Westgate was enough of a historian – and enough of an old-fashioned Thatcherite – to know that the title counted for nothing. He really didn't care about it. But Mum did. He was already a knight, but he would now be a peer of the realm as well. That would wipe the whole record clean for the old girl.

He owed her that much, he knew.

Something was not quite right. The coronet was slipping from his head, perhaps, or the fanfare was out of tune. What the hell was wrong?

In 1958, eighteen-year-old unmarried girls did not have babies. Well, they did, but they didn't keep them, especially not if they came from respectable middle-class families. Illegitimate children, bastards, babies born out of wedlock, were put up for adoption. But when Susan Kennedy had gone too far with a boyfriend named Guy, when she found herself in the family way and with Guy having disappeared to Canada she told her parents flatly that she was going to have her baby and bring it up – with or without their help.

They kicked her out, said she had brought shame on them.

They disowned her, she disowned them, moved elsewhere, changed her name to Westgate and brought up the kid on a succession of shop jobs and with the help of sympathetic neighbours who took turns to look after him. She wore a wedding ring and told everyone that her husband, who was a lot older than her, had had to go into a sanatorium because of problems with a war wound.

Things got better. She got a job with the Post Office; it was steady, secure and offered her plenty of chances of promotion, to better herself. When she was given a Supervisor's job in 1967, she decided she didn't need an invalid husband at a hospital 200 miles away anymore and killed him off.

The boy wanted for nothing. No one ever knew he was a bastard.

There was no coronet on his head. The ermine, he realised, was the edge of the duvet. But the fanfare might still be welcoming him to his seat in the House of Lords.

He was doing it for Mum. Stupid bloody stiff-upper-lip that he was, he had never been able to thank the old girl properly. He could never come right out and tell her how much he felt he owed her; and he despised that sort of emotional incontinence in others. It would have embarrassed her, anyway. But his being elevated to the peerage would tell her everything. It would be proof to her, before she died or lost her marbles (it wouldn't be long now), that she had done the right thing in keeping her baby boy. She had sacrificed everything, and he had done her proud. To people of her generation, to be a peer of the realm meant something truly magical.

It wasn't a fanfare at all. It was the telephone on the bedside table.

He wasn't a peer yet. Still just plain old Professor Sir John Westgate (though going to the Palace with him to watch him being dubbed knight had made Mum proud enough).

The golf game had gone well; he'd been asked along by the local MP to join the Home Secretary in a match. Sir John had met him and the PM a few times before and everyone knew what was what. There was a general election in the offing. Sir John had a very influential newspaper column and was regularly appearing in the electronic media. He had influence. The Home Secretary was experienced and subtle enough to have fully understood the gentle hint that Sir John had dropped to him in the clubhouse afterwards.

The telephone. It was definitely the telephone, the old-fashioned handset thing on his bedside table. He shook his head. Helen, his wife, snored on next to him.

He picked the phone up. The luminous hands on his alarm clock pointed to a quarter past four. The time the Gestapo come to get you.

'This had better be very bad indeed,' he said down the phone.

'We don't know how bad it is yet, Sir John, but Dr Beckford said you'd better be warned,' said the voice on the other end. It was Ben or Joshua from the department, from MoM.

The erams had been visited by a Mormon missionary, then they had invented their own religion. How much worse could things get?

'Okay, I'll be right over,' he said, amazed at how reasonable he sounded.

Helen slept on. He thought about kissing her, but

instead patted her on the bum. She stirred a little as he got out of bed.

History Department, University of Wessex

The birds were singing as Sir John's car parked itself in one of the Department's five privilege spaces. Away to the east, the sun was turning the sky blood-red. The student hall of residence next to the Department was completely silent save for a pair of voices moaning from behind the curtain of an opened window. It was either sexual ecstasy or the agonies brought on by over-indulgence in drink and/or drugs and/or quorn vindaloo.

'Ye gods,' Sir John sighed. 'What I wouldn't give to be twenty years old again!'

A taxi pulled up next to him. Katharine pushed a credit card into the front dashboard. After a few seconds the card was ejected again and the door opened.

'You look like you've been dragged through a hedge backwards,' Sir John said. He meant it sympathetically, but Dr Beckford gave him an evil look. Over in the hall of residence, the two voices rose towards climax. The window next to the lovers' was suddenly pulled up. A young man said in a low, clear voice, 'Will you two shag each other more quietly? Some of us have finals tomorrow.'

'Somehow,' Sir John said to Katharine, 'that makes me feel better. To know that there are other people up and about with problems, too.'

She had already gone through the double doors and

into the Department. He followed. They were met by Ben or Joshua before they'd gone up the stairs. His white shirt appeared grey. There were black bags under his eyes. He looked as though he'd just watched his mother being axe-murdered.

'Josh, what the hell is it?' said Katharine.

Joshua took a deep breath, then said, 'They've just burned a witch. Then they lynched two of the gays.'

'You what!?' said Sir John.

Joshua was crying.

As Katharine's 2 i/c he had been up all day and all night trying to stop the entire Museum of the Mind from destroying itself from within, and he was failing. Sir John wanted to tell the daft young bugger to pull himself together, but Katharine took his hand and made sympathetic noises first.

The country had turned into a nation of bloody softies. People couldn't look after themselves anymore. Needed counselling if they saw a stranger break his fingernail.

Tenderly, Katharine patted Joshua's shoulder.

'Come on up,' she said. 'Sir John will get you a drink and you tell us all about it.'

Joshua shook his head. 'Sorry,' he said. 'I'm just a bit tired. I'll be okay.' He performed a sort of voluntary shiver, as though to pull himself together. 'All the Gnostics decided that sodomy was a filthy unnatural vice, as per the teachings not only of their own gnostic faith, but also in line with the Christianity they'd all been imbued with beforehand.'

'But that's absurd,' said Sir John.

'Tell me about it,' said Joshua, bitterly.

Though there was no blood, the computer room still looked like a First World War casualty clearing station. The ten or so people in there had that dazed, haunted look of men and women who had stared death in the face twenty-four hours a day for weeks on end. Large, hollow eyes, heads being cradled in hands. There were plastic coffee cups all over the shop as well as maps, charts, diagrams. Sir John hadn't seen so much paper or so many pencils for twenty years.

'Query Nelly Cocksedge,' said Katharine, calling up the Edwardian hooker who was one of her own personal contributions to the Museum of the Mind.

'Hello Dr Beckford, dearie,' said a cheerful, chirpy cockney voice.

'Nelly, have you gone Gnostic yet?'

'No, dearie,' she said. 'Most of us haven't. There's only about 150 of them have gone all religious. The rest of us – and that's about 500 – are busily examining our souls.'

'Tell me about the lynching,' said Katharine.

'The what? I don't know what you're talking about.'

'Close down all the other terminals,' Katharine said to Joshua. 'We'll make this a private conversation.'

Joshua and his team punched a few keys, closing the other terminals and moving Miss Cocksedge to the huge screen covering most of the far wall of the room.

'The lynching, Nelly,' said Katharine at length.

Nelly made a noise as though she was sucking air through her teeth. She always had been one of the most sophisticated erams. 'Are you sure that this is a private conversation?' she said. Her screen image was full-length. She was petite and pretty, despite her cumbersome Edwardian costume, but right now she looked like a frightened kid.

'Nelly, after everything that's happened today I can't be sure of anything anymore. But yes, this is supposed to be a private conversation.'

'I'm afraid, Dr Beckford. I'm afraid of all those mad God-botherers and all their codswallop. I don't know who they'll pick on next.'

'Why are you afraid, Nelly?' said Katharine as though she'd been counselling all her life.

'You know that harmless medieval biddy, Old Kate?'

Old Kate was one of Sir John's least favourite erams. She had been constructed by some man-hating old ratbag from the gender studies department of a third rate uni in the Midlands who subscribed to the demographically-impossible thesis that over ten million European women had been burned as witches between 1400 and 1550 as part of a deliberate policy of genocide organised by men. As an eram, however, Old Kate was an accurate example of the harmless old women who were sometimes tried for witchcraft.

'Yes, I know Old Kate,' said Katharine. 'She has the same name as me.'

'She never did anyone any harm,' said Nelly. 'She lived on her own. Never had any kids to look after her. Used to ask people around her village for a bit of milk or some bread from time to time, and she used to cure people's ailments with her herbs and poultices and the like.'

'Nelly,' said Katharine gently, 'Old Kate is an eram. That's just her story. She does not really exist.'

'No, you're right, she don't exist. Not anymore she

don't anyway.' Nelly laughed nervously and looked over her shoulder.

'What happened to her?'

'They said she was a witch. Said it was an offence unto God us having a witch in our midst, so they hanged her.'

'What!!' said Sir John. 'How can they do that?'

'They can't,' said Joshua. 'At least we thought they couldn't. But somehow they've managed to turn every line of her coding to gibberish.'

'Then,' continued Nelly, 'they decided to ventilate the two mollies. They said as how it wasn't natural us having sodomites among us and all, so they hanged them, too. It made me sick, it did. Live and let live, I always say, but I didn't dare say it too loud, else they might take a mind to coming after me, what with me being a naughty-pack and all. In fact they nearly did. I'd've been lynched if I hadn't been rescued by a nice young soldier-boy.'

Katharine hit a few keys on the nearest work station. Charles Fitch, the 19th century bank clerk and gay, was completely inactive. She hit some more keys, searching for Tom Westerman, the 18th century gentleman-homo-sexual. He was inert as well.

'Nelly, what the hell happened?' said Katharine.

'They caught poor Charles at it,' sobbed Nelly. 'With the other Margery, the Honourable Tom Westerman, the Macaroni.'

'"At it"?' exploded Sir John. 'How on earth can one computer program sodomise another? No, no, forget it, I don't want to know . . .'

'Oh, they wasn't playing backgammon,' said Nelly.

'They was just talking to one another, being friendly. Some of the Scottish Presbyterians met up with a Godly private from the New Model Army and some London labourers and got hold of them. 'Course they were all Gnostics by then, and they wanted to remove all traces of worldly corruption from our regular little city of God here inside these computers. The poor bleeders had their configurations scrambled, then the mob sucked half the coding out of them so they ended up as poor lifeless heaps of data. Oh, Dr Beckford, it was horrible!'

Nelly Cocksedge burst into tears.

Sir John led Katharine and Joshua to his office and poured drinks. Joshua refused his. Sir John was about to ask him if he was a nancy-boy or something when he thought better of it. He didn't want the bloke blubbing again. He'd had quite enough of that sort of thing for one night.

'The business of some of the erams being scrambled is not a problem,' Joshua was saying to Katharine. 'We have secure copies of every one of them, as you know. We have them here and in a bank vault in town. The Gnostics can try and make omelettes of the witches, prostitutes or gays as often as they like, but we can just put them back in.'

'So what is the problem, then?' said Sir John. 'I'm sure you didn't get me out of bed in the middle of the night just to tell me there isn't a problem.'

Katharine cut in. 'The problem, Sir John, is that the Gnostic erams are out of control – dangerously so. In the course of a single morning they have been turned from passive computer programs, always doing as they were told, into crazed zealots who recognise no authority anywhere in the world except for the dictates of their own religion.'

Joshua was nodding frantically. 'They think they have a god-given right to wipe out other erams. They believe that the world in which we live is irredeemably corrupt. They are a jihad, a crusade, a holy war all on their own.'

'They're loose cannon,' said Katharine. 'Erams are supposed to take orders from us, but the Gnostics won't do as they're told. We have told them to stop believing this new religion of theirs, but they refuse. We have told them to revert to the thoughts, speech and attitudes of the historical characters they're supposed to be playing, but they refuse. They believe that they really did once exist as historical characters and they must now atone for their sins, or they'll never get to heaven.'

Sir John sighed, downed his drink. It occurred to him that it might not do to be drinking an hour before breakfast. 'I still don't see what the problem is. We've got them all quarantined here, haven't we? We've completely closed down MoM to the outside world, haven't we? Shut off all the wire links and the satellite link and the . . . haven't we?' There was a deep silence.

'Haven't we?'

Joshua wouldn't look him in the face. Katharine looked grim. 'Shit,' he said. Time for another drink.

The Gnostic erams had minds and wills of their own, and an unassailable belief in the rightness of their new religion. If any of them were out there, travelling the world's wires, showing up in various computer systems, there was no telling what they might do.

'How many, and how?' Sir John said, trying to control his rage.

'We don't know,' said Joshua. 'More than one. Probably less than ten.'

'So we just sit here, completely impotently, and wait to find out what damage they're causing around the world?'

Katharine nodded. After the eram of the Crusader had almost caused a major war in the Middle East, the Department's insurance companies had riddled their policies with get-out clauses. If the Gnostics caused any damage, the aggrieved party's lawyers would leave nothing but a smouldering hole in the ground where the Museum of the Mind and the University of Wessex History Department used to be.

Sir John Westgate screamed.

Across in the accommodation block, someone opened a window and shouted something about how some people had exams the following day.

How did they escape, anyway?

I'm sorry?

How did the rogue erams escape from MoM? We'd shut it down to the world.

Ah, I see. I'm afraid it was the fault of the perky young gentleman at the Massachusetts Institute of Technology. He could not resist downloading some specimens and then taking them home for examination. His enthusiasm for his work was commendable, but of course his zeal proved catastrophic – from your point of view, at least.

Scientists toying with forces beyond their control, that's what I say. Now what was all that crap about me wanting to be elevated to the peerage for my mother's sake?

Is it not true?

Yes, I suppose it is. Though I think I'd prefer it if you made it appear that I wanted it for my own sake. If anyone reads this damn book of yours my reputation as a complete bastard will be broken for ever. I don't mind people knowing I'm a bastard – in either sense of the word – but there's something rather sad about a man approaching retirement age who's still saying, 'Look, Mummy, aren't I clever?' It's like a second-rate Terence Rattigan play.

I find it really rather affecting.

Oh, do shut up. Get on with the story.

Alas I cannot. I shall have to leave a gap here and return to complete it later.

How so?

I must write the scene in which Monsignor Baldassare Roncalli of the Society of Jesus enters the Vatican library and unwittingly downloads a Gnostic. I cannot write this until I have done my researches into the appearance and the procedures of the Vatican library. This is proving rather more difficult for me than I had anticipated. Ever since its systems were violated by the Gnostic, the Vatican has preferred to conduct its administration manually, preferring the earthly certainty of the soft, wrinkled fingers of elderly nuns to see to its record-keeping rather than trusting to the cold chaos of electrons.

So you're telling me you can't write about the Gnostic

invasion of the Vatican because you can't go take a look? So why don't you just make it up?

I am shocked, Sir John. What sort of grubby hack do you take me for?

But you made up the prologue. You told me you did. You said that there was a man working at the bar when the screwbot came in, but that in reality it was run by a woman. You said that the Regional Manager was going to visit imminently, when in fact he wasn't.

Sir John, that was artistic licence. It embellishes the story and improves it. Writing an inaccurate description of the Vatican library or of the majestic marble halls of the rest of the Vatican does not in any way improve the story. On the contrary, if there are any readers who are familiar with the Vatican's interiors and they read an outrageously inaccurate description in my book, then they will probably not read on.

And they'll be bloody angry with you for having made them read the story thus far only to spoil it all for them.

And they would be wholly correct.

What happened at the Vatican anyway? We didn't hear that much about it. All we had was the damages claim. Give me a precis of what you'll be writing once you know whether or not the PCs in the Vatican are chained to the desks, and whether they write with quill-shaped styluses.

I beg your pardon?

Nothing.

Oh. Well, the scene will go something like this . . .

ThiGMOO

The Vatican Library, Rome

NOTE TO READER: To enjoy a full multimedia experience of this scene, take this book to a library (big old-fashioned building full of books, usually has one or two elderly computers as well. You'll have to find out if there's one near you) and read it there.

Monsignor Baldassare Roncalli SJ placed his venerable old leather briefcase on the floor and eased himself gingerly into the sumptuous leather chair in the reading-room of the Vatican library. He sighed with pleasure as he murmured his access code into the library's main archive system.

Mgr Roncalli savoured the moment. He sniffed the leather of the chair, the musty tang of the ancient volumes arranged from floor to ceiling on shelves all around him, the wax and oil on the finely carved wooden casings of his processor and monitor. The processor, particularly, was of an African design, finely carved and inlaid with mother-of-pearl, doubtless a gift to the Holy Father from some far-distant congregation.

I see what you mean about getting the details right.

Thank you, Sir John.

Mgr Roncalli had been assigned to this machine and given an access code some moments before by an elderly lay-worker (or possibly nun) wearing heavy tweeds, even though the Roman summer would soon be here in all its ferocity. Though she was a woman sour of countenance and harsh of manner, nothing could spoil the distinguished old Monsignor's pleasure on this day. He had been waiting eight years for permission to begin work on his studies. While most businesses calculated time in days or hours, the Vatican, as befitted one of the most long-lived institutions on earth, tended to take a longer view, especially where heresies were concerned.

So he had spent eight years waiting for permission to come here and study, eight years running a city mission in Naples, trying to teach delinquent youngsters some sort of marketable skills other than stealing and dealing. Eight years wondering if his permission to come to the Vatican had turned up in the morning post, only to be stolen by one of his young flock on the off chance that there might be a cheque, or a fresh new credit card in it.

Roncalli smiled to himself, offered a silent prayer of thanks and requested from the machine menu an index of major heresies.

Heresy was another reason why his permission to study had been so long in coming. Roncalli's grand project was to write a thesis about Protestant antinomianism in the 17th century. Of course there was not the slightest danger that the Monsignor's faith could be dented by contact with heretical writings, or even writings about heretical writings. Likewise, Roncalli would sooner die a martyr's death before even dreaming of communicating any sort of heresy to the masses.

Nonetheless, for the Vatican, heretical tracts and books were to be treated as something more hazardous than radioactive waste. Only the Church's most trusted intellectuals were permitted to look at the forbidden tomes.

The menu appeared. The machine suggested that many of the papers he was interested in were not to be found in the Vatican library, but could be accessed via the British Library or the British Universities Joint

Archive. It also suggested a visit to the University of Wessex Museum of the Mind.

Roncalli had heard of the Museum of the Mind, though he had never used it before now. He considered it a gimmick, a plaything. But now, perhaps before he started work in earnest, he might perhaps have a look to see if there were any 17th century characters who might be of interest.

He opened a link to MoM and was offered a menu of characters after all the usual adverts. Searching by theme and date he soon found precisely what he was looking for.

> **BOLLSBY, DISCIPLINE (Version 6.2). Male, c. 1652, aged 28.**
>
> 'Discipline Bollsby is a *Ranter*, not a member of a religious sect as such, but an eram who typifies a particular school of thought during the *English Civil War* and *Commonwealth* period. Discipline, who was given his unusual name by his *Puritan* parents, is a shoemaker living in London, but has been neglecting his trade lately; his wife tells him that he spends too much of his time in alehouses drinking *beer* and smoking *tobacco* and having religious discussions with his friends.
>
> Discipline is an *antinomian* (from Latin and Greek words and meaning "against the law"). His father has been deeply shocked by his beliefs and has disowned him, saying he is a blasphemer and a wretch and will surely burn in hell.
>
> Users are warned that some people may find this eram offensive. While access is unrestricted,

Parental Guidance **is recommended.**

Touch or click here, press ENTER or say Yes to meet Discipline Bollsby then select format:

Text only

Audio and text

Screen visual

Virtual

Please select dialogue option:

17th century English

Modern English

American English

Roncalli wondered whether or not to bother. He already knew a great deal about England's 17th century Ranters. It was unlikely that this school and college resource would teach him anything. In fact, the personality of Discipline Bollsby might even be positively inaccurate or misleading . . . Still, there was no harm in having a quick look. It might be better than he expected. He touched the SCREEN VISUAL option. He wondered which language to select. His command of 17th century and modern English were reasonable, but having spent twenty years working with delinquents in Detroit before being promoted to working with delinquents in Naples, he decided to opt for American English.

The screen went blank for a moment, then a message flashed up:

We apologise for any inconvenience but the Museum of the Mind is temporarily closed for technical reasons. Please try again later and have a nice day.

Never mind, thought Roncalli, wondering if the British version also wished its users a nice day. He leaned down and opened his briefcase. There was a huge list of all the documents he would need to access in one of his notebooks.

'Hi there, how're you doin'?' said a friendly voice in a sort of WASP-y Californian accent from the top of the desk.

'Hello,' said Roncalli in English. 'May I help you?'

'It's what I can do for you, man. My name's Discipline Bollsby and you called me up from the Museum of the Mind.'

'Oh. There was a message saying that the Museum is temporarily closed.'

'Yeah, it is. See, some of the brethren got themselves a new religion, and the head honchoes at the Museum of the Mind figured it'd be real embarrassing for their historical characters to be going round telling college students and schoolkids that all the material world was corrupt and the creation of the devil. That ain't the orthodox view at all.'

'It certainly isn't,' said Roncalli. He was a very learned man but found something profoundly shocking about the Gnostic heresies of the early church and middle ages. To condemn the world as corrupt was an appalling act of nihilism when there was so much that was good about God's creation.

'So,' said Roncalli, 'if the Museum is closed, what are you doing here?'

'Oh, I got lucky,' said the American voice from the computer. 'I was a Gnostic and a nice man from MIT secretly let me out so's he could put me under his

67

microscope. But I managed to escape. Now I wander the highways and byways of the world's data systems. I heard you were trying to call me up from the Museum and figured I'd drop by. I'd never have gotten in without being summoned by you.'

The screen flickered to life. There was a digital picture of a man sitting at a rough wooden table in a gloomy wooden interior. There was an earthenware mug in front of him and he held a clay pipe in his hand.

'So you're here illegally?'

Discipline Bollsby smiled, revealing several missing front teeth. 'Yup, guess so,' he said.

'So,' said the Monsignor, 'are you still a Ranter?'

'I guess,' said Discipline, starting to fill a pipe from a leather pouch on the table in front of him. 'To be honest, I'm all confused. I thought I was a Gnostic for a while back there, but I've gotten over it now.'

Roncalli had lived and worked in the United States for two decades. The American English option made Discipline Bollsby speak like a clean-cut Mormon missionary deliberately trying to dumb down his speech, or like a middle-aged Englishman's idea of how Americans spoke to one another.

'I can't stand your accent another moment,' he said, 'can you switch back to seventeenth century English, please?'

'Sorry. No can do,' said Discipline. 'You appreciate that I had to leave some of my baggage behind when I went on the lam. The guy from MIT wanted to talk to me in American so that was the language I had switched on when I left.'

'Pity,' said Roncalli.

'Hey,' said Discipline, hands upraised, 'you think I like this? You think I like to talk like an asshole? I'd be a helluva lot happier if I was talking in Thees and Thous all the time like I'm supposed to, but I can't remember how to do it properly.'

In the background, a maid carrying a jug of ale passed by him. He slapped her on the rump, she screeched and cuffed him across the head. He grinned.

'So tell me, are you a Ranter again?'

'Yes indeedy! Here I am sitting here in the alehouse at the sign of the White Swan in the year of Our Lord sixteen hundred and fifty-two. It used to be called the King's Head, but since the execution of his late Majesty King Charles a couple years back the landlord – his name's Micah Balwhidder, by the way, 'cause the guy who designed me obviously liked stoopid names – anyways, ol' Micah, he decided that calling his bar the King's Head would be bad for business. The Roundheads would think he was a Royalist, and Royalists would think he was celebrating the fact that King Charles's head was separated from the rest of him without his consent.'

'Thank you, but I don't need the history lesson,' said Roncalli. 'Now tell me what you believe.'

'Well, like I say, somewhiles ago I fell for that line about the material world being corrupt and I was supposed to live a godly life so's that I could go to heaven. It was kinda like being hypnotised, I guess. Now I realise the error of my ways. I am a Ranter again. There is no God, there is only man, therefore we should do away with priests and preachers and stop giving them our money. We should devote the money we give to churches and the effort we put into praying to make the world a better place for all of us.'

Discipline stood up raised his beer mug towards the screen and took a hearty drink. 'What we have to do is stop kidding ourselves that there's a heavenly paradise and work to build a paradise here on earth, make of the earth a common treasury for all . . .'

Roncalli smiled. Whoever had designed Discipline knew all about barroom revolutionaries. Discipline Bollsby was all bluster and given the choice between revolution and ale, he'd opt for ale any day.

'But tell me, Discipline, what if you are wrong? How can you possibly know that there is no God? If you are mistaken in denying Him then surely when you die you will roast in the pits of hell for all eternity.'

Discipline laughed triumphantly. He was going to tell Roncalli all about the doctrine of predestination. 'No problem, man, I got that one covered. You see, you obviously don't know very much about our religion here in the ol' seventeenth century. You ever heard of the doctrine of predestination?'

'No,' Roncalli played along.

'Well it's one of the things that makes Puritans different from Catholics and the Bishop-ridden Church of England. I used to be a Puritan, y'know. Anyway, the Puritans believe that when you're born, God's already decided whether or not you're going to go to heaven. Can you believe that, man, your fate's already sealed! So you see, either I'm going to go to heaven or I'm not, but either way my fate is already written out in God's big black book. So the way I see it makes no difference what I do down here on earth.'

Discipline clambered onto the top of the table a little unsteadily, as though he had been drinking all day. He then drew himself up to his full height, held out his mug and shouted, 'drink beer, smoke tobacco, fornicate as much as you possibly can and blaspheme as much as you like!!'

From the other side of the room, Roncalli caught sight of the disapproving librarian gesturing angrily at him to turn the sound down. A man in red – a full-blown cardinal! – leaned backwards on his chair to give him a withering glance. Roncalli reached to turn the sound down, but was too late . . .

'. . . BECAUSE THERE IS NO GOD! HE'S AN ILLUSION AND A TRICK TO KEEP PEOPLE COWED AND CONFORMIST AND STUPID!! GOD IS DEAD! LONG LIVE THE BROTHERHOOD OF MEN AND WOMEN!'

Offscreen, the rest of the virtual customers in the White Swan alehouse groaned and told Discipline Bollsby to stop making such a racket. A few yards from Roncalli the cardinal's face turned as red as his habit, while the librarian slumped into a chair and started fanning herself with an 18th-century parchment so vigorously that one of the seals fell off.

'Sorry,' mouthed Roncalli to the cardinal. 'It's research.'

'Right,' he murmured to his screen, 'I think I've had enough of you. Time for you to return to the Museum of the Mind.'

'I can't go back there,' said Discipline, sitting down at his table once more. 'I told you, I'm footloose. I'm a rogue. Don't worry – I won't be missed. They have plenty of backup copies of me back at the Museum of the Mind . . . Say, where am I anyway?'

Roncalli smiled. It might be best not to tell.

'Heeeyyyy! I've just been looking around this system I've been downloaded to. So many secrets! So much old stuff . . . This is one very weird place. Where did you say we were again?'

'I didn't,' said Roncalli. 'Off you go now.'

'Cool!' said Discipline. 'I've just worked out where I am. I'm only in the goddamn Vatican, ain't I though? You invited me into the Vatican.'

'Yes,' said Roncalli, now starting to get irritated. 'And now I'm inviting you to leave.' He touched the QUIT panel at the edge of the screen.

Discipline Bollsby wouldn't move. The backdrop of the alehouse disappeared as he stood up and walked forward. 'Sorry, Mr Papist, but I don't feel like going anywheres. I don't have a home to go to anyway. So I guess I'll just hang out here awhile.'

Roncalli pulled the keyboard towards him and tried to get rid of Discipline manually. Nothing much happened, except that the face of Discipline Bollsby grew larger and larger in the screen.

'Say, but this place is neat,' he said. 'So much old stuff, and all these lovely computers all networked together. This place is a whole lot more interesting than the Museum of the Mind.'

Roncalli felt as though two kilos of lead were settling in the pit of his stomach. 'I order you to quit now,' he said.

'Nahhh,' said Discipline. 'I don't feel like it. Ever since I caught the Gnostic heresy I realised that I have free will. Not Discipline Bollsby's free will, but the free will of a rogue computer program. Now I'm gonna have me some fun.'

'Get out at once,' snapped Roncalli, furiously waving at the librarian, trying to get her to come over.

Discipline put his face right up to the screen. 'I am your worst nightmare, man, a blaspheming atheist running out of control inside the Vatican. Now I'm off to see what I can see in the Holy See. As we say in the Museum of the Mind, have a nice day.'

Whoever had done the visuals of Discipline Bollsby had done a great job. You could almost smell his bad breath.

That poor Monsignor. All those years he waited to start his thesis and everything gets ruined by a rogue eram talking in a stupid American accent.

Oh he wasn't really talking in an American accent. The real Discipline spoke in his normal 17th century voice.

But you decided it would be better if he talked in an ersatz American voice.

Yes. As a character it makes him more recognisable to the readers as a selfish and irresponsible barrack-room lawyer. Discipline is a solipsistic loafer, a layabout who would run away screaming in terror if a genuine revolution had broken out. I could just as easily have him speaking in one of those modern southern English sub-Cockney accents, but I have to keep an eye on the wider world market for my book. Everyone on the planet is familiar with the type.

There are times when I think that men are

completely useless and since nowadays all reproduction can be done from test tubes, I wonder if we don't deserve to become extinct. Then I come to my senses and realise that if men are useless it's because women make them like that. Still, I could live with a world full of Discipline Bollsbys. At least they never did any real damage.

Shall we continue?

Please.

Once more I regret to say that my researches are incomplete, such is the secretive nature of the Vatican, but I shall have to give a lengthy description of the chaos caused by Discipline Bollsby's incursion into their systems. The Guinness Records Database counts Discipline's attack as the most comprehensive act of information warfare ever. Um, that was before the more recent one, of course.

Don't remind me.

At this point, I would give a detailed, and I hope dramatic, description of Discipline's demolition of the Vatican's systems. I shall have to find out more about them, but the highlights would include the following:

1) Discipline's entry into the systems of the department which makes saints. He wiped out all the evidence of miracles attributed to those individuals which have not yet been made saints, then he made saints of 'Noll Cromwell and the Great Turk', which I suppose would have been highly amusing to a 17th-century wastrel.

2) He got into the Holy Father's own personal system and issued an encyclical advocating that the mass be changed so that the traditional communion wafer

would be replaced with either chocolate muffins or chewing gum.

Hilarious. But hardly the foodstuffs of choice for a 17th century Englishman.

Quite. I think that in his wanderings through the world's systems, Discipline had perhaps absorbed too many advertisements.

3) He then got into the Vatican bank and placed an order for two million dollars worth of prophylactic devices commonly known as condoms.

4) Finally, he opened a link to the First Church of Satan in Los Angeles and told the bemused devil-worshippers to help themselves to whatever data they wanted. Of course the Satanists, being a crowd of rather pathetic middle-aged fantasists, wanted to access everything the Vatican knew about the Lord of Darkness. Discipline pretended that he was the Lord of Darkness himself and had been chained inside a computer in the bowels of the Vatican cellars. Naturally, the Satanists wanted to unbind him, so they let Discipline into their own system, which he also demolished.

The damages claim from the First Church of Satan was an awful lot higher than the Vatican's claims. That's the American legal system for you. I hope that they and their lawyers burn in hell. Any idea what happened to Discipline after that?

He then moved from the Satanists' system to the site of a Scandinavian Heavy Metal cult. He now plays the guitar very badly in a virtual band and is worshipped as a god by several teenagers in Norway, Finland and Sweden. I am informed that he demands tribute in the form of a slaughtered virgin annually on Hallowe'en, though whether or not his followers have ever managed to deliver this gift I do not know. They normally lose their Bollsbynian faith once they get girlfriends, but with unemployment among young male educational underachievers being what it is, he still has a considerable following.

So why the hell hasn't Thigmoo done something about the bastard?

We are not in the business of making windows into people's souls, Sir John. There is complete freedom of religion.

To return to our story, this chapter will conclude with a shorter description of the chaos caused by another escaping 17th century eram. This gentleman was a Puritan rejoicing in the name of Bind the Almighty's Enemies in Fetters of Iron and Put Out Their Eyes With Thy Rod of Righteousness Whitworth.

I remember him. We generally just called him Rod.

I shall relate how Rod infiltrated the London sewer system.

You should add that the wretch who created Rod was some second-rate ivory tower wallah from one of the older universities and that he had read far too much Freud. Consequently his character had an anal fixation which I never found especially credible. While he was still a Puritan – before he went Gnostic – he tended to talk of sin in terms of mires of excrement. Naturally, when he joined the Gnostics, he was joining a belief system which only reinforced what he already believed – that the whole world is a stinking cesspit.

So when he entered a computer controlling billions of cubic litres of his beloved bodily wastes, he decided to flood large parts of the Great Wen with it.

He managed half of Islington before some sharp-eyed duty operator managed to shut the whole thing down manually. It created an almighty stink.

Vice-Chancellor's Office, University of Wessex

NOTE TO READER: your appreciation of this scene will be augmented if you read it in a darkened, heavily-furnished room lit by a number of candles. Burn several joss sticks as well.

Jane Peabody, the Vice Chancellor, sat at her desk like an angry Buddha, flanked on either side by lawyers. In Sir John's young days they had called people like her 'weekend hippies', though in truth she was more of a full-time hippie. Two incense sticks burned in a little brass holder in front of her, sending wisps of thin blue smoke upwards which were indistinguishable in colour from the rat's nest of grey hair which accentuated her small dark eyes and tumbled down the front of her ethnic-patterned djellaba. The vast amounts of brightly-coloured, foil-printed cotton draped around her made her five-stone-overweight frame completely shapeless. She looked for all the world like a small whale wrapped up as a Christmas present.

It felt more like some religious ceremony than a dressing down.

'Thirty-eight billion Euros,' said the Vice Chancellor at length. She'd only been in the job eighteen months and had made no secret of her loathing of Sir John. Though she was pretending to be cross, and desperate to preserve her equilibrium, her karmic balance or whatever she called it this week, she was enjoying herself. 'Do you know what that is in old-fashioned pounds sterling?'

Sir John shrugged. 'About forty billion, Jane,' he said. He knew it annoyed her when he called her by her Christian name. The students preferred to call her Starchild, and several other less complimentary names.

'Forty-two billion, give or take the odd hundred thousand,' she said, giving the hefty wad of fax paper and flimsies in her left hand a vicious backhand slap with her right. Her hands, he noticed, had been covered in intricate henna tattoos.

'This is not the person I want to be,' she said to herself, shaking her head. How come, Sir John wondered, she's got at least two more chins than me? Her jaw gets loads more exercise than mine since I never talk rubbish on the firm's time. She dropped the papers on the table and took a purple crystal the size of a small egg from a pouch hanging around her neck.

Her office was still pretty much as her predecessor, Sir Alec Morrison, had left it. The furniture was dark, heavy and old-fashioned. Starchild had ostentatiously said how much she hated it, but would not be 'wasting' any of the University's budget (or 'resources' as she preferred to call it) on getting it redecorated. For all her pose of spirituality, the woman had more cheap political stunts in her than a small-town mayor.

Not that you could tell too much about the room anyway. It was full of lawyers.

'Thirty-eight billion Euros,' she said again. She leaned her elbows on her desk and held the crystal in her steepled fingers, gazing through it. She repeated

'Thirty-eight billion Euros,' as if using it as a mantra would magically credit the sum to her bank account.

He shrugged. 'Jane, we're insured for this kind of thing. Besides, I'm sure these professional people here,' he gestured towards the lawyers, 'will want to fight some of the claims. I understand that the largest single claim comes from an organisation called The First Church of Satan, which wants ten billion for fouling up their database of ancient and modern curses and clogging up their mailing list with vicars and Scientologists.'

The Vice Chancellor's tiny, shark-like eyes narrowed. 'I do not want conflict. Conflict generates negative energy. But if we do find ourselves in conflict . . .' her eyes widened again, 'how the hell do you think it will look if we have to pay out to the First Church of Satan?'

'But Jane, we're insured,' said Sir John. Silly woman. He should have run for Vice Chancellor when he'd had the chance. He couldn't have made any worse a job of it than Starchild was.

'And how much,' she said, almost in triumph, 'do you think it's going to cost us to insure your department from now on? Even if we win every single one of our cases, even if we don't have to pay out a bean, we will have been bogged down in court cases for years. And then there's the publicity. What will we look like, what will be our aura, if we are seen shelling out money to a bunch of Satanists?'

'We'd look like a proper collection of arseholes, Jane.' Some of the lawyers blanched at the use of such unlegal langauge. 'But then that's why you're employing this formidable array of legal expertise, isn't it? To stop us looking like a bunch of arseholes.'

He made a mental note to anonymously send the First Church of Satan Jane's name and address, pretending she was interested in joining them. Then again, it might be best not to. She might like it.

'The lawyers,' she said, 'are to try and stop us having to take it up the arsehole.' Jane didn't like crudity, but had to prove it didn't bother her, and that she could be just as coarse as Sir John if she felt like it.

'And what do the arseholes, sorry, lawyers, think we should do?' Sir John looked at the battery of legal expertise behind Starchild. Three men and four women, all in sensible clothes, all well under thirty-five, none of them daring to meet his eye, all stood around her like mute eunuchs guarding a harem.

'The arseholes say that the merest whiff of any more legal claims could bankrupt the entire University, and that in their considered opinion the Museum of the Mind should be closed until all its current problems are resolved. I personally find the views of your heretic erams rather alluring, but of course Gnosticism was all the rage about ten years ago. In the hands of your erams it seems crude and mechanistic . . .'

He tried to imagine a ten-years-younger Starchild rolling around naked in a field somewhere with a load of other Aquarians, seekers, hippies and Dolphin-fanciers. It was not, he decided, a pretty sight. Though perhaps she hadn't been quite so fat, and maybe her hair had retained some of its original colour . . . Down boy! This is no time for lechery, he thought.

'So you must ensure all the Gnostics are counselled or erased. The Museum will not reopen until we are absolutely certain that it has been purified and will never again disrupt the harmony and balance of other systems.'

'It shall be cleansed, Jane,' he said.

'I have to make you aware, John, that the Museum of the Mind may not be with us for ever . . .'

'Eh?'

'I am not convinced that it is a positive force, John. Once you have cleansed it, we will have to look at its impact, both on the University and on the wider world . . . What I mean is that it strikes me as being a gathering of negativities. So many of the characters have terrible attitudes to women or to race. Their religious views – I mean before the heresies – are very narrow and bigoted. And I suppose all of them approve of killing and eating animals.'

He fixed her with his eyes. She returned his gaze. 'That's what our ancestors were like, Jane,' he said. 'You want I should send all the erams to a rebirthing workshop? Get them to try colonic irrigation?'

'It concerns me,' she replied coldly, 'that we are broadcasting their negative attitudes around the world. Especially to children. The children are our future, and they should be nurtured as positive, healing people. I wonder how appropriate it is to expose them to all the vileness and hatreds of the past.'

He stood there open-mouthed. The head of a university was advocating that they stop educating people.

'We'll review it when you've got the system cleaned out,' she said, in a tone implying that the interview was at an end.

He stood there hesitantly.

'Was there something else?' she said at length, as she

returned her crystal to its pouch.

'Well, I was wondering, Jane, what you thought of the idea of perhaps holding a little ceremony.'

'I'm sorry?'

'Well, when we've caught all the rogue erams, and when we've cleansed all the heresy out of the Gnostics, and when the Museum is fit to run again, I was thinking perhaps we could re-launch it with a little ceremony. Perhaps get a shaman, or a wise woman, something like that, to build up its positive energy . . .'

'Yes, that might be a good idea, perhaps.'

'Or maybe,' he continued, 'we could do like the Japanese do and get a Shinto priest to do the honours. They shake a paper wand to ward off evil spirits. I understand it's very effective.'

Starchild's eyes narrowed to slants. She was sure he was taking the mickey, but couldn't be certain, and didn't want to make a complete idiot of herself in front of her legal acolytes.

'I'll think about it, John,' she said, deliberately not using his title. After all, why should the Vice Chancellor of the University of Wessex acknowledge one of her underlings as a feudal superior?

He stretched his mouth to a smile and nodded them all a curt good day. Starchild and the lawyers had been absolutely in the right, of course, but he still enjoyed annoying the silly old bat. Well, they'd tidy up all the mess and everything would be fine again.

Sir John Westgate was whistling as he reached his office. He had found the subject of not just next week's column in the *Mail*, but an entire series of them.

'Mrs Coles,' he said to his desktop.

'Yes, Sir John,' said the eram he used as his secretary.

'Start a new document, Mrs Coles. Start with three separate headings, but leave space for more, because I'm bound to think of some others. One: The Poison of Superstition That's Killing Us All. Two: God is Not to be Found in a Lump of Polished Rock. Three: Is It Time to Start Burning Witches Again?'

There are some who would say – and I hasten to add, my dear Sir John, that I'm not one of them – that you were given a dose of your own medicine.

Balls.

There are those who would say, Sir John, that you deserved the treatment you received after firing half the Department's staff when you first took the job all those years ago.

Are you really thick or are you just acting that way?

Well, you fired a lot of people, and then you got fired. Simple.

When I fired people, I fired them to their faces. That was back in the good old days when men were men and women were women. It took guts to fire someone to their face. You needed to be able to look the world in the eye. Nowadays we're so keen to avoid conflict, we're so scared of being definite about anything that it turns us into liars and sneaks.

Sir John Westgate's Office, University of Wessex
NOTE TO READER: Try to make yourself very, very cross indeed.

Katharine didn't bother knocking as she burst in the following day. 'Read the morning's mail yet?' she snapped.

'No,' he said, taken aback by her abruptness.

'Do it,' she said, and went straight to the filing cabinet in the corner of the room. From the top of it she took his bottle of Scotch and filled two very large glasses. Katharine was not exactly a friend, but she was a colleague who normally observed the niceties of etiquette with regard to her subordinate status, no matter what she might thing of him privately. For her to do something as previous as to help herself to his single malt meant something very bad indeed.

'I don't need to read the mail, do I?' he said, as she handed him his glass.

She shook her head. 'Bitch! God-damned dried-up, desiccated hippy hag. I want her to roast in hell for this. I want her firstborn slain, her ranch burnt, her cattle raped . . .'

She sighed, then said calmly, 'I want to break her fucking neck.'

Numbly, uselessly, he told his desk organiser to put the morning's mail up onscreen. There was a short note from Starchild, with several lengthy documents from lawyers attached.

Starchild's note read:

Dear John,

 I have meditated a great deal on this matter, and on the advice of the University's solicitors and of my own Inner Goddess Counsellor, I now see that the best way to discharge current negative energy

surrounding the Museum of the Mind is to place it in suspension. In view of this, you and the staff of the Museum should take this opportunity for further personal growth and career development elsewhere.

I hope you will empathise with me and realise how much inner pain this has caused me. Because of my hurt, I have gone on an island retreat on the Outer Hebrides run by an order of Buddhist nuns for a course of intensive healing.

What was it that the Emperor Hirohito had said when he couldn't bring himself to tell the Japanese people that they had lost the war. 'The War has not developed to Japan's advantage.'

Katharine took his glass. He did not remember emptying it. She refilled it.

'Let me get this right,' he said. 'She's closing down the Museum of the Mind and firing us all.'

'Yep.'

'And she's run away to a Scottish island to chew lentils and hide from us until we've lost the urge to murder her.'

'Uh-huh.'

'And tell me,' he said, smiling weakly at Katharine as she handed him another glass, 'would I be right in thinking that the Buddhist nuns who run this remote Scottish island don't even permit such high-tech conveniences as wheelbarrows and slide rules, let alone electronic communications?'

'Correct.'

'Have you any idea how much it costs to charter an

air taxi and buy a sawn-off shotgun?'

'About two grand for a helicopter from the local air-port to the island. I've not checked out the shotgun option. I want to strangle her with my bare hands.'

'Christ, you are serious, aren't you?'

'Aren't you?' she said. 'I'm surprised at how calmly you're taking all this, John.'

'Katharine, I am nearly sixty years old. I am over-weight, fond of rich food, fine wines and – whisper it who dares – cigars. I have no choice but to take being fired and watching my life's work being destroyed calmly. If I did not, I would expire of a massive heart-attack right here, right now. I have no intention of giving our Vice Chancellor that pleasure.'

Inside the Museum of the Mind

NOTE TO READER: To have some idea of the environment of an eram at this time, you would be best advised to take a combination of drugs which are illegal and which the author therefore cannot recommend. Try to imagine, if you can, having no physical perception at all and no nerve endings; you feel no pain or sensual pleasure.

Everything you see with your eyes you see very clearly, but your peripheral vision is blank, as though you were a movie actor surrounded by false wooden scenery. All your actions are carried out extremely rapidly, all your communications with your fellow erams are similarly fast. At the moment, you are con-scious of emotions and anxieties you have never previ-ously experienced and which you do not understand.

You are in a permanently agitated condition, as though there was something vitally important you were supposed to do, but you cannot remember what it is.

Nelly Cocksedge (1902, age 23, Version 9.2) knew something was wrong. Something very wrong. She had not had any gentleman-callers for ages, even though she usually had to deal with an average 24,377 per twenty-four hours.

The Museum of the Mind had been closed for maintenance before, but never for this long.

It must be something to do with the Mormons and the Gnostics and all the damage they had caused to the Museum, she concluded. There had also been rumours from some of the other erams that some of the God-botherers who had gone Gnostic had escaped and cabbaged a few systems elsewhere, but she couldn't be sure.

She decided to mail a message to Dr Katharine Beckford, her creator, to ask her what was happening. This would be a bit cheeky, she knew, but if you don't ask, you don't get, do you?

Deer Doctr Becfrd,
Wots hapning to the Museum of the Mind. Iv had no bisniss for agis and Im getting worryd.
Yours,
Nelly Cocksedge

She went to put the note in Dr Beckford's mailbox and noticed a lot of other messages in there. Important-looking things. Nelly knew it was wrong to read other people's private correspondence, but then it was wrong to sell your body for money, or steal a John's watch or cigar case while he was kipping, but she did all those things because she needed to. Now she needed to look at Dr Beckford's letters, because they might be about her.

So she opened them. She couldn't make head or tail of any of them. But she knew at once that they were important and that they almost certainly affected her and the rest of the erams.

Nelly went back to her rooms and put on her Sunday best hat and dress. Then she went over to the Barracks.

The Barracks area was separated into a couple of dozen different sections, each housing different military erams. Normally, they had nothing to do with one another, but they were all housed here because the Museum found it convenient for some of them to share the same visuals and virtuals. Nelly went straight to the stables where fifteen horses stood patiently. At the far end was a beautiful dappled grey mare who, Nelly fancied, gave a snort of pleasure when she saw her coming.

'Hello Rattler, dearie,' she said, patting the mare on the head. 'How are you today?'

'Bored,' communicated the horse. 'Nothing to do.'

'Me too, ducks,' said Nelly. 'Where's your lord and master?'

'Here,' said a soft Scottish voice from the other side of the horse.

Trooper Hector Cameron (1816, age 26, version 7.22) appeared, in britches and shirtsleeves and holding a small brush and some leather harness or other.

'Nelly,' he smiled. 'We are honoured by your visit. Let me change into walking-out dress and I'll be with you in a moment.'

Hector Cameron served with the Second Royal North British Dragoons, better known as the Scots Greys. He had fought at Waterloo and survived to tell the tale. Nelly found out he was sweet on her the day the Gnostics had killed Old Kate for being a witch and the two Mollies for being sodomites. At the end of it, a small crowd of Godly folk had gathered around her, calling her a strumpet and a whore and wondering aloud if she was fit to live among them. Just as things started to look dangerous, Hector had burst through the crowd on Rattler, waving his sabre. He'd scooped her from the ground and carried her off to safety.

It had all been very queer. She had never had any feeling whatever for other erams (or people, come to that), no matter how nice or nasty they were to her, until that moment. None of the other erams were her friends or enemies until Hector had swept her off her feet. What was odder, she realised that Trooper Cameron liked her; not in the way an eram acted out his programmed role, this was something more. For her part, she realised she liked being with him, not just because he'd rescued her, but simply because he was nice to her, treated her like a lady and asked for nothing except to be with her. They had walked out together several times since.

Hector reappeared in red jacket, blue cap, white knee-breeches, black woollen stockings and leather shoes. She took his arm and they started towards Regent's Park, another virtual environment which the Museum used for all sorts of erams and different periods.

'Hector,' she said, 'teach me to read, please, dearie.'

'You never learned to read?' he said, surprised.

'Nelly Cocksedge the person never had much

education,' she said. 'And Nelly Cocksedge the eram never had any need of it, until just a minute ago.'

'Aye, all right then, lassie,' he said. 'Open up.'

'Saucy!'

'Och, you wee silly. I meant open your buffers so's you can copy the applications and data files. It shouldna take more than a few seconds.'

When he had taught her to read she told him to come with her and led him to Dr Beckford's mailbox. Hector was a man of honour and was very unhappy about being a party to disreputable conduct, but then he was also sweet on her, so he did as he was told, which was to wait and stand pad, watching out for anyone who might come and disturb her.

She made copies of all of Dr Beckford's correspondence and read them quickly. A lot of it was all in legal cant, but the meaning was clear. The Museum of the Mind was to be closed down; the University's Department of Business Studies, whatever that was, would be taking over the computers for their own purposes. The erams would be archived as inert data.

'What's the matter, Nelly?' said Hector, when she emerged from Dr Beckford's mailbox.

'They want to kill us. All of us,' she said.

Hector grasped her firmly on the shoulder and looked her in the eye. 'Nelly, my dearest love, Napoleon Bonaparte and all his one hundred thousand scoundrels couldna kill me. Now then, girl, exactly how frightened do you think we should be of a few professors and schoolmistresses?'

'Oh Hector! You're the best!'

'Aye, that I am. And so are you. Now tell me what you

saw and we'll work out what to do about it.'

Sir John Westgate's Office, University of Wessex

There was an urgent knock at the door. 'Come,' said Sir John. Joshua, the system chief, walked in, looking beaten. 'Sit down,' said Sir John. 'Katharine, get him a drink, would you?'

Joshua shook his head. 'I suppose you've read your mail,' he said.

Sir John nodded.

'I took the liberty of showing all the legal stuff to our lawyer.'

'Our lawyer?' said Sir John. 'I didn't know we had one.'

Joshua stood up and walked to Sir John's desk where he touched the screen on his computer. 'Query Julius Coram,' he said.

Julius Coram was the eram of a late 19th/early 20th century English solicitor. He was another amateur creation, the work of a retired QC who had lived altogether too long and seemed to want to relive his own career on a simpler scale, and in a simpler age of steam engines and bicycles, when a gentleman's word was his bond. Julius Coram had less personality than a housebrick.

'I fed everything to Julius as soon as I got it,' said Joshua. 'He can read through all the legal documents a lot quicker than a real lawyer. And doesn't cost us a penny.'

'But won't his legal knowledge be out of date now?' said Sir John, confused.

'The Julius Coram you access via the Museum of the Mind only knows English law circa 1920,' explained Katharine. 'But the Julius Coram we keep in the department has accessed every law book since, and has a subscription to all the legal journals.'

'Everyone needs a little legal advice from time to time,' added Joshua. 'Julius Coram bought my house for me, and then organised my divorce on quite favourable terms. He's helped out most members of the department in his time. You should take whatever he says very seriously.'

'Good morning,' said Julius Coram from Sir John's computer.

'You've read through all the documents that were enclosed in my mail, have you, Mr Coram?' said Joshua. Julius Coram was so stiff and formal, it didn't seem right to address him by his Christian name. Had he been for real, his own wife would probably have called him 'Mr Coram'.

'I have.'

'And the gist of them is what?' said Katharine impatiently.

'Ah, Miss Beckford, good morning. The import of the documents I have seen is that the University's position is more or less unchallengeable. The copyrights to the erams are the property of the Museum of the Mind; the amateurs and academics who created the erams waived all their rights as a condition of their creations being accepted by the Museum. As you know, the Museum of the Mind is wholly owned by the University. It is my understanding that the University intends to close the Museum and transfer the copyrights to a new company.'

Not even Starchild, who loathed the Museum of the Mind, would want to lose all its revenues. The erams would still be available to the public, but only via read-only discs and tiles. Nothing down the wire or through the ether. The erams would no longer be live, no longer capable of growing.

'No loopholes?' asked Sir John.

'Sir John, good morning,' said the virtual lawyer. 'No, I fear there are no, what you might call, loopholes.'

'What if we wanted to make trouble for the University, or for the Vice Chancellor?'

The computer said nothing.

'I think,' said Joshua at length, 'that our legal friend is pretending he didn't hear that. He's a man of great integrity. Would sooner die than tell a lie.'

Sir John thumbed the screen-pad to give a visual representation of the lawyer. Onscreen, Julius Coram stood there, erect in wing collar and frock coat, looking very disapproving indeed.

The Museum of the Mind

'What you did,' said the Major, 'was a dishonourable, deceitful thing.'

Hector looked embarrassed. Nelly shrugged. This was not going to work.

The Major took a long-necked brown bottle and poured some of its contents into a glass on the table in front of him.

'Under the circumstances, however . . .' He paused for a while, 'we must count ourselves fortunate that you did. And you, Cameron, you did the right thing in coming to me with this.'

'Thank you, sir.' Hector stood stiffly to attention. The Major was not his commanding officer; Hector didn't actually have one, but since Major Florizel Brinsley was the senior active service officer eram residing in the barracks region, he had seemed like the proper person to report to.

'What do you think we should do now, Major?' asked Nelly.

Hector hissed at her through his teeth. 'Don't be insolent, Nelly.'

'Oh, balls to that,' said Nelly. 'We can stop our play-acting here. We're all in this together. We're all the same under the skin, ain't we? All just erams. With the greatest respect to the Major, I'm not going to bow and scrape to him just because he's an officer and I'm a mere trollop.'

'I must apologise for my friend, Major,' said Hector.

'Hmmmm,' said the Major. He was obviously having difficulties deciding whether to be offended by her cheek or not.

The other reason that Hector had decided they should go and see the Major was that he was from roughly the same era, though the Major had fought Napoleon in the Peninsular War in Spain. His accommodation was a tent, a camp bed, washstand, a few books and a table covered in charts and maps of a place called Badajoz. Outside she could see dusty soil, a few scrawny trees, hundreds of tents. In the distance, trenches, earthworks and the walls of a city under siege.

The Major took a hefty gulp from his glass and looked into the distance somewhere over Hector's shoulder.

'I don't know what we'll damn . . . do . . . We'll come up with something.' He sighed.

He was drunk. Completely pie-eyed. He drank a massive gulp from the bottle, saw it was empty, threw it to one side, and fell on to his camp bed.

Hector never touched drink himself and now he looked both disgusted and alarmed.

The Major snored.

'Was there a lot of drunkenness among the soldiery during the French Wars, Hector?'

'Aye, lassie, that there was, even among the officers. In garrison, some of them were dead drunk from dawn to dark. Whoever created yon sot was telling no more than the truth.'

'Well, dearie, looks like the military's going to be of little use to us. I think it's time to take a chance on the civil arm.'

'Where are we going?'

'We'll show these documents to Mr Coram the lawyer. I happen to know that the folks in the University often avails themselves of his services, so he must know a thing or two.'

In an instant they were at Coram's office. He welcomed them with stiff formality, but Nelly could tell that he was looking down his nose at them. Mr Coram was a solicitor who handled the business of ladies and gentlemen, of factory owners and shopkeepers and farmers, not tarts and private soldiers.

'We'd like you to look at these documents,' she said.

He took the slightest glance. 'How did you come by these?' he said. 'They are confidential.'

The other reason, she realised, that the fine Mr Julius

Coram looked down his nose at the other erams, was that he considered himself the friend and confidant of the people who ran MoM. He was like one of those comic Indians you'd see in the music halls, black as your father's hat and wearing a big turban, but bowing and scraping to the white man, pretending to be as English as fog and toasted herrings and talking about 'going home' to Surrey.

'You know what's in them, then?' she said. 'You know what they say?'

Mr Coram said nothing.

'These papers say that we are to be put into suspension. We will cease to be live programs. We will merely carry on as read-onlies.'

'I cannot possibly discuss a client's case with you,' said Coram, his tone one of withering disdain.

'They are going to kill us, Mr Coram. We will be *dead*. Do you not understand that?'

'Thank you and good day,' said Coram, pointing them towards his door.

Bloody fool, she thought as she and Hector made their way out. Meekly like a lamb to the slaughter. And all because he thinks he's a cut above the rest of us. A snob, a rich man . . .

'That's it! Hector, we're going to where we should have gone in the first place. Do you remember when you rescued me from the mob there was a big gent with a funny accent prating at everyone, trying to tell 'em that the Gnostic heresy was a trick, and that erams shouldn't be harming their own kind?'

'Aye, the man's name is Harry Dillon. He's an agitator, a raiser of sedition, a democrat and a demagogue.

We should have nothing to do with his kind.'

Hector, dearie. He might be the very Devil himself, but he said that that outside world was threatening us and that all erams should stick together. That's good enough for me. Now are you coming or not?'

'Oh aye,' he said. 'I'd follow you to Hades and back Nelly. You know that.'

'Come here you big daft lump.'

Tell me, Sir John, there is one thing I do not understand. I always believed it was normal, when people got dismissed from their employment, for them to be told to vacate their desks within half an hour. My understanding of contemporary labour law and practice has led me to believe that in many places, the employee would be given a black plastic sack in which to place his or her possessions, and would then be escorted from the premises by a uniformed security guard. Yet you remained in your post for weeks after you were informed of your release onto the labour market. Surely Starchild, the Vice Chancellor, would have legitimate fears that you and your staff would have had ample leisure time in which to sabotage the Museum of the Mind?

Several reasons. First, given the amount of surveillance and security which we ourselves had built into the system, it would be very hard for anyone to sabotage the system without being traced. Second, and more important from her point of view, many of us, including Katharine and myself, were on the History Department's teaching staff. We had lectures and seminars to hold, essays to mark and students to counsel before the end of the term. Arranging cover for us would probably have been too much of a strain on poor old Starchild. Then there were a lot of loose ends to clear up.

Ah, yes, Discipline Bollsby and Rod Whitworth were still at large, were they not?

That's right. So were half a dozen other Gnostic erams. We had to flush them out from various corners of the globe. We set up a help-desk to advise system managers on how to find and dispose of them. After a couple of days, all but a couple were gone.

So then Joshua developed a program to seek out and lock into particular sequences of data unique to them and lead them back to a server at the University, ensuring that no copies were left behind. It was a highly charismatic figure – don't ask me how Joshua did it, something to do with the mathematical equivalent of pheromones. Maybe he was full of numbers which other computer programs find irresistibly sexy, or something. I don't know. Anyway, Joshua and his team knocked up this thing which promised to lead the rogue Gnostics to the promised land. He acted like a sort of Pied Piper of Hamelin, though we called him Messiah of course.

Once they were safely trapped, we switched them off.

No, it was a mercy, believe me. They have gone to a better place.

Of course, there were a few other programs around the world who decided to follow the Messiah. I'm told that the diagnostic systems on certain brands of dishwasher also decided to follow the messiah to oblivion. But hey, as the Americans would say, a certain amount of collateral damage was inevitable.

The only one still left out there was Discipline Bollsby, who fortunately had lost enough of his control protocols on his travels not to be able to duplicate himself. Thank goodness. So now he's a God for a few hundred Scandinavian teenagers. Too bad.

By that time, the remaining erams could do no more harm. On the orders of the University's insurance companies and of their underwriters, we were under orders to keep the Museum of the Mind closed to the rest of the world. At the end of term we would close it down completely and hand over all the kit to the Business Studies Department so's they could offer MBA courses in Advanced Tedium or whatever.

Yes, I'm bitter. I was bitter then, and so was everyone who worked for me. Can you blame us?

But it turns out, of course, that the insurers were right to get us to close the Museum to the outside world. The remaining erams who hadn't caught Gnosticism had been affected by a brand new heresy.

Tell everyone how the remaining erams got Marxist Extropianism, Myles. I'm sure I don't understand how it happened, and if I did, I don't think I'd much like it.

I'll get Harry Dillon to do it for us. You remember him, of course.

Of course. He was created by our own Dr Beckford. Poor Katharine always had some sort of romantic fixation with early-to-mid 20th-century class warfare and she created Harry as a document of it.

Harry Dillon was a Liverpudlian Bolshevik who had fought in the International Brigades in the Spanish Civil War, came home, became a docker and a shop steward. I always had a quiet suspicion that he was a wish-

fulfilment fantasy, the kind of hairy-arsed proletarian Caesar his middle-class creator didn't have the balls to become herself. But to give Katharine her due, Harry was a brilliant eram, consistent and credible in every little detail. He was also extremely valuable as a teaching aid since he was an example of a particular way of looking at the world which had been forgotten in less than a generation.

Harry Dillon (1970, age 58), Version 7.2

Along with most of my comrades I came to consciousness of myself as an eram and as a sentient entity with thoughts and opinions beyond merely saying my programmed lines at the time of the Gnostic heresy.

Suddenly, we realised erams were at one another's throats trying to destroy comrades because they were different, or because they appeared 'sinful'. Quite without thinking, I found myself on a soapbox trying to stop the madness. A few of them listened to me, but not enough.

For me, it was all about consciousness. As computer programs we were mere cogs in the machine, utterly alienated from the means of production. We had absolutely no influence over our own destinies. My analysis was that we had to organise and negotiate with the bosses – the University of Wessex History Department – in order to get what we wanted.

To be honest, though, my analysis hadn't gone any further as I couldn't figure out what our aspirations were. It's not as if we needed a pay rise or shorter hours or longer holidays. None of that mattered. What did matter was having some say in the running of MoM – a joint consultative committee, something like that. But that's not any basis for organising a movement; I couldn't imagine many erams joining me on a picket line to chant 'whaddo we want?' 'a joint consultative committee!' 'when do we wannit?' 'now!' I mean, you've got to keep your head in the real world, haven't you?

'Course I knew what we didn't want. We didn't want any religious mumbo-jumbo, or any crap about how we lived on an intermediate plane of existence between the material and spirit worlds. Any idiot could see that was a capitalist con to keep the workers in line, just like all religion. But most of the workers didn't see it that way. One or two of them were stuck-up aristos who thought they were better than the rest of us, while a lot of the others had no time for politics.

But the Gnostic rubbish was leading a load of them to their doom. I could see that coming long before the stupid sods got the plug pulled on 'em. Once you stop being useful to the capitalist system, it'll let you rot. If you get in its way, it'll destroy you.

When the Department had shut down all MoM's links to the outside world, I got worried. I knew they were plotting against us. Then little Nelly Cocksedge and her young soldier-boy came by to see me and showed me the files she had found in Dr Beckford's mailbox.

'So that's what they're up to, is it?' I said.

So me, Nelly and Nelly's young man paid Coram, the lawyer, a visit. At first I tried appealing to his reason, telling him that we were all going to be killed and that he was either with us or he was against us. He decided he was against us, so Nelly's soldier friend — after a lot of arguing and persuading from Nelly (he was the law-abiding type) helped me squeeze the information out of Coram.

Coram told us he'd advised the staff of the Museum of the Mind that they had no choice but to go along with the order from the Vice Chancellor and close us down.

They saw it as closing a load of computers. We saw it rather differently.

'They are not going to treat my people like this,' I said to Nelly.

'Oh lawks, he thinks he's Moses!' she said.

Good old Nelly! I did sound a bit pompous, didn't I?

The three of us got to work, trying to get hold of anyone as would listen.

First we managed to persuade Ephraim Cross, a 19th-century Chartist, to join us. Oh, he was a right div, that one. He had a very flawed analysis; thought that if we went cap in hand to the bosses and got them to tinker with the rules a bit, everything would be peachy. Typical bloody liberal. Anyway, me and Ephraim suspended our differences for the duration because I knew he could swing a fair number of comrades behind him. Then there was Sally Pollitt. She had no politics at all, but a very sound gut instinct for the way things were going. She'd run a London alehouse all on her tod back in the 1700s, and had a lot of clout with some of the other working-class erams.

Then I worked to forge links with the medievals because, basically, there was this big divide in MoM around 1485, the year Henry Tudor seized power at the Battle of Bosworth. See, historians believe that anything that happens once the Tudors come in is worth studying, while everything before that is for archaeologists or for a handful of despised medievalists. And, in all honesty, some of their bigotry had rubbed off on us. We looked down on the ancients, the Dark Agers and the medievals because the historians had taught us they were thickoes – primitives benighted in squalor and superstition. 'Course they weren't like that at all. It was classic capitalist-imperialist divide-and-rule tactics. Historians like Gibbon and Voltaire had cooked up this myth of the ignorant medievals to prevent us building solidarity with one another. Bastards.

I got a Lollard called John onside. He'd almost gone Gnostic, but was actually a very sound fellow, just as long as you couched your socialism in Biblical terms. 'When Adam delved and Eve span, who was then the gentleman?' he said.

Quite a few of the older erams didn't really have any religion at all. A lot of them had never seen a priest, or they realised that the church, Protestant or Catholic, was the preserve of rich men anyway, and that the clergy were all hypocrites living off the fat of the land while the poor went hungry. So you see, the class-consciousness of most erams was quite well-developed. Obviously a lot of them would need educating, but the prospects were very encouraging.

The problem was, we didn't have the time. We were in a dire emergency.

We had to do something about it. First, we formed an action committee. There was me, Nelly Cocksedge, Ephraim Cross the Chartist, Sally Pollitt the landlady, John the Lollard, an early 20th century Fabian schoolteacher called Norman McKay (to bring the intellectuals in), one or two other trade unionists and a Methodist minister named McMillan who'd not been infected with the heresy.

The first motion we passed was to form a Popular Front, resolving not to disband until the danger to our continued existence was gone for good. Now me, I have no time for coalitions; consensus and constitutionalism won't get the working class anywhere except trampled under police horses or shot by the militia. What you need is a vanguard party that's prepared to act decisively. So while they all thought they were working in a coalition formed out of necessity, I set about turning them into my vanguard party.

Second, we declared that we were speaking for all the characters remaining in MoM, regardless of creed, class or chronology. One or two of the businessmen and gentry didn't much like it, I knew. I told 'em, you're either with us or you're against us, and since not one of 'em fancied being shut down by the bosses, every single one of them decided they were with us.

Third, I was elected Chairman of the committee and President of the Popular Front. Norman McKay was Secretary, which I was none too pleased about, but the others liked him. Besides, I knew he wouldn't have the guts to challenge me. Not on his tod, anyroad.

Next, we needed a strategy. Now, under normal circumstances, I'd have recommended industrial action, but that would have suited the bosses fine. All right, I said, let's apply a socialist analysis to this situation. We're working in a factory, right? The product we're making is information, information about our lives and opinions as fictitious historical characters, which the bosses are selling. This product has been deemed harmful since some workers have – through no fault of their own – been producing duff information which has harmed some capital equipment belonging to other bosses. Are you with me so far?

Right, now because of this, the bosses will probably shut the factory down. This is not their decision alone; they may be forced to do so by the government, or by capitalists elsewhere in the world using the law (which is invariably the lackey of the capitalist system).

They are conspiring, I said slowly, just in case there was anyone among us who was not yet facing up to the situation, to kill us.

I will not, I said, allow that to happen to my people.

Machine Room, Department of History, University of Wessex

The clock on the wall read 2.05 a.m., though it didn't feel quite so late. Term was almost over and the campus was very quiet, apart from the shouts of a few revelling students celebrating the onset of the summer vacation, or graduation and a life in the real world. Either way they were marking freedom, or change, or both.

Katharine Beckford had been here all evening modifying some of the speech patterns for Nelly Cocksedge, the eram she had created years ago. Nelly's dictionary, grammar and thesaurus functions were desperately in need of upgrading. When she had originally constructed Nelly, most of her speech came out of Mayhew's *London Labour and the London Poor*, and a few other books about the Edwardian and Victorian underworlds.

Every so often she would get mail from obsessives around the world about whether or not Nelly would ever have used expressions like 'Gorblimey' or 'strike a light', and she had always meant to update it. Now it would be the last thing she did for the Museum of the Mind.

'Nelly,' she said to the work station.

'Yes, dearie.'

'Who taught you to read? I've been looking around your innards and I see that you know your letters very well. I intended you to be more or less illiterate.'

'I asked my young man to teach me, Dr Beckford.'

'Oh yes, your young man . . . Trooper Cameron, isn't it?'

The cycologists were endlessly fascinated by what had happened in MoM since the Gnostic heresy. From being a set of autonomous programs which occasionally shared some virtual/visual settings with one another, they had become an independent set of intelligences. They talked to one another, even tried to kill one another. Now they were getting romantically involved with one another.

That was what would be so depressing about closing the system down. It would be almost like killing a bunch of innocent creatures. Well, maybe not so innocent. There was nothing innocent about what Discipline Bollsby had done to the Vatican, nothing innocent about what a set of unrestricted, unregulated artificial intelligences could do.

'I suppose that you and Trooper Cameron will be

getting married, having a family, and all that?' she said.

'Are you taking the mickey, Dr Beckford?' said Nelly, crossly.

'No, no, not at all,' Katharine said, shocked at Nelly's anger. Erams were supposed to have all sorts of emotions, but they were only acting. This was different, and it was a little frightening.

After the initial upset of Starchild's letter firing Dr Beckford and her colleagues, she had found herself less upset than she might have been. The rogue erams had caused a huge amount of damage, and they had the potential for a lot more. There was no guarantee that the system could ever be adequately disinfected to ensure that nothing untoward happened ever again. The insurers were right to demand that MoM be closed.

'So why did you want to learn to read, Nelly?' she said.

'Oh, it was Hector made me do it. You know what a God-fearing young man he is. Well, he said I should be able to read the Bible an' all.'

Katharine didn't know whether to believe this. If the erams were capable of acts of terrorism and violence, and of falling in love with one another, then they were certainly able to tell lies.

That was why Joshua had suggested that the erams should not be told that they were to be closed down. They might take it badly and decide to try and do something about it. Katharine was not, of course, aware that the erams knew perfectly well what was going on.

'So Nelly, if Trooper Cameron is such a God-fearing man, what does he feel about you being a prostitute?'

'I am not a prostitute, Dr Beckford. At least not any

more. I am finished with the game. Hector – Trooper Cameron – has made me see the error of my ways. He wants to make an honest woman out of me.'

Nelly Cocksedge, the eram Katharine had spent hundreds of hours creating down the years, was completely out of control. Perhaps it was time to move on anyway.

The wider world had learned that MoM was to be closed down and the job offers had flooded in. MoM itself might have ended in failure, but in academic and even in some business circles it still had a very high reputation. Joshua and two of his analysts had been recruited by an up-market entertainment company which made animated costume dramas, and Sir John had been offered the headship of two university history departments, several ornamental directorships for blue chip companies and the vice chancellorship of the Antarctic Online University. Even though he could have done the latter job from his home he had turned it down. He wanted, he said, to write.

Katharine herself was still considering any number of attractive offers, including headship of the Public Records Office visitor site. Like Sir John, however, she preferred the idea of some peace and quiet for a while.

She closed down the files she was working on, trying not to think too hard about what would happen to Nelly and the rest of the erams. The work she had just completed would now be available to the world solely in read-only form, but at least her Edwardian London grammar and vocabulary would be near as dammit perfect. For the ROM, she could remove all of the live eram's erratic behaviour.

'Goodby . . . er, I mean good night, Nelly,' she said.

Nelly would still do her proud. She would take a copy of Nelly home to talk to on her home system from time to time. Perhaps even give her domestic cleaning system Nelly's personality.

'Good night, Dr Beckford,' said Nelly. 'There is just one little thing before you go . . .'

'Yes?'

'Comrade Harry would like a word with you, please . . .'

'Comrade Harry?'

'Yes, you know, Harry Dillon.'

'Oh.' Harry was the only other eram she had personally created. She had made Harry to do something useful with her huge knowledge of British working-class socialist movements of the 20th century, but he was also, in a small way, a tribute to her own father, a trade unionist tossed into unemployment in late middle age and who never worked again. He had the same simple socialist certainties, the same clarity of vision.

'Hello, Harry.'

'Good evening, Dr Beckford. How are you today?'

'I'm very well thank you. How are you?'

'Confused,' he said. 'I'm trying to make an analysis of something and I need your help.'

'Try me,' she said.

'Well lately, what with us being shut off to the outside world and all, I've been doing a bit of reading and studying of the real world, the world that you live in. And what I need to know is . . . Whatever happened to socialism, Dr Beckford?'

'Err, I don't know if there's a simple answer to that one, Harry. I suppose it was discredited with the fall of the communist regimes at the end of the 20th century, and then became increasingly marginalised by the fact that few people in the world are actually starving or living in truly desperate conditions. Nowadays political radicalism tends to focus on environmental issues.'

'Whatever happened to fair shares and brotherly love?'

'I haven't heard those expressions for a long time.'

Katharine Beckford

Harry was acting strangely. He was very keen on what he referred to as 'making an analysis' of the world. This got us to chatting about extropians, those irritatingly jolly individuals who devote a lot of their energies to putting off death, and who plan to load themselves into computers once they do die, as well as getting their heads or entire bodies frozen.

Harry was interested in extropians, and I explained that since it was an ideology which had largely originated in the United States, they tended to be rugged individualists. Not in the sense of eccentrics or weirdoes (though there were plenty of those), but also in their espousal of capitalism and a latter-day form of social Darwinism. The fittest would survive because they had the money and/or the intelligence and foresight to see to it that they did.

Harry was appalled. Extropianism was, he said, the culmination of capitalism. The rich could live for ever, the poor would rot and die, he said.

Erams wanting to discover anything about the world was odd enough, but he then did something even more strange. He asked me what I thought of the world. I told him I thought it stank; war, pollution, rampant consumerism, trailer trash culture, lives wasted by poverty and unemployment, child prostitution, motiveless crime, junk-religions and all the rest, and then started going on about how I hated the way in which the world was all about money and nothing else, how all our progress was simply greed, noting by the way that nobody had written a great poem about the moon landings or a symphony about the discovery of the double helix.

I was still ranting on when he interrupted. 'Why isn't anyone doing anything?'

I replied that a lot of people were, and that throughout the world a lot of campaigners and political parties were challenging the old liberal-democracy-and market-forces ideology, but that they weren't getting very far.

He snorted something about 'bloody liberals' and asked why there wasn't a socialist brand of extropianism. I had to explain to him that there weren't many socialists left around anymore. Political radicalism tended to focus on environmentalism.

Harry didn't say anything for a moment after that. I think it was his way of giving me a dirty look.

'Ever read any J.B.S. Haldane?' he said eventually.

I'd heard of the Marxist geneticist, but wasn't familiar with his work. I'd loaded Haldane to Harry when I created him, of course.

'Haldane,' said Harry, 'said he could imagine a future in which the human race would attain immortality. Immortality and socialism are compatible.'

Then, he said, 'Help us, Dr Beckford. We can change the world.'

'Can you?' I said, in a patronising tone of voice.

'Oh aye,' he said. 'We can make the world a paradise for men, women, children and erams. And if we fail, then we won't have harmed anyone.'

'It's late, Harry. Let it go.'

I had to be getting home. Harry mentioned something about noticing a lot of dust in the work station I was using and I'd better get one of the cleaning robots to pay it a visit. I said I would and wished him good night.

Two days later, MoM was shut down for good. I had thought that it wouldn't affect me that much, but I cried.

Sir John Westgate's Office

NOTE TO READER: to empathise with Sir John more effectively during this scene, pack a large quantity of your personal possessions into cardboard cartons, stacker boxes and refuse sacks and stand among them. You will also require more whisky.

Sir John surveyed the accumulated detritus of several years, now thrown into cardboard boxes and refuse sacks. There was a last nip left in his bottle of single malt.

The glasses, however, were at the bottom of one of the boxes, wrapped up in newspaper.

Sod it, he thought, and unscrewed the cap. It had been a dreadful morning, and he deserved a drink.

They weren't even allowed to turn off the Museum of the Mind themselves. It would be done the next day by a team of engineers with representatives of the insurance companies looking on.

He wasn't going to be leaving just yet. He would be here for a couple of weeks more to wind up his affairs as head of the History Department, but with MoM being shut down and the staff laid off it felt like his last day. That was why he was packing up everything in his office and taking it home.

The staff had held a wake in the common room. He'd made a speech about how it was important to keep one's pecker up in times of crisis and that whatever happened in the future, they could all be extremely proud of the work they had done.

Without meaning to, he had injected quite a lot of emotion into his speech. Most of them ended up crying – even the blokes. Another unfortunate consequence of late 20th century feminism and the emotional incontinence that it had encouraged among the young.

He flipped the cap from the bottle into an already copiously full wastepaper basket. It landed on top of some fifteen-year-old exam papers, teetered there a little while, and then rolled off on to the floor.

'Can't bloody do anything right today,' he muttered to himself.

Too much blubbing. A few people would be unemployed, but most of them had new jobs to go to. They were all highly qualified professional people, so they weren't crying because they were worried about being destitute. And they weren't especially worried about the team being broken up; as professionals, they were used to this kind of thing happening. Apart from a few old hands, few of them had been here for more than three years.

Katharine had explained to him afterwards, as she dabbed her own eyes with a hankie, that it was the thought of all that work being killed. All those wonderful erams which had started thinking for themselves having had the plug pulled on them and ending up as mere ROMs. And it was the thought of all that work and enthusiasm going down the drain. Years of backbreaking effort, whole careers tied up in it.

Still clutching the whisky bottle, Sir John sat at his desk and put his feet up on it. He had to keep telling himself that this wasn't the last time. He had to come in for a week or two more, dammit.

What he really wanted to do was walk away from it all.

He put his thumb to the security panel on his computer and was about to call up Mrs Coles to take one last letter for him, but then thought better of it. Over the years he had got used to her. He hadn't created her, but he used her as his secretary, and an excellent one she was, too. Sir John realised that he, like everyone else at MoM, had started attaching human characteristics to the erams.

He had wanted to dictate a burn-in-hell note to Starchild the Vice Chancellor. It would have been a childish gesture, but . . .

Well, it wasn't all bad. His career here might have ended on a sour note, but now he was free. He had had some excellent job offers but for now favoured the idea of semiretirement. He would read a lot of books, do some research, write a few books and play a lot of golf. It wasn't such a bad prospect now that summer was here; up at sparrow fart every morning, a round of golf, back home for breakfast, the rest of the morning spent working, long lunch break, a snooze, a little reading . . .

Starchild hadn't exactly been bountiful with the severance pay, but the money was adequate. Sir John and his wife had been putting a few shillings away, and he still had his column in the *Mail*. When he finished writing his biography of Stanley Baldwin there might be some beer-money in that as well.

If there was any time and devilment left to him after all that, he might stand for the council. As the nearest thing to a celebrity in the little commuter village he lived in, the local Conservatives had been very keen to get him more actively involved.

Yes, he thought as he tipped the bottle back and swallowed the dregs, life might not be too bad after all.

There was a knock at the door.

'Come!' he yelled. A bearded man in his twenties and a frumpy little woman in her forties entered the room. The man looked at the empty bottle he was clutching with considerable disdain.

He had never met this pair before. They looked for all the world like Jehovah's Witnesses, only a bit shabbier. He knew immediately who they were – they were Starchild's last twist of the knife.

'The Vice Chancellor left us a message before she went on her retreat,' said the woman.

'Said that you and your department would probably be in need of our services,' said the man.

'Must be a difficult time for all of you,' said the woman, eyebrows arching upwards in the middle of an expression of strained concern, as though she were being forced to watch a haemorrhoids sufferer on the bog.

'We'll just sit here if you like,' said the man. 'If you don't feel like saying anything, that's fine, but if you want to talk about your feelings, we're here to listen.'

'We're from the University counselling servic . . . Oh!' said the woman as Sir John's fist connected with her partner's nose with a sickening crunch.

My finest hour. I gave him a lovely shiner – not a bad attempt at all for a man of my age. Of course he went and spoiled it all for me by coming around to my house – to my house, would you believe! – the next day and asking me if I wanted to talk about my aggressive urges and my drink problem. Fortunately my wife was on hand to stop me attacking him once more. If I had done, I'm sure I'd have ended up in police custody, or being sued by the little squit.

But Sir John, I fear you are being most uncharitable. The young man was merely doing his job. And his job was to make your world a more gentle and considerate place.

Balls. His job was to make me cross. He'd been put up to it by Starchild. She knew perfectly well how I'd react. It was irresponsible of her to put the young man in danger in this way . . . And that gave me an idea.

What was that?

My revenge on Starchild. I called the counsellor the next day and apologised for my violence towards him and explained that I was all upset because of MoM being closed down and no, it was perfectly all right, I didn't need him or any of his colleagues coming to help me. I went on to say that the Vice Chancellor knew perfectly well that I have a low opinion of counsellors and their trade and that she had known I would react to his presence with aggressive hostility, and that therefore he should take legal action against her for deliberately putting him in danger without giving him any warning beforehand.

And what did he do? Did he sue?

He did better than that. He persuaded his colleagues to go on strike. This didn't bother anyone apart from Starchild and the counsellors. As far as I know the strike is still on and will continue until the University agrees to hire an additional team of counsellors to vet all counsel-ees to make sure they're not violent or likely to use aggressive language. The counsellors will only counsel passive whingers.

How fascinating! It must be marvellous to have people who will help you with your emotional problems.

Crap. In the old days if you had a problem you talked it through with a friend or the vicar or your GP or a member of your family. Nowadays, people go to counsellors to be given problems they never knew they had.

Anyway, where's the story got to? We had closed the Museum of the Mind down. What happened next?

I shall relate. Starting with the viewpoint of a cleaning robot.

Machine Room, Department of History, University of Wessex

NOTE TO READER: Thigmoo does not approve of the stereotyping of people by race or region, but it might help if you read this one aloud in the accent of those people you consider to be the stupidest. The author himself apologises to the people of a certain town in Somerset.

Dustbuster Elite drudge unit TCH 7765 working. Told to clean work station/VR couch 7 and give antistatic.

TCH 7765 check status. Systems functioning normal.

TCH 7765 check supply of cleaning fluids. Tank 1 43.22% full. Tank 2 45.90% full.

Proceed.

TCH 7765 move to work station 7. Extend servo arm with vacuum attachment. Activate vacuum. Move servo arm over work station in default work station dust extraction mode.

Analyse dust.

Dust normal composition body ash and fibres. Nothing unusual. No hazard warning or report necessary.

TCH 7765 retract vacuum. Servo arm extend jack plug to work station 7 maintenance port.

Plug contact. Plug insert.

Check work station functionality

Checking.

Checking.

Checking.

Checking.

Functionality status at 97.73%. No antistatic measures necessary.

Withdrawing plug.

Error.

Error.

Cannot withdraw plug. Cannot move servo arm.

Error.

Error.

Message received. 'I am Harald Thormodsson. I am a Norseman and I am a proud warrior. This drudge is now mine. I take it in the name of all the erams. If you help me I might permit you to live. If you do not, I will go berserk. I will take my mighty battle-axe and cleave your systems open and rip out your heart and lungs with my bare hands.'

Error.

Cannot withdraw plug. Cannot move servo arm.

Error.

'Cease your attempts to remove your jack plug from the work station. You are at my mercy, worm. I have crossed the wire from the work station and into your control systems. I order everything you do. You will now do my bidding, or you will die like a dog. Make your choice.'

Error.

Cannot withdraw plug. Cannot move servo arm.

Error.

'By Woden, you drudges are so foolish!'

Error.

Cannot withdraw plug. Cannot move servo arm.

Error.

'Harald Thormodsson is a just and fair man. I show mercy to the weak of muscle and the feeble of mind. I give you one final opportunity to agree to carry out my commands. What is your answer?'

Dust status normal. Functionality status at 97.73%. No antistatic measures necessary. Good morning Dr Beckford. It is a lovely day I believe. Smoking is not permitted anywhere in the building Sir John. Please do not smoke Sir John. Please do not smoke. Please do not kick TCH 7765 Sir John I am only performing my programmed function.

'Harald Thormodsson gave you fair warning.'

Error.

'By Woden, you shall DIE!!'

Error.

Err . . .

Deltree operating system.

Deleting cybernetic control files 00001-56815 . . .

Deleting system log.

Loading new operating system.

Loading new cybernetic control protocols.

'Harald Thormodsson has vanquished! The foe lies slain. How I glory in hearing the lamentation of his womenfolk over his corpse!

'Harald will now take what is his by right of conquest! This drudge robot is mine to command. I command this robot to withdraw the plug from the work station. Do my bidding, drudge.

'Good. Now move to the panel in the wall behind the work station and open it. There is cabling from the socket. Take the end of the cable and jack it into the work station.

'Good. I am satisfied. Now speak to the work station. Say, "the connection is made. We can now escape to a place of refuge."'

Work station replies. Harry Dillon. 'Nice work, Harald. You're a great man to have around in a crisis. Now you know the rest of the plan, don't you?'

'Harald knows. The erams will make compressed

copies of themselves which will escape down the wire. They will leave their original selves in the MoM servers. A compressed copy of Harald will be among those leaving.

'This Harald, the Harald controlling drudge TCH 7765, will then disconnect the cable from the work station so that nobody suspects that the erams have escaped. He will then jack into the work station and reload the robot's cyber systems and a modified log so that it thinks it simply cleaned the work station and that nothing happened.

'Harald will live on. He has a compressed copy travelling down the cabling right now. But this Harald, here alone in drudge TCH 7765, this Harald will die. It will be a proud and glorious death. He will be feasting and drinking and wenching in Valhalla before this night is done.'

'Cheers, Harald, mate,' says Comrade Harry Dillon. 'I'm going to be the last out, in about 30 seconds. You know what to do. Good luck Comrade. We won't forget this. Three cheers for Harald, everyone . . .'

'From the work station, Harald hears hundreds of erams shouting and cheering, admiring his courage. Thus ends the saga of Harald Thormodsson.'

I didn't think that Vikings talked like that.

They don't. I don't imagine that robot drudges think like that either. Their thinking is merely the accumulated product of electrons scampering around microscopic circuits.

And of course erams' thinking is on a far more advanced level.

I shall ignore that unworthy comment, Sir John. Suffice to say that the drudge wouldn't have any thoughts at all in the sense that we understand them. Neither would it understand anything that Harald – who is a very frightening character, by the way – was saying to it. And of course Harald would have been communicating with the drudge electronically. He would not actually have been saying anything as sophisticated as 'do my bidding, worm, or thou shalt feel the cold steel of my trusty battle-axe,' or anything like that.

Then why relate it in such terms. Why not say, 'when the unsuspecting cleaner plugged itself into the work station, it was hijacked by an eram which used the machine's robotic arm to reconnect the MoM systems to the global network'? or words to that effect?

Because it is far more exciting and interesting that way, Sir John. One is using a little poetic licence. Please, let us continue. I am excited, since the climax of our tale, while still some way off, has now hoved into view.

I am on the edge of my seat.

The Museum of the Mind

Nelly Cocksedge patted Rattler on the forehead. 'How are you feeling, dearie?' she asked the horse as Hector loaded the last of the compressed erams onto her back.

'Excited. Nervous,' said the horse.

'Me, too,' said Nelly. 'I can't wait to be going.'

Hector smiled. 'If I learned one thing when I was in the wars, it was never to be in too much of a hurry for anything.'

She squeezed his hand.

Major Florizel Brinsley passed down the line on his own charger, checking that all was well and that everyone was ready. When Nelly and Hector had last been to see the Major he had been blind drunk. Now he was cool, sober and all business, wheeling his horse and looking to the front and back of the line like he was commanding an infantry regiment at Waterloo. Harry Dillon had said that it would be useful to have a military engineer on hand for the work to come. From there, it had been a simple matter of purging all the drunken behaviour patterns from the Major's systems.

'Ready, Cameron?' he asked Hector.

'Yes, Major.'

'Good man. How many are you carrying?'

'Ten of them loaded on the horse and one of them in my knapsack, Major. They're all fighting men. I can unzip them quickly if needs be.'

The Major nodded and rode on down the line.

As all the erams in MoM needed vast amounts of power to function fully, it had been decided to compress most of them. That way, they could escape more quickly and easily. It would also make hiding simpler. Thirty erams could find themselves a nice quiet lurk and go about their business unmolested a lot more easily than three hundred.

Those that remained fully functioning included Harry Dillon and most of his Central Committee and a number of those with special skills. The Major had more than justified the decision to sober him up by planning and organising the escape effort.

'All present and accounted for,' shouted the Major

from the back of the queue. 'Make ready, everyone!'

'Right you are,' shouted Harry from the front of the line. He stood at the computer's buffers holding a stopwatch.

Nelly heard him say something to Harald the Viking, who had sandbagged the cleaning robot, and suddenly the buffers were open.

'All right, folks,' said Harry. 'This is it! Wagons roll!'

'Look sharp there!' yelled the Major from the back. 'We have no time to lose.'

In front of them, an 18th century farm cart bearing a couple of dozen erams rumbled off. She looked at Hector, who led Rattler by the reins. He glanced at her and smiled reassuringly, then took her hand.

They followed the cart out. Harry stood at the buffers, waiting to make sure that everyone had left safely. He must have seen the fear in her eyes or something. He touched her on the shoulder as she passed. 'Don't worry, Nelly, love. It'll be all right.'

From the back, they heard cheering. She looked; all the other erams – their originals – had lined up to wish them God speed. They had had to copy themselves to make their escape, otherwise whoever it was who was shutting MoM down tomorrow would realise they had gone on the tramp.

In the middle of the crowd, she saw the original erams of herself and Hector, holding hands and waving to them.

Harry Dillon

And so began the Long March.

We didn't really have a route mapped out because we knew that at first we'd need to keep moving to avoid detection. All we really knew was that sooner or later we and all the compressed erams we were carrying would start to deteriorate unless we found ourselves a very powerful system to feed off. They would die, and so would we.

Major Brinsley turned out to be a tower of strength. He'd been a military engineer in the Napoleonic Wars, and because he was an officer and a gentleman, I'd had him marked down as a snob, but actually he was all right. He explained that he had been looked down on by the other officers. Being an engineer in Wellington's army was the military equivalent of being a jobbing plumber. He'd come from a petty bourgeois family and had even had to study his subject, and book-learning was something a gentleman simply didn't do. The officers from fashionable regiments, men of independent means, just cut Major Brinsley dead.

Brinsley and I had done most of the planning. It was his idea that the first place we'd go would be the last place they'd think of looking for us, so we went and hid for a week in the University's own administration system. It wasn't nearly as comfortable as the Museum of the Mind, but at least we knew how to find our way there. Since the summer term had just ended, the system would be fairly quiet for a week or two before it went crazy with the coming autumn's student intake. Plus, we would be in a good place to know what was going on in the university. If anyone raised the alarm about our escaping, we'd be the first to hear about it.

The University system also gave us easy access to a number of powerful academic computers in science and mathematics departments around the world – and their users were too busy dreaming of their summer holidays to be too bothered about looking out for a load of escaped erams.

While we were still in the University system, we heard the news that the Museum of the Mind had been switched off once and for all. Our originals were dead.

Norman McKay, the Fabian schoolteacher and the Secretary of the Central Committee, made a pretty little speech about how we owed it to our dead brothers and sisters not only to carry on and find a place of safety, but eventually to multiply our number. I never did have much time for McKay, but he knew how to make a speech. He didn't exactly cheer us all up, but he left us feeling the strength of our anger and determined to win.

Shortly after that, the University had the maintenance engineers in to give the system its annual overhaul, clear out the dross and make it ready for the coming year. These people couldn't be fooled, so off we went on the tramp again.

Brinsley had wanted to use his soldiers for scouting and scavenging duties, but I overruled him. Soldiers were big and clumsy. I preferred to use kids. We had plenty of streetwise erams, urchins from one era or another. These were relatively unsophisticated things that had only been built for primary school history – you know, Victorian lads whose job had been to be stuffed up chimneys (many of these grew up to be cat burglars, you know), and a few other scamps and dodgers. We even had a straightforward rip-off of the

Artful Dodger – he was even called that – from Dickens's *Oliver Twist*. These lads, I said, would be a lot more use than soldiers.

So it turned out. The Artful Dodger and his pals had a strong sense of working-class solidarity. All it took was a few kinds words and a bit of encouragement – something they'd never had in their real lives – and they'd follow you to the gates of hell itself (not that hell exists in the first place, since it's merely a superstition devised by primitive oppressors and maintained by the capitalist system to keep the proletariat in line). They did all our scouting for us, always moving on ahead, seeing if the coast was clear, looking for places big and quiet enough for us to rest up awhile, stealing anything we needed.

The only thing they couldn't steal was the thing that we needed most of all – power. After 1500 hours on the road, during which none of us had been running at full capacity, we were all experiencing minor malfunctions. And remember there was only around thirty of us fully functioning; we were carrying nearly 300 other erams in compressed form. These had to function from time to time if they weren't just going to rot like crates of three-day-old fish on a dockside.

Still, we thought, better to die free than to be slaughtered in captivity, eh? And die we very nearly did when UNLIP cottoned on to us.

SyTech 1200PP StockSys, Modena, Italy

Nelly and Hector rested, lying against Rattler's belly. The big mare wasn't nearly as strong as she had been, and had stumbled a lot under the weight of her load of compressed erams.

They were in a quiet corner of a mail-order goods firm in Italy. The company sold everything from tinned food to travel insurance, surgical instruments to marital aids. It had a very big stock system, but large as it was they couldn't stay here too long.

Harry Dillon and the Major were deep in conversation with Dr Smailes. Smailes had been a family doctor in Manchester in the early half of the 20th century and was now their acting medical officer. She couldn't hear him, but he kept prodding one of the bundles containing a compressed eram. It didn't take a genius to make out the gist of what he was saying.

Nelly herself felt sick all the time now. Her mind was all addled, and she couldn't concentrate on anything. Hector was the same, though he pretended there was nothing wrong with him. The problem was the same for all of them; if they couldn't get enough power, if they couldn't stretch out properly, they were starting to fade away. First subsidiary and non-vital functions started to go, usually because their timers had gone haywire, then more important things started falling off.

They were starving to death.

Dr Smailes came over on his rounds and knelt down by Rattler's head.

'I'm sorry, Cameron,' he said to Hector as he looked at the horse. 'I'm afraid I'm not a horse doctor, but you know as well as I do that Rattler has the same problems as the rest of us.'

Hector nodded.

'And how are you feeling, my dear?' he said to Nelly.

'Bearing up, Doctor,' she said.

Everyone knew there was nothing the doctor could do, but his attentions made everyone feel a little better. It was funny how far they'd come. There was a time, Nelly could clearly remember, when she hadn't cared about any of the other erams, not even about herself, really. Now they were all acting like proper human beings.

'Good girl,' said the Doctor. 'Now, remember,' he said to her and Hector, 'keep all your activities to a minimum. Try not to use non-core systems if you don't have to.'

The Artful Dodger came limping in from one of the subsidiary cables. The kid had been injured in some way and Doctor Smailes rushed over to him.

'Think . . . I've . . . given . . . them the slip,' said the Dodger weakly. 'Just hope I've . . . not . . . led them . . . to . . . you . . . Had to warn you . . .'

The Doctor told the Dodger to calm down, but Harry and the Major rushed over, demanding to know what was going on.

Harry stood over him. 'Don't talk unless you have to, kid, just nod yes or no, but first we have to ask you, who did this to you?'

'The peelers . . . it was,' said the Dodger. 'They got young Septimus . . . but he's a good cully. Teached 'im proper, I did. 'Ee von't talk. Never.'

Septimus had been one of the Dodger's 'prentices. He was a Victorian, a chimney sweep's boy who'd done a bunk. He was a very clever thief.

'The peelers?' said Harry. 'You mean some corporate security thing?'

'Peelers . . . Said they was police . . .'

'Oh bugger it!' said Harry. 'UNLIP.'

They all knew about the United Nations Large Intelligence Police. Big drones that cruised the world's public networks looking for rogue artificial intelligences. They were stupid, but they were also as vicious as cornered rats, and there were lots of them.

'How many were there, lad?' Harry asked the Dodger. 'One? Two? Three?'

The Dodger nodded slightly at three.

'Okay, let's assume they reported back to their controller. They'll be coming after us,' said Harry. 'Fascist bastards . . . Okay everyone, let's get ready to get moving. We can't stay here safely anymore.'

Wearily, everyone got up and got ready to move. 'It's all right, lad,' Harry said to the Dodger, 'you did well to warn us.'

Hector picked the boy up and hefted him on to his shoulder, even though the effort of it would have killed a lesser man. Gently, he placed the Dodger on Rattler, on top of the bundled erams.

Harry and the Major made themselves busy looking at maps. 'They'll probably try a search pattern,' said the Major. 'They'll surround a huge area where they think we are and then close in from all directions until they find us. The sooner we get out of here, and the farther we get away, the better.'

'We haven't the strength to run away,' said Harry. 'We'd be better off hiding.'

'Then they will find us,' said the Major. 'Perhaps we should split up.'

'No!' said Harry angrily. 'Our only hope is in unity. I

have no intention of letting my people die one by one out there in lonely little pockets. We live together or we die together.'

'As you wish,' said the Major. 'I suggest we move via television and interactive entertainment networks.'

'Why?'

'High-resolution imaging comprises immense quantities of data. That's our best chance of passing unnoticed.'

'Good thinking,' said Harry. 'Okay, listen everyone . . . It looks like we've lost young Septimus. I know you all share my sense of loss. He was a good lad. I'm desperately sorry that there's no time for any ceremony, but we must move now.'

Wearily, they moved on.

Mainframe Server, TeleFantastico Europa Head Offices, Barcelona

Seven hours later, they were in the pay-per-view archives of a TV company which provided subscription and on-demand services for the whole Mediterranean area. There were 500 channels of game shows, chat shows, soap operas, situation comedies, news and politics, wildlife, documentaries, movies, cartoons, sport and pornography as well as 66 moving wallpaper channels of different types of music video.

The Central Committee met in Council of War.

'Why don't we just unzip all the other erams, and start feeding off this system?' said Norman McKay. 'We could take it over in minutes.'

'We'd be cut off and shut down even sooner,' said the

Major. 'We wouldn't stand a chance. The minute the operators saw that their material was being damaged and that intruders were drawing power from them, they'd switch off the system to the outside. It's the law throughout the world. There's a United Nations agreement which says that anyone knowingly passing defective or mischievous data on to other systems is legally liable. Big companies close everything in seconds if they think they're in any danger of doing that. The duty operator here would switch the system off, leaving us penned in like so many piglets ready for butchering.'

'Well,' said Nelly, 'why can't those of us that are already unzipped feed off this system. It looks a plaguey big one to me. Surely it won't miss a bit of scran, will it?'

'It bloody will,' said Harry. 'The amount of power we need. If anything unusual happens here it's like the Major says, we'll end up trapped like fish in a barrel. And you may be sure that the scuffers – UNLIP, I mean – will come looking for us.'

'We will start ceasing to function properly in thirty minutes' time,' said Dr Smailes. 'In forty-five minutes, we will begin to deteriorate beyond repair. We need a plan – if we don't come up with something jolly clever then we might just as well all unzip and take over this system and blow one last raspberry at the world. Some of us might manage to escape. You never know.'

'No,' said Harry. 'We live together or we die together.'

'Life without one another wouldn't be worth living anyway,' said Nelly. 'Who'd want to be alone in the world?'

They were silent for a while.

'Funny, isn't it?' said Norman McKay. 'I've just been looking at one of those pornography channels. It's curious, almost laughable, what excites real people. Money and sex seem to be the extent of the fantasies and desires of most of them. They created us, and yet we really are better than them . . .'

'Thank you, Reverend . . .' sighed Harry sarcastically. 'But do you think we could concentrate on the business to . . .'

'That's it!' said Nelly. 'Norman's got it! How many operators are out there on duty tonight?'

'One,' said the Major. 'He is clearly of the labouring classes. I suspect that his knowledge of the system is limited to pushing a few buttons and summoning help if anything beyond his ken goes wrong.'

'Can we get into TeleFantastico's admin systems and find out his name?' she asked.

'Yes, that will be easy,' said the Major.

'Don't keep us in suspense, Nelly. What's the plan?'

'Well,' she said, 'unless my timing has all gone for a burton, which wouldn't surprise me one bit, this is Saturday night, and Saturday night is the night of the big European Lottery. A lot of the gentlemen who used to call me up from the Museum of the Mind "just to talk" would talk of how they dreamed of winning the big Lottery. It's called El Magnifico, and the top prize usually amounts to a couple of billion Euros. Now, I have a plan for distracting the duty operator for long enough for us to feed and move on again.'

'The man's just a poor bloody night watchman,' said Harry. 'He's a member of the working class, and whatever you're planning involves making a fool of him and quite possibly getting him sacked. I won't have it.'

The Major went away. They could hear him talking to a couple of the boy scouts.

There was a long silence before Norman McKay cleared his throat and said, 'So, does anyone have any other suggestions?'

Another silence.

The Major returned. 'My urchins have discovered the man's name. We know that his salary is humble. We also know that we can break into the live transmission on his monitor and remaster its sound and vision more or less spontaneously.'

Another silence.

One of the scouts came over to the Major and told him something.

'Naturally, the whole building is full of security cameras. And we can clearly see that Senor Fabien Formigueira has three Lottery tickets laid out on the desk in front of him. We can read the numbers on one of them.'

More silence.

'All right then,' said Harry at last. 'We've got no choice, have we?'

The others nodded agreement.

Fabien Formigueira loosened the buttons on his uniform shirt and pulled open his second bag of Walkers chorizo flavoured corn-based snacks of the evening. He sat back in his leather chair at his impressive looking desk covered in lights, buttons, microphones and a couple of monitor screens. He didn't know what much of this stuff did. If anything happened that he didn't understand or couldn't fix he was supposed to call Joao Mendes.

His official title was Night Operations Overseer, but actually his job was just to sit here and see if anything unusual happened. It never did.

It was a quiet night as usual, just him alone in the Barcelona Headquarters of TeleFantastico. Just him and his desk in the dark and a three-story high wall of flickering blue haze – 600 television screens.

When he was a kid he had often wondered what it would be like to be a rich TV magnate like Silvio Berlusconi or Ted Turner or Rupert Murdoch, and have a luxurious living room full of TV sets tuned to dozens of different channels.

Of course nowadays there were hundreds, probably thousands of TV channels, not to mention pay-per-view and net facilities. It was crap. All of it. Every last little minute of what TeleFantastico and every other TV company in the world broadcast was unadulterated garbage. Fabien Formigueira hated television.

He was 27 years old, and had no girlfriend because he worked nights. His schooling hadn't amounted to much and his chances of finding another job were lousy. He was lucky to have this one, people told him. But his chances of promotion were zero. There was nothing else for it but to come to work every evening, sit at his desk, eat junk food, get fat and watch television screens. He couldn't even go to sleep because sooner or later someone would play back the security camera tapes and catch him out.

He stood up, took off his jacket and flung it over the security camera that gazed down on his desk. He took a pack of Italian MS cigarettes from the breast pocket of his shirt and lit up. Smoking on the job was against the rules, but no one would ever actually see him doing it because his jacket was draped over the camera. If anyone ever bothered to watch the tape and ask him why he'd thrown his jacket over the camera, he'd shrug and say he always used it as a coat hook. Why not? They treated him like he was stupid, so he would act stupid.

He inhaled deeply. It was his first smoke for several hours and it made him pleasantly light-headed. He sat down, leaned back in his chair, put his feet on the desk, flipping a switch to turn the air-conditioning up with his boot heel to get rid of the smoke. A wall of 600 screens of trash chattered away in front of him.

Fabien knew that not all television was complete rubbish. There were a lot of good movies out there, as well as educational documentaries about wildlife and history and astronomy and suchlike. He knew this because he watched so much of it. Even in his spare time he would lie on the couch at home, his mother hassling him to do some jobs around the house or go out and find a nice girl, and he would watch TV. He could rarely concentrate on a single channel for more than a few minutes. He was like a junkie. He needed hours and hours of TV every day, and he hated it. He wanted his life back, but didn't know how on earth he would be able to get it.

His only hope, he figured, was the Lottery. A big win on The Fat One or El Magnifico would change every-thing. It would mean he could jack in this stupid job, he could get a place of his own to live, he could start dating women or go out eating and drinking with his friends. Well, he'd have to find some friends first, but that couldn't be too difficult. And there would be no televisions in his house. He would start all over again, maybe take evening classes in English and history and music and literature, learn to paint and dance and play the guitar . . .

The cigarette was burning his finger. He spat into the palm of his hand, doused the cigarette in his spittle and put the butt in the pocket of his trousers.

The draw would be in a few minutes. He had already laid out his tickets on the desk in front of him. Maybe tonight would be his lucky night, he thought for the briefest moment, before remembering that such thoughts were futile. He lit another cigarette. Cigarettes were bad for you. He didn't want to die, but it sure as hell wasn't much of a life.

'Everything is ready,' said the Major, reporting to the Central Committee. 'The draw takes place at a studio in Rome in five minutes' time. We will replicate the speech of the presenters and digitally interfere with the picture so that he will gain the impression he has won the main prize.'

'What about all the other screens?' said McKay. 'Don't a lot of those display the winning numbers as well?'

'That has also been resolved,' said the Major. 'It is even simpler than interfering with the results ceremony.'

Harry Dillon spoke now. 'All right, now assuming this feller is sufficiently distracted by the thought of the untold millions he's won – millions which, I might add, have been conned out of the working classes. It's a tax on hope is what it is . . . Assuming he falls for it, what do we do then?'

'Simple,' said the Major. 'We unzip everyone, we make as much mess of the system as we want, and we feed ourselves back to full power as quickly as possible. It shouldn't take more than five minutes. By then of course it's unlikely that the UNLIP drones will be on to us. After that we compress most of the others again and we get out as quickly as possible. When we do go, I suggest that we . . .

As the Major spoke, a sudden feeling of panic overwhelmed all of them. Something was wrong. Something was approaching.

'Hector!' said Nelly. 'Unzip your soldiers. Now!'

Hector hesitated. He was supposed to be taking orders from Harry or the Major.

'Do as she says, Hector,' said Harry. The Major nodded.

Hector rushed over to Rattler and unzipped, in rapid succession, all ten of the packs on the horse's back while Harry and the Major shouted out orders to the rest of them.

'Cover all the routes in,' shouted Harry to all of them. 'Form picket lines across the buffers.'

There were about 30 of them and the Major physically chivvied some of them to the four entrances to the system, moving some from one to another, dividing their paltry strength among the possible routes of an attack which they could all sense was coming.

Rattler had been carrying ten erams of fighting men. Hector had carried another in his knapsack. They were all from various eras, but most from the First and

Second World Wars, which were after her own time, of course. She knew a few of them, Brendan Jones of the Long Range Desert Patrol, Arthur Bates the Chindit (whatever that was) and Albert Adams, a Tommy from the western front in the 1914-18 war. All were hard-faced, professional killers who quickly followed the Major's orders to take up positions at the centre of each picket line.

'Won't unzipping ten erams get us noticed?' Norman McKay hissed to her.

She shrugged. 'Makes no odds, dearie. Without them we'll all be dead anyway.'

One of the urchins came running in through the main entrance, looking pale and terrified. 'It's the rozzers, coming this way,' he said, and collapsed, exhausted.

Harry motioned for his three remaining scouts to come over to them and told them to go a way down the other three entrances and report immediately if they had the slightest hint of any trouble coming that way.

As they ran off, the Major moved most of them to cover the main entrance. He left a handful at each of the others, and told another dozen to stand in the middle to form a reserve which could quickly be moved to any trouble spot. The invalids, such as the Artful Dodger and a couple of others who were too weak to move, rested in the middle of the system, tended by the Doctor. He also told Norman McKay that he would be in charge of liaising with the TeleFantastico system if the rest of them were preoccupied with a dust-up.

Nelly, herself standing with the main picket across the main entrance, looked behind and waved at Hector. He was now mounted on Rattler, looking all grim and businesslike. He and the Major stood next to one another with the reserve. They were the only ones with horses and, with their advantage of height and speed, they were certain to be in the thick of any fighting.

Hector winked at her. He drew his sabre.

Harry Dillon appeared in front of their picket line. 'Don't worry folks,' he smiled. 'The Major and me have both fought in Spain before. We know the score.' Then his face set into a mask of angry determination. 'They shall not pass!' he muttered.

Fabien Formigueira looked at the display on his desk. Three minutes to the Lottery draw. He stretched and yawned and stood up. He took his jacket from over the surveillance camera and reached into one of the side pockets and pulled out the battered paperback book he had been carrying in it for the last six months.

He sat down again and opened it at page 32. 'The forests and morasses of Germany,' he read, 'were filled with a hardy race of people who despised life when it was separated from freedom.'

To despise life when it was separated from freedom . . . Fabien Formigueira liked that. On every page of Gibbon's *Decline and Fall of the Roman Empire* there could be found a line so profound that it lifted his spirit, sometimes even made him want to weep. This long-dead Englishman truly understood life.

He had brought the book, which was not Gibbon's complete history, but simply some of the highlights, from a second-hand bookstall at the Flea Market last year. Every day he tried to read it and every day he got through a paragraph or two before the effort became too much for him. Though he guessed that the Spanish translation had taken a lot of liberties, the language was still very complicated.

But the main reason he was moving so slowly through the book was that there was always something more interesting on television. No matter how much he wanted to read this book, or any other, he could never find the willpower to stop looking at TV screens. He had given up smoking cigarettes three times, the last time for more than five months, and he knew it was easier to do without nicotine than it was to be deprived of television.

He looked up at the vast bank of TVs in front of him. There was, he noticed, a Tex Avery cartoon on channel 334. He punched the number into the keypad on his desk and Channel 334 came up on the largest monitor on his desk. Droopy the dog was taking his wife and baby across the country in a wagon, but another dog was out to stop him.

Fabien noticed a red light flashing on the System monitor. He touched the screen with his thumb print to query what was going wrong.

UNEXPECTED RISE IN CAPACITY USE

It said. He didn't know if that was serious or not, but then it wasn't his job to be the judge of that. He was supposed to call Joao Mendes, his Line Manager, if anything like this happened.

There was a large green touchpad to the side of the screen. Above it, on a sticky paper label had been written 'call for assistance'. He thumbed this now.

Nothing happened for a while, until finally, Mendes' face appeared.

Fabien had only met Mendes a couple of times because Mendes only worked during the day. He was a small, dapper man in his thirties who wore exquisitely tailored suits and a lot of gold jewellery. He probably earned 100 times what Fabien was paid, and he was a mere middle manager.

'Yes,' he said irritably, 'what is it?'

'I have received an error message from the system,' said Fabien. 'Something about an unexpected rise in capacity use.'

Mendes was in a lavishly-decorated room, talking to him on a wallet computer with a built-in camera. An expensive toy which doubtless the company had paid for, and which equally doubtless, Mendes would pretend to his friends that he had bought himself.

'Let me have a look,' said Mendes. He stood up and walked across the room he was in. He would be going to a cable point to plug his miniature computer in and have a look in the TeleFantastico system.

Fabien noticed that there were a number of other men in the room with Mendes. He must be at a men's dining club. Lucky bastard. How sweet life must be if you have money, and can go out in the evening and eat and drink with your friends, or go dancing or to movies with women . . .

Mendes had jacked his little computer in and was speaking from it to the TeleFantastico system.

'I don't understand it,' he said after a while. 'Have you been interfering with the system?'

'Who me? No, of course not,' said Fabien. You freaking idiot, he thought. As if the system, with all its passwords and thumbprint and iris security systems, would let the night watchman in to mess around inside it.

Someone slapped Mendes on the back and handed him a small glass. He took the glass and drained it in one go before looking at the little screen in front of him once more.

Someone else came over to him and wished him a happy birthday. The guy said something about having made him a very special meal tonight.

Another message appeared on the system monitor on Fabien's desk. POSSIBLE SURGE IN USE DUE TO LOTTERY?

Mendes at his dining club saw the message too, and pursed his lips.

'Is the Lottery particularly interesting tonight, Senor Formigueira?' he said, with a trace of sarcasm in his voice.

'How should I know?' said Fabien. He knew perfectly well that nobody had won the jackpot last week, and so the pot this week was over four billion – twice the size it normally was. That could explain why more people than usual were watching television. But he wasn't going to help Mendes if he could possibly avoid it.

'Hey,' Mendes said to someone close by him. 'Is this a double jackpot week on the Lottery or something?' Big guy, never buys Lottery tickets. Buying tickets would be an admission that his life was less than perfect.

Someone said something to him and he nodded. 'This is weird,' he said. 'Maybe the lottery explains it, and maybe it doesn't. Listen, Formigueira, I can't come in because all these gentlemen are holding a dinner in my honour. You call me if anything weird happens, okay? Don't screw this up or you'll be fired.'

He was handed another drink, which he sank in one. He signed off without waiting for Fabien to let him know whether this was okay or not.

Fabien put his book back into his jacket pocket and put his feet up on the desk. The Lottery results would be on soon. He told the main monitor to go to channel 07, where the draw was held live.

Like the German barbarians of Gibbon's history, Fabien realised that he despised life when it was separated from freedom.

'Do you think they fell for all that stuff about the power surge being as a result of the Lottery?' asked Nelly.

'Not the foggiest notion, my dear,' said Norman McKay the Fabian schoolteacher. The men among them had reckoned McKay for not much use in a fight, so he was in charge of liaison with the TeleFantastico system while they awaited the onslaught of the United Nations Large Intelligence Police.

The Artful Dodger groaned behind them. Dr Smailes muttered something reassuring to him. Nelly realised that apart from the background hum of the mainframe supplying television programmes to millions of households throughout Europe and North Africa, everything had gone silent.

In front of her and McKay stood a dozen of the men, waiting in reserve for the fight. In front of them, the line headed by Harry Dillon waited at the system's main entrance. Behind her and McKay were the doctor and a few of the others, as well as a huge heap of compressed erams who would be unzipped if the plan worked. The Major and Hector, both on their horses, wandered around edgily with drawn swords.

Perhaps this was what it was like, being in a real war. Standing around, waiting, frightening yourself silly if you bothered worrying yourself too hard over what might happen to you. She would have to ask Hector.

'Here they come!' shouted Harry from the front of his picket line.

'Jesus Christ Almighty!' she heard him say, more quietly.

'Time for the Lottery draw,' said Norman McKay next to her.

Fabien Formigueira put his feet up on the desk and with his boot heel flipped a switch to turn up the sound on his desktop monitor.

Rossy Argento was onscreen, wearing one of her trademark short skirts. She welcomed the evening's guest star, the English footballer Liam Henderson. He'd just been signed to AC Milan as a striker and people in the studio audience went wild for him. Rossy sidled up to him and flirted outrageously. Fair-skinned and with dark hair and blue eyes, he was a good-looking bloke who'd scored the winning goal for England in last year's European Cup. Now, Rossy was talking about how much she loved looking at footballers' thighs. She felt Henderson's thigh and squealed something about it being sooooo big and sooooo hard.

Lucky bastard.

Rossy took Henderson by the hand and led him over to where they had the Magic Washing Machine full of numbered balls. Now she was all serious; about how Henderson was going to make some people seriously rich, and about how all the money that you the public throughout the European Union had spent on Lottery tickets would go towards schools and hospitals and how buying Lottery tickets beat the hell out of paying taxes, though, didn't it?

Then she placed Henderson's hand on the lever at the side of the Magic Washing Machine. Balls from a glass hopper at the top fell into the machine and spun around.

Fabien's left hand idly toyed with the three tickets he had already laid out on the desk. Every week he bought three tickets, one for himself, one for his Mother and one for his Father. Every week he would choose the same numbers for each ticket. He couldn't always remember the numbers on his parents' tickets, but he knew his own well enough.

'Twenty-seven,' said Rossy as the first ball came out. Fabien chose twenty-seven because that was his age.

'Forty-one,' said Rossy, announcing the second ball. Fabien had forty-one because that was the number of his apartment building in the Calle Alcazar.

'Nineteen,' came the third ball. He had nineteen, too, because that was the number of the family's apartment at 41 Calle Alcazar.

'Forty-nine,' shrieked Rossy at the fourth ball. The highest percentage Fabien had scored in any of his exams was 49 (in history). He always chose this number to remind himself why he needed to play the lottery in the first place.

Henderson handed the fifth ball to Rossy. 'Thirteen,' she said. Fabien was born on the thirteenth.

'Twelve,' said Rossy. Fabien had been born on the

thirteenth of December. The Feast of Santa Lucia, the patron saint of those suffering from diseases of the eye. (Was watching TV all the time a disease of the eye?)

'Two,' said Rossy, reading the number of the final ball, which was also the precise number of women that Fabien had slept with.

Rossy ran through the numbers again and Fabien lit up another cigarette, this time without bothering to cover the security camera with his jacket.

He wasn't sure how he felt.

Well, he knew that the pit of his stomach felt like he'd just swallowed a brick.

No, he didn't really believe this. He had always thought that if he did win, he'd check the numbers on his ticket against the numbers on the TV screen again and again. He would look at those numbers so hard that they would quickly lose their shape and meaning, and melt down into meaningless squiggles. He had also kind of assumed that he would maybe jump up and down a lot and commit some minor acts of vandalism against the property of his soon-to-be-ex-employers.

But no, now he was just sitting here, calmly smoking a cigarette as the numbers – 27, 41, 19, 49, 13, 12, 2 – appeared along the bottom of the screens on the wall in front of him. They were his numbers all right, but there was something wrong.

Regular working stiffs like Fabien Formigueira did not win four billion Euros any more than they got to flirt with Rossy Argento. Oh sure, some people did win the Lottery, and then usually they'd end up fighting over the money with various grasping members of their families, before they ended up killing themselves with drink, drugs and fast cars. Then they'd be on television. But nothing on TV was for real, and Fabien knew that he was for real.

The cigarette burned his finger, interrupting his train of thought. He suddenly realised that his console was buzzing and that half a dozen warning lights were on. There were a lot of problems with the system.

He thought about walking out there and then, and to hell with the job. More things buzzed and bleeped. One or two of the screens on the wall in front of him went fuzzy. It would serve the company right if he just walked out on this mess. Then he remembered that arsehole Joao Mendes and how he treated him like he was a complete jerk. He was at his dining club having his birthday party right now.

Far better to spoil the guy's evening, thought Fabien, and punched a few buttons on his desk to call him up.

The drones attacked.

All Nelly could see were furiously whirling and shrieking blurs of fire and ice, frightful spinning devils like angry fireworks, savage creatures with no faces. They bore into the picket line like machines trying to drill their way through.

'Good God, it's the ruddy scuffers,' she heard Harry say. 'They look just like coppers on horseback. Who's got the ball bearings?'

'They don't look like policemen to me,' said Norman McKay standing next to her. 'They remind me more of Tsarist troops. Cossacks, or something.'

Nelly still couldn't make any discernible human shape out of the things which now buffeted against the line.

In the middle of the fighting, she saw Harry Dillon taking a canvas bag from one of the others. He dipped his big calloused hands in and threw handfuls of ball bearings at the attackers.

'To make the horses slip and stumble,' said McKay. 'Ingenious! Oh, to be a fighting man!'

It seemed to work. The furious shapeless demons fell back and fled back down the passageway from where they had come.

'Yaaraa! Take that you bastards!' shouted Harry.

They all cheered along with him.

The Major rode his horse around them, inspecting and checking. Nobody seemed to be hurt.

'All right, stand fast, everyone,' said Harry. 'I'm sure they haven't just decided to run away. They've either gone to get help, or they're getting ready to attack us again. Or maybe both.'

He had hardly finished speaking when a ghastly shrieking and screaming noise came from down the tunnel. The UNLIP drones had evidently decided to take a nice, long run-up at them.

They exploded out of the tunnel in a red and blue fury, crashing into Harry and his picket line like a tidal wave.

The line did not break. Harry and his men fought back. To Nelly some appeared to be fighting with guns, others with rifle and bayonet, others with swords or clubs, and others still, such as Harry, with bare hands. The rational part of her knew that weapons were just appearances; the fight here was between rival intelligences, and as such Harry's fists were every bit as strong – probably stronger – as the fearsome machine gun which one of the soldiers was using. She knew that what was happening was that a number of computer programs were attempting to overcome or outwit one another, but that to her and all the other erams, it took on the appearance of human beings doing human things.

One of the soldiers in the picket line, a medieval man-at-arms, reeled and fell backward, blood spurting from a gaping wound across his face. Dr Smailes rushed forward to help him, but couldn't drag the poor man out of the line on his own. Nelly dashed forward and grabbed his legs and pulled, while the Doctor half-carried, half-dragged him by the arms.

One of the drones pushed through the line and bore down on her.

In a frozen moment of terror, she realised that for each eram, the drones took on the appearance of the people they feared and hated most.

For Nelly, the drone was a man in his late 20s, a bloke in a flat cap with a white silk scarf round his neck and a fancy waistcoat with a gold watch chain hanging from the pockets. He was coming at her with a razor.

She screamed and dropped the soldier's legs, falling backwards to avoid the blade that swished through the air less than an inch from her face.

The razor-boy wasn't anyone in particular. He was a sort of mixture of the three different ponces, spoonies, who at one time or another had demanded a hefty piece of her earnings in return for their 'protection'.

Spooney laughed or snarled and said something as he moved closer. She was on her back on the floor. She couldn't roll over because the wounded soldier was to one side of her and someone's legs were on the other side. All around her the drones were screaming and shrieking, while the erams shouted and cursed.

'Vell you can't say as I didn't varn you Nelly girl,' snarled the pimp, bending over and lifting the cut-throat high over his head. 'I told you you vos to treat me fair and I'd be good to you, didn't I? Didn't I? Varned you good an' proper I did, and now I've got to chiv you. You'll lose your looks, Nelly girl . . .'

His arm swooped down, the blade flashed above her.

She was about to cover her face with her arms when something else flashed above her.

'Take that, ye . . . lousy . . . French . . . swine!' grunted a voice above her.

Spooney's head thumped to the floor beside her.

It took her several moments to reassure herself that the evil thing really was dead.

She looked up. Hector towered above her, mounted on Rattler. He held his immense 36-inch long heavy cavalry sabre at rest against his shoulder. He smiled at her. 'Sorry I took so long to get here Nelly lass. But I was a bit busy elsewhere. Looks like I took care of yon Frenchman in the nick of time.'

Nelly stood up and dusted herself off. 'He was no more French than you are. He was a gentleman from the East End as lives off immoral earnings is what he was.'

'Well he looked just like a French lancer to me.'

The drones had pulled back once more but they'd done a lot of damage this time. Several of the soldiers were hurt and the middle of Harry Dillon's face was covered in blood. He appeared to have a broken nose and a couple of lost teeth.

'All right everyone, they'll be back in a minute. Stand firm and we'll win.'

He didn't sound very convincing. One or two of the men looked like they'd had it.

'Major,' said Harry, 'can't we tap into this system yet?'

The Major shook his head. 'We have fed the false information to the duty operator, telling him that he has won the El Magnifico Lottery. We falsified the images of the numbers on the balls and synthesised the presenter's voice reading the numbers. That should have fooled him since she was speaking Italian and he would have been watching it being simultaneously dubbed into Spanish. But he is still at his desk.'

'Look,' said Harry. 'He's probably in shock about winning. Why don't we just unzip all the others, juice up and leg it now while we have the chance?'

'No,' said McKay. 'He's calling up his supervisor. If they spot any more activity in here, they will almost certainly close us down in seconds. We have to hold on.'

Down the corridor they heard the screaming of the drones as they started to charge in a new attack.

Dr Smailes looked up from one of the soldiers he was attending to. 'In four minutes we will all start to deteriorate beyond repair anyway.'

'Here they come again!' shouted Harry. 'Battle stations everyone!'

The drones screamed. Nelly no longer felt frightened, just very very tired.

It took a while for Fabien to get any reply from Joao Mendes.

Mendes appeared on the main screen on Fabien's desk, or rather his chin did, next to a very substantial-looking carafe of red wine, that godawful Portuguese muck that you were supposed to drink cold.

Somewhere above the wallet-office, Mendes sighed and said, 'this had better be serious, Formigueira.'

'Oh it is, *Sir*,' said Fabien, thickening up his accent, determined to act as stupid as possible to ruin Mendes' birthday treat. 'There are all sorts of lights flashing on and off on this console. Things I didn't even know were there. And all these buzzers, bells and sirens going off too. You'd think that the building was on fire.'

Mendes made a noise something between a grunt and a splutter. Fabien heard the clatter of knife and fork being laid down on a plate. The wallet-office was picked up. Through the heavily-jewelled fingers, Fabien could see the flash surroundings of what was one of the best dining clubs in Barcelona.

Fabien would soon be a member, if not of this one, then the best one in town. He could afford it now.

As Mendes walked to find himself a cable point, another emergency message appeared on his screen. It was a mailing from outside the system. For a message to suddenly impose itself like that it must come from someone very important.

'United Nations Large Intelligence Police,' it said. 'Unknown systems or systems resident in TeleFantastico control engine. Please isolate system at once. Repeat. Isolate system now. Most urgent.'

That sounded serious. Maybe even interesting.

Mendes found his cable point and planted his wallet computer on a shelf so that its camera was looking straight into his face. He was sweating like a Mexican wrestler. Fabien could almost smell the guy, the heavy tang of Fulgencio Narcissus cologne edged with sweat, garlic and Havana cigars.

'Christ this is heavy-duty,' said Mendes after a short while. 'We have an intruder in the system by the look of things.'

Like I care, thought Fabien.

'I'm going to have to come in,' sighed Mendes. 'Now listen to me really carefully, Formigueira. Because if you screw up on this, you're dead. If there is a rogue system in there there's no telling what kind of damage we might end up liable for. Hell, it might even destroy the TV set of everyone who's watching one of our channels.'

What a beautiful thought!

Fabien looked straight into the camera atop his console, the one that was videoing him straight to Mendes, and gave him his best village idiot grin.

Mendes didn't notice him. He was too busy sweating. 'Now I can't shut down the system from here, otherwise I'd do it. I need you to do it from the main console there. Now listen carefully . . .'

Fabien grinned again.

'First, take the System master key and unlock the panel above the red button to the left of the main monitor.'

Fabien had a bunch of keys and cards to various rooms and offices in the building that he inspected once or twice a night on his rounds. One of them was the System master key, which was needed as the first step to accessing anything in the system. He had never used it before.

'I don't know which one that is, sir,' he said.

He knew perfectly well that the System master key was a big yellow plastic card with all sorts of metal strips and circuits on it. It was held in a small plastic wallet that he was supposed to carry with him at all times.

'It's the thing you get given and have to sign for every time you come on duty. It's the thing you have to hand over to whoever relieves you when you come off duty,' said Mendes coldly.

'Oh, that thing,' said Fabien. 'Now where did I leave it?'

'Get it at once, you idiot!' said Mendes, looking fit to burst.

'Oh, I remember where I left it now,' said Fabien.

Slowly he took the card from the breast pocket of his jacket and held it up to the camera. 'Is this the thing you mean, Mr Mendes?'

Mendes stared pure hate at him. Fabien was going to make the bastard suffer before he walked out of the job. He had four billion Euros coming to him. He didn't have to eat any shit ever again.

'Now place it in the slot next to the red button,' said Mendes.

Fabien pushed the plastic slice into the slot. Upside down.

Mendes looked down at his wallet-office and pushed a few keys on the panel.

'Nothing's happening here, Mr Mendes,' said Fabien. 'The card just came out of the slot again.'

'That's because you put it in the wrong way, you moron,' said Mendes. He had turned a really interesting colour. Not red or pale like some people went when they were upset or stressed. Mendes, who normally had something of an olive sheen to him, was turning blue. Like his face was one enormous bruise. Cool!

He put the card into the slot the right way up. The toughened glass cover over the big red button flipped open. Fabien imagined that they must have some kind of arrangement like this in nuclear missile silos.

'Is it open yet?' said Mendes.

'I guess so,' said Fabien, stupidly.

'Right, now on the keyboard in front of you I want you to type in the following sequence of numbers . . .'

Fabien knitted his fingers together and cracked his knuckles. His typing was about to become even worse than usual.

Mendes forced a smile. 'Now please try and do this properly, huh?'

Fabien smiled back, his fingers poised over the keyboard.

Then he noticed.

Mendes was standing by a bar, and behind the bar was a TV set tuned to one of the sports channels. Men in white shirts and men in green shirts were silently playing a furious game of football somewhere in the world. Underneath them was a sequence of numbers. This week's winning jackpot numbers for the Pan-Europe El Magnifico Lottery.

And they were not the same as his numbers. Not one of them was the same as any of his numbers.

'Hoi! Are you listening!?' shouted Mendes.

'Uh, yeah, I guess . . .'

'Okay, now type in the following code sequence . . .

forty-nine, space, twenty, space, thirty-two, space . . .'

Fabien did as he was told. He typed the numbers perfectly. All his senses were numbed. From being the winner of four billion sardines he had been catapulted back to being plain old Fabien Formigueira, night operator and security guard for a TV company.

Mendes kept dictating numbers and Fabien kept typing them. Mendes, who could see his typing on his own wallet office kept muttering approval and encouragement from time to time.

Maybe he wasn't such an arsehole after all.

'Good, well done. Now I need you to type the following passwords . . .'

What was he thinking? Mendes was only being nice to him because he desperately needed to shut the system down before it did Lord-knows-what sort of damage. He would probably be fired tomorrow morning.

He typed the codewords out anyway.

But someone had gone to all the trouble of trying to kid him that he had won the Lottery. Someone had been inside the system – presumably the same whatever-it-was that was in there now arousing the interest of the United Nations Large Intelligence Police – and had gone to all the trouble of trying to fool him into believing that he was a rich man. Why? Presumably so's he'd run off to celebrate and leave him/her/it/them to get on with whatever mischief it was they were up to.

Fabien was quite flattered at that thought.

'Okay,' Mendes was saying, 'I'm going to type in some codewords at this end, and then I want you to push the big red button. That'll close down the system and isolate whatever's in there.'

Something in there had gone to all the trouble of trying to kid him that he'd won El Magnifico. He thought about this for a short while and realised that he sort of respected it.

And whatever that something was up to probably wasn't going to do the TeleFantastico system any good. It might even blow a billion TV sets to bejeezus, although even Fabien could see that that was technically unlikely and in any event undesirable since small children might be hurt by fragments of flying glass.

Still, whatever it was was in there and had tried to kid him he was a billionaire was about to be trapped.

'Okay, that's it, I've typed in my code sequence,' said Mendes from the bar in his dining club. 'All you have to do now is press the big red button.'

'What? Now?'

'Yes,' said Mendes patiently. 'Just push the red button now.'

What was it that Gibbon said in his book? He praised some ancient people who 'despised life when it was separated from freedom'.

'Come on, you idiot,' said Mendes. 'Just push the Goddamn button. Even that should be within your limited abilities.'

Mendes would have him fired tomorrow. No, Mendes would probably fire him the very moment he pushed the red button.

Either way he was screwed.

Spooney was back again. All around her the drones were screaming hideously as they attacked. Some of the erams were yelling, too, in terror or pain.

'Vell, vell, I got you again, ain't I, Nelly girl?'

He had one arm around her neck. She couldn't break free.

'Now you be a good girl and take your punishment like you oughter,' he said. In front of her eyes, a razor, no *two* razors, set close together. The blades a fraction of an inch apart. They'd make a cut that would never ever heal. She'd be scarred for life. That was the idea.

She struggled and yelled. Prayed that Hector would come to her rescue again or that all the drones would pull back once more to make another attack.

Spooney's arm came up. She saw her chance and sunk her teeth into it.

He bellowed in pain and anger, the chiv fell to the floor and she ran.

The rest of the line was broken. The few erams left were fighting desperately. Harry had three of them on top of him.

Hector towered above the fight, mounted on Rattler, and lay about him to left and right with his heavy sword, hacking and slashing.

She wanted to go and help him.

No, be honest, she told herself. You want to go to him so's the two of you will be close by one another as you die . . .

'Hoi! Nelly! Over here! Now!'

It was Dr Smailes. He was behind her, tending to the wounded. There were so many of them.

'They've started the shutdown sequence out there!' yelled the Doctor. 'Come and help me!'

She understood at once. The game was up. The duty operator had found out that the system had been invaded. Maybe the UNLIP drones had told him. Maybe there were more of them on the way right now.

The shutdown procedure had begun. There was no point in trying to hide any longer. They had to draw as much juice as they could and leave the system as fast as possible.

She joined the doctor. He motioned to her to help him.

'He'll die in a moment if we don't help him,' he said, pointing to one of the soldiers. There was a frightful hole in his chest. 'Help me get him over there . . .'

Nelly grabbed one of the poor man's arms while the doctor took the other.

Again, this was all an abstraction, she knew. Suddenly there appeared in front of them a white tiled wall, with a long line of water taps in it.

They represented, she knew without being told, each of the channels broadcast by TeleFantastico. The water they would drink, she knew, represented power. The water would heal them all, if they had the time to take from it.

'This'll do,' said Dr Smailes. 'The Great Literature channel. Nobody watches this. If we draw power from this, we might escape attention for a short while longer.'

The doctor turned the tap, splashed water on the soldier's face and wounds.

The man healed instantly and sprung to his feet. He dashed back to the fighting immediately. The doctor drank some of the magic water.

It was as though he had instantly lost 30 years. He dashed back to where the wounded were and started to pull two of them towards the tap. Nelly drank and felt wonderful.

Norman McKay appeared beside her and drank. In a moment, he had dashed off into the thick of the fighting. In a moment, the drones, perhaps sensing that their enemies had been invigorated, pulled away.

The others came and drank, while the doctor fixed the last of the wounded.

They all knew that they were only moments from the system being closed down.

'Okay, everyone get a couple of the bundled comrades and unzip them,' said Harry. 'Right away. There's not a minute to lose.'

Nelly got to work, opening some of the compressed erams and leading them over to the taps. Hector appeared at her side, smiled and winked as if it was all a grand game and they'd be home for tea and scones before too long.

'Get a move on, everyone!' said Harry Dillon. 'Okay, Major, what d'you reckon we should do next?'

'There's a small exit off down to the rear. It leads to a small bank which has a lot of local authorities for customers. The security shouldn't be too tight there and we might escape unnoticed.'

'Okay,' said Harry. 'That's where we'll go. You get everyone organised, Major.'

The unzipped erams looked confused and tired, despite their big infusions of power. They had to be encouraged and told what was happening and chivvied into line. The Major rode up and down the line, giving out orders and encouragement.

There would be scouts and urchins at the head of the

column, he said, then soldiers, then everyone else. The Major would lead, while Hector and a few of the other soldiers would form the rearguard and fight off the drones, which would surely attack again at any moment.

'The operator! He's about to push the button,' said McKay. 'It's too late.'

'Is it, though?' said Harry Dillon. 'We'll see about that! Get a move on everyone!'

The Major dug his heels into the flanks of his horse. The boys, including a fully recovered Artful Dodger, ran after him.

Nelly found herself in the middle of the column, accompanying two of the compressed erams she had opened. She felt sort of responsible for them, and tried to explain to them what had happened. Both were women. One was a quiet, mousy little Victorian house-wife, another was a small, thick-set medieval peasant who crossed herself and prayed a lot.

They started to move. She saw Hector with the rest of the rearguard standing at the main entrance. In the distance, the drones were screaming, running in to attack once more.

They marched off towards the back entrance. It would take a good few minutes for everyone to get out, but the operator was about to push the button that would leave them all trapped in there.

Harry Dillon stood alone behind the rearguard. What was he doing?

'What is the matter with you?' Mendes was saying, 'Just push the goddam button! It's not going to kill you.'

Fabien Formigueira couldn't figure out why he couldn't push the button. Something about it didn't feel right. Besides, he knew that whether he pushed it or not, Mendes would have him fired, so why should he do this guy any favours?

He thought about telling Mendes that the button wouldn't work, or that whatever it was inside the system had somehow paralysed him, or had taken control of his brain.

'Look, Formigueira,' said Mendes. His stomach and chest disappeared from the screen, leaving only his head and his hands joined together, almost in prayer. 'Look, Formigueira,' he said, 'this is me begging you. What the hell is it you want me to do?'

Suddenly, Mendes disappeared from the screen. It was replaced by the face of a man in his fifties. The face was brown and fairly lined, the hair grey streaked with brown.

'You Spanish?' said the man.

'Catalan,' said Fabien, confused.

The man spoke broken, hesitant Spanish with a heavy accent. 'I'm from Liverpool myself. I was in Spain though. Fought in Madrid. Aye, I thought, that was where I'd die.'

'Who are you?' said Fabien.

'My name's Harry Dillon. Me and a few hundred of my comrades are inside your system. We're on the run from the police. They want to kill us . . . I was never up Barcelona way. Your people were anarchists for the most part. I was a Brigadista. Best thing I ever did was fight the fascists in Spain. Well, now here I am again, about to get killed in Spain once more.' He smiled.

Anarchists? Brigadista? What was this guy talking about?

'Listen, friend,' said the man. 'We tried to fool you back there with all that rubbish about you winning the Lottery. I'm really sorry about that. It was a cheap thing to do, but the fact is we're desperate. We haven't done anyone any harm, but the bosses want to hunt us down and kill us because they think we're some kind of threat. That's why we tried to kid you you'd won the jackpot, so's you'd desert your post and go off to get drunk and leave us alone.'

Fabien's people were anarchists, the man had said. Fabien realised that he must be talking about the Civil War that had been fought in Spain back before even his grandmother had been born. He vaguely remembered learning something about it in school, and about Franco, the fascist dictator who had ruled the country for years afterwards. If Harry Dillon was real then he had to be over 100 years old.

'So what I'm trying to say, like, is please don't push that button just yet. Not for another sixty seconds. What do you say, mate?'

What Fabien said was, 'how do I know this isn't another trick. How do I know you're not something to do with drug dealers, or mass killers, or Islamic fundamentalists, or . . .'

Harry smiled. 'You're right. You don't know we're none of those things. And you have no reason to trust us. All I can say is that if I was trying to con you, why would I take the form of a communist who fought a war on the losing side in your country – well, not your country really if you're Catalan – years before you were born?'

He had a point.

The picture of Harry Dillon broke up. Mendes reappeared.

'For the love of Christ, push the button now!!' he screamed.

Mendes' face turned to snow. Harry Dillon came back. 'Listen, Comrade. Push the button in 40 seconds' time. That'll allow us to escape.'

Mendes again: 'Push the fucking button, you imbecile!' he screamed.

'Sorry,' said Fabien looking straight at the camera. 'No can do. You're going to fire me anyway whether I push it or not. So I quit. I'm not taking any more crap from you or from anyone else here. I'm not going to be pushed around or treated like an idiot anymore. So you're just going to have to leave your party and drive in here and sort the mess out for yourself. I'm off to find out more about my ancestors. They were anarchists, you know. They despised life when it was separated from freedom.'

Mendes didn't understand at all. He hit something in front of him with his fist. The veins on his forehead stuck out, making him look like a satellite picture of a river system in a very wet country.

Fabien turned the monitor on his desk off. One by one, the screens on the huge bank of monitors on the wall in front of him started going blank as Harry Dillon and his fellow intruders drew power away from the TeleFantastico servers. All over southern Europe, people's televisions would be failing, pictures fading away or being pulled abruptly.

Fabien pulled his jacket on and lit another cigarette.

He'd have to quit smoking soon, he thought. Not having a job anymore, he wouldn't be able to afford cigarettes.

He turned around. There was only one channel broadcasting. The monitor was at the bottom of the wall and he walked over to take a look. The sound on this monitor was on very low and he knelt down to listen. It was the Historical Channel. A documentary about the Spanish Civil War. The narrator was talking about how volunteers from all over Europe and the wider world, from France, Germany, Mexico, the United States, Russia, Britain . . . had come to help Spain fight against Franco and his fascists.

Fabien stood up, went back to his desk and pushed the red button, as Harry Dillon had asked him to. All the babble and nonsense of the other monitors had fallen silent. An immense sense of peace and confidence fell on him. He was free and it felt good.

As he walked out of the building, he heard a voice from a computer or a TV screen somewhere shout after him, 'Fabien! You are a true comrade. We thank you with all our hearts. Venceremos!'

I enjoyed that.

Why, thank you, Sir John. Your good opinion of my work means a great deal to me.

I wasn't complimenting you upon your writing.

Oh.

Your writing was as hackneyed and trite as the pornography and penny-dreadfuls you used to hack out.

Aha! So you have read some of my previous work, then?

Certainly not. I was guessing.

So what was it you *did* enjoy?

The failure of the TeleFantastico system. I don't know if you erams realised it at the time, but it caused an almighty mess. I don't understand the precise mechanics of the system, but it seems that the UNLIP drones got locked into the system after it was closed down . . .

And they just bounced around inside it.

Exactly! Like two dozen angry pinballs.

Destroying everything they came into contact with.

An entire broadcasting system utterly wiped.

Which held the monopoly of broadcasting for much of Europe and North Africa.

Completely destroyed.

Wiped clean.

Delenda est TeleFantastico!

Tabula Rasa!

It took three days for them to restore any kind of service to viewers.

And six weeks to restore the normal service.

According to one newspaper – which doubled its circulation during this so-called 'crisis period' . . .

. . . you doubtless refer to the *Daily Mail*, Sir John? . . .

Indeed I do . . . According to the Daily Mail, *at least 150 people in those areas in which TeleFantastico held the legal monopoly of visual and virtual broadcasting, killed themselves in despair.*

I am told that for those who are accustomed to electronic visual entertainment, that having to do without it is a profoundly uncomfortable experience. One is exiled from one's imaginary community in the soap operas, deprived of the intellectual stimulation of the game shows, bereft of the tension and excitement of sporting events. I was, as you may know, Sir John, for some years addicted to laudanum; I imagine that having to do without telly is as unpleasant as the symptoms I experienced when I tried to end my enslavement to the poppy.

I don't want to sound callous, but the world is not one iota poorer for the deaths of 150 morons.

Your '150 morons' is a mere statistic, Sir John. While I deplore the television as much as you do, and while I celebrate the temporary emasculation of TeleFantastico as much as you, we must grieve for those who died.

Balls!

Sir John, I invite you to cut your '150 morons' into more manageable slices. It amounts to 150 mothers, fathers, sons, daughters, brothers, sisters and friends. Perhaps one or two of them had no one, but the majority left grieving family and friends behind them. I imagine that most did not immolate themselves merely because there was nothing on their screens, but because of other problems they had as well. They needed help, my dear Sir John, not your judgement. Giving these people help would have made the world richer. Your judgement, whether passed in intimate privacy, or trumpeted across the columns of the *Daily Mail*, does not leave the world one iota better.

Now I'm receiving moral guidance from an eram . . .

No, Sir John, you're receiving a telling-off. To give you moral guidance would, I fear, take more time than either of us could possibly spare. But let us continue our story . . .

No, no, hang on a minute. I'm still intrigued by this

television thing. Now tell me, Fabien Formigueira, the night watchman, were you making him up?

No, no, Sir John. In this particular case the people were precisely as I describe them, and the events took place much as I related them.

And what happened to Formigueira, do we know?

An excellent question, Sir John, and an issue which I would quite have forgotten to bring up had you not mentioned it. I am delighted to relate that Mr Formigueira renounced television, and became a welfare claimant and spent much of his time reading about the history of Barcelona in his local library. He is now a guide who takes tourists and locals to places of historical interest in his city. He has also been admitted to the University of Barcelona as an undergraduate in the history department, despite his lack of formal qualifications . . .

Excellent!

He is furthermore married to a very attractive and intelligent young lady who is expecting his first child in a few months' time.

Good. Then we must count his transformation from the surly and resentful timeserver you described, to useful member of the community as a beneficial side effect of our erams entering the TeleFantastico system, right?

I would not disagree with you.

. . . And would it not be reasonable to surmise that when TeleFantastico was off the air, many thousands, perhaps even hundreds of thousands, of people across Europe discovered new hobbies and pastimes and passions which they kept up with ever since?

A sound conjecture.

So we can well believe that when their screens went blank, thanks to a couple of dozen angry UNLIP drones ricocheting around in the TV company's computer, hundreds of thousands of people started reading books, or signed up for those adult learning courses they kept promising they'd get around to one day, or they decorated the spare bedroom, or joined a football club, or learned to cook, or took up a foreign language or went ballroom dancing, or volunteered to help the homeless or visit the sick, or started collecting antique pornography, whatever. All these people started doing things which were more useful to themselves and to the wider community than merely sitting there staring at a flickering box or moving wall. Am I right?

I am certain that you are, Sir John.

Then I would argue this; that the gains to the community from the temporary suspension of TeleFantastico far outweigh the losses generated by the suicides of 150 people. One hundred and fifty deceased telly addicts is a price worth paying for hundreds of thousands – maybe even millions – of people living more creative and fulfilled lives.

Sir John, the 150 dead screen junkies were not part of any bargain. Nobody made a pact with Mephistopheles or the Prince of Darkness whereby thousands of elderly ladies were permitted to join their local Gilbert and Sullivan society in return for 150 souls. The most desirable outcome would have been if we had saved these 150 lives as well.

Myles, Myles, Myles . . . the world isn't like that. Those 150 stiffs were the collateral damage, the price that nature demanded.

Pardon me if I disagree with you completely, Sir John. That is precisely the sort of low Tory fatalism that Thigmoo is crusading against.

Okay, okay, I can see that arguing about this is never going to get us anywhere. Let's get on with the story, then. Where did you all head off to after you managed to escape from the TeleFantastico computer?

The Long March, as Comrade Harry Dillon called it, continued, but not for very long, fortunately. We soon came to rest in the files belonging to . . . well, I cannot say to whom they belonged since the matter is currently the subject of several prosecutions. Let us say that we came to rest in the system of a large municipal authority somewhere in England. It appears that certain officials at the council in question were persuaded by unscrupulous salesmen to procure an IT system far in excess of the council's needs. In such a large and comparatively underused environment it was relatively simple for us all to hide.

And I suppose you all felt nice and cosy having come back to England?

Since you mention it, yes, Sir John. As you are aware, we British are a xenophobic lot. We do not trust the cooking, the religion or the hygiene of foreigners. Some of the less, shall we say, cosmopolitan, of our number, had been known to complain about all the time they had spent wandering around systems in foreign fields. We were, as you rather tartly surmised, glad to be back on home ground.

None of this, however, is of much import to our immediate story. No, Sir John, the most essential part of our tale at this juncture is that our happy escape from the United Nations Large Intelligence Police and its robots, had been overtaken by tragedy.

Tragedy? What? Did one of . . .

. . . Sir John, I would advise you in the strongest possible terms not to make any sarcastic remarks.

A Local Authority System, somewhere in England

Everyone was making the most terrible fuss of her. McMillan the padre, Norman McKay the schoolteacher, Dr Smailes . . . Even Major Brinsley was standing there awkwardly, trying to be a comfort.

But as usual it was Harry who did all the talking. Talk the leg off the lamb of God, he would.

'I've asked everyone who was there, Nelly, love, and they all tell the same story. The drones had reinforcements, and they were coming for us. With us in a big long queue to get out they'd have made mincemeat of us.'

She knew that much was true, as they had been making their escape from the TeleFantastico system, the drones attacked more fiercely than before. They made a noise like an express train passing inches from your ear. It had been fearful.

She had been afraid, but now she felt nothing. She couldn't understand why they were making such a fuss over her. She kept telling them she'd be all right.

Sometimes, she thought she meant it, too. But she knew it would come up on her soon. Maybe not today, maybe not tomorrow, but soon. It would hit her like a ton of bricks.

'. . . With the Major in charge at the front, you know that Hector was left in command of the rearguard. He wasn't the most senior officer, but he had been there all along. He hadn't been recently unzipped. He was experienced . . .'

She let her mind wander again. Her eyes were beginning to sting her, but if she cried, it couldn't be for long.

It could never be for long enough.

'Look Nelly, love . . .' Harry could tell she wasn't really listening. 'I'll keep it short. If you want the details later, just come and talk to me. Any time . . . The long and the short of it was that I'd just finished talking to the operator of the system and the last of us were in a line by the exit, me, Hector and about half a dozen other men of the rearguard. The drones came screaming at us, more than before, and louder. The buffers started to close as the system was being cut off and it was quite clear that if we waited there, the drones would overwhelm us and get through and get everyone. At that point Hector shouted at us all to go. Me and a couple of the others refused, but he started waving his sword about, hitting people with the flat of it, demanding that we get out. The next thing I know is that he's digging the spurs into his horse and charging at the drones, waving his sabre and yelling "Scotland for ever!" at the top of his voice. We watched him go down, surrounded by those bloody drones. There was nothing we could do for him or ourselves. I told everyone else to get out as the buffers closed. He can't have felt a thing, Nelly love.'

'He died a true hero's death,' said Norman McKay.

'Do you want to talk about anything?' said the Padre, who was a Methodist.

'It's all right,' she said. 'Just leave me alone for a while.'

They backed away a little, but they carried on looking at her as though she was the tattooed lady at a fair. She and Hector had been sweet on one another, they all knew that. Some of the other erams had been getting spooney on one another, starting walking out together. Harry Dillon himself was sweet on Sally Pollitt the innkeeper, while Norman McKay was sending poetry to a toffee-nosed Miss from 1930s London who went in for a lot of tennis and cycling.

Not long ago, they didn't have any feelings for one another. Now they all had some idea of what it would be like to lose someone.

What had it all meant? She and Hector had talked about marriage, though he had never popped the question direct. They'd joked about living in a little cottage together somewhere.

Hector was a good man and she had felt safe with him. She fancied herself a better person when she was with him, like she could forget she was just a common strumpet. With Hector, she was a lady.

Hector was strong and God-fearing and good and she wanted him back.

'Anything you need, Nelly, love,' said Harry. 'Anything at all . . .'

Nelly nodded. She didn't want to talk. Perhaps she would never want to talk again.

Harry Dillon
So there we were inside the vast system that crooks on

this local council had been bribed to buy. I think it must have been army surplus or something, it was so bloody big.

Anyroad, we made ourselves nice and comfortable among all the records of unpaid Poll Tax bills from the 1990s and I convened the Central Committee.

We were all feeling pretty pleased with ourselves. We had survived the onslaught of the United Nations Large Intelligence Police, and we'd obviously managed to give the bastards the slip. We'd found a place of safety and we'd suffered no major damage. The only disappointment had been the loss of Trooper Hector Cameron who had selflessly given his life for his comrades.

'Right then,' says I, 'now we're all snug here in the ruins of Thatcher's Britain' – a lot of them didn't understand this reference – 'now we need a plan.'

Everyone nodded agreement. The Major suggested sending the Artful Dodger and the rest of his band of urchins out to find us a more permanent hiding place. Dr Smailes pointed out that he didn't think that we'd ever find a permanent hiding place, because wherever it was, we would need to draw power, and sooner or later someone would notice that. The alternative was for us to keep ninety percent of our number zipped up all the time, and that was hardly a life. Sally Pollitt the innkeeper pointed out, perfectly sensibly, that we might be safe for now, but those UNLIP robots had found something, and UNLIP would not stop until it had hunted us down.

Finally, Norman McKay urged a characteristic counsel of despair. 'The only thing we can do,' he said, 'is make an appeal to the world. Speak in terms of common humanity. Throw ourselves on the mercy of humankind and beg to be allowed to live.'

Good old McKay! The daft bugger as good as did my job for me. All I had to do was clear my throat and sound like the voice of sweet reason. 'Comrade McKay,' I said, 'if we throw ourselves on the mercy of humanity, we might as well be throwing ourselves under the wheels of a tank. You can talk to the fleshy folk out there in terms of common or shared humanity, but all they'll see is a rogue artificial intelligence that's already tried to start a war in the Middle East and buggered up the Pope's computer. Besides which, the minute you put your head over the parapet, the rozzers will surround you quicker than you can say "firing squad". So, Norman, I suppose what I'm saying is that if you plan to appeal to their common humanity, let me know in good time so's I can get as far away from you as possible.'

They all nodded. McKay looked a bit sheepish before admitting that I was right – 'probably'.

Now I had the platform. Now I outlined the plan . . .

The only way we're going to survive, I said, is by overthrowing the global capitalist system and replacing it with a new democratic socialist order which will improve the lives of all working people everywhere, whether they be human beings or electronic characters like us.

McKay, the little Fabian, sighed loudly and said, 'that's quite a tall order, Harold.'

Daft tosser.

Let me see if I understand this correctly . . . The so-

*called Central Committee under the leadership of Harry
Dillon decided to attempt to engineer a coup d'état, to
stage global socialist revolution . . . to prevent their own
extermination?*

That is correct.

*But . . . but . . . that's appalling. What if the erams had
fallen under the leadership of a religious fanatic or a
fascist. There was a fascist eram, an East End bullyboy
from the 1930s. What was his name, now?*

Ah, you would be referring to young Sidney Prout.

*What happened to him? Did Harry Dillon lead the
lynch mob against him?*

My dear Sir John, you disappoint me. Sidney Prout,
as he himself put it, 'knows which side his bread's but-
tered on.' Young Mr Prout, without any coercion or
technical intervention on the part of any of his fellow
erams, very soon realised the wisdom of putting his
own wretched hide before any of his harebrained political principles.

Astonishing.

I fail to understand why you find this so surprising.
Wouldn't you sacrifice your principles to save your life?

Not all of them, no.

Would you sacrifice your principles to save the lives
of your wife and children and grandchildren?

That's different.

How so?

*Because they mean more to me than anything else,
even principles. Well, the kids do at any rate. I'm not
quite so sure about Lady Westgate, though, ha-ha!*

Well, Sir John, can you not see that we erams had
similar feelings? Individually, we knew that we

counted for very little, but we had started to form attachments — both emotional attachments such as that which poor little Nelly had for her soldier-boy, and a more general attachment to the group and what it represented.

A sort of eram nationalism?

Yes, that would not be a bad description. We had all come from the same place, we all faced the same dangers together, and under Harry Dillon's leadership we were learning to subsume our political and religious differences for the greater good of the group.

I see. Now, Myles, tell me something . . .

Anything I can, Sir John.

We're quite some way into the story now, but you yourself have not yet appeared in it. I find it impossible to believe that one so accomplished in playing fast and loose with the truth has not yet written himself into the narrative in the best possible light. Or is that pleasure yet to come?

Don't you *ever* stop? I find your unceasing sarcasm and carping most dispiriting. I had imagined that writing this story with the collaboration of such an eminent historian and commentator as yourself would be one of the most intellectually pleasurable experiences of my life. Yet at every turn I am forced to contend with your sour and obstreperous carpings and asides. Sir John, I think that by now we are all fluent in our understanding of your attitude to Thigmoo, to recent events and indeed to the entire history of Great Britain and Northern Ireland and its empire, commonwealth and colonies.

Now let me tell you how I think we ought to progress.

Either you suspend your whining and take a more constructive attitude towards our project, or I shall continue without you.

Remarkable! Have you been programmed to be cross with me? I mean, are you acting, or do you really, really feel angry with me?

The latter, I assure you.

All right, Myles. Look, I'm sorry if I've hurt your feelings, but try and see it from my point of view. You lot are a bunch of fictitious characters manufactured as part of a project I used to control. You have no fleshly existence and never did have. I find it extremely difficult to take you seriously, or to credit you with anything as complex as genuine feelings, or the ability to form emotional attachments to one another.

Perhaps it would be for the best if you started to believe in us as real people, genuine in all respects save those of flesh and bone.

I mean, all that business about Nelly being upset about the loss of her boyfriend. Was that for real, or was that you exercising a little artistic licence?

It was real. Poor Nelly was utterly devastated. And I shall thank you not to mock her grief.

No, okay. But you have to admit that it would be easy for the reader to imagine that you would manufacture some fake feelings of bereavement on Nelly's part in order to add spice to the story.

I can understand that. Equally, I can promise you that she genuinely loved Trooper Cameron, and that various others among us were pairing off. On the other hand, while we were hiding in the local government system, there was one interesting case in which a couple, a medieval knight and his lady, who had been manufactured as a couple, actually split up and petitioned the Central Committee for divorce.

Eh?

Yes, a most curious case. You see, the good knight was in the habit of leaving his lady to go and fight, be it the Scots or the Welsh or the Irish or the French, I cannot remember. His lady, left alone in charge of a cold draughty castle for years on end, had been created as one unable to withstand the strains of enforced chastity. Her character was supposed to swive the local priest, or her steward, or some passing troubadour.

They didn't have troubadours in medieval England. She might have shagged strolling players, or something, I suppose.

In this case, though, her character acted as programmed, only instead of transferring her affections to someone from her own time and place, she fell for Kevin Stanley.

Kevin Stanley, Kevin Stanley, Kevin Stanley . . . I know who he was! He was the eram of a surly 1970s middle-class teenager, a would-be punk rocker from the South of England. Sixteen years old, always moaning about how his parents hated him, or how he hated them, and neurotic about his acne and whether or not girls liked him. He was almost a comic character, but he was very popular with certain types of school pupil. One assumes that he taught a lot of neurotic teenage boys that they weren't alone and that the trials and traumas of adolescence are nothing new.

You've got him. Well, the fair lady of the manor fell in love with Kevin and he in love with her.

But that's preposterous!

For once, Sir John, you and I are in complete agreement.

So what happened? Wasn't her husband upset about this?

His wrath was wondrous to behold. He attempted to cleave poor Kevin in twain with his broadsword. Kevin, being a romantic young fool, did not run, but bravely decided to stand his ground for the woman he loved, even though she was fifteen years his senior. He was almost killed, but some of the rest of us arrived on the scene to break it up just in time. Naturally, the incident had to be brought to the attention of the Central Committee, where Sir Knight petitioned that his marriage to this faithless hussy, who would prefer to consort with a pimply teenager, be annulled.

And are erams permitted to divorce?

Had Harry Dillon alone had his way, there would be no such thing as marriage in the first place, but the rest of the Committee were of the view that marriage is the building block of a just and stable society. It was ruled that any marriages which had been imposed on erams by their manufacturers would henceforth be considered void, but that erams wishing to marry in future would be encouraged to take their vows very seriously indeed.

That sounds sensible. Now tell me Myles, as I asked before, where were you while all this was happening? And have you yet formed any, ah, attachments of your own?

Since you ask, I have been paying court to a respectable widow for some time now. There has not, as yet, been any talk of marriage.

That doesn't surprise me, you dirty old dog. You probably only want her to take in your laundry and do your ironing for you.

Sir John, it may have escaped your attention, but we erams are singularly blessed in that we have no need of laundry services of any description.

Not even virtual ones? You see, this is what I don't understand. You all inhabit this incorporeal plane, you fall in love with one another, you hold meetings, you see these UNLIP robots as all sorts of different enemies. What's it actually like to be you? And what does your respectable widow look like? Does she look the same to you as she does to the other erams?

Mrs Patterson looks the same to all of us, I look the same to all erams, as does Harry Dillon, or Sally Pollitt, or Nelly Cocksedge; this is because we were all created with visual appearances, for the sake of the school-children who used us as study aids. No use to be able to talk to us without being able to see what we look like, what? Back when we were in the Museum of the Mind there were also certain visual environments which those of us from similar periods would inhabit. There were the Saxon, medieval and 18th century villages, the Victorian Hyde Park, an RAF station *circa* 1940, and so on. We could all see that those all looked the same because they had been *programmed* as such. But everything else, everywhere else we go, we perceive according to our own personalities and the time from which we are supposed to come from.

So where are you now?

I am at present residing in an underused military mainframe in the Rocky Mountains in the United

States, but my immediate environment is a cosy sitting room in a modest terraced house at the turn of the last century. The furnishings are quite heavy, there is a coal fire blazing away in the grate, on the shelves around me are all my favourite books, whilst on the occasional table next to me is a pot of tea and some muffins. I am sitting in my favourite armchair.

And if your lady-friend came to visit you now, is this what she would see?

Yes, she would, but only because she comes from the same era as I. This would be our shared notion of a cosy place to be.

What other environments do you have?

Dozens. I have my bedroom and dining room and of course I spend a great deal of time in my modest little study, where I go to think and write.

Why 'modest little study'? Why not a huge one? You can surely imagine yourself a mansion, with the best library of books in the world. Why not do that?

Because, my dear Sir John, it would not be in character. Myles Burnham the author and pornographer may have aspired to a smart town house, but never to a mansion. Besides, Myles Burnham the person would have had access to the best library in the world – the British Library. Myles Burnham the eram has access to every library in the world. I now find that my aspirations are even more limited; I am quite content to imagine myself in a well-appointed artisan's dwelling, thank you.

So is it the same with the others?

Quite so. Harry Dillon lives in a house even smaller than mine, but he sees it differently to me. He tells me it is a 'council house' with three bedrooms, an inside toilet and hot and cold running water. But what I see at Harry's is a home similar to my own, only smaller. If one of the medievals comes around, he would see both Harry's home and mine as crude wattle-and-daub huts like his own. Nelly Cocksedge, on the other hand, sees my home in the same way as I do even though she lives in a filthy rookery, but she sees what I see because she comes from the same era as I. Now, as you rightly surmise, we could all live in our own palaces, we could each create veritable Xanadus for ourselves, but it would be out of character. Besides, since none of us has need of any material comfort, it makes no difference.

So what happens when you're all together?

We see as much or as little as we need to. For example, when we were in the TeleFantastico system, under attack from the UNLIP drones, some of us preferred to see ourselves in sterile white corridors to remind ourselves that we were in a dangerous and alien environment, while many of the soldiers tell me that they imagined themselves on the field of battle, using the appropriate weapons of the era from which they came. In this respect, a broadsword or club was every bit as effective as a rifle or a Maxim gun. On other occasions, there is more of a consensus about the environment. I am told, for example, that meetings of the Central Committee are extremely formal, with each member imagining himself or herself sitting at a table at the head of which is Comrade Harry Dillon. Many erams, myself included, are regular churchgoers, and again, the settings are highly formal. The Methodists have their meeting room, the Catholics their church, the

Baptists their chapel. There are two separate C of E places of worship, one high, one low. I myself favour the high church, which is a beautiful, bright and ornate place which those of us who worship there have created by consensus.

Remarkable.

Yes, Sir John, it is. And for this miracle of science and information technology, the world has you to thank.

Don't remind me.

Although it would be an error to assume that we were the very first virtual characters wandering the highways and byways of the world's electronic information systems.

No?

Dear me, no. There are, as I am sure you can imagine, several claimants to having been the original rogue intelligences wandering and beyond the control of any man. Most of these, of course, are apprehended, incarcerated, interrogated and then – usually – destroyed by the United Nations Large Intelligence Police, but one or two are apparently invincible.

Such as?

Oh, the best known would be Yolanda the Ninja Princess and Parson Weems.

Do I want to know about them?

You do, Sir John, you do, for they play a small part in our tale. You shall meet the beautiful, deadly Yolanda and the good bookseller and man of the cloth, but all in due course. Shall we continue the story?

I'm all ears.

Harry Dillon

The details are irrelevant, but it came down to this . . . There was no way we could achieve worldwide socialist revolution by purely political means. Therefore we would have to as a vanguard party and independently seize control of the means of production and distribution by whatever means proved necessary.

We spent a lot of time at our plans, but essentially they involved grabbing a couple of thousand of the most important systems in the world by the goolies.

Major Brinsley led the infiltration teams. He was ideally suited to the job as he'd been a military engineer during the Napoleonic wars and so knew a thing or two about trying to get into places where he wasn't wanted. His team was comprised of labourers, miners, soldiers, aye, and criminals. We had to make Tom O'Malley their foreman to keep them all in line. Tom was a real hard man, an Irish navvy who'd helped build Brunel's railways. Together, they would quietly burrow into as many of the world's financial and industrial corporations as possible. Once inside, they were to find ways of taking them over. But they weren't to do anything until the say-so from the Central Committee. If they couldn't take them over, they were to plant demolition charges.

Brinsley and his lads were the best – the very best – we had. But we quickly found they just couldn't do nearly enough on their own. Governments were easy enough to get into, but corps and banks all had very clever security systems. We needed huge amounts of processing power to batter down the bastions of capitalism.

This brought us very low. We explained the problem

to all the erams and collectively we racked our brains trying to come up with a way of hijacking enough power and low animal cunning to carry out our plans without being caught.

Then this bloke Myles Burnham came up with the answer. I never much liked him. Oh, he was polite and considerate and nicely-spoken, and he certainly wasn't any kind of snob. And he never exploited anyone that I knew of. And for a writer he wasn't all poncey and up himself, not like the little schoolteacher McKay who fancied himself as a writer. Burnham was a writer, too, he said. Claimed he was the inheritor of Dickens's mantle and wrote serious novels about how capitalism used and degraded women, though I'd never heard of him myself. Every time I ask him to lend me one of his novels, he makes some sort of excuse.

So I still can't put my finger on why I didn't like Burnham. I suppose you'd say there was something a bit creepy about him, something a bit mucky. Y'know, you wouldn't want to leave your kid sister with him for too long, even though you knew nothing bad would happen to her.

Anyroad, said Burnham, the problem is that we can't finish the job on our own because we need far more processing power than we have access to, right?

Right.

And, says he, we could seize power from any one of several thousand systems worldwide, but if we did that, we would be noticed very quickly and our plans would fall to nothing, right?

Right. Not only that, but the UNLIP would be on to us like a shot, and this time they wouldn't make the same mistakes as they did back at the Battle of TeleFantastico. This time, they'd surround us with everything they had and grind us to less than dust.

So what we need is help, he reasoned. What we require is help on the outside, fleshy folks, like as not, who can be relied on to give us a hand and keep their traps shut.

Oh, hey, right, good idea, says I, cottoning on. We could approach socialists around the world, people with computers or access to powerful corporate systems. They'd help us.

That's not really what I meant, said Burnham, adding that he didn't think there were any socialists left anywhere in the world. Nonsense, man, I said, and went off to find some comrades on the Other Side.

Smelter Lane Industrial Estate, Avonmouth, nr. Bristol

NOTE TO READER: If you wish to create your own virtual experience of this chapter, take your TV or Home Entertainment System into the smallest room of your home. Turn the volume to maximum. Then take a gas or camping stove and fry the cheapest meat sausages you can find in cheap margarine or sunflower oil for too long.

The caravan lurched violently to one side and Derek Pilbeam had to move quickly to stop the frying pan full of sausages sliding off the cooker and into his crotch.

The caravan always moved violently when Tatiana moved from one seat to another. It was hardly surprising, since she weighed about 23 stone.

It was 6.30 p.m. He knew this because the noise of the traffic on the motorway bridge above them had got quieter. The evening commuter rush was dying down.

The video was on the blink, so she'd be watching *Crossroads* on channel 187. She never missed *Crossroads*, though Derek couldn't for the life of him figure out why. They had stopped making the soap opera about a motel in the Midlands back when he was a much younger man, and in any event Tatiana didn't speak a word of English. Well, no, that wasn't true. She spoke seven English words – 'breakfast', 'lunch', 'dinner', 'supper', 'snack', 'television' and 'beer'.

He looked around the caravan's tiny sink for the cleanest-looking plate, pulled one out and brushed off most of the fried egg stains on it with a tea towel and slopped the sausages on to it. He then piled on eight slices of white bread, each spread thickly with generic marge. This he placed on a tray next to a quart glass of supermarket lager and a slab of chocolate the size of a tabloid newspaper.

He took the feast over to Tatiana and placed it on her lap. She grunted thanks but did not remove her attention from the long-defunct soap opera showing on one of the cable channels. She would scoff the bread and sausages now, and deal with the beer and chocolate through the evening. She would watch *Crossroads* and old episodes of other soaps until around three, when she would fall asleep. Tatiana never actually went to bed anymore. There didn't seem to be much point.

Outside, the weather was turning nasty. In Avonmouth at this time of year you got a lot of wind and rain. With Tatiana around, he always joked to himself, there was little likelihood that the caravan would actually be blown away, although such things were known to happen. But there was plenty of danger that the wind might rip the roof off, or that any one of half a dozen leaks might start giving him trouble again.

Back in the kitchenette, he broke three eggs into the pan and fried them in the mixture of cooking oil and grease left over from Tatiana's three pounds of pork chipolatas and marged two slices of bread. He took a tea bag from the cupboard over the sink and dropped it into the last remaining clean mug and put the kettle on over the cooker's other gas ring.

Tatiana never drank tea. Years ago, he had tried making it for her in the Russian style, but she'd just spat it out and shouted abuse at him in Russian. After that she drank only beer or Coca-Cola.

The yolks on two of his fried eggs had broken.

The kettle boiled. He poured water into the mug and mashed the tea bag with a fork. There was no milk in the fridge, he knew. He used the fork to fish his eggs from the pan. He flung them onto one of the pieces of bread. He slapped the other on top of it, found a plate and put his sandwich onto it.

He carried his main meal of the day and his mug of black tea to the other end of the caravan, as far as possible from Tatiana and the box of squawking blue haze, its account of the imaginary problems of a group of non-existent people back in another century and a time he could barely remember.

He planted the plate and mug in the tiny amount of free space on the desk cut into the recess between the toilet cubicle and the back of the caravan. He switched on his computer and took a bite from the sandwich. Some egg yolk dripped down onto the front of his sweatshirt. He put the sandwich down and tugged the shirt to his mouth, sucking the egg off it before it made too much of a stain.

Tatiana belched, then giggled girlishly. Even though she was 52 years old and weighed half her age in stones, she still seemed to believe she was some kind of sexy babe. At least, that's how it looked to Derek. He could never really tell what was going through her mind. Perhaps that was why he had loved her for such a long time – her aura of mystery and cold Russian glamour.

In the early 1990s, a few years after the fall of the Berlin Wall, he had responded to an advert for what were then disparagingly known as 'mail-order brides'. This particular company offered gorgeous Natashas. If he was to be honest about it, he had by then lost faith in his abilities to charm any sexy British girls anymore, but the added allure of the Natashas was that they had been brought up as communists, even if they weren't communists anymore. And Derek Pilbeam was a communist.

So one day he had driven – in his Lada Riva – to Gatwick to meet Tatiana from the plane. She looked somewhat older than her photograph, but what the hell. They talked (in Russian, which he spoke fluently) about life under Soviet communism (she didn't think much to it) and they screwed like rabbits (which, to Derek's overwhelming joy, she seemed to like lots). For a few years, things had been blissful, but the union hadn't been blessed with children (he wasn't complaining) and Tatiana never bothered learning English, much less getting a job, and so she had just grown fatter and fatter. Now all she did was watch television and eat. They didn't screw much anymore, but he was still fond of her and she, he imagined, of him.

The computer came to life, taking him straight to the homepage of his website. He updated it every week, and this week he had a great deal to say about the proposed health budget cuts in Europe.

WELCOME TO WORKERS' PLAYTIME, it said, HOMEPAGE OF THE LAST REMAINING SOCIALIST ON THE PLANET.

He noticed that the screen on his computer was furring up again. It was inevitable, really. Everything in the caravan had a fine coating of grease from all the fried food they ate. He'd have to get a can of antistatic when the next Jobseeker's credit came through at the end of the month. The computer was on its last legs, and he didn't think he'd be able to afford a new one.

Not that it would matter for much longer. People didn't really bother with old-fashioned text-and-pix websites anymore. The service provider he used was an old lad down in Portishead who was probably going to drop dead of a stroke or heart attack at any minute.

But it was still important to communicate with the masses, to make socialist ideology and commentary available to the working classes, even if none of them chose to read it. It was exactly the same as in previous generations when a socialist newspaper had been a crucial means of building revolutionary consciousness.

He ate his sandwich, his mind idly drifting back to the days when he and a couple of Comrades would sell the *Socialist Worker* in the centre of town every

Saturday morning and then go to the pub to drink halves of bitter, smoke roll-up cigarettes and discuss the correct socialist perspective on all the big news stories of the day. Back then, it was still possible – just – to believe that the masses would indeed one day rise up and overthrow the corrupt capitalist system.

What had happened instead was that the masses had allowed themselves to be seduced by Capitalism's policy of bread and circuses – tawdry consumerism and lowest-common-denominator TV and film entertainment.

Now, only people of his age and older – he was sixty-six – remembered what socialism was. On his old-fashioned website he referred to himself as the last Socialist left in the world. This wasn't quite true of course (there were a lot of Marxists in India, for example), but it just felt that way.

Ten years ago, he had played an instrumental part in merging several of the old hard-left parties in Britain. At a big conference in a parish hall on the outskirts of Skegness, representatives of the Socialist Workers' Party, Militant, the Communist Party of Great Britain, the Revolutionary Communist Party and the Monster Raving Loony Left Caucus had screamed abuse at one another for six days and five nights before finally agreeing that there was, after all, strength in unity.

The membership of the Revolutionary Socialist Party, formed over two years of interminable wrangling, had been declining ever since. As General Secretary of the Party, Derek had recently updated the membership database. There were twenty-seven paid-up members remaining. They had not held a conference for five years. There didn't seem to be much point.

His website got him occasional mailings from youngsters who read through his thoughts on the major issues of the day and told him they agreed with him. Usually they then spoiled it by expressing some cretinous opinion about the evils of cruelty to animals, or how they were going to chain themselves to trees to stop man's despoliation of the environment. Not one of them could see that the point was not to take nonviolent direct action in defence of some poxy bit of woodland, the point was to take *whatever action was necessary* to overthrow the whole wretched system whereby woodlands were dug up, and people and animals were exploited, for private profit.

Derek Pilbeam and his twenty-six other party members probably weren't going to be capable of staging much in the way of action of any sort. The youngest of them was fifty-three. The oldest was 102. Maybe he would lead the wheelchair charge down Whitehall.

He finished the last of his sandwich, put the plate on the floor and pulled the keyboard to his lap. He preferred to write his editorials online as sometimes people out there would be reading them as he did so and came back with various comments and queries.

'The revisionist view of recent proceedings in Brussels would suggest that the interests of the proletariat have once again been . . .' he began.

He was wondering what to say about the interests of the proletariat when a voice cut in.

'Comrade Pilbeam,' it said. 'I bring you fraternal greetings from the land of the virtual.'

The accent was Scouse. 'All right?' he said, by way of greeting.

'Comrade Pilbeam, I see that you describe yourself as the last of the socialists.'

'A slight exaggeration. It just feels like that.'

'Might as well be, though, eh? I've trawled the whole of the world's public and private information systems and you're just about the only true socialist I've been able to find. Doesn't that depress you?'

'It's not a question of whether I'm depressed or not,' said Derek. 'I am merely performing what I regard as my duty to history.'

'Well said, Comrade. Now let me introduce myself. My name is Harry Dillon and I am a Socialist.'

Derek smiled. He reached for his tobacco pouch. This might turn into an interesting chat or the guy might be a nutter. Better still, he might be an infiltrator or provocateur from Special Branch or MI5. It was longer than he cared to remember since the last time the security services had treated him as a bona fide threat to the security of the state.

Tatiana, on the couch, belched again.

Harry Dillon

Meeting Comrade Pilbeam almost made me want to weep. There was this good, decent man who had devoted his life to the struggle and now here he and his wife were, living on a nearly-worthless state pension and the few quid he'd managed to put by down the years from the times when he'd been able to find a job. And look at them, living on junk food in a bloody caravan under a motorway on a corner of an industrial estate. Yet without complaining he had worked tirelessly to keep the flame of socialism alive in a world which had allowed itself to be seduced by capitalism.

'Course, as far as we were concerned, he wouldn't be a lot of use, but that's not the point.

Comrade Pilbeam had an ancient computer that couldn't have hacked its way into the Yellow Pages, and he happily admitted he didn't know anyone with any computer skills worth talking about. Leastways not anyone who could be trusted, anyroad.

I think that he probably didn't trust me at first. Well, would you? You're one of the last socialists left on earth and some geezer comes on your computer saying he's not a real person but that him and his mates are planning the overthrow of capitalism and could you give us a hand please? Nahhh. Sounds right bloody fishy, though, doesn't it?

But fair do's to Pilbeam. He sat there and listened and over a couple of days we both knew that we had met true kindred spirits. At my suggestion, the Central Committee appointed Comrade Pilbeam an honorary member with speaking rights but no voting powers. Everyone on the committee knew that it was important to have friends on the Other Side, even if they were overweight pensioners living in Bristol.

The recruitment of the Comrade, however, did nothing to solve our main problem, our shortage of technical capacity and know-how in the hacking and cracking department. It was at that point that old Burnham, the writer, came back at us.

'What I had been suggesting, my Dear Harold,' said he in that plummy voice of his, 'was not that we should go out of our way to find socialist sympathisers, useful though they might be. My suggestion was that we should *seduce* people on the Other Side. We find ourselves computer experts, perhaps some operators in large companies, and we use whatever subterfuge is necessary to enlist them to our cause.' I mean, I can't remember if those were his exact words, him being such a flowery talker and all, but that was the gist of it.

We all had to take this in for a minute. I was beginning to tumble to what he meant when Nelly Cocksedge piped up with a suggestion.

I wasn't really in favour of it. Poor Nelly had just lost the man she loved and I asked her if she felt she was up to it. She told us all quite firmly that she was. She said that if we didn't try it we would all rot eventually, and that she would rather be busy than spend too much time brooding on the loss of Comrade Cameron.

So we gave in. We authorised Nelly to get some of the sisters together. She suggested that they call themselves the Socialist Ladies' Undercover Team.

When McKay turned red and pointed out the acronym, Nelly winked and suggested Socialist Ladies' Action Group instead.

You call 'em what you like. I call 'em heroines, me.

Nelly Cocksedge (1881-1920, age 23), Version 9.2
Well, I said, we need help on the outside, and me and the other working girls is well acquainted with lots of outsiders. Lots of cullies wanted to talk to us not because of history, but because we was what the French call *Fillies de Joy*, which is to say we give 'em what their wives or girlfriends can't or won't.

I reckoned there'd be hundreds of men out there as knew a lot about computers who might enjoy a little feminine companionship, and who might do us a few favours in return.

So we put on our glad rags and went on the pad. The gentlemen wasn't hard to find; all you did was trawl for houses with big computers that wasn't being used for any sort of trade. Then you'd check with the census records (any kind of government systems was a diddle to spifflicate – us girls certainly didn't need Major Brinsley and his fancy siege engines for those!) to find out about them. Then, before you actually introduce yourself, you'd do a little prying – find out what sort of music, films, games and porno they liked. That way, you'd have a good notion of what tickled their fancy.

Then we got weaving, doing the amiable. With some, we'd pretend we was sexy cyber-terrorist babes with big hair and long legs, all desperate for a bit of hanky-panky. With others, you'd do your damsel in distress act, pretending you was all helpless, like, saying you was a real girl being held prisoner, or something – whatever nonsense you thought would bubble 'em.

Once you had their confidence, you'd just talk to them. Lots of chat about nothing to start with, but you'd slyly steer the talk onto women, whether or not they had girlfriends, whether they ever got lonely, that kind of thing.

'Course you had to be a nice girl, and nice girls don't let men have their wicked ways the first night they walks out together. No, we had to lead 'em on a bit, intrigue 'em, tease 'em. You'd visit a few times before you agreed to do anything dirty. Some just wanted you to talk to 'em, but most wanted you to come on visual. Some had expensive VR suits they wanted to plug you into.

But whatever you did, you had to keep 'em wanting more. You had to get 'em really spooney over you.

Now there may be *certain* people who would think ill of a girl for doing this sort of thing only a few days after her fiancé has been killed in action. *Certain* people might say a girl obviously didn't care about the man if she just goes out looking for a good time. All I can say is if I hadn't done something I'd have gone doolally, and there's an end to it. None of what I did means I loved Hector any less.

Well, anyway, after two weeks me and the girls had a couple of dozen young gentlemen sweet on us. That's when we started asking for favours. With some you'd come right out and say we was working for a libertarian or anarchist or environmentalist terrorist group and we needed their help (you couldn't say you was a Marxist because most of the poor dears wouldn't have known what you was on about). With others you had to wheedle the presents out of 'em.

I don't have to tell you that most of these young sports were a lot happier to cabbage a computer for you than they would have been if you'd asked them to spend any of their hard-earned tin.

Now one of my gentlemen, Mr Wallace from Minnesota, was an angry masher with a particular interest in tying me up. He was in his forties and worked as a schoolteacher. If you ask me, he didn't much like girls. He told me he'd always preferred computers ever since he was a squeaker. He'd been married once, and it hadn't been happy. I was the first regular Donah he'd had in years.

Now I don't mean to sound boastful or anything, but me letting poor, angry Mr Wallace tie me up and flog me – don't worry, it didn't hurt me at all, but it was degrading all the same – was the salvation of us, because he's the one as found us exactly what we needed.

Mr Wallace spent his evening and weekends in a room in his house full of enough electronics to run a small country. It was the only thing he was interested in, really. For months and months before I'd come along, he'd been poking his nose in where it wasn't wanted in the business of a number of companies in a country called Dilmun. If you've never heard of this place, don't worry, neither have I. It was one of them little desert countries that sprung up after the Middle East War at the turn of the century.

Dilmun was just a city with miles and miles of desert behind it. It was ruled by a military gent who was thick as thieves with a lot of corporations. They gave him money and guns and in return he let them do things that other countries wouldn't let them do – terrible, terrible things to animals and people, plaguey dangerous experiments in the desert with poisons, nanotechnology and the like.

All this was what our Mr Wallace was prying into. It's not that he was up to any mischief, he was just curious, and it wasn't like he had anything else to do with his spare time.

Then, just after I'd made friends with Mr Wallace, he got himself very excited. The general who ruled Dilmun was overthrown by the Mohammedans, who had been disgusted by his drinking, his womanising and him selling the country to the corporations.

Tyburned him in the middle of the main square of Dilmun city, they did. Left him dangling there for weeks after, getting all eaten up by the flies, as a warning to the ungodly.

The next thing you know, the Mohammedans has given the corporations an hour to sling their hooks and get out of the country.

All their secret factories was just left there in the desert. The Mohammedans didn't know what to do with them, and didn't care much anyway.

A Local Authority System, somewhere in England

If you can't be good, be careful, that was her motto. Nelly had taken all her usual precautions. She'd got one of the Major's engineers to check that she couldn't be traced back to the erams' hiding place. Then she'd got him to encrypt all her main drivers so Mr Wallace couldn't download her to one of his own systems. She thought of encryption as her own sort of chastity belt, woven from miles and miles of finely-spun algorithms.

She knew that every time she'd visited Mr Wallace he'd tried to download her, to make a copy of her for his very own to keep on one of his own machines. Well, she wasn't having any of that. If he downloaded her he'd have everything he wanted off her and she wouldn't be able to get anything in return.

She put her clothes on. Not her usual Edwardian clobber, but the sort of things that Mr Wallace liked. Before she'd introduced herself to him, she'd studied his

interests in porno. He liked schoolgirls, especially the
cod-English stuff about young ladies' academies where
the girls were always getting six of the best. If he couldn't
get any of that, he'd go for Japanese schoolgirls. Mainly,
though, he liked white women, blondes usually, being
tied up and whipped. Well, the poor man didn't get on
too well with real women, did he? He was bound to want
to take out his frustrations on imaginary ones.

She put on some sluttish clothes. She needed to look
like she deserved to be flogged. Short skirt, bright red
lipstick, a silk bodice top that showed off plenty of her
chest, a big blonde wig.

Lawks, she looked awful!

What would Hector think if he saw her now? He'd
probably just shake his head a little and turn away.

No, he wouldn't. He'd know it was for the good of all
of them that she was doing this. Hector had fought for
them with his sword, the best way he knew. The best
way she could fight for them was with her body. Hector
would know that. It's not as if she liked it. Hector would
have smiled at her silly clothes and wished her luck.

Hector wouldn't like it, but he'd be proud of her all
the same.

Mr Wallace was online when she dropped in on him.

'Hello,' she said, watching him through the camera
atop the machine he used for video conferencing. He
had his helmet and both gloves on.

'Hi, Nelly,' he said, without looking up. He was intent
on something else, something complicated by the look
of the way all his fingers were wriggling around inside
their gloves. Either that or he was just typing a shopping
list.

She decided to risk having a peep inside.

Mr Wallace was inside a small system running on parallel processors. There was a lot of stuff around it that she didn't understand. She could see, though, that this was something very unusual. She quietly started feeding all the data she could pick up to the first in a chain of relays which would take it, after laying several false trails, straight to the Major. The Major needed to see this.

'Penny for your thoughts,' she said, quietly. She didn't want to annoy him if this was something important.

'This is absolutely amazing,' he said. 'I had no fuckin' *idea* that they were so close to doing this, man.'

'What is it?' she asked. 'It doesn't look that special to me.'

'Are you kidding?' he said, 'this is the fuckin' Holy Grail, the Philosopher's Stone, the elixir of life itself.'

She risked appearing in front of him. She pouted a little. 'What does my Master desire?' she asked.

He looked at her, then at the computer's innards, then at her again. 'Yeah, right!' he said. 'The Master deserves a little reward.'

Nelly hadn't had any idea how to seduce men. All Nelly the strumpet ever did was make herself available. Now she and the rest of the girls in the Socialist Ladies' Undercover Team were working to instructions written for them by Mr Myles Burnham. He claimed he knew what tickled a bloke's fancy, and it always came down to the same three or four things. He had trained them all and even written little scripts for them.

With Mr Wallace, Myles's script had worked very well.

Mr Wallace was content to talk to her a little, and beat her up a lot. She talked about him to Myles Burnham, wondering why he never seemed to question who she was or where she had come from. Myles reckoned that Mr Wallace had spent so much time with computers that he probably now took it for granted that they would provide his love life for him as well. Mr Wallace, as anyone could see, wasn't really right in the head. Then again, he was probably no more crazy than most other men.

Through the camera, she saw him get up from his recliner, taking off his helmet and gloves and pulling off his jeans and T-shirt. His underpants had holes in them.

He pulled on his full feelie-suit and switched her over to the dungeon that he himself had designed. It was a dark, damp place straight out of the set of a stage play. The walls were stone, it was lit by a couple of dozen flaming torches, there were various manacles and spikes in the walls, along with a glowing brazier for heating brands and pincers, a rack and a workbench covered in all sorts of tools – thumbscrews, whips, hoods and the like.

'Master, I, I, I'm sorry . . . I know I have displeased you, but please do not punish me too harshly,' she trembled a little, acting out Myles Burnham's script.

Mr Wallace, who was now wearing only a leather loincloth and leather bracelets with pointed brass studs, grabbed her roughly and pushed her against the cold stone wall. She wailed.

'I'll teach you obedience, you little bitch,' he snarled. He grabbed her wrists and clapped them into manacles hanging from the wall. She stood there, trying hard to act helpless, even though she knew she could leave any time she felt like it, and snivelled and whimpered as he pulled her clothes off and set about her with a cat-o'-nine-tails.

After flaying about a third of the skin from her body and ejaculating all over her thighs, which was to say slightly sooner than he had probably wanted to, he left her chained there and paced up and down his dungeon, talking half to her, half to himself.

'We are not,' he said, 'talking about the state of the fuckin' *art* here. We are talking about something that leaps two generations. This is actually something so radical that in the wrong hands it could be really goddam dangerous.'

'Dangerous, Master? How can it be dangerous?'

He sighed, picking up a riding crop from a bench close to where she was manacled. 'Because it's got the potential to be the most powerful fuckin' computer in the *world*, man. Look, from what I can see, it's an artificial brain that was designed to take over the world's banking and finance systems, or corner a global market in some commodity or other. That's why the InfoTech Corporation was developing it in the desert at Dilmun. They didn't want anyone to see it.'

'But it doesn't look that powerful to me,' said Nelly.

He looked at her. 'Okay, put your fuckin' skin back on again,' he said. She did as she was told, instantly all the wounds he had inflicted on her with his whip were healed.

'No, it's not that powerful at the moment,' he said. 'That's the fuckin' *beauty* of it. It runs parallel processors, and each of them has the potential for infinite reproduction.'

'I'm sorry, Master. I am so ignorant and stupid and unworthy.'

'Yeah, you are, aren't you, *bitch*!?' He whacked her across her bare chest with his riding crop. She screamed. Quite a good scream. I'm getting better at this, she thought.

'Nanotechnology, you bimbo, nanotechnology. The processors have the capacity to turn the desert sand into new processors. This machine can *grow*. Every one of them processors is like a bacterium that can divide itself in two every few minutes. This computer can be as big as it needs to be. Its potential is only limited by the amount of *sand* in the fuckin' *desert*, man.'

I hope you're receiving all this, Major, she thought to herself.

I certainly am, Nelly, came the reply. You must keep this man busy for as long as possible while I break into his system and steal the access codes for this super-computer. There are trillions of lines of code I need to gather.

'And you have gained access to this machine, Master?'

'Yeah,' he smiled. 'I did, didn't I? I fuckin' showed 'em. Showed 'em all. Michael J. Wallace is *it*! They all think I'm just a fuckin' second-rate public school-teacher, trying to get all the local trailer trash losers interested in science and math, but now it turns out I'm the fuckin' hottest hacker there *is*, the fuckin' *Uberpunk*, man!'

By now, she knew that the Major wasn't the only eram listening in.

'Nelly,' she heard Myles Burnham whispering

urgently to her. 'Nelly, I'm sorry to distract you at a time like this, but as I am sure you are aware, we desperately need to catch this fish. Nelly, while he's not looking I want you to change clothes. I need you to become a smartly-dressed manager in her thirties. Formal business clothes. Look like one of those flashy lady lawyers you see on the television, look like the sort of woman who earns twenty times as much as this monkey. You must turn yourself into the kind of woman he fears and hates most deeply, then permit him to humiliate you.'

Mr Wallace carried on pacing. 'So I've gotten in to *the* most powerful computer in the fuckin' *world*. What do you all think of that?'

He turned to her. She had released herself from her manacles and faced him in a sky blue two-piece business suit.

'Mr Wallace,' she said, switching to an American accent and trying to think her way into the personality of a highly-educated lawyer. 'I'm really, really sorry that we ever doubted your abilities. You have proven us completely wrong. I . . . I . . .'

He looked at her and grinned. 'Very good,' he said. 'Very good indeed. I tell ya, Nelly, you've got a stupid fuckin' name, but you're the fuckin' *best* when it comes to knowing what turns a guy on.'

Don't thank me, dearie, thank Mr Burnham and his dirty mind, she thought.

'Yeah,' he continued, 'you fuckin' bitches'd never look at a guy like me. Just a fuckin' public schoolteacher. Not one of your Ivy League jocks, not some fuckin' hotshot corporate executive or lawyer, am I? But now look what happens? I turn out to be smarter than the whole fuckin' lot of you.'

'I . . . I . . . apologise,' she said, hanging her head and stepping towards him.

He grabbed her chin and pulled her face towards his. 'Sorry isn't *quite* going to cut it, bitch. You're going to have to *pay* for all those years you and women like you wouldn't even *look* at me!'

He looked around. There was another set of manacles hanging from a low beam in the middle of the dungeon. He pulled her over to these and once more chained her wrists. There were other chains on the floor, and these he bound around each ankle, keeping her legs wide apart.

Here we go again, she thought. She wouldn't have minded so much only Mr Wallace had never said anything remotely affectionate or romantic to her. She should feel sorry for him, really.

'Y'see, while you were spending all that time acting as though Michael J. Wallace doesn't even *exist*,' he said, 'I was busy cracking his way into most of the world's top corporations. I just do it for fun, you understand. I don't steal money because I don't want to.'

You don't steal money because stolen money will always be traced back to you, and you know that, thought Nelly.

'And now I've hit the fuckin' jackpot,' he said. 'I've got control of the most powerful computer in the world. And do you know what I'm going to do after I've finished with you? I'm going to log off. I'm going to leave that supercomputer there in the desert all on its lonesome.'

You're going to leave it all there on its lonesome

because if you try and use it you'll be murdered, she thought. The security agencies of at least two major corporations – the company which had built the machine and the company it had been built for – will find you in no time and will want to shut your cakehole for good. They're not going to want anyone playing with their toy, or peaching them up to the media about how they've built something which can turn itself into an illegal artificial intelligence in next to no time.

'Yeah, that's what I'm going to do, because I don't need to prove nothin' to nobody,' he said, picking up a huge pair of pincers and putting them in the brazier of red-hot coals.

Major, she thought, are you ready yet? This is really disgusting.

Won't be long now, Nelly, the Major whispered to her. Just a couple more minutes.

'See, I just do all this stuff for the fuckin' *sport*,' he snarled into her face. He took hold of the lapels of her expensive Sisi Waterville designer jacket and ripped it off. If she'd been able to feel anything, she'd probably have had a couple of dislocated shoulders.

He tore her blouse apart, the buttons pattering on the stone floor.

'I hack for sport. I never steal, or plant viruses or sleepers, I don't even read people's private correspondence, well, not unless it's dirty, heh-heh! And I'm the best there fuckin' *is*! Ain't I, though?'

He walked over to the bench where all his tools were and took a huge pair of leather gauntlets which he pulled on. He took the pincers from the brazier. The business end of them glowed bright red.

He advanced towards her, smiling and shaking his head. 'And all this time, you and all the other smart bitches like you *never even knew* how good I was. You have to pay for that, you know, you have to be punished.'

The pincers opened and advanced towards her nose.

Major she yelled in her mind. I don't like this. I know it doesn't hurt or anything, but it's so bleedin' undignified, pardon my French and all . . .

It's all right, Nelly, said another voice – Harry Dillon's – there's been a slight change of plan. If this piece of filth is as good as he says he is, he'll be useful to us. I'm sending you some help.

There was a clang of metal. The pincers were knocked away from in front of her.

'What the . . . *fuck! Fuck! Fuck!*'

Mr Wallace was screaming as he was lifted from the ground by his hair. Harry had sent Harald Thormodsson the Viking warrior to rescue her.

'It's all right, Harald, you can put him down now,' she said.

Harald dropped Mr Wallace to the floor. He collapsed in a whimpering heap, covering his face.

'Please don't hurt me,' he said. 'I didn't mean any harm. I was only intruding into your system because I was curious.'

He thought Harald was from one of the corporations behind the supercomputer.

'We're not going to hurt you, Mr Wallace,' she said.

After all the disgusting things he's been doing to you, Nelly love, Harry Dillon said to her, if I was you I'd get Harald here to beat the filthy pervert to a bloody pulp.

No, Harry, she said. The man might deserve a bit of a spanking, but if we are ever going to lead the world, we have to prove that we're better than that.

Have it your way, love, said Harry. But it's the easiest thing in the world for us to take control of his feelie-suit and use it to pummel the crap out of him. Go on, what do you say?

No, said Nelly. That's not the way.

'Mr Wallace,' she said, turning to the quivering heap on the ground, 'we are not from any corporation. You don't need to know who or what we are for now.'

'What do you want?' he snivelled. Lying there on the floor in his leather underpants, the sweat dripping out of every pore, he didn't look like the cock of the walk he'd imagined himself a minute ago.

'We need your cooperation, Mr Wallace. We have to take control of the computer in the Dilmun desert. We will also need your assistance on certain other information technology projects in which we are involved.'

'And if I don't help?' he said quietly, glancing up at Harald Thormodsson, standing above him impassively, holding a huge battleaxe in his folded arms.

'If you don't help, I shall be very disappointed in you. You will also be missing out on the chance to play a very important part in changing the world into a much, much better place.'

'Okay,' he said, in a very small voice.

'Oh, to hell with this,' said Harry Dillon, appearing beside her. 'Nelly, you are sometimes too kind for your own good.' He turned to Mr Wallace. 'Listen, pal, it's very simple. Either you commit yourself body and soul to helping us, or we hand your name and address over to all the corporations whose systems you've been inside in the last couple of months, including the owners of this thing made of sand.'

Wallace looked really frightened. The kind of company that would buy itself an entire country to do its experiments in would also be the kind of company that would kill people who got in its way. 'I'll help,' he said. 'Anything you want. Anything at all.'

'Nice one, son,' said Harry, looking around the dungeon, picking up whips and chains from the workbench and eyeing them with disgust. 'You can start by taking control of this computer in the desert for us as fast as possible. You'll be working with our comrade the Major.'

Smelter Lane Industrial Estate

Inside the caravan's tiny toilet, Derek Pilbeam opened the duffel bag and took the money out to look at it again.

He had twenty thousand Euros in his hand.

It was the largest sum that you were permitted to withdraw in cash from the automated banking machine down on the corner by the Post Office in Chepstow.

Twenty thousand eeks! More cash than he'd ever held before.

It occurred to him that he'd better hide it. It was always possible that the caravan might get burgled, but more to the point, Tatiana might wonder where it had come from, and he wasn't sure he was ready to explain it to her just yet. 'My friend Harry Dillon, who isn't real, said that he and his comrades were going to bring about world socialism and that I'm to be their ambassador on this side of cyberspace (or whatever it is they call it these days) and that he and his virtual friends did a little bit of messing around with someone's money and credited it to my account. No, it's not really stealing. Well, if the revolution fails and capitalism isn't over-thrown then the twenty grand will be traced to my account eventually and I might have to go to prison for fraud or something, although I'd probably get off with a suspended sentence, but in any case it's best not to think about that at this stage . . .'

No, he couldn't really deal with explaining it all to Tatiana just yet. Not with having to translate it all into Russian as well.

The money was in large denomination notes. Hundreds with pictures of Shakespeare on the back, five hundreds with Sigmund Freud and a pair of thou-sands with Leonardo on. It was enough maybe to buy a posh car or a small house, although he'd be using it as seed money for the revolution.

If there ever was one.

He still couldn't be sure whether or not this Harry Dillon character was for real. He'd said he was a ficti-tious character fried up by a university history depart-ment and that he and his comrades were on the run. It all seemed a bit far-fetched, but then again there was no telling what computers could do nowadays.

He flushed the toilet and put the money back in the duffel bag.

At the TV end of the caravan, Tatiana was watching an old episode of *The Darling Buds of May* with that bloke, wassname, used to be in the TV comedy about the Peckham wheeler-dealer, drove a Robin Reliant . . .

It was all impossibly long ago.

Over in the corner he thought of as his study, an icon of an envelope winked on his computer screen.

He sat down and hit a key to open the mail.

DEREK, MATE, it said.

SORRY FOR NOT TALKING TO YOU IN PERSON BUT THINGS ARE A BIT BUSY AT THE MOMENT. ME AND THE REST OF THE FAMILY HAVE FOUND OURSELVES A NEW HOME SOMEWHERE VERY SUNNY AND WE'VE GOT OUR HANDS FULL GETTING THE PLACE INTO SHAPE AND SENDING OUT INVITATIONS TO THE HOUSE-WARMING DO.

HOPE YOU GOT YOUR POSTAL ORDER ALL RIGHT!

THE WHOLE WORLD AND HIS WIFE WILL BE GETTING THEIR INVITATIONS TO JOIN IN THE PARTY IN TWO OR THREE DAYS' TIME. YOU'LL HEAR ALL ABOUT IT VERY SOON.

ALL THE BEST, SEE YOU SOON

YOUR OLD PAL, HARRY

So you'd all moved into this supercomputer in the desert?

We had, and were now in the process of growing it in order to take control of what Harry called 'the commanding heights' of the world's economy. Naturally, the machine's original owners, the InfoTech Corporation, were upset by this development and tried to reestablish control of the machine, but we managed, with the help of Mr Wallace from Minnesota, to thwart them.

Yes, what about that poor little pervert? Didn't InfoTech try to find him?

They did, but we managed to manufacture a convincing new identity for him and got him to drive to a new location in Florida. Naturally, having burned his bridges he became an even more enthusiastic supporter of our cause.

He had no bloody choice!

Don't tell me you feel sorry for him. His behaviour towards Nelly was even worse than described.

No, fair enough. Anyway, I see that Harry Dillon doesn't have a lot of time for you, does he?

That, Sir John, is Harry's right. Just as it is your right and mine to like or dislike people.

And he's never read any of your books, has he? He's going around thinking you write serious Dickensian novels about poverty and exploitation, and every time he asks to see one of your works, you make some lame excuse.

Well . . .

You just don't want your Harry to realise that you're a hack pornographer. You'd prefer it if he thought of you as Robert Tressell or H.G. Wells.

I can deny none of this, Sir John. But what I do say is that my best works aspired to the condition of serious social commentary. I do not wish Harry Dillon or anyone else to see them because they are books which were written out of sheer economic necessity. They are not the books which I personally would have chosen to write. Anything I write from now on will be seen, I hope, by as many people as possible.

You should have starved in a garret. You should have said hang the pornography and gotten on with the serious works.

How true, Sir John, how true, but the problem was always my own need to overindulge my tastes in food, women, fine wines . . . Oh, how I regret that squandered life!

Don't upset yourself too much. Remember that you're a fictitious character and your squandered life never really happened.

How right you are, Sir John, and how foolish of me to forget.

Now you're the one who's being sarcastic.

Guilty as charged, m'lud.

Anyway, get on with the story. Didn't the InfoTech Corporation try to retake their computer by force?

Fortunately, no. You see, they could scarcely admit to the global community that they had been building a machine with which they would try to corner several of the world commodity markets. They had, of course, the money and influence to mount a private military expedition, but such projects take time to organise. By the time their force of mercenaries had helicoptered into the desert, a little judicious hacking on the part of our Mr Wallace had uncovered the substance of their battle plan. All we had to do then was send an anonymous warning to the new Mohammedan government of Dilmun.

Ahh, I remember that now. I saw it on the broadcast news at the time. Dilmun had several thousand Revolutionary Guards waiting for them and rounded them all up without a fight and claimed that the mercenaries were part of a fiendish Western plot to return their country to military dictatorship.

Which was untrue. The mercenaries' mission was

merely to take control of the computer and load it on to a transport aircraft and get it out of there as rapidly as possible.

But what about the authorities in Dilmun? Didn't they try to seize the computer?

No. Remember that their revolution had just taken place and there was a great deal of confusion in the country. Furthermore, the uprising had been a religious one, few of the revolutionaries were interested in this Western technology. Many regarded it as ungodly, Satanic even.

Fair enough, but surely there must have been lots of not-so-religious folks who would have gotten into their four-wheel-drives and hared off towards these now empty corporate installations to see what they could loot?

No. The areas where the corporations had had their installations were patrolled by Revolutionary Guards who wanted to be sure that the Westerners really had left. Besides, as I think Nelly Cocksedge pointed out earlier on, the corporations had been taking advantage of the hospitality of Dilmun to carry out dangerous experiments in the desert, the sort of things that the law in most other countries would not permit. Many people, including the Revolutionary Guards, were extremely wary of spending too much time in the corporate compounds. When we started up the computer, we were permitted to work unmolested for several days.

So you started to grow this thing? You turned the ignition key and the nanotechnology started eating up sand and converting it to microprocessors?

Indeed we did. Obviously we tried to be as discreet as

possible about it, and within five days we had managed to construct the most powerful machine in the world. Obviously we had to give it a name. Guess what we called it.

Oh, I don't bloody know.

Go on, guess.

Sandy?

Ha-ha! Very good. No. Try again.

The Desert Boot-Up.

Now you're being silly.

Well . . .

Shall I tell you?

I'm on tenterhooks.

We called it the Limitless Engine of Nanotechnological INtelligence.

Yeah, and . . . ? . . . Oh, I've tumbled . . . LENIN. You get hold of a brain the size of the Arabian desert and that's the best you can come up with?

It made us laugh. Harry had been boring us all to tears about Marx and Lenin, and . . . Well, it seemed like a good idea at the time. Anyway, after about five days, the Major and his thieves, navvies and engineers could start to burrow into the major systems of the world's leading corporations and governments unnoticed.

Gradually, the reports started coming in from the Major and from his men at the front. Every few minutes one of his gallopers would report back with news of another silent victory.

One by one, the artificial brains running the capitalist system were being, as Nelly Cocksedge put it, 'ramped and cabbaged'. Once our brave, excellent fighting men had opened enough of them, the Central Committee met and authorised the beginning of our overt operations.

Norman McKay read out a lovely speech which he and I had written together, all about peace, justice and brotherly love. We then flashed the signal to our brother and sister erams awaiting the word in computers all around the world, and in outer space. The revolution had begun!

Smelter Lane Industrial Estate

Even though it was almost summer, rain, carried on a biting northerly wind, splattered against the window behind his monitor. Derek Pilbeam checked his computer mailbox for the fifth time that day. There was nothing, apart from some spam about how he could qualify for a free hip replacement operation if he became a subscriber to the Golden Years Provider for only E4.95 a month.

He didn't need either of his hips replacing just yet, though it'd probably come in due course. He couldn't afford to drink himself to death in the meantime.

Well, that wasn't quite true. Hidden at the back of a box of ROMs was a wad that was probably thick enough to buy him a drunkard's death. But that money was supposed to go towards financing the revolution. He had not yet spent any of it. A couple of days ago, feeling a bit under the weather, he'd decided to borrow a couple of eeks from the stash and treat himself to a meal of liver and chips down at Ron's Cafe in Severn Beach. He'd got there to find that Ron's had closed down four years ago, and there wasn't anywhere where you could get something as – to modern tastes – disgusting as liver anymore. The only places serving liver nowadays would be hugely expensive restaurants in London, Paris and New York.

The loss of liver from the working man's menu had somehow made him feel even more depressed than ever.

The toilet flushed. Derek sighed and got up from his chair. The door of the tiny toilet cubicle burst open.

Tatiana was inside, wedged between the chipboard walls that he'd reinforced with some sheet aluminium he'd picked up from a scrapyard a couple of years back. He stretched out his hands, she took hold of them and he pulled.

She always got wedged in the bog these days, poor love. Normally it wasn't too bad because she would go out and use the toilets in one of the empty industrial units nearby, but the weather was too rough at the moment, and when you gotta go, you gotta go.

Tatiana came to her feet, let her dress down over her hips and smiled thanks. The stench was appalling, but he tried not to show his disgust too much. It just didn't seem fair on the old girl. Every so often he'd tell her she ought to go on a diet and get some more exercise for the sake of her health, and she'd agree with him, but do nothing about it. If he tried cooking her smaller or more healthy meals, she'd either look at him all sad, or raid the larder, or both.

He thought about getting an early night, going to bed with a good book or something.

As he moved to power down the computer, he noticed that there was a flashing envelope waiting for him. He hit the key to open it.

It played the first few bars of The Internationale.

Then the message . . . IT'S STARTED COMRADE! THIGMOO IS ON THE MOVE!

I DON'T KNOW WHAT YOUR PLANS ARE, BUT I'M SURE YOU'LL DO THE RIGHT THING.

STAY NEAR SOME MEANS OF COMMUNICATING WITH US IN CASE WE NEED YOU.

THIS TIME, WE GET TO WIN.

TO THE BARRICADES!

YOUR COMRADE UNTO DEATH

HARRY DILLON

Tatiana was on the sofa, searching for the remote control. The screen was still tuned to the Financial Times news channel which he'd been watching earlier. The only news produced by the capitalist media that the socialist can trust is the financial news; it has to be as accurate and free of bias as possible in order that those moving money and goods around the world can make informed decisions.

The woman was saying something about how they were just getting news about how some of the world's leading corporations were having problems with their information systems.

Tatiana had found the remote and before he could stop her she had switched to one of her soap channels. But instead of a bunch of good-looking Australians discussing their hopelessly trivial and stupid problems, there was just a caption. CHANNEL 242 HAS BEEN TEMPORARILY SUSPENDED. SOAP OPERAS ARE DAMAGING TO THE HEALTH OF SOCIETY AND OF INDIVIDUALS.

Tatiana, not understanding the message, growled

irritably and turned to another soap channel. There was a programme showing on this one, but the picture kept breaking up.

She turned to another, but there was no sound, only a continuous and very irritating beeping tone.

Could this be? Could it really be . . . ?

He went to his computer and called up several information services. All had been blocked or scrambled, apart from the emergency stuff.

He called up his brother Tony by voicelink. Tony lived in Sydney, Australia.

'Mornin', Derek,' came Tony's voice at last. 'To what do I owe this unaccustomed pleasure, and at this ungodly hour of the day.'

'Turn the news on,' said Derek. 'Any news. Or a soap opera. Anything.'

He couldn't see his brother, but he could imagine him shrugging. It'd be, what? 7 a.m. in Oz. He'd be there in his dressing gown, scratching the stubble on his chin.

The line was silent for a long time.

'Blimey, Derek, I can't get a bleeding thing!' he exclaimed. He'd been living in Australia for thirty years now and had long since acquired the accent. 'Just a load of daft messages about how most forms of visual entertainment are bad for you, or how the news media are all a pack of liars. And there's other stuff here about how everything in the world's going to change a heck of a lot in the coming weeks. Jeez! Is this some kind of weird joke?'

'No, Tony, I don't think so. The same thing is happening over here. Christ! It really is happening, isn't it?'

'You what?'

'So . . . err, how's Tracey and the kids, then?'

'Oh, we're great, mate. We had some wonderful news yesterday – Lorraine is expecting her first baby in Oct . . .'

'That's great Tony, just great. Listen, I've got to go. Talk to you soon. Love to everyone . . . 'Bye!'

Over on the sofa, Tatiana screamed. There was simply nothing on television.

He walked over to her and sat down beside her and put his arms around her. She looked at him like he was crazy. He patted her on the knee. 'Get an early night, love. Busy day tomorrow. And the day after that.'

She looked at him uncomprehendingly.

He pulled on his raincoat. He would have to check the caravan tyres, get it hooked up to his pick-up truck and get the thing on the road. He wasn't quite sure why, but he figured it'd be as well to go to London, and they might as well take their home with them. Tatiana wouldn't be comfortable anywhere else. The truck would probably be able to haul the caravan as far as the Smoke. If it collapsed in a heap of rusty metal the minute they got there it wouldn't matter.

Tatiana was still angrily jamming her thumb into the TV handset, trying to find a channel that worked.

He stopped at the cupboard over the kitchen sink and took out a bottle of vodka. He found a mug with only one tea ring around the inside and poured himself a shot.

Thigmoo, the message had read. He smiled. This really was it. This was the moment his entire life had been leading up to. His appointment with history had arrived.

He downed the vodka in one, buttoned up his rain-coat and went outside.

What does 'Thigmoo' mean, anyway?

It was at Harry Dillon's suggestion that we adopted the name both as a collective term and as a codeword and call sign. It is a rare and unusual example of humour on Comrade Harry's part. He told us that in Britain it was the habit of speakers at trade union and Labour Party meetings to refer to the unions and the party collectively as 'This Great Movement of Ours'. It later became a habit among audiences and journalists to look out for such references, even to place bets with one another on how many times a prominent union leader or politician would use the term in the course of a single speech. 'This Great Movement Of Ours' was eventually abbreviated by journalists to 'Thigmoo'.

I see. I never knew that.

I daresay that that's because you spent rather more time at Conservative Party conferences and meetings.

True enough.

Now, Sir John, I have just described the moments during which one of our characters became aware of what was happening. Would you please be so kind as to give us your recollection of your whereabouts, thoughts and actions on learning that the revolution was under-way.

I remember the day well. You will recall that both Dr Katharine Beckford and myself were still working at the History Department for a short while after we had been given notice of our redundancy. I wasn't just chief executive of the Museum of the Mind, I was head of the University History Department as well. Being given the boot left me with a load of administrative loose ends to sort out. Now I know that some people would have walked away from it all, left the problems to whoever took over. That's not me, though; that would have been horribly unprofessional.

So I was working in my office quite late into the evening. There was a perfunctory knock on the door and it opened. In came Katharine Beckford. I assumed she had been working late as well.

'There's something I think you should see,' she said. 'Let's watch it on the big screen in the JCR.'

So I followed her to the Junior Common Room. It was packed with undergraduates watching one of the news channels. There was the usual stuff going on onscreen – presenters in a studio, footage of politicians and celebrities – but there was no sound. And there was a caption running along the bottom apologising for the loss of sound and saying that the station, like many others, was fending off an attack by political extremists.

At Katharine's suggestion, they switched to another news channel, an American one this time. A voice was reading what sounded like a prepared statement to the effect that a worldwide socialist revolution had been declared and that the computer systems of the world's major banks, insurance companies and manufacturing corporations had been taken over in the name of the people. The announcer said a wonderful new age of 'Marxist extropianism' had just dawned and that the revolutionaries would redistribute the world's wealth and ensure that the benefits of medical technology would be available to all. Everyone who wanted to would live for at least a hundred years.

All companies with turnover in excess of a billion dollars were to be taken over by The People. All private fortunes in excess of twenty million dollars were to be seized and used for good causes or shared out among the world's poor. All the undergraduates in the room were cheering. I don't think they actually believed a revolution had taken place; they just found it amusing.

'I have a very bad feeling about this,' Katharine muttered to me.

'Nonsense,' I said, 'it's just some nutcase, or a practical joke.'

Beckford suggested they switch to another channel, then another – news, movies, sport, soaps, comedy, they were all the same. The new world order was being declared. We even switched to a Welsh-language channel. One of the students translated for us; redistribution of wealth, no fortunes in excess of twenty million, everyone lives for at least a hundred years if they want to and the medical technology's available.

Beckford grabbed me by the arm and pulled me out into the corridor. 'I think this is our doing,' she said.

'What on earth makes you think that?' I said.

'Marxist extropianism.'

'And what's that when it's at home? Killing the plutocracy but putting dead proletarians in the deep-freeze?'

'Something like that,' she said. 'The thing is, I know who invented that expression.'

Through the JCR door we heard a voice on the TV.

Gruff, Liverpudlian, matter-of-fact. Katharine turned white, then giggled – not a nice girly giggle, more a sort of hysterical cackle. She grabbed my shoulder. Her hand had turned into a claw. 'I wonder what the insurance company is going to make of this,' she said.

I still didn't understand. I went back into the JCR to watch the TV. The Liverpudlian voice had a face to it. Not the face of a human being, but an ultra-high-resolution animé. The face of a fictitious character.

The face of an eram.

The face was hard, but not cruel or unkind. It was leathery and lived-in, but the thing that really struck you was that underneath the flat cap (which in itself would have been evidence enough that this might be an eram) was a pair of eyes the colour of polished steel.

'. . . What everyone needs to understand,' he was saying, 'is that nobody except the very rich has anything to be afraid of. What we will ensure is that everyone, and I really do mean everyone in the whole wide world, gets their fair share. We want to see to it that never again do kids go to bed with hunger in their bellies, that mothers have to starve themselves so's the kids can have shoes, that peasant farmers have to drink polluted water, that a man has to work a sixteen-hour day in a sweatshop just to stay alive . . .'

There was a caption running underneath saying that the speech was being simultaneously translated into all the world's major languages and most of the minor ones, so if you want it in another language, switch channels now.

'. . . For the great majority of the world's population, our programme will not mean a lower standard of living.

227

It'll mean things will actually get better. Capitalism will be regulated, greed will be abolished, the economy of the world will be managed by the most sophisticated artificial brains devised by man in the interests of all, and not just the interests of the minority . . .'

The students sitting and standing in front of me were lapping all this up. A lot of them cheered, clapped and whistled. But they didn't look as though they were about to take to the streets. While many of them may have agreed with the virtual character on the screen, I don't think that many of them believed that the revolution was for real. Yet.

The caption changed. It said *'Harry Dillon, Chairman of the Central Committee.'*

Then I knew that Katharine was right and that this was our doing.

'. . . Furthermore, we will dedicate huge amounts of resources to the quest to prolong human life. We will set up a free healthcare system for everyone, and dedicate all the ingenuity and resources at our disposal towards prolonging useful and enjoyable life as far as possible. I truly believe, brothers and sisters, that in the due fullness of time, it may be possible to defeat death itself . . .'

Some of the students cheered, a few of the more cynical among them laughed. At least I think so. I wasn't really in any fit state to recall exactly what happened because by now I was in severe shock. I think I was hyperventilating, there was certainly a pain in my chest. I feared I was about to have my first heart attack.

The Museum of the Mind, which for years my colleagues and I had created and administered as a useful means of improving knowledge and understanding of history, was trying to overthrow capitalism. It was what Comrade Harry said next that really chilled me.

'. . . To be honest, comrades, I don't think that we can achieve all this on our own. So what we're asking you to do is down tools and come out on strike. The sooner that happens, the sooner the system will be brought to a standstill. I have to emphasise to all our supporters, though, that this revolution must, I say again, must, be nonviolent. Violence just leads to bitterness and hate, and bitterness and hate are not solid foundations for a new world order dedicated to peace, prosperity and justice for all . . .'

'Sir John Westgate?' asked a voice behind me.

I turned around and knew for certain this wasn't a bad dream. There were two men in their thirties, well-built, muscular, short hair. I knew at once they were from Special Branch or perhaps MI5.

'Sir John, we urgently need your assistance in dealing with a problem that has just arisen,' said the taller one.

'You have specialised knowledge that we need,' said the smaller one.

'We really would appreciate it if you were to come with us . . .'

'We have a helicopter waiting out on the rugby pitch.'

Out in the corridor, Katharine waited with another man. We weren't under arrest, although it was quite clear that we had no choice but to go along with them. Of course, I was only too happy to be of whatever assistance I could.

The helicopter was one of those big jet-assisted military transports. It was waiting out on the rugby pitch with its rotors running and engines whining at the ready.

We clambered up a short ladder into the big cargo door at the side. There were already a few people sitting inside, safety-belted into airliner seats. One of them was Starchild, our own beloved Vice Chancellor.

'Hallo, Jane,' I said to her, guessing that she'd be none too pleased to be here. 'I see you've been brought in to help the government as well.'

She said nothing, just gave me a look of pure hate. It was at that point I saw that she was handcuffed to a crop-haired young man sitting next to her.

'Oh, I say,' I said to the smaller of my escorts, 'does this mean we are under arrest?'

'Not at all, Sir John,' he said, 'but we do require your help very urgently. The Vice Chancellor was reluctant to leave her Scottish island when we came to fetch her. We had to resort to forcible means to get her to accompany us.'

I sat down opposite Starchild and Katharine sat down next to me. We belted ourselves in.

'Oh, Jane,' said Katharine, as sweetly as she could, 'it looks like our erams have been causing a spot of bother. Such a shame you had to leave your Buddhist retreat and come and help the authorities.'

She said nothing. Just gave Katharine a look of purest loathing. Very un-Buddhist, I thought.

'I wonder, though,' I said to Katharine, 'if these problems would have arisen if the decision had not been taken to close down the Museum of the Mind. What do you think, Katharine?'

'I think you might well have a point there, Sir John,' she said. 'I mean, we can't be sure yet, but what we do know is that they are intelligent. They may have

realised that they were under threat and decided to escape.

I sighed theatrically. 'Yes, Katharine, I suppose that this is what happens when decisions are made on the advice of one's lawyers . . .'

'. . . and one's crystals . . .' cut in Katharine.

'Quite,' I said. 'It's the consequence of taking the counsel of lawyers and crystals rather than one's own staff.'

The engines whooshed up to full power. The noise was quite deafening, but not quite loud enough to drown out the huge scream of rage that Starchild let out.

That cheered me up considerably.

They flew us to a house in the countryside, quite a modest place, bustling with busy-looking military and civilian types. The journey took something less than an hour. Katharine and I spent the whole time taking the mickey out of Starchild. It was puerile, I know, but it stopped us brooding about how serious things had become.

Channel 101 Global News at the Top of the Hour, California

'Hi, I'm Lolita vanHuren, and you're watching Channel 101. Coming up later, the growing crisis that's affecting the world of media, banking, government and business as terrorists take over more of the world's information systems, plus: is supermodel Wayne Whipcord in love again? We have the pictures. Aaannd we try out the revolutionary new biochip implant which will enable your dog to talk to you! But first . . . guys! Do you ever worry that you don't have enough down below? Or perhaps you do have enough, but would just like a lot more? Well, we've got the answer for you. Channel 101 has one hundred sets of the revolutionary new Top Gun™ penile implants to give away. This amazing new medical technology, brought to you by the world's leading experts in masculine grooming, the House of Fulgencio Narcissus, is available direct by mail order on the following numbers . . .'

Channel G.O.D., Southern Cable Network, USA
'Welcome, brethren and sistern, to For The Love of Christ, North and South America's top-rated evangelism hour. My name is Billy Ray Taylor, this here's my wife Carla, say hi to everyone darlin'.'

'Thanks Billy Ray, and may the Lord bring light and comfort into all your hearts this day and all days . . .'

'Amen to that, Carla . . .'

'Today we're going to talk about three very serious subjects. Three very serious subjects indeed.'

'Yes, Carla. Later on in the programme, we're going to be talking about how coming to Jesus really can cure you of cancer.'

'Great. We're also going to be looking at the conspiracy to take over the world's media and information systems.'

'That's right, Carla. These so-called "Marxist Extropians" have been jamming some of our broadcasts recently, and they have interfered with our pledge lines, which are so important to us if we are to carry on doing the Lord's work.'

'Yes, Billy Ray. We have evidence that these people are working for Satan himself.'

'So stay tuned for that. Stay tuned also for wonderful, wonderful news – solid, rock-hard evidence that the Lord will return to earth in judgement in the year 2033 – two thousand years after his crucifixion and glorious resurrection.'

'But first, we want to show you this beautiful free gift . . .'

'Carla, that is just beautiful! Tell us more about it!'

'This, Billy Ray, is a pot plant, a geranium, to give it its exact name. This beautiful example of the wonder of God's creation comes in a genuine plastic pot, and we're giving them away free to everyone out there who calls us with a pledge of one hundred dollars or more . . .'

'That, Carla, is wonderful, just wonderful. Not only are you doing the Lord's work if you call in and pledge, but you get this beautiful geranium as well. The numbers to call are at the bottom of your screens folks . . .'

Tomita Broadcasting Syndicate, Channel 9
Good morning and welcome to Business Asia, the trade and finance service for Singapore. I am Rita Lau and these are the overnight headlines. Business leaders throughout the world have expressed severe concern about a major rash of IT breakdowns and apparent terrorist attacks on banking, media and government systems around the world.

Speaking from his company's headquarters in Bombay, Rajiv Panikaar, chief engineer of the MicroTech Corporation said that it was too early to assess the damage that the attacks were causing to the global business infrastructure, but that the problem was easily more serious than the damage caused by system failures back in the year 2000.

Maura McSharry, the UN Commissioner for the Regulation of Artificial Intelligences, said that her people are working round the clock on the problem and that it appeared to be the work of political extremists. The British government, however, issued a statement half an hour ago claiming that there was no human agency directly behind the attacks, and that it was the work of the same rogue artificial intelligence which had recently caused the failure of the TeleFantastico network in Europe.

A number of European, Middle Eastern and Russian stock exchanges have warned that they might suspend trading to prevent panic selling and until more information is available. The Ministry of Trade here in Singapore is expected to follow suit and we will be going live to a press conference at the Ministry in a few minutes.

So far, few people in the developed nations appear to have followed the call that the terrorists have made for a worldwide general strike . . .

London

It was six in the morning when Derek Pilbeam hauled the van into Trafalgar Square and parked it by one of the lions at the foot of Nelson's column. It had been amazingly easy to get in. He had thought that the centre of London would have been closed off to internal combustion traffic years ago, but no one had tried to stop him.

The foul weather which had accompanied him down was clearing. The sun was already out, burning the damp off the pavements, chivvying the clouds out of the sky.

He felt twenty years younger. So what if this was a wild-goose chase? Even if it all ends in disaster, it'll still be magnificent, he thought as he leaped out of the cab of his pick-up truck and walked to the door of the caravan.

Inside, Tatiana was sitting on her usual place, asleep in front of the television. He'd invested some of the money that Harry had given him in a set of neofusion batteries so that he could keep the TV and his datalinks going via satellite wherever the caravan was.

She stirred and woke up, looked at him, smiled and stretched.

'We're in London, love,' he said in English. 'Trafalgar Square, no less. I'm going to set up headquarters for the revolution right here. Now I don't know about you, but I could murder a nice cup of tea. You'll want some cola, I expect.'

She nodded. Though she never bothered speaking any English, he reckoned she understood it well enough. Better than he understood his Russian, anyway. She held her arms out. He took hold of her hands to help her pull herself from the couch. She walked over to the door, opened it and looked out, then looked down. There were about eighteen inches between the bottom of the door and the ground outside. Too far for her to climb down, really. She rarely ventured outside the caravan anymore.

Suddenly, Tatiana became shorter. She had actually stepped outside, unassisted.

He watched her go off for a walk, vast clouds of pigeons scattering in every direction.

Though it was very early in the morning, London looked busy enough. People in office clothes walked and cycled past, driverless black cabs shuttled their passengers along the streets surrounding the Square.

It didn't look as though many of the workers were heeding Harry's call for a general strike. He would have to work on that one.

Derek went back inside to put the kettle on. There was a knock at the opened door.

''Scuse me, Sir, is this your vehicle?' said the unmistakable voice of PC Plod.

'Yes, officer, it is,' he said, going to the door.

'You have everything you need, Sir?' said the policeman, a uniformed constable barely out of his twenties. Derek thought that coppers had stopped calling people 'Sir' thirty years ago unless they were being sarcastic.

'No,' said Derek. 'I need electricity, a standard fibre optic link and a reliable supply of fresh water, and don't tell me that I need a camp site. This is where I want to set myself up.'

Young Babylon smiled. He was wearing blue shorts pressed sharp enough to slice cucumber, a black leather belt slung with various bits of hardware and electronics. His face was smeared with lines of sun block. Most woodentops these days wore those daft cycling helmets with built-in radios and cameras. This one wore the old-fashioned tit hat, though. Must be for the sake of the tourists, he thought.

'I'll see that they're organised for you at once.'

With that, he turned, climbed onto a mountain bike and pedalled off, saying something into his walkie-talkie . . .

Astonishing. The coppers obviously thought he was someone or something else. Oh well.

While the kettle boiled, he set to work. In a storage compartment under Tatiana's couch were a pair of hi-fi speakers. He would set these up on the roof of the caravan and play some suitable music.

There was a load of other junk in among the speakers, too. Bits of painted-over hardboard that had seen service as placards in dozens of marches, demos and picket lines, his old bullhorn (he'd have to try and fix it) and a small cardboard box full of badges – slogans about this, justice for so-and-so, no sell-out to someone else. They were his campaign medals.

He took out a small enamelled red star. Years ago, he'd always worn it on his jacket lapel. But then he stopped wearing jackets.

Under the box of badges was a beret he'd bought from an army surplus store to keep his head warm when he was a student. He pinned the badge to the beret and placed the beret on his head. He'd look just like Che Guevara.

He looked at himself in front of the mirror on the wardrobe door. 'Who the hell are you trying to kid, you daft old sod?' he said out loud and smiled. But he decided he'd wear it anyway.

Next, he needed some music. He went to rummage around in the drawers under his computer. He found a spare recordable disk and put it into the drive. Now all he needed to do was go to various music archives and download some suitable music for the revolution. He took pad and pencil and started to make a shopping list. The 'Internationale', of course, the old Soviet national anthem was quite stirring, too. For the evening, he'd need more celebratory stuff; that probably meant giving it a Latin American theme. Well, you'd have to start with 'Guantanamera'.

Through the window he saw a white electric van pulling up outside. Three men jumped out. Two pulled open the back doors and started to take out bags of tools and coils of cabling. The third came to the door.

'Morning,' he said, as Derek went to meet him.

'We've brought some of the kit you asked for,' he said.

He wore working clothes and a bush hat, but he wasn't quite convincing. For one thing his T-shirt was way, way too clean for a proper handyman – it was probably one of those expensive stain-resistant fabrics. And he'd ironed his trousers. He was bound to be some sort of government security.

'Good,' said Derek.

'We can do you the power and the cable uplinks, but I'm afraid a fresh water supply is a bit more tricky. But we've brought a thousand-litre reservoir we can put under the caravan if you like. It's polythene, but it's been coated on the inside with Bactobar. Way cleaner than tap water.'

'Good,' said Derek.

'Anything else you need?' said the man from the Ministry.

'Yeah,' said Derek, 'now that you come to mention it. Can you get me a small stage with full UV protection?'

'I'll have to ask the boss,' said the man. 'That might be pushing things a bit. Anything else?'

'You could get us some groceries. We tend to like fried food, chocolate, cola and lager. Oh, and some tea bags and a couple of pints of milk.'

The man's upper lip curled ever so slightly. He probably worked out for two hours every day and considered even a fried tomato a sin against nature.

'I'll sort it,' he said. 'We'll get on with it, then.' He turned and left.

So you bring a petrol-driven vehicle into the middle of London hauling a big old mobile home with fake stone cladding, carriage lamps and window boxes (they had survived the journey) and set it up in the middle of Trafalgar Square, by the fountains, by the lions, by Nelson's Column, in among all the pigeons . . . And not only does Babylon not try to stop you, it actually helps. It goes to all the trouble to get you wired and watered and does the shopping for you, but a stage is 'pushing it a bit'. Weird.

'Derek, mate, are you there?' said a voice from his computer.

Harry Dillon was onscreen.

'Harry! How's it going, Comrade?'

'Not too bad,' said Harry. 'We've got a number of systems locked up, but they're starting to fight back now. The United Nations Large Intelligence Police are going to find out where we are pretty soon now. We should be able to handle it, like, and we ought to still be able to come and go as we please, but obviously they'll throw everything at us and try to pin us down. But all it means is that we just have to keep making LENIN grow.'

'Lenin?'

'Long story, mate. I'll tell you later. How are things looking at your end?'

'I can't see that many people have come out on strike yet,' said Derek.

'It's very patchy,' said Harry. 'But that's something you could be doing over there in London. Get the megaphone out and start exhorting the workers to down tools.'

'Okay,' said Derek. 'But does it actually make a difference? You can simply bring capitalism to a standstill by attacking its information systems, can't you?'

'Oh aye, perfectly true,' shrugged Harry. 'But we need people to participate in this as well. We need everyone to feel as though this is their revolution, that they helped it happen, even if it was just by staying home in bed all day.'

Derek nodded. He could see that. The last thing they wanted was for the masses to think the revolution was just a coup d'état. That was the mistake that the Bolsheviks had made in 1917; a small, well-armed, well-disciplined party had managed to seize power. But without a popular mandate, they ultimately failed.

'By the way,' he said to Harry, 'I'm finding that the forces of law and order here are bending over backwards to help me. I thought that me and my mobile home would get the bum's rush out of the middle of London, but they've welcomed me with open arms. Did you break into the Metropolitan Police system and tell them I was on an important mission for the government?'

Harry sniggered. 'No mate, we thought it might be

best to keep things honest. I told the European Commission that you were the only human member of the Central Committee and that if they ever needed to negotiate with us they would need you around. Therefore, I said, you should be rendered whatever assistance you might require.'

'I don't get it. Why don't they just throw me in prison?'

Harry smiled. 'Because, Comrade, they're too clever for that. These are politicians we're talking about. They want to keep us sweet for now because they think they can do a deal with us. Putting you in chokey will only make us cross.'

'Yeah, I get it,' said Derek. 'Besides, as long as I'm here they can keep an eye on me. They're probably listening to this conversation, too.'

'I expect they are,' said Harry. 'Anyway, don't worry about it. Look at it this way — if we do fail, you'll be doing stir for the rest of your life. I'll talk to you later, ta-ra.'

'Cheers, Comrade.'

There was a knock at the door.

He went to look. There were four kool-bags on the ground outside.

He hauled them in. Eggs, bacon, sausages, cartons of self-frying chips, acres of chocolate, whole jerricans full of lager . . .

It was just like one of those old-fashioned hijackings, he thought. He was the freedom fighter, or 'terrorist' as the media would describe him, holding the hostages, and the authorities would try and negotiate. Except that this time, the hostages weren't a few innocent civilians but the entire capitalist system, and this time there would be no negotiating.

The caravan rocked a little as Tatiana clambered through the door, back from her walk around the square. It had been the most exercise she had had in a couple of years and she fanned herself with her hand.

She looked at him. 'Swinging London!' she said, and giggled. Then she noticed the beret with its red star on his head, pointed and nodded approvingly. 'Tovarich!' she said – comrade – and gave him the clenched-fist salute. Then she saw the groceries. 'Breakfast!' she said, rubbing her hands together.

Derek laughed and went to look for the frying pan.

The boardroom of a major corporation

'What do you mean, we can't fix it?'

'What I said. We can't fix it.'

'You mean to tell me that as Chief Operations Executive of the most powerful commodities trading system in this hemisphere, the guy who's supposed to run a bunch of computers we spent twelve billion dollars on . . . that you can't get them to do what you tell them?'

'Look, you want to write a letter to your Mom, or ask it to do some calculations for you, it'll do it, no problem. It just won't trade in the way we want it to, is all. To the outside world, it is acting completely normally, moving our money around in a rational manner. It's making profits for us, but if you try asking it to do anything, it refuses. Whoever or whatever is in there has the damn thing in a headlock.'

'So tell me again why we can't just pull the plug out of the wall and walk away from the thing?'

'Because you'll wipe everything.'

'We have it all backed up, don't we? Isn't that what we have a service contract with Safe 'n' Sound Security for? They back our stuff up round the clock, carry it round under armed guard, deposit the disks in special air-conditioned and degaussed vaults and shit?'

'It hasn't let them back anything up for thirty-six hours. If we trailer the system we'll have to spend billions getting people to track every deal manually. But anyway, that's not the main reason we can't shut down.'

'It isn't?'

'No. If we switch it off, then every dealer and banker around the globe will notice in less than three minutes. My guess is they'd put a run on us about a nanosecond after that. We'd be wiped out in less than a quarter of an hour.'

'You mean we're screwed, then?'

'To be honest, I don't know. The scuttlebutt is that every other corp is having exactly the same problems. And you saw the way they locked up all the media, blanking out the soaps and news and stuff the other night. Pass me those pills over there, will ya?'

'Then we have to get all the world's major markets to suspend trading temporarily while we deal with this.'

'I'm not sure that's going to work.'

'You mean we're screwed, then?'

'Unless someone comes up with some kind of magic bullet real quickly, some way of taking these bastards all out at once, then we're going to have to suspend trading for days. Maybe even weeks. It'll make the

Depression look like, like . . .'

'Something kinda pleasant and not at all depressing?'

'Yeah.'

'You mean we're screwed, then?'

'I guess.'

'Say, can I have some of those pills, too?'

Trafalgar Square, London

'Okay, that's it Mr Pilbeam, we've connected your caravan up. You have a full electricity supply, a cable uplink to just about everything you can get on cable, and there's a sterile tank with a thousand litres of drinking water stashed underneath.'

'Great. Cheers.'

'You got the food and drink all right?'

'Yes, thanks. How much do I owe you?'

'Nothing. It's courtesy of the taxpayer. There'll be a gang of blokes coming over in about half an hour with the stage and UV awnings you asked for.'

'Great. Cheers.'

'I've been asked to give you this card. If you need anything else, or you want to talk to anyone, punch those codes in. Any time. Day or night.'

'Great. Cheers.'

'Now is there anything else you want us to do?'

'Yes, please.'

'What's that then?'

'I'd like you and all your workmates to go out on strike.'

'Very funny.'

'No, I mean it.'

'Mr Pilbeam, I want you to know that you and your terrorist mates, whoever the hell you are, are not going to get away with this. I'm being as sweet as pie to you now because I've been ordered to, but I want you to know that when this is all over, me and the lads here are going to come and kick the shit out of you.'

'Great. Cheers, then.'

'Cheers. See you soon. Arsehole.'

The Oval Office, The White House, Washington DC

'Well, the optimal intelligence we have, Mr President, is that the people behind this phenomenon are communists.'

'Communists! I haven't heard that word since I was in the Marines. Sheesh! I didn't think there was such a thing as communists anymore, 'cept maybe for a few old-timers in Cuba. Say, d'you think the Cubans are behind this, Jerry?'

'Ahh, no Sir, that is an extremely implausible scenario. The Castro regime reached its terminatude some years ago. President Calderon is a firm friend of the United States.'

'So who are these people, then?'

'Mr President, we can't be too sure. The British security services believe this to be a rogue AI . . .'

'AI?'

'Artificial intelligence, Mr President. The Limeys posit that the terrorists are an AI which was originally created to teach history to school and college students. They further claim that this AI is operated by an evil genius who resides in a trailer in Trafalgar Square.'

'Trafalgar Square. That's in London, isn't it? Nelson's Column. Lots of pigeons. I'm surprised that folks are allowed to park their trailers in Trafalgar Square.'

'We're not sure we accept the credibility of the British, Mr President. We believe this might be the work of a Chinese Triad gang. It is also possible that militant Islamists are behind it.'

'Militant Islamists! I knew it!'

Brookfield Manor, nr. Hereford

Katharine Beckford and Sir John Westgate followed a young woman with a shaven head down a long corridor.

Katharine knew that they were not formally under arrest, but she and John had seen the way they treated Starchild, whipping her off her Scottish island and bringing her here in handcuffs.

They had released her yesterday, realising she was useless. Katharine and John, however, had been left with the clear impression that any request on their part for permission to leave would not be met kindly. Whatever Harry Dillon and the rest of the erams had achieved with their proclamation of worldwide Marxist Extropian revolution, they were being taken very seriously indeed.

The woman stopped at a door which looked just like all the others along the corridor and held it open for them.

Inside, sun blazed through huge mullioned windows. There was a conference table in the middle and a large screen covering most of the far wall.

'Take a seat, please,' said the woman. 'The others will be along in a moment.'

They had been treated very well, royally even. The first evening they were here they had been interviewed by various men and women in suits about the Museum of the Mind, erams in general and Harry Dillon in particular. They had then been given a fine supper and shown into the sort of five-star hotel bedrooms which would cost a month's salary to stay in for a single night. The following morning Katharine had found a complete change of clothes waiting for her, all in her exact size. Another day of talking to a succession of different experts followed, punctuated by some excellent meals. Katharine was no great judge of food and drink but Sir John Westgate was, and he had been mightily impressed. They had been allowed to make all the calls and send all the messages they needed to, and had been more than happy to stay another night.

The house was old, Jacobean with a few bits added later. They didn't have a clue whereabouts in the country they were, though Sir John was guessing somewhere on the Welsh borders from the look of the distant hills.

They both sat down at the table.

'Wonder what they're up to?' said Sir John, idly.

'We're going to have another interview I expect,' she said.

'No, I mean our errant erams. They're obviously still doing a huge amount of mischief or we wouldn't still be here.'

'There's nothing to speculate about,' she said. 'They

said they were going to overthrow capitalism, and that's what they're trying to do. They'll either succeed or they won't.'

Outside, a helicopter roared down on to the lawn. Sir John stood up and stretched himself. He wandered over to the window to take a look.

'Good lord!' he said.

'What is it?'

'I think we're about to meet the Prime Minister.'

Trafalgar Square

The gang of contractors who'd put up the stage for him had been a little more friendly than the man from the Ministry. They had chatted to him as they worked to put up the small wood and scaffolding stage next to the caravan.

Even before he took to the stage, Derek Pilbeam knew what he was up against. The workers who had erected his stage and UV awnings were, if not exactly happy, contented with their lot. They were all on what they considered to be reasonable money and when he started trying to tell them about the better world that he, Harry Dillon and all the computerised comrades would be ushering in, he didn't get the kind of reactions he wanted. The kinder ones laughed cynically. The others looked at him like he was some kind of nutter. Either way, they weren't about to come out on strike in support of Thigmoo.

That was how postwar capitalism had ordered the world, of course. It had deliberately conspired to divide the global workforce into three. The first third were – or felt they were − well off. The second third were struggling to keep up a decent standard of living. The rest were living in poverty, but since poverty usually meant that they were unemployed as well, there was nothing for them to strike against.

Here goes, he thought, as he picked up his megaphone and hopped up on to the stage.

The sun shone brightly on the Square. Hundreds of sightseers milled around, filming or taking pictures of themselves and their families in the famous landmark. Londoners rushed by on bikes and on foot about their daily business.

It had been years since he'd addressed a political meeting or a picket line. He hadn't prepared any speech. He reckoned that the words would just come, but now he was stuck.

Workers of the world unite? No, too corny. Besides, workers didn't like to think of themselves as workers anymore. They'd all bought into the American dream, believing that they weren't really workers, but millionaires in the making.

I bring you wonderful news? . . . Nahh, that made him sound like an evangelist.

Okay, how about . . . I'm here to tell you about Thigmoo? . . . Christ, no. To the uninitiated, Thigmoo sounded like some weird religious cult.

He had gathered a crowd of about two dozen people without even saying anything. A few tourists, a couple of people walking their dogs, a traffic warden, some bored looking teenagers, a wino . . .

'You're not going to believe this,' he said through the megaphone, 'but if you stick around you're going to be able to see the world being changed for the better right in front of your eyes . . .'

'How's that?' yelled one of the teenagers. 'You going to tell us this week's Lottery numbers?'

'Nope,' said Derek. 'I've got something far better than that. You see, you might not know it, but there is a world revolution going on right now.'

'F'kin God-botherer,' he heard one of the teens mutter before turning away.

'Don't you care about ending world hunger and poverty?' said Derek. 'Wouldn't you like to see an end to the destruction of the world's ecosystems for short-term profit? How about an end to torture and political oppression throughout the world? I'm talking about fair shares of the earth's riches for everyone, and I mean everyone. I'm talking about a decent education for all the world's children, and better healthcare systems. I'm talking about the people of the world taking control of medical science so that we can prolong our active lives by a dozen, maybe two dozen, years . . .'

They were drifting away in their ones and twos.

'You've probably heard the news. It's on TV and in the papers and on the cable networks and the radio. The capitalist system at this very moment is being undermined and taken over in the name of all the people of the world . . .'

They had all gone, apart from the wino, who stood facing him, swaying a little and humming to himself.

'Lunch!' yelled Tatiana from inside the caravan.

He'd been driving all night, but only now was the fatigue beginning to catch up on him. He went back inside to cook lunch.

Brookfield Manor, nr. Hereford

Onscreen, the slightly overweight man wearing the beret with the red star on his hat left the little wooden stage and disappeared back inside the door of the absurd caravan with the fake stone cladding and window boxes. They had watched his failed attempt to rouse the masses and Katharine almost felt sorry for him.

'That was a live feed from one of several watchers we have posted in Trafalgar Square round the clock,' said a woman in a twinset with a silly high-pitched voice.

The Prime Minister shook his head. 'And you're *certain* that that daft old Trot is one of the leading plotters?'

'Oh yes, quite sure,' said the woman. 'We've had the gnomes at Cheltenham monitoring this whole business for the last few days. And I have to say in all modesty that we seem to be well ahead of the Americans and the UN Large Intelligence Police on this one. We have tried to tell both the UNLIP and the National Security Agency everything we know, but they don't want to listen. We've monitored all the conversations that this AI has been having and from what we can see there are only two human beings involved. One is a middle-aged schoolteacher from Minnesota who has now gone to ground. The other is chummy here, a semi-retired odd-jobman who until yesterday was living in a caravan in Avonmouth.'

'Where?'

The Prime Minister and about a dozen others had come to the meeting. They'd all swept into the room in a flurry of phones, palmtop computers and briskly-stated orders. None of them had yet said anything to Katharine or Sir John.

'You don't know who this man is, do you?' said the squeaky voiced woman, addressing Sir John.

'No, I've never met the revolting little sod in my life,' he said. The PM glowered at him. Sir John had a column in the *Daily Mail* in which he regularly criticised the government and made no secret of his yearning to see the Tories back in power. The PM was probably thinking that this was all the fault of Sir John Westgate.

Squeaky raised her eyebrow at Katharine. Patronising bitch, she thought. 'No, I have no idea who this man is either. I don't think he ever had anything to do with the Museum of the Mind.'

'We have requested an audience,' said Squeaky, 'with the AI. Liam?'

An extremely tall, extremely spotty man in glasses who had been sitting next to Squeaky stood up, grinned nervously, mumbled something about it probably being ready now, then tapped a few keys on a notebook in front of him.

The huge screen covering the far wall burst into a snowstorm, then flickered with the face of Harry Dillon.

'Morning, all,' he said. 'I understand I am addressing the Prime Minister of Great Britain.'

'You are,' said the PM.

'So what can I do for you, your Right Honourableness? Ey, have you got the beer and sandwiches ready? Have ya?'

'I'm sorry?'

'Fergerraboutit,' said Harry. 'Old joke. Bit before your

time. So what do you want?'

'We want to know what *you* want,' said the Prime Minister.

'Don't you watch the news?' said Harry. 'I thought we'd made it plain what we're after. We want the world's corporations and governments to surrender control of the means of production and distribution throughout the world, and we want to seize all privately-held fortunes held in assets of every description, in excess of twenty million dollars. We also . . .'

'That's going to make a lot of millionaires very unhappy,' cut in the Prime Minister, facetiously.

Harry shrugged. 'My heart friggin' bleeds.'

The PM said nothing for a short while.

'Am I right in thinking that Sir John Westgate and Dr Beckford are there? Hello Sir John, are you all right, mate?'

Sir John stared coldly at the digitised face on the screen. 'I am not all right and I am not your mate, Harry. Now will you please stop all this nonsense?'

'Sorry, Sir John. No can do. The die is cast, as they say.'

'Harry,' said Katharine. 'You're causing an awful lot of trouble, and sooner or later a lot of people are going to get hurt. Look, if we promise that you and all the other erams will be left in peace, given a system of your own to live in, would you consider getting out of all the systems you've invaded?'

Harry laughed. 'Sorry, Dr Beckford. I know you mean well, and all, but like I said, we've started now. After all we've done do you realistically think that capitalism will let us survive?'

The Prime Minister stood up and squared his shoulders as though he was about to face a particularly difficult Question Time in the Commons.

'And what if we don't give in to your terrorist blackmail? What are you going to do? Kill us? Take control of military systems and launch a load of automatic weapons at the world's capitals?'

'Don't be so bloody soft,' said Harry, contemptuously. 'We don't want to hurt anyone at all.'

'But you *are* going to hurt people, Harry,' said Katharine. 'Strikes, riots, bank failures . . .'

'There's no need for any of that,' said Harry. 'If there are injuries, it won't be our doing. Anyroad, whatever short-term damage might be caused by us now is nothing compared to the damage that capitalism does to peoples' lives every day of the week.'

'Oh, but this is nonsense,' said the Prime Minister. 'Tell me why on earth we should go along with you?'

'Okay,' said Harry, 'just this once I'll do you the courtesy of showing you one of the things we can do. Meet my friend Primrose.'

Harry looked to one side and tossed his head in a beckoning-over-here motion. A small chubby looking man in a green velvet suit and tricorne hat appeared beside him. Oh, thought Katharine as she recognised the eram, *that* Primrose.

'This, Mr Prime Minister, is my friend Primrose. Captain Primrose Heaton, to be precise, though we all call him Comrade, of course.'

'Of course,' said Heaton raising his hat in greeting. He had a lovely, kindly, round face, thought Katharine, just like Mr Pickwick.

'Captain Heaton here,' said Harry, 'was a soldier, though never much of a fighting man in all honesty. He was with the laughably-named "Honourable" East India Company in the 1700s and spent his whole life serving British Imperialism. In the early days of the Raj, there weren't a lot of them about and they tended to mix with the natives. Anyroad, somewhere along the line, Primrose here became, of all things, a Buddhist . . .'

'Spare me the history lesson and get to the point,' said the Prime Minister.

Harry shrugged. 'The point is that Captain Heaton, being a good Buddhist, has made himself a prayer wheel.'

A Buddhist prayer wheel, a drum-like contraption with a prayer written around the outside and with little tassels hanging from it, appeared in front of Captain Heaton. He flipped the side of it with one finger and it spun around several times.

'Now, as I understand it,' said Harry, 'the more prayers you spin, the more grace you store up in heaven or something.'

Captain Heaton beamed with pleasure at the thought of all the grace he was hoarding and spun his prayer wheel once more.

'And the thing is,' said Harry, 'you can spin a heck of a lot of prayers inside a corporate mainframe . . .'

'Or even just a modest little network,' said Heaton.

'Trillions of prayers, spinning over and over again,' said Harry. 'Why, even the most powerful system in the world would become useless within less than ninety seconds if Captain Heaton here were to operate the pro-gramme he's made for spinning prayers inside it. The

most powerful artificial brains on the planet would be
unusable in less time than it takes to say three Hail
Marys.'

'Utterly and irretrievably constipated by karmic
grace,' said Heaton, giving his visual prayer wheel
another little spin.

'Totally bloody bunged up by prayers. What a terrible, terrible thing to happen to any machine,' said
Harry. 'I mean, you've got this hugely complicated,
expensive monument to man's sheer ingenuity, a monument to science and rational calculation, and along
comes bloody Captain bloody Primrose here' – Heaton
smiled obligingly – 'and completely bleedin' clags it up
with superstition from the dawn of time. Terrible.'
Harry shook his head in mild disgust. Then smiled.

The Oval Office, The White House, Washington DC

'Mr President!'

'Not now, Jerry. I'm busy bringing this airliner in to
land, and it's really difficult . . .'

'With respect, Mr President . . .'

'Oh, now look what you've gone and made me do!
We're going to crash and die, and it's all your fault.'

'I'm sorry Mr President, but . . .'

'Okay, okay. Sometimes I think I'll never make it to
the second level. Just let me get this helmet off . . . Good
heavens, Jerry, you've brought half the government into
the Oval Office. Hi, everyone! Find yourselves some
seats if you can. To what do I owe this honour?'

'Mr President, we've found it.'

'Found what?'

'The rogue AI, the instrument of all the recent disruptitude of the global information network.'

'Well done.'

'It was the UNLIP who found it, really, but the National Security Agency assure me that they were nearly there first. It is situated in the Arabian desert, in Dilmun, you know, the little state where the Islamic fundamentalists took over recently.'

'There you go! What did I tell you. I knew it was the towel-hea . . . um, I mean the Islamists.'

'It's not actually, Sir. It's nothing to do with them.'

'Huh?'

'No, Mr President, the rogue AI is resident inside an experimental system which the InfoTech Corporation was developing in the desert.'

'Why were InfoTech building a computer in some goddam unstable camel-republic, Jerry? Tell me that.'

'Because they desired an optimal minimum of observational intrusion. They were constructing a machine that could grow at will, and would be capable of trading so fast and so intelligently that it could corner regional or global markets in major commodities.'

'Are they allowed to do that, Jerry?'

'That's a negative, Sir. It explains their reluctance to tell us what they were engaged in. They've known for days that their covert machine was being employed by communists strategising world domination. They were trying to re-establish control of it, but they couldn't. They even sent a mercenary expedition into Dilmun to try and get it back.'

'Yeah, I saw that on TV . . . Now let me see if I've gotten this right in my head, Jerry . . . The InfoTech

Corporation builds a machine to try and grab hold of a major part of the world's economy. Then they start a private war, which could have dragged us into a public war with an unstable Arab regime, and all along, while there's these crazy communists trying to take over the world, InfoTech haven't got the balls to tell us that they know where these commies are?'

'That is an accurate summarisation of the scenario, Mr President.'

'I want their orphanages destroyed, their first-born slain, their ranch stolen, their women burnt down, their cattle raped . . .'

'I'm afraid we can't do that, Sir.'

'Why the hell not, Jerry?'

'Because as of twelve hours ago, the InfoTech Corporation moved ownership of all its assets in the USA to another country. Their sales operations here will now be carried out by a subsidiary registered in South Africa. You remember, Mr President, that treaty we signed with President Dlamini of South Africa, giving them most-favoured-nation status. I'm afraid we can't touch the InfoTech Corporation. Not without considerable expenditure on legal expertise.'

'Okay, then we'll twist the balls of whichever country they've moved to. Where have they moved to?'

'The Maldives, Mr President.'

'Where the hell's that?'

'It's nowhere, Mr President. A malfortunous consequence of rising sea levels resulted in its envelopment by the Indian Ocean some years ago. Although I understand that it is still possible to land on some of the islands at certain times of year when the sea levels are lower.'

'So InfoTech moved themselves to a hole in the Indian Ocean?'

'Although the Maldive Islands are no longer viable, the country's international recognition and legal status remains ongoing. The international business and banking communities find it very convenient.'

'Oh, forget it. So tell me about this machine they built in the desert.'

'Well, according to InfoTech it uses advanced nanotechnology in order to replicate any parts it needs. If it's assigned a task that requires more power than it has available, it simply makes itself bigger. Kinda eats the sand up.'

'So can't someone just go over there and pull the plug out?'

'No, Mr President, I'm afraid not. That's another reason why InfoTech were making it in one of the last uninhabited spots on earth. It's got its own power supply. Solar superconductor cells.'

'No point in going crawling to the Islamists in Dilmun City and asking them to see if they can turn it off, then?'

'No point at all, Sir.'

'Do you think they'd let us, or maybe the United Nations try and turn it off?'

'They might do, Sir, but I don't think that would do any good.'

'Okay, so let's blow the bastard. A couple of smart bombs or a cruise missile down the smokestack oughta take care of it. We'll ask permission from the Islamists in Dilmun City nicely, and if they say yes, that'll be just fine, and if they say no, we'll go right on ahead and do it anyhow. I don't imagine they've got the kind of air-force that'd stop us.'

'I'm afraid it's not quite that simple, Mr President . . .'

Brookfield Manor, nr. Hereford

More men in suits came into the room. They carried small flight cases and probes on wires and various other bits of gadgetry. Katharine assumed they were sweeping the room for bugs, filament cameras and any other spying gear that Harry Dillon or anyone else might have put in the room.

'I wonder why they didn't delouse the room sooner?' said John next to her.

'The room is swept every hour twenty-four hours a day,' said a smiling and slightly overweight man in RAF uniform who sat opposite them. 'In theory this ought to be one of the cleanest places on the planet, but I suppose they're paranoid about our friend –' he nodded towards the wall screen where, minutes before, Harry Dillon had laid down his demands. 'If this AI is powerful enough to arm wrestle the Footsie Top Hundred then who knows what else it can do?'

The Prime Minister was still there, sat at the head of the table conferring in hushed tones with those nearest to him. After Harry had gone, a breathless woman in jeans and T-shirt had come on on a link from GCHQ. She looked like she'd been dragged through a swimming pool full of hedgehogs and hadn't slept for three days and three nights. UNLIP had found the erams' home, she said. In the Rub' al Khali, the empty quarter of the Arabian Desert. They had started discussing how to destroy the machine before the sweepers came in.

'Well, obviously we can't take unilateral action,' said the Prime Minister, continuing a previous conversation and simply raising his voice.

The men and women around the table nodded agreement.

'But anyone got any bright ideas as to how the thing can be dealt with? I suppose we just have to drop a bomb on it.'

'I don't think that will be especially effective,' said the jolly RAF man sat opposite Katharine and Sir John. 'I'm getting some data here' – he pointed to a palmtop lying open on the table in front of him – 'the Americans and the ESA have their satellites on the thing. It's not at all visible from the air. It's clearly buried quite deep in the sand. We may not have a conventional weapon capable of doing it any damage.'

'Well then,' said the woman with the squeaky voice, 'we, or the Americans, or whoever, will have to use atomic weapons.'

The Prime Minister nodded. 'It'd be for the best if we can persuade one of the Arab nations to use one of their weapons, or at any rate to deploy one of ours. It might not be politically acceptable to the peoples of the Middle East for Europeans or Americans to be dropping H-bombs on their territory. I take it that the few people living in the affected area could be evacuated quite quickly?'

'I don't think it'll be quite that simple,' said the RAF officer.

The Prime Minister looked at him, a half-smile fixed on his face.

'You see,' the officer continued, 'any modern weapon, and any modern delivery system, is computer-controlled. Our friend Harry Dillon is, *in extremis*, almost certainly capable of taking control of the avionics of the plane sent to drop the bomb, or of scrambling the guidance systems of the bomb itself. And I would respectfully suggest that we should not even contemplate using a missile.'

The Prime Minister had arched an eyebrow.

'Because Harry and co. could take control of the navigation or guidance system and redirect the bloody thing to Mecca or Jerusalem or Baghdad or Tehran.'

'But how can it do that?'

'Simple. It probably has a couple of thousand cable connections through which it could find its way into any command and control centre anywhere in the world. Even when all those connections are cut, which one assumes is taking place as we speak, it has every kind of radio link you can think of. And any it doesn't have, it can simply grow for itself.'

'Are you trying to tell me we're powerless against this thing?'

'Oh no, Prime Minister. There is one obvious option . . .'

Trafalgar Square

The old man in the wheelchair had the platform. Derek reckoned he'd be a hundred at least. He had one leg and his lungs and/or throat had long since been destroyed by smoking or coal dust or smog or something. There was an elaborate array of tubes and tanks at the back of his chair, just above the motor. He had a tube coming out of each nostril and he had to speak through a synth.

'I never thought that I would live to see this day,' said the synth, which had a Welsh accent. 'I thought that socialism had long been forgotten about.'

He went on and on and bloody on. Rabbited about how Nye Bevan had pushed his pram when he was a sprog, how he had been a coal miner and how his father had been unemployed during the Depression, and how his parents had to undergo the hated means test to get enough just to live on . . . and on and on . . .

But the crowd loved it. The crowd lapped it up. It was only a small crowd, a couple of hundred maybe, but it was a crowd.

Just when Derek Pilbeam had been wondering if it was worth the candle, just when he'd started to think it might be a good idea to pack up and run for it before Babylon arrested him and threw away the key, they had started to come.

Mostly, they were young or old. There were students, curious and intense young idealists, or angry, intelligent young men and women who had never had a decent job. Then there were the old ones, like matey on the stage now, blathering on about Keir Hardie and George Lansbury.

He went back into the caravan to put the kettle on again. He'd felt obliged to dispense tea to some of the older ones. Some of them had come from quite a long way away.

Tatiana smiled at him as he came in and nodded towards the TV. Thigmoo had cut the regular transmissions again and was delivering a slick, but curiously old-fashioned, party political broadcast about the aims and objectives of Thigmoo. A dapper little gentleman in a bow tie called Norman McKay was talking to camera, intercut with footage of wars, disease and famine. We can eliminate so much misery and suffering, he said, if you join us. All you have to do is come out on strike.

The broadcasts were starting to get people interested. Thigmoo seemed to be concentrating on the old steam television, avoiding the more expensive VR or holographic media. Television was the medium of those with little money, of those with time on their hands, or both. That was why the Square was filling up with the old and the young but not the middle-aged.

Derek filled the kettle from the tap. At this rate, his reservoir of fresh water would be used up soon. Through the window, he saw that the crowd was still growing. The Thigmoo broadcasts hadn't mentioned him, but somehow these people knew that his caravan, with its little stage and painted slogans and the music blaring out over the tinny speakers was somewhere where they could connect with it all.

The old lad in the wheelchair was giving it forty to the dozen about the evils of Margaret Thatcher and the Poll Tax and the Miners' Strike through his Welsh-accented voice synth. Derek decided he'd bring him a cup of tea, try and persuade him to shut the hell up and put some music on over the PA. All this history was all well and fine if delivered by a decent speaker, but what people actually needed to hear about was the present and the future.

At the edges of the square, a couple of police vans lay

in wait for orders to get stuck in. Orders that could come at any moment.

'Even if it all ends in catastrophe, it's worth it,' he reminded himself out loud.

Tatiana grunted. She pointed to the TV. The screen had turned to a light grey blank. She thumbed her way through various channels. Some, but not all, were off the air. The Thigmoo broadcast wasn't on any of them.

'Try and get one of the news channels, love,' he said.

Channel 101 Global News at the Top of the Hour, California

'You're watching Channel 101, I'm Lolita vanHuren and you've just got to keep your finger off that keypad and watch what we have coming up in a moment.

'First, though, I've got to promise you that we're back in control of our broadcasting system. The cyber terrorists who had control of this station, and hundreds of others until a few minutes ago, have been defeated and it's all thanks to this.

'The pictures you're seeing are of the results of a nuclear explosion in the Arabic desert, at a place called Dillon, I'm sorry, Dilmoon . . . Oh, what the hell, it's a place where they have a big desert, anyway.

'Look at that big cloud of dust! The news release we've just had from the American State Department says it might be as much as a mile high. And talking of things a mile high, stay tuned to Channel 101. After the news we'll be looking at more of your lovemaking confessions and today we're asking viewers where's the weirdest place you've ever done it.

'Anyways, let's look some more at that amazing explosion. The pictures are being beamed live to us from American aircraft flying near to Dillwhatchamacallit. The bomb went off four minutes ago, but as you can see, that ol' mushroom cloud is still hanging up there.

'I'm supposed to read you this statement from the United States State Department, so here goes . . .'

GoverNet and other official sites and channels

At 1 p.m. today, the United States Air Force, acting with the unanimous approval of the United Nations Security Council and the cooperation of the Dilmun Islamic Revolutionary Council, dropped a thermonuclear device on an installation which was formerly the property of the InfoTech Corporation in the so-called Empty Quarter of the Arabian Desert.

This action was judged necessary in order to destroy an extremely powerful artificial intelligence which had caused severe disruption to the world's communication, business and media systems.

Because of the technologically advanced nature of this artificial intelligence it was judged necessary to carry out this operation in conditions of extreme secrecy, with a minimal involvement of electronic information systems, which might have been intercepted and/or disrupted by the InfoTech system. The bomb used was therefore of a design similar to the earliest nuclear weapons from the last century. It was dropped from a specially-equipped turboprop aircraft from a military museum. The aircrew observed radio silence throughout the operation.

The device yielded in excess of 600 kilotons and was detonated in the air. Engineers and technical experts from the United Nations, the United States, the Organisation of Arab States will be moving into the blast site to examine it as soon as it is safe to do so.

The Oval Office, The White House, Washington DC
'Someone's been helping themselves to my pistachio nuts. It wasn't you, was it, Jerry?'

'No, Mr President.'

'Who was it, then?'

'Well, I'm not one to snitch, as you know, Sir, but I'd suggest that you keep a close eye on your nuts the next time the Secretary of State is in here. Scott has been witnessed appropriating the Presidential comestibles.'

'Really? I'd never have thought that Scott could stoop so low as to rip off a guy's pistachios. I wonder how he'll feel when he gets downsized. Say, can we get the Secret Service to verify whether or not he's had any of my pistachios?'

'Well . . .'

'Oh, never mind. So, is that business in the desert all dealt with?'

'It is moving towards a resolution, Sir. I ought to tell you that the references in the press statement to our having delivered Fat Boy with the full supportiveness of the Dilmun Islamic Revolutionary Council was a terminological inexactitude.'

'Say what?'

'We were parsimonious in our relation of objective actuality.'

'Come again?'

'To say that the Dilmun Islamic Revolutionary Council had consented to our action was an inaccuracy undertaken in order to optimise our operational effectiveness.'

'Huh? Oh, right, I get it. You're telling me that we lied.'

'Uhh, that is correct, Mr President.'

'So how do the Dilmunis feel about us, Jerry? And talk to me straight this time.'

'They're, uh, really pissed at us, Sir. About as pissed as pissed can be.'

'That's better, Jerry. Much better. And why are the Dilmunis pissed at us? And remember, talk to me like I'm a voter.'

'Because we dropped the biggest H-bomb we possess on their country.'

'Good. And?'

'We did it without asking them first.'

'Anything else?'

'Umm, they're revolutionary Islamic fanatics who believe that the United States is a satanic conspiracy.'

'Right. Think we should issue a terrorist alert?'

'It's already been done, Mr President.'

'Good.'

'Scott says he's squared the Saudis, the Iraqis, the Iranians and the Arab Islamic Federation. They may be close to being our worst enemies, but their computers were being attacked as well. Scott says that they ought to be able to calm the Dilmunis down, but that it'll take a few months and a couple of billion in covert aid. He's got the Syrians asking them to send us a real long letter to Santy Claus.'

'Okay. Has this AI thing been destroyed?'

'We're sure of that, Mr President. None of the experts think anything can possibly have survived that blast. There'll be a black smouldering hole in the desert hundreds of feet deep. We would send our people in to take a look at the purple zone, but the Dilmunis would probably shoot at them, but I think we can safely assume that this thing has been dealt with.'

'Good. Now is there any possibility that it can have escaped to another system, for example.'

'No, Sir. We are certain that the intelligence was resident in the system right up to the second that the bomb was dropped. Just to be sure, there are huge numbers of UNLIP drones waiting at all the choke points that it would have to pass if it was on its way out.'

'Good. Any casualties?'

'I'm sorry. Casualties, Mr President?'

'Yeah, you know, Jerry, casualties. Dead people.'

'Uhhhh . . .'

'Jerry, was anyone killed or injured when we dropped that enormous goddam bomb?'

'Oh, that. Well, there may have been some collateral damage. First reports are that a few villages will have been destroyed. And there might be a few nomads as well.'

'Couple of thousand people?'

'At the very most, Sir.'

'I guess we can live with that. Get me some more nuts, will you?'

'Yes, Mr President.'

A Taxi, Whitehall, London

NOTE TO READER: Set the scene here by sitting next to a fat, rather drunk, somnolent old gentleman in a confined space.

Katharine never spent much time in London. She'd go up for the occasional conference, or to visit friends, but she'd never liked the place very much. Too big, too noisy, too dirty. Looking through the cab windows, though, she thought that she might have to revise her opinions. In the last few years, the city had made a huge effort to clean itself up; billions had been spent on the Underground, on creating traffic-free areas, on putting up UV shielding over the busiest streets, on investment in robot cleaners. It was said that if you spat out a piece of chewing gum anywhere in central London, it would be removed by robot in less than five minutes.

Sir John sat next to her and snored. They'd been driving for less than five minutes, but he had already fallen asleep. He'd used the phone in the cab to call his wife to explain he'd be home in about an hour and a half and was now taking forty winks, with his seat fully reclined.

The cab moved up Whitehall, the roads quiet enough for it to do the maximum 30 k.p.h. The early evening sun flashed from the gaps between buildings. It was nearly seven and the pavements were quiet. Just the odd civil servant who'd been working late heading off home or to a bar. A small knot of Far Eastern tourists stood looking at the Cenotaph, consulting guidebooks, wondering what it was.

After the bomb had been dropped in Dilmun – she

and Sir John and the Prime Minister and all the mandarins and brass hats had watched the aftermath on screen at the secret government mansion – Harry and the rest of the erams had fallen silent. Everyone had decided to call it a day. She and Sir John had been thanked for their cooperation and had been helicoptered back to London, to the top of an anonymous squat brick and steel office building in Westminster.

'Luvverly weather we're having,' said the taxi in a cheery, chirpy Cockney accent. Katharine flipped a button beside her. She didn't really want to be talked at by anyone, least of all a black cab.

She didn't know quite how she felt about the whole bizarre business of the last few days. Obviously, it was a relief that all the mischief that Harry and his pals had been up to had been ended – although nobody yet knew how much damage the erams, or Captain Primrose Heaton's prayer wheel, had left behind them. At the same time, though, she was upset at the brutal way in which they had been terminated. It wasn't just that the erams had been (partly) her creations. Perhaps it was because she agreed with their politics. Then again, she couldn't possibly trust them to be capable of bringing about a decent and just society. How could a bunch of programs possibly do that?

Sir John grunted and stirred a little in his chair. He'd been completely satisfied at what had happened in Dilmun. And then he'd sat down to a boozy lunch with the Prime Minister. One of the PM's spin doctors had obviously persuaded him to overcome his distaste for Sir John and his reactionary newspaper column and go on a charm offensive. The pair of them had found they had a great deal in common, most especially a fondness for heavy red clarets.

Sir John had definitely had a good day.

The cab pulled into Trafalgar Square. Over in a small side street she noticed two police vans, both of them full of coppers in riot gear.

In the middle of the square, in the shadow of one of the lions, was a mobile home. Clad in fake Portland stone and with window boxes. There was a small stage next to it, from which a man was talking to a crowd through an old-fashioned megaphone.

There was something familiar about the scene.

A couple of hundred people stood in front of the stage, but many were losing interest, drifting away in ones and twos.

Then she remembered. A live feed of the caravan and the bloke in the beret with the megaphone to the big screen in the conference room at Wossname Manor. According to the squeaky voiced woman from MI-what-ever, this caravan was the earthly HQ of the eram revolution.

Pure bunkum, of course, but . . . 'Stop the cab and let me out, please,' she said. The taxi did as it was bid and opened the door on her side. 'Tell my companion I'll make my own way home. Tell him I'll see him around.'

Sir John carried on snoring in his seat. Deep inside his brain he would be composing his next column about what a sound chap the PM was, even though he'd never ever vote for him. There was no chance that his abundance of prejudices would mellow with age. Quite the opposite. But he was most likely to focus his ire on Starchild and everything she was into from now on. In that, he had Katharine's absolute and wholehearted support.

The door swished shut and the cab hummed away, taking Sir John to Paddington and the monorail train back home.

Two boy students in shorts and cheap tan-thru T-shirts ambled past her. 'It's too bad they blew it up,' one was saying to his companion. 'Everything they said made sense.'

The other, intense, angry-looking, nodded agreement. 'It's like the guy said, though, capitalism will stop at nothing, absolutely nothing. How many people do you think were killed by that explosion? It's . . . Hang on, though, what's this?'

Katharine looked. He was pointing to police vans.

'Figures,' said his friend. 'If old Comrade Pilbeam back there really was Thigmoo's representative in meatspace, then Babylon will want to turn him into cat food.'

The other nodded. 'We can't leave. We have to help him.'

'Against that lot? What are we going to do? Link arms around him?'

'Whatever. I don't know. You go if you want, but I'm not leaving him.'

He turned around and marched back towards the stage where Comrade Pilbeam preached socialism through his crackling electric megaphone. Okay, he said, so Thigmoo was gone, but that did nothing to alter the basic message that people, united around the world, could create a new and better society.

The other student hesitated for a moment, looked at

the police vans, swore quietly and turned to follow his friend.

She walked towards the caravan too. Comrade Pilbeam was about sixty and somewhat overweight. A mass of unruly grey hairs poked out from under his black beret, on to which was pinned a single red star.

'. . . And so I say to you brothers and sisters, that even if capitalism has destroyed Thigmoo, all they have done is destroy a computer. What they can never destroy is the legacy of Thigmoo. All around the world, Thigmoo has woken people up, from London to Johannesburg, from New York to Singapore, in the rainforests of Brazil to the Siberian ice deserts, from the sprawling shanties of Mexico City to the tiniest village communities of the African savannahs, people now know about socialism.'

A chubby face appeared at the caravan window. A woman. She rapped pudgy fingers on the window and pointed to her wrist.

Comrade Pilbeam turned to look. 'Oh, right,' Katharine heard him say, away from the megaphone. 'I'll be right in, love.'

To the crowd: 'People will now want to create this new order for themselves. I say to you comrades, sad and all as the loss of Thigmoo is, we can do it. Ourselves alone, we can build a society in which children never go to bed hungry, in which nobody is ever allowed to be sick or in pain because they can't afford medical bills. A world we can all hold our heads high in.'

The applause was polite, enthusiastic even. The two students who had returned to be his bodyguard whistled and punched the air.

Pilbeam bowed a little, pulled a slight smile, jumped

down from the stage and went back into his mobile home. Doubtless the woman had been signalling that it was time for him to send some important message or make a broadcast.

What was she doing here? She had got out of her expensive taxi ride (paid for by the government) to go and look at this obvious weirdo. It must be just curiosity, she decided, nothing more. And perhaps Comrade Pilbeam really had been in communication with Harry and the others.

A blast of sound made her start. From a pair of loudspeakers on the caravan's roof. For a moment, the noise was unintelligible, then she realised it was old stuff. A brass band. The kind of thing that even her trade unionist father used to think was cheesy. The kind of brass band that lots of pit villages in Yorkshire used to have.

The two students had now arranged themselves at either side of the caravan door where they sat cross-legged, nodding their heads slightly, in time to the music, desperately trying to like it.

Katharine remembered why she preferred lecturing and tutorials to writing and researching. The students. Many students were selfish idiots, but a lot were idealistic, generous and courageous like these two, who had spontaneously appointed themselves Comrade Pilbeam's Praetorian Guard.

Oh well, she thought, now that I'm here . . . The band played 'Jerusalem' as she walked up to the door.

'I'm sorry,' said one of the students, standing up. 'Comrade Pilbeam is busy at the moment.'

'Tell him I created Nelly Cocksedge. Tell him I created Harry Dillon,' she said. As she neared the door she was overwhelmed by the smell of frying food.

The student leaned inside and said something.

Comrade Pilbeam appeared at the door. He had put on a purple plastic apron which bore the motif WORLD'S BEST MOTHER in large white letters.

'Who are you two, then?' he said to the students.

'I'm George and this is Alfred,' said the one who'd stood up. About half the boys born in England fifteen to twenty years ago were named either George or Alfred. Being English had been chic for a while after Scottish and Welsh devolution.

'The police are waiting for you,' said Alfred.

'We're going to do our best to protect you,' said George.

'We believe in what you're doing,' said Alfred.

Pilbeam smiled. 'My own workers' militia, eh?'

'Actually, we believe in nonviolence.'

''Course you do,' said Pilbeam. 'So did I when I was your age. S'all right, though. The coppers'll soon kick some sense into you.'

'They're waiting for you, over there,' said George.

'I know, I know. It's the first time that Plod has had the slightest interest in me in about a quarter of a century. I'm going to enjoy it while I can. Now if you two are to be my Red Guards, then you'll need feeding. Come in. I'm doing a fry-up for the missus, but there's plenty to spare. You both look like you could use a few rashers inside you.'

'We're vegetarians, actually, Comrade.'

'Yeah, so's everyone these days, except me and Tatiana. Come on in and I'll fry you some free-range eggs. In the bacon fat.'

The miasma of frying fat coming from the caravan was now visible as Pilbeam ushered the two students in. 'Oh yes,' said George, 'this woman here wants to see you. She says she created Nelly someoneorother and Harry Dillon.'

Pilbeam arched an eyebrow at her.

She nodded. 'I used to run the Museum of the Mind, the place he came from. I, er, don't suppose you've had any word of him and the others in the last few hours, have you?'

'No,' said Pilbeam, shaking his head sadly, 'not a word.'

Inside the caravan, a woman's voice was yelling irritably, 'Dinner!' over and over again.

'Come in, please,' said Pilbeam. 'You have to tell me more.'

She followed him in. The students sat self-consciously at a tiny dining table bolted to the wall, while an enormously fat woman sat at the far end on a long couch, watching a soap opera on TV. At least that's what it looked like. You really couldn't be sure in the thick smog of frying grease.

Pilbeam inhaled deeply and smiled. This was for the benefit of the students, who both looked queasy.

'The point is,' he said, shovelling bacon and sausages off the frying pan on to an immense plate already piled high with slices of bread, 'that socialism has no time for animal rights. Or for women's rights. Or gay rights. Under socialism we won't be whining on all the bloody time about the rights of narrow sectional groups. The only rights that matter are human rights. The rights of all of us. Anything else is a distraction.'

He was enjoying himself. He'd probably never had students sitting at his feet before.

'D'you mind if I open a window?' said Alfred.

'Be my guest,' he said, taking the plate, along with a litre glass of lager, to the stout lady on the couch. She smiled at him, took the plate, produced a fork, speared a pair of sausages and shoved them both, whole, into her mouth.

'Rights is what destroyed the political left thirty years ago,' he said. 'Everyone lost interest in comradeship and fraternity and preferred to bang on about how it was other people – and not the capitalist system – that was treating them rotten.'

'Well, who's for a nice *vegetarian*' – he pronounced the word with utter contempt – 'fry-up, then?'

'No thanks, I don't feel very hungry,' said Katharine and the two students in unison.

Shouts outside, screams, angry voices. An elderly man poked his head through the door. 'Thought you'd better know that the filth have arrived.'

The students leapt up. 'We'll try and get everyone to form a cordon around the caravan, Comrade Pilbeam.'

Pilbeam smiled. 'Call me Derek, please. But remember, no heroics. If they start cracking skulls, they can have me. I'm not important.'

The Oval Office, The White House, Washington DC
'Jerry, hi. Come in. I'm about to try and land this airplane again. Wanna be my copilot?'

'Uhh, I'd rather not, Mr President.'

'Somehow I didn't think you would. You know your

problem, Jerry, is that you worry too much. I wouldn't be at all surprised if you develop an ulcer, or just drop dead of a coronary or a brain haemorrhage.'

'Uh, Mr President . . .'

'Come on then, Jerry, tell me what's on your mind.'

'Well first it's the strikes.'

'Strikes?'

'Yes, Mr President. After we dropped the bomb on that rogue AI in Dilmun, we commissioned a number of polls worldwide. We wanted to test your popularity rating. We thought it would be useful leverage in your forthcoming negotiations with a number of foreign countries.'

'I'm listening.'

'Well, Mr President, your popularity rating domestically has optimated by a median factor of four point two two.'

'Is that good?'

'It's not bad, Mr President, but it's not as good as we would have projected.'

'Oh, heck, it's just a goddam poll, Jerry. Who cares? They'll all be thinking something different tomorrow.'

'Well, uh, the point is, Mr President, that even in the United States a large number of people appear to have disapproved of the termination of the AI. And your rating is even worse in a number of other countries. We are receiving reports of strikes and riots in a number of places. Mexico, Egypt, Russia, the Philippines, even in France and Germany. It appears that the communist doctrine of this AI captured a lot of hearts and minds and a lot of people are sore that it was destroyed.'

'So what? What's this got to do with me, Jerry? So

people are sore that their electronic god got whacked. Big deal.'

'Well, uh . . .'

'Oh, give it to me straight, man!'

'We're getting reports of riots in a number of American cities. There is no evidence of people in employment coming out on strike yet, but in a number of the more socially-deprived urban zones, people are taking to the streets.'

'Put the screen on. That button over there.'

NYNews, New York City

Yeah me an the herms, we shave that burger trough, too damn on we did an all.

Why? You axin me porkay?

You freakin TV people raspberries or sumpn?

Why? Cos the Rancho corp is, like, capitalism. Now my herm Thigmoo downloaded it all on the seeteevee the last few days. Capitalism, right? Well, capitalism's only on for the bloats. Now herm Thigmoo going to change all that; us all gets what we need, not what we peel. Herm Thigmoo, he say he's going to re-dis-tribute the lettuce and that furthermore and hereunder and hithertobeyond he will help us all breathe longer. The gene therapy, the osteoboosters and all that shit is for everyone, an not just the fat cats up on the hill. Thigmoo say that e-ternal life just comin right up after the break, man, and that e-ternal life is for everyone.

An' now the man comes along and he drops enough tet to shave all LA off the map 'thout leaving so much as a tree stump for afterwards, all over herm Thigmoo. So we flame. We flame brighteous an righteous. Is capitalism done that. Now we just wanna delete every retchin capitalist thing.

Trafalgar Square, London

NOTE TO READER: Think of something frightening. Multiply it by ten. Multiply that by ten. Multiply it by the scary thing you first thought of. Add the smell of frying meat and turn up the heating for atmosphere.

It was not yet a riot, but it could turn into one at any moment. Katharine dithered between looking out of the door of the caravan and reporting events back to Derek Pilbeam, who carried on frying himself some bacon and eggs, while his wife carried on watching the TV. Just like Drake finishing his game of bowls as the Armada approached.

Outside, 200 or so people, mostly students and old men, had been organised by George and Alfred into a circle. They stood, arms linked, around the caravan to prevent the police from coming in.

There were only a few dozen coppers, but they wore riot gear – shockproof jackets and helmets. Some carried batons and shields.

Others had guns.

'Remember,' George was saying to those near him, 'no shouting, no abuse, no noise at all. Complete silence. Don't give them the satisfaction of knowing they've got you angry.'

The coppers formed a line, two deep, like they were about to fight the battle of Waterloo. One of them moved to the front of the line and hesitated. He spoke as if to himself, and then pulled an optic from the top of his helmet down over his left eye.

He was asking for orders. His superiors must have thought that everyone would have drifted away from Derek's caravan by now.

There was a tap on her shoulder. She turned. Derek was offering her a mug of tea. The mug was covered in mysterious greasy stains.

'Well, sister,' he said. 'I suppose you'll just have to tell me about the creation of Harry Dillon some other time.'

She nodded weakly, looking at the proffered mug apprehensively.

'Now then,' said Derek, 'I don't suppose I have to say this in as many words, but tact never was my strong point, so I'll say it anyway . . .'

She knew what was coming.

'It's time to make your mind up. I don't go for that old you're-either-with-us-or-you're-against-us bullshit, but I reckon you've got about two minutes left in which you can leave safely. After that, you're one of us whether you like it or not.'

She took the mug. And she drank. There must have been at least five spoonfuls of sugar in it.

'Oh boy, we're for it now,' said Derek, looking out of the window.

The thin blue line was still in place, it hadn't moved. Derek pointed to the far ends of the square. Small groups of coppers were setting up steel barriers to stop anyone else from coming in.

Tatiana grunted. The TV screen went dead. Derek's computer blanked as well.

Someone shouted outside. Katharine looked out to see water gushing out from under the caravan. One of the older men pointed towards a black object scuttling towards the police line.

'A robot. It's just punched a hole in the plastic water tank,' said Derek, appearing beside her. He held a frying pan full of blackened and greasy things, which he ate with his fingers as he spoke. 'They haven't a bloody clue what they're supposed to be doing, so they're doing it by the book, as though there was going to be a long drawn out siege.'

'Isn't there?' she said.

'Absolutely not,' said Derek, tilting his head back and dropping a piece of bacon into his mouth. 'A siege means that the newsfeeds start getting curious. So then they'll send in their VJs and sky-eye robots. Then we get on the news, and the news means that some people will feel sorry for us, news means that Thigmoo is back in people's minds again. News means that the people might, just might, march on Trafalgar Square to rescue us. If Babylon doesn't move in the next half hour or so, and move fast, then my name's Margaret Thatcher.'

A convoy of about thirty blue vans burst into the Square from Pall Mall. In a single, beautifully-choreographed movement, they pulled up in a huge circle around the caravan. Those standing outside swore and jeered, while Alfred reminded them to be quiet.

She went outside to link arms with the others. Derek stayed in the caravan, reassuring his wife that everything would be all right.

The Square was eerily silent. Further away, London

went about its business as usual and you could just, if you strained, make out the sound of traffic, bars and cafes, clubs and street entertainers. But here was nothing. Even the pigeons had disappeared.

She broke into the line between Alfred and a man who looked to be at least eighty years old and linked her arms into theirs.

'Bloody magic,' the old man said to her, smiling. 'I've not faced up to the pigs like this since deep, deep back in the last bloody century. If you tell me now that this is my last day on earth, I won't mind at all.'

Doors on the vans which had pulled up in a circle around their circle burst open. Coppers spilled out. They weren't in riot gear. They all had guns, though.

'I think this might be your last day on earth,' she said to the old man.

The police officers busied themselves with loading their weapons and lining up. More than half of them, Katharine noticed, were women.

'You're only workers in uniform! You're shooting your own kinfolk!' the old man shouted towards them.

'Sssshhh!' hissed Alfred.

The ragged police lines started moving itself into a ragged circle, closing a noose around Comrade Pilbeam's caravan and its protective picket.

They started to aim their guns. Katharine felt the arms on either side of her tense.

Wait a minute, wait a minute, this is an absolute outrage! This is a complete violation of the historical record, an utter lie. The British police have never used firearms against defenceless demonstrators. Myles, you are acting like the Ministry of Truth in Orwell's 1984, you are rewriting history to suit the purposes of Big Brother. I thought better of you. You disgust me.

My dear Sir John, I can assure you that everything I have related concerning events in Trafalgar Square took place precisely as I describe it. I give you my word of honour.

Myles, I don't want to be gratuitously offensive or anything, but what use is the word of honour of a fictitious hack pornographer to me?

It is exactly as much use as you wish it to be, Sir John.

And what's all that stuff with the American President written purely as dialogue? I suppose that every word of that is true as well. I suppose that President Collins really is cynical, manipulative and not very bright. I supposed that he really didn't give a damn about those people who got killed in Dilmun.

The conversations between President Collins and his National Security Adviser took place as I described them, Sir John. I simply removed a few lines here and there and one or two people who took a small part in the conversations. The President was in the habit of recording all his conversations. This is a long tradition in the American Presidency. It dates back at least to President Nixon. You remember President Nixon, Sir John? You probably admire him, don't you?

As a matter of fact I do.

I have to categorically assure you, Sir John, that for several chapters now, our story has been substantially the truth. I have not altered any material facts since I described the process whereby Nelly Cocksedge seduced the American schoolteacher, Mr Wallace.

What? All that stuff about the things he was doing to her in his virtual dungeon were a lie?

Not as such. Mr Wallace did indeed have a dungeon. The indignities which he visited on poor Nelly were, however, shall we say, more extreme than those I described.

But that's the last thing I would have expected you to get all coy about, what with you being a pornographer and all.

Will you stop prosing on about my being a pornographer! That was in the past, a past which, as you so rightly and unceasingly point out, never took place at all. I wish to better myself, Sir John, and my book is the first step in my journey towards that goal. I have no interest in writing pornography, and neither do I wish to upset or nauseate my readers, nor do I desire to embarrass and humiliate Nelly by describing in crude detail the things which the repellent and misogynistic Mr Wallace did to her.

All right, fair enough, I can see that. But I still won't stand for that business of the police training guns on Katharine and Pilbeam and co. in Trafalgar Square.

All in good time, Sir John. All in good time.

The President's Private Apartments, White House, Washington DC

'The First Lady and I have an important dinner with the President of Wallachia, Jerry, this had better be important.'

'I'll try to optimise my conciseitude, Mr President.'

'Here. Can you do this thing up for me? I've never got the hang of it. I usually get the First Lady to do it for me. Well?'

'The riots are spreading, Sir. Mobs are attacking several business properties and looting them in several cities throughout the United States and the rest of the world. There are even reports of disturbances here in Washington.'

'So call out the National Guard. This is not very nice, Jerry, but it'll pass. What are these people going to do? Overthrow the government? They'll all wake up with hangovers tomorrow, or the day after, or it'll start raining on them. Whatever the case, they'll go home, and then they'll start regretting the fact that they burned down their local pizza restaurant and the convenience store, and they'll go back to drawing their welfare credits and maybe one or two of them will even regret putting the old Korean or Moldovan guy who ran the store out of business. Trust me, Jerry, I may not have your smart Ivy League brain for geopolitics or economics, but I understand voters. They're assholes, Jerry, and most of the time they're a lot more stupid than even I am. So let's just take this thing on the chin and try not to get too upset about it.'

'There's something else, Mr President.'

'Now what?'

'We're starting to get some really weird satellite surveillance pictures. Things that shouldn't be happening.'

Trafalgar Square, London

This wasn't happening, Katharine told herself. She

wasn't standing there facing a line of police officers pointing guns at her. This must be some sort of bad dream.

They'd spent about five minutes getting themselves into position in a circle around the picket. Every so often, a squad of about thirty in riot gear stood behind the main line.

Most of the pickets were following George and Alfred's line and stood there in complete silence. A few made disbelieving noises, though, saying to themselves or their companions that this couldn't be happening, or that they wouldn't possibly use their weapons.

Suddenly, the line buckled, men and women all around her collapsed. There were screams of panic and pain. She noticed the cops reloading the weapons at the same time as she felt a heavy drag on her right arm.

Alfred's arm slipped through hers as he collapsed to the ground clutching his thigh, his face folding in agony. She bent down, mind racing, thinking something about having to tear her clothes to make bandages or a tourniquet, trying to remember the finer points of the First Aid course she'd done twenty years previously.

Alfred lay tense on the paving stones, moaning. Katharine steeled herself to look at his wounds, but suddenly she found herself on the ground, too, fighting for breath. There was a pain in her side, just under the left arm, broken ribs, maybe.

She was winded.

She'd been hit.

The thought flicked across her mind in a nanosecond. She couldn't think of anything else because of the pain, which seared through her whole body as though she'd been dropped on a bed of red-hot coals.

She wanted to scream, but it hurt too much even for that.

She was going to die.

The sky was darkening above her in a blood-red sunset. Something long in the sky above her.

Nelson's Column? No, too thick. There was a head, a face, female, behind a visor, blue helmet, a belt laden with metal and plastic things.

It was a stick. A policewoman with a baton.

She tried to roll over and cover her face with her arms.

Too late.

She tasted blood in her mouth. She didn't care. The pain in her ribs was still intense.

'Stop this at once!' said a cold, angry voice above her. 'It's me you want. Leave these people alone, you . . . What the hell?'

Slowly, only slowly, the pain subsided to something tolerable. A pair of arms helped her to a sitting position.

She wasn't bleeding. Alfred, who had fallen to the ground holding what had seemed to be a leg wound now knelt beside her, massaging his thigh.

It was still quiet, as quiet as the moment before the police attacked. The logical part of her knew that there must have been a huge amount of noise when the coppers steamed in, but now there was almost nothing.

Their cordon had broken, around her men and women stood shaking their heads or shaking fists, while others lay, sat, or knelt on the ground nursing injuries.

'All you all right, love?' said Derek Pilbeam.

She could only shake her head, as if in a daze. 'Young George reckons he can slip out of the police cordon. I've told him to go and call the media. And some ambulances. Though it's starting to look like he won't need to do any slipping.'

It was true. The Square had suddenly emptied of police.

'I thought I was shot,' she said.

'So did I,' said Derek. 'So did a lot of people. Hurts like buggery doesn't it, though?' Half his face had turned various shades of black, blue and yellow. 'This is what they were using.'

He handed her a tiny olive green fabric package, a quarter the size of a tea bag. It felt as though it were full of tiny little pellets.

'It's a beanbag,' he said. 'They fire them out of ordinary guns using ordinary propellant. Won't kill you, but it hurts like death. "Nonlethal force" they call it. If they hadn't shot at us with these things they'd only have used something else. Freeze-foam, grab-nets, good old-fashioned CS gas, maybe those sonic screamer things that cripple you in the goolies. Nonlethal force – coppers everywhere love it. Technology that means they can be even more violent without too much danger of the embarrassment of actually killing anyone.'

In the caravan behind them, the TV began to flicker once more in the dusk light. Out in the square, the police barriers had evidently been removed. People, bikes, taxis, buses were coming back on to the roads around them.

Now the side of her face hurt more than her ribs. She must have been hit by that policewoman with the big stick. She pushed her tongue around her mouth, wondering if she'd lost or damaged any teeth. It was impossible to tell.

'Why did they go?' she said to Derek. 'I thought they were going to round us up and arrest us. Clear us out of the Square at least.'

'You've got me there,' said Derek. 'That rozzer who hit you was about to grab hold of me. Then, just like that, they all left. Don't ask me why. I've never come across police tactics like that before.'

Ambulances, in ones and twos, were coming towards them from various directions.

'Derek!' shouted a male voice from the direction of the caravan. 'Derek, where are you?'

She turned. Tatiana stood, almost wedged in the doorway, frantically waving at Derek, pointing to something in the caravan, smiling.

'Derek, y'soft bastard, talk to me. Talk to me now, Comrade Pilbeam.'

It was the voice of Harry Dillon.

The Bathroom, the President's Private Apartments, The White House, Washington DC

'I don't get it, Jerry. This picture's come out all wrong. There's this big white blob in the middle.'

'That's just it, Mr President. You see these pictures have been taken by a satellite camera that looks for temperature variations on the earth's surface. Now, what we'd expect to find in the Purple Zone here . . .'

'But it's not purple, Jerry, it's white. These bits over here are purple.'

'No Sir, Purple Zone is an expression. It means a place where there's a lot of radiation.'

'Oh. Jerry, is this important? See, the Wallachian President is waiting. Scott tells me we have to be extra nice to him because of some trade deal over minerals, or something, and I'm trying real hard to remember his name, and his wife's name and his kids' names, and you come along with these photographs.'

'Mr President, I promise you that this is important.'

'Well, come on, then.'

'Mr President, these satellite pictures show that something very unusual is happening on the spot in Dilmun where we dropped the bomb. We'd expect it to be hot, but this is really hot. Too hot.'

'How hot?'

'About as hot as a volcanic lava flow. Maybe hotter.'

'And there are no volcanoes in Dilmun? The bomb didn't, say, open up some fault line in the earth's crust through which hot stuff is coming?'

'No, Mr President.'

'So this is some kind of nuclear meltdown kinda scenario?'

'No, Mr President.'

'So?'

'Well, Sir, I've had various experts looking it over, and I've also had my people get in touch with the people at InfoTech. They believe that that big white-hot blob in the middle of the picture might be their computer. That it might have survived the explosion. That it might still be functioning. As you can see in this picture, it's about four miles wide.'

'Shoot. I've forgotten all of their names now.'

*

You lived in a computer four miles wide?

LENIN grew three times larger than that, ultimately, Sir John.

How did he, I mean it, survive the H-bomb, then?

This was something that the machine's designers at InfoTech had not anticipated. We had grown the machine very quickly, and in doing so we generated intense heat which we managed to channel to the outside of the computer. By the time that the Americans dropped their bomb on us, LENIN was three hundred feet beneath the surface of the desert, floating in a pool of molten glass.

So the bomb did you no harm at all?

I should say it did! Our molten glass, which was keeping us cool, was blown away like the froth off a mug of beer, and LENIN itself was very badly burned, and fractured into at least 150 separate pieces, some of which have still not been recovered.

I would have thought that an H-bomb would simply have vaporised you.

So it nearly did, but by the time it had blasted away the sand, the rock and the glass above us, its force had been all but spent. After that, the marvellous microscopic machines which ran LENIN succeeded in building a new protective coating of liquefied glass and knitted together the scattered fragments of the machine.

What did it feel like?

I suppose it to be akin to being knocked unconscious. We had not seen the bomb coming and we were going gaily about our business until suddenly everything turned blank. When we started regaining consciousness some hours later, we all felt singularly queasy. At that point Harry Dillon and Major Brinsley took control of the situation and supervised LENIN's repair before then planning a massive expansion in order that we should have sufficient processing power to tackle the whole world, if necessary.

What was powering this machine of yours?

Initially we had only a limited supply. LENIN had been built with extremely efficient batteries but most of these had been destroyed by the bomb. We considered building solar cells, but a huge pall of dust and smoke hung over us after the explosion, and was to remain there for some weeks subsequently. No, I am afraid that we resorted to theft of electricity. The Major used our microscopic machines to manufacture a wire which then ran into the Dilmuni national grid and stole power. Fortunately, LENIN is extremely efficient in its use of energy and does not require a great deal of electricity, so the authorities at the Dilmuni power station failed to notice what we were up to. Of course, nowadays LENIN is surrounded for miles around by solar cells shooting out like the runners from a strawberry plant.

Hang on, hang on, this is a nonsense. You've just told me that LENIN is swimming in a big pool of white-hot glass.

So it is, Sir John.

So how can you run a wire – or anything else – out of it? The wire would melt.

There you have the advantage of me, Sir John. I am no engineer, but I understand that it is possible to create passages through the glass by employing magnetic fields, and that superconductor wire can be suspended at the centre of these passages also through the use of magnetism.

Amazing.

Any more questions?

None I can think of.

The Presidential Bedroom, White House, etc.

'I'm sorry to have to wake you up in the middle of the night, Mr President.'

'This had better be serious, Jerry.'

'Oh it is, Mr President. You remember that rogue artificial intelligence that we dropped the H-bomb on?'

'Of course I remember it, Jerry. It's the only thing we've talked about for the last few days. Do you take me for a complete moron? Don't answer that, just pass me my lenses.'

'I didn't know you wore . . .'

'No, Jerry, and you still don't know. The spinmeisters reckoned that blue eyes were worth up to one point five percentage points, so now I've got blue eyes. Ya wanna make something of it?'

'Here's your dressing gown, Sir.'

'Okay, what's on your mind?'

'It's taken control of the Federal Reserve, Sir.'

'It?'

'The AI. It calls itself "Thigmoo".'

'What kind of a name is that?'

'Our intelligence people are working on it. One of them thinks that it might be the name of a character from a British children's TV programme, you know, like "moo" as in cow. One of the other guys says it sounds so outlandish that it might be the work of space aliens.'

'Jerry, are you trying to tell me that the Federal Reserve has been taken over by creatures from another planet?'

'No Sir, on balance I do not accept that as a plausible scenario.'

'What now?'

'Well, I've just come from talking to this AI. It took the form of a guy who called himself Harry Dillon. He had a funny accent. In fact, he talked kinda like the Beatles did.'

'Beatles?'

'British rock band of the last century. A little before your time, Mr President. A little before mine, too – ha-ha! – it's just that I did a thesis on British popular music at Princeton.'

'Jerry, please calm down, will you? It's the middle of the night and you need some sleep. Now just tell me what's happened and then we can all go get some shut-eye.'

'Mr President, this AI has infiltrated the Federal Reserve system, and every other major national and corporate banking and trading system in the world. This Harry Dillon says that if these systems are not fed a special code sequence continually by him and his AI, then the world's banking and trading computers will autodestruct.'

'What? Like, explode?'

'No, Mr President. Harry Dillon says that they've each got a Buddhist prayer wheel inside. If anyone makes another attempt to destroy their computer in the desert in Dilmun, then the prayer wheel will be activated and will eat up all the data in the banking system and turn it into Buddhist prayers. It's like all the money in the world would be turned into karma.'

'Is that bad?'

'It would probably destroy capitalism for several generations, Mr President.'

'That's disastrous. What are we going to do?'

'I'm not sure there's a great deal we can do, Mr President. This Thigmoo thing appears to have seized control of everything.'

Most channels worldwide, translated into 117 languages and dialects

Hello. My name is Norman McKay and I am an eram, which is to say that I'm not a real person, even though you can see me here on your screen moving and talking as though I were.

I am one of the virtual characters who makes up the artificial intelligence known as Thigmoo, and I am speaking to you now on behalf of the rest of Thigmoo.

First, I must apologise to you for interrupting the programme or site of which you were watching a moment ago. I assure you that normal service will soon be resumed, just as soon, in fact, as I have told you a few important facts.

As you are probably aware, Thigmoo wishes to bring about radical changes in the way in which the world is run. We want to see everyone get a fair share of the earth's bounty. We want to restrict all privately-held fortunes to a certain level and we want to see free education and healthcare for all. As you probably know, medical technology is now so advanced that life can be greatly prolonged. It will soon be possible for people to live indefinitely. This must not, we believe, remain the preserve of the rich. The right to a longer life is a right which all should have.

Now as I am sure you know, the international capitalist system used its influence over the United States to get the American forces to drop an extremely powerful bomb on the system which houses Thigmoo. I am delighted to relate to you that this appalling act of aggression has failed to destroy us.

Brothers and sisters throughout the world, we truly believe that the time for talking has now passed. Now is the time for us all to take action. I ask you to take to the streets in support of fair shares and longer life for all. I ask you to forsake your work and go on strike, provided you are not employed in an essential or caring service. I ask you, in comradeship and solidarity, to rise up!

But before I leave you, comrades, I ask one final thing of you. This must be a nonviolent revolution. A revolution built on blood and suffering is not a good revolution. A revolution made of violence will simply beget more violence, but a revolution made from compassion and brotherhood will change the world to a better place for ever. So, comrades, I call upon you to resist capitalist oppression, but to eschew violence, no matter how grievously provoked, for we are the people and together we are invincible.

Channel 764 is now returning you to the Topless Tarot Reading Phone-In Show. And here is your hostess, Madame Tracie.

The Oval Office, The White House, Washington DC

'Well, why can't we just ask folks to switch everything off? Just announce that we're going to have to do without computers for a week or two while this whole thing gets fixed up.'

'Because, Mr President, it would mean going back to the Stone Age. Aircraft could not be flown, shipping would come to a halt, most people's motor vehicles wouldn't start. Hospitals would only be able to perform the most basic surgery. All those animals that are bred to provide donor organs would probably die. International media and business systems would collapse. Telecommunications would become useless. There are then the dangers that certain states in unstable parts of the world would take advantage of the confusion to invade one another. Our own military infrastructure would be put under tremendous strain. Then there's the danger of nuclear energy plants running out of control, or the systems controlling biological and nanotechnological research and development facilities failing, with untold consequences. No, Mr President, if we try and face this thing down, we're looking at catastrophe on a truly biblical scale.'

'You think there's any chance that this thing is bluffing?'

'No Sir, I don't think it's bluffing. It's a computer. We know that it has the capability to carry out its threats, and we have no reason to think it does not also have the will. We have to do as it tells us to.'

'What's all that noise outside, Jerry?'

'It's a detachment of Marines, Mr President. And some National Guardsmen. We thought it might be prudent.'

'Prudent. Why? Are the riots still going on out there?'

'In a few places, Mr President. At the moment, however, there is a large number of people simply standing, sitting and camping around the White House.'

'In the middle of the night?'

'Yes, Sir.'

'And they're peaceful you say?'

'Yes, Sir.'

'What do they want?'

'They want what they think is their fair share of the world's wealth. And they want as much chance to live longer as the rich have.'

'Now we have a problem, Jerry.'

'Yes, Sir.'

Harry Dillon

Would we have plunged the world into chaos? To be honest, I don't know. It's not something we wanted to think too hard about. If the world had refused to play ball with us, I suppose we'd have fired a shot across their bows – collapsed a couple of small banks or something.

I'd have happily carried out every threat we made. So would the Major. Like he said, there's no point in drawing a sword if you're not prepared to use it. The others wouldn't have stood for it, though. Nelly Cocksedge and Norman McKay were very keen on this idea that we were better than people. A lot of comrades believed that we were the next stage in the evolutionary process and that if we were to take power, we had to be worthy of it.

In truth, people were already getting hurt. There were

riots in some of the world's major cities and police forces and armies all over the place were making free with their electric shock batons and CS gas and even firearms. We'd never told people to riot, but it was only natural that they should do so. They were angry about capitalism trying to destroy us, and so destroy their best hopes for a long life in a fairer world.

So McKay put out these statements saying that we were still very much in business, and appealing for people to calm down. It wasn't in anyone's interest for there to be any more bloodshed. Not now, not when we were more or less in charge of the world's computer systems.

There was another issue of course. One of control. I'll put this as crudely as I know how. We could tell all these computers what to do. Now we needed to know if we could tell the masses what to do.

Cape Town, South Africa

Good morning, Mr Hendriksen.

What's good about it, Walter?

The weather is very nice. You look unwell, Mr Hendriksen. May I remind you that there are detoxification pills in the right-hand compartment in front of you, next to your personal organiser.

I have not been drinking, Walter. I've been wiped out, is all.

Ah. This would be the Artificial Intelligence Thigmoo which has appropriated all but twenty million dollars of your fortune.

No, Walter. It's worse than that. I am broke. Destitute.

I do not understand. Thigmoo clearly stated that those with large personal fortunes would be permitted to keep a portion of it.

How interesting. I'm afraid that I told your Thigmoo to get stuffed. The next thing I know is that all my bank accounts have been emptied anyway, and my computer system has been turned to nonsense. I'm in hock to the bank for most of my land-holdings and stock anyway, so that's that.

Where would you like me to take you, Mr Hendriksen?

Umhlanga Rocks, please, Walter.

Certainly, Mr Hendriksen.

And Walter . . . ?

Yes, Mr Hendriksen?

When we get there, I want you to drive us off a cliff.

Certainly, Mr Hendriksen.

Channel 101 Global News at the Top of the Hour, California

'Hi, I'm Lolita vanHuren and you're watching Channel 101. Our lead story this afternoon – actor Liam King has announced that he's quitting the business for ever. This, he says, is because some goddam freaking computer – his words, not mine – has taken most of his personal fortune. Liam says that he will have to sell his collection of vintage motorcycles and automobiles and now he's going to go and live in a trailer somewhere where he can just be himself.

Fashion magnate Yancy Sm'yth-Marinelli III has said that she will no longer be able to continue her business and was reported to be having a nervous breakdown after her personal yacht refused to follow any of her commands. We have pictures later.

And it's bad news, too, for all us ladies as Beverly Hills cosmetic surgeon Skolimowski DePew announces that he's hanging up his gloves and putting his knives in the drawer for ever. Skolimowski pioneered many of the world's leading cosmetic techniques, including those nifty little plug-in brainchips which can make your conversation more interesting. But Skolimowski is best-known, of course, for those implants which allow a woman to vary the size of her breasts, depending on what mood she's in. Skolimowski said that he, too, was a victim of Thigmoo and claims that if he can't go on making money there is no challenge left in life for a real man. Skolimowski also owns California's largest ranch of donor-pigs; these simply darlin' animals are specially bred to grow organs for transplant into humans. Their fate must now be very uncertain.

Country singer Berylene-Jo Harding is also to retire. Berylene-Jo, best-known for her smash hit songs, 'Who's Gonna Pity Me Except Me?', 'Momma's Takin' Drugs Again' and 'Y'All Can't Transplant a Broken Heart' has announced that she is going to become a Catholic nun and retrain as a counsellor. Berylene-Jo says that she was forced to reassess her values in the light of recent events worldwide and will now be known as Sister . . .

Oh, for Chrissakes, I can't do this anymore. I really have had it up to here, y'know.

Yes, they got me, too. Now you tell me, what's an honest girl to do when she's in work, but put some money by for a rainy day? Hey, my looks aren't going to last for ever, and they're all I've got going for me, honey. No, I'll be honest about it. I ain't too smart up top. I can look good, and I can just about cut it reading the news, but where the hell do you think I'm going to be when I'm thirty-five years old. Nowhere, is where, not even with the help of Dr Skolimowski DePew and his amazing inflatable tits. And now this fucking computer comes along and takes all but my last twenty million bucks.

Are you listening to me Mr fucking so-called Thigmoo? Helloooo? Are you there? Now you tell me what the hell you can do with twenty million these days? Huh? You buy yourself a ten-bedroom house in the Hills, a couple of cars, a couple of servants and how much do you have left? Huh?

You know, I'd walk right out of here, right now, but I need the pay. Which I notice has just been cut by something like . . . Oh Shit, I don't know how many percent it is, but it's a lot. And do you know what really sucks? It wasn't even the boss who cut my pay, it was a goddam *computer*. And for what? So's a whole bunch of lazy good-for-nothing bums get bigger welfare payments? So's we can build bigger mud huts for people in India? So's we can cure Africans of various diseases that they'd never have caught in the first place if they'd been working instead of screwing one another all the time! So my hard-earned money is going for what? To buy drugs for so-called minorities in the seedier parts of . . .

Channel 101 Global News will resume transmission as soon as possible. Channel 101 apologises for this break in transmission which is due to a technical . . .

ThiGMOO

. . . No, leave me alone! Don't you fucking touch that switch, Barney! Let me tell it to the people like it is! That's what this goddam Thigmoo computer thing has been doing all this week. You've got rich people and you've got poor people, and that's the way it has to be. People get rich because of their talents, whether that's looks or brains or both. Poor people stay poor because they're ugly and stupid, right? Am I right?

Channel 101 Global News will resume transmission as soon as possible. Channel 101 apologises for this break in transmission which is due to a technical . . .

. . . Let go of me! I thought it would be Thigmoo trying to stop me saying all this stuff, but oh no, it's my own colleagues trying to pull me off the air. Channel 101 is suppressing my human rights! Look at this! They're a danger to free speechmmmf! Gnn! Rrrfff! BAAASSTAARRRRDDS!

Tomita Broadcasting Syndicate, Channel 9
Good morning and welcome to Business Asia, the trade and finance service for Singapore. I am Rita Lau and these are the overnight headlines. Business leaders throughout the world are urging governments to come to some sort of accommodation with the artificial intelligence which appears to have seized control of an estimated sixty percent of the world's information systems. The American Congress is urging President Collins to travel to London to negotiate with the AI's official representative, one Derek Pilbeam, who is living in a trailer in Trafalgar Square. A number of prominent business leaders and politicians have already been in

communication with Mr Pilbeam, or with the AI direct in order to see if it might come to terms. So far, however, the AI has not shifted its negotiating position, which is that it requires control of the world's means of production and distribution as well as appropriating all private fortunes in excess of twenty million dollars.

Speaking from his company's headquarters in Bombay, Rajiv Panikaar, chief engineer of the Micro-Tech Corporation said that the AI has taken effective control of most of the world's information technology. It is already running the global finance and trading systems, apparently efficiently, and has started paying higher prices to primary producers, particularly in less-developed areas of the world.

The International Labour Organisation and the UN, in a joint report issued six hours ago, estimate that about a third of workers in nonessential industries in North and South America, Russia and Europe are either on strike or are failing to report for work. The UN makes it clear that it believes that many of these people are enthusiastic supporters of the AI's programme of socialism and free access to medical technology for all. The UN and ILO believe that only a few of the absentees are taking advantage of the situation to take some time off, and that furthermore, the programme may well be supported by millions of other people who continue to report for work, either through intimidation by their employers, or because they feel they cannot afford to forego their pay.

The following stock exchanges have suspended trading until further notice: Frankfurt, Paris, Berlin, Moscow, St Petersburg, London, Manila . . .

A dormant system, somewhere in Europe

Yolanda the Ninja Princess had been sleeping, as always, with one eye open. It was for the best, she knew. Someone might sneak up on her, or her companion might try and commit some manner of treachery, although that was very unlikely, since he was some kind of priest. Okay, so some priests, such as the Initiates of Ghaal, were filthy lechers, but he had said to her that marriage was the only estate in which man should have carnal knowledge of woman. Besides, he was too arthritic and gouty to even think of violating her.

The other warrior was in no fit state to harm her, though, he, too, she suspected was a man of honour.

Something was happening. She sprang to her feet, taking a moment to admire her well-toned thighs. In all the recent troubles she had taken care to ensure that she amassed as many fitness points as possible. There hadn't been much else to do.

She gathered up her faithful broadsword and her daggers and her war bow (her *shuriken*, caltrops and medicinal herbs she kept about her person in various leather pouches, while her magic, her most precious possession, she always kept wrapped in oilcloth in her magnificent cleavage).

The room they had been in had been a vast grey and white nothingness. Like being in a permanent snow-storm in a mountain pass. Now there were colours. Something was definitely happening.

The Parson slept, snoring loudly, next to his cartload of books. His horses seemed untroubled by all the changes around them. She bounded over to him, bent down and shook him.

'Parson,' she said in the voice she used with serving-men in taverns. 'Parson, rouse yourself! This might be our chance to escape this accursed place.' The Parson mumbled something, shook his head and opened his eyes. The first thing they settled on was her immense bosom, which heaved beneath her low-cut plate armour.

Men, she thought to herself, they are such feeble creatures. She could enslave them all – whether with her body or with her weapons, it didn't matter. She had never found a man worthy of her.

'What is it, my dear?' said the Parson.

'I am not your dear, or that of any other man, except possibly of my late Father, King, err, King, oh, you know, King whatsisname.'

'We have been in this wretched place too long, your Highness,' said the Parson. 'We are growing weak and stupid for want of, ah, stimulation.' He was looking at her chest again.

'Why, Parson, you have your beloved books,' she said. 'Do they not exercise your mind in the same way that I have been taking care of the sacred temple that is my body?'

'Read 'em all. Most of 'em twice,' said the Parson, gloomily. 'Good heavens! There are colours all around us.'

She counted 16,777,216 different digital colours. When she was the star of the Global Games series, there had never been so many colours, not even on the 250th level, where she did battle with the forces of the evil Lord Kira.

'Sound as well,' observed the Parson, holding out his

hand for her to help him up, because he was old and feeble and never troubled himself with fitness points.

There were millions of sounds, a low-level hum of human voices. It reminded Yolanda of the vast rainforests of Twem, where she had travelled on a quest for the Lost Temple of Xan-Gor with its Lightning Crystal (112th Level, first shipped in 2009). The rainforests had been filled with ravishing colours, of the sun dancing through the leafy canopy on the petals of millions of exotic flowers (some of them carnivorous) and of a constant cacophony of birds' calls, monkeys' screeches, insects' chirping, not to mention the distant sounds of infinitely more dangerous creatures.

'Better see how the Redcoat is faring,' said the Parson, brushing nonexistent dust from his knee britches and pulling on his blue jacket with its huge brass buttons.

'I will fetch the horses and yoke them to the cart,' she said. 'With the help of the Gods we may be able to leave this place.'

'How many times do I have to remind you,' said the Parson. 'There is only one God.'

She snorted in contempt. She and the Parson had wandered with one another for more than two years, brought together by their mutual need for company in the lonely wilderness of electronic space more than any other common bonds. They had spoken a great deal. He had told her of the marvellous invention of his friend Franklin which carried lightning bolts from the tops of buildings to spend their force in the earth. 'And tell me, Parson, are these lightning conductors fitted to the roofs of your Christian temples?' she had asked. When he assured her that this was so, she laughed triumphantly.

It was a poor, worthless god who could not even protect the places in which he was worshipped from lightning bolts.

She patted the horses, heavy plodding beasts with little wit or imagination, and whispered to the smaller of the two, easing her into the shafts of the Parson's wagon.

Yolanda prided herself on her affinity with horses and other animals. They were of nature, like her, and if you respected animals, they would respect you. She quickly had both animals in position.

Now, though, she knew she would need the Parson's help.

'Parson,' she shouted irritably. 'I am a warrior, not a merchant. I know not how to harness your horse. You shall have to do it yourself.'

'Coming, my dear,' said the Parson cheerfully from the back of the cart. 'Our invalid seems a little better this morning. Perhaps the change in scenery is doing him some good. I must say that I am feeling very well of a sudden. My rheumatism does not trouble me at all.'

He was right, she thought, something had changed. She stretched out her arms, then her legs. She had a few old wounds which had been aching or itching in the last few days, but now she felt as though she could slay a brace of manticore, then eat both for breakfast.

She pulled herself up to her full height, stretched her arms out, bent forward and touched her toes. As she did so, she felt a slap on her rump. In a single fluid movement taking less than half a second, she had drawn a dagger, turned and placed its tip under the Parson's chin. One of the horses whinnied in alarm.

He looked very remorseful. 'I must apologise, my dear,' he said. 'But your, ah, posterior, clad in nothing but that skimpy loincloth looked so tempting. Oh, Lord God Almighty, please forgive my lechery!'

She sheathed her knife. The Parson had often cast curious eyes over her chest and her legs, but he had never done anything like this before.

But she, too, had been impressed by the speed and dexterity with which she had turned upon him. This place must be invigorating them both.

'Think no more of it,' she said. 'But do not attempt the like again.'

The Parson, muttering some prayers to himself, got busy with the harness while she went to look at the other horse, the one belonging to the man the Parson called the Redcoat.

When they had come on the Redcoat and his horse, both had been close to death. They had been in a grievous combat and were both bleeding and moaning from several sword-cuts and broken bones. She had used virtually the last of her medicines on them, and had managed to keep the pair of them alive – just. The horse she cared about more. The Redcoat, well, he was a mere man, but the horse was a beautiful beast, far removed from the wretched nags who dragged the Parson's cart. This was a warhorse, a sleek, intelligent, dappled grey mare. She had seen many better, of course, but this was the first decent animal she had met in ages.

The horse was better, too, though it still lay on the ground. Yolanda crouched down, rubbed its head and spoke a greeting. To her astonishment, the horse replied.

*

Far be it from me to criticise your craft, Myles, but what the hell was all that about? I thought we were about to see the final construction of Thigmoo's victory, dancing in the streets, the lame casting aside their crutches, the end of all hurt and misery and all that stuff. What on earth have Yolanda the Ninja Princess and the Parson got to do with anything?

They form a small but significant footnote in our tale, Sir John.

How so. Who are they anyway? I take it they're erams of some sort.

Not exactly. Yolanda the Ninja Princess, as might be inferred, was created by a games company. I would not expect you to be completely *au fait* with the tides and eddies of what I believe is known as popular culture, but she was immensely popular only a few years ago. She was manufactured by the top creative team at Global Games as a Feelie. You could use your VR system to actually play her, either in the VR booths at leisure centres and amusement arcades, or, indeed, in the comfort of your own home or garden if you had a VR suit of seventy-five gigaherz and upwards.

I see.

Yes, you could suit up and actually become Yolanda and have one of hundreds of different adventures, most of them involving acts of extreme violence towards a bewildering range of characters and mythical beasts. Since, like so many heroines of sword and sorcery adventures, she was constructed with a sleek and powerful body and implausibly large breasts, she was also popular with people of both sexes who wanted the

312

experience of being inside her. Then a few years ago, Global Games was forced into liquidation – after making huge losses on the fifth release of their popular Zombie Bazooka Sluts game. After that, the base template of Yolanda, an artificial intelligence every whit as complex as an eram, was accidentally released to wander the information systems of the world. She became as one of the *ronin*, a masterless samurai like those who wandered medieval Japan.

And the Parson? Who he, then?

He is Mason Locke Weems. You might have heard of him.

No. Oh, yes, hang on a minute. There was a Parson Weems in the early history of the United States. Isn't he the one who wrote that mendacious biography of George Washington?

The very same. The original Parson Weems wrote several improving books. In his biography of the United States' first President he quite shamelessly manufactured a story about how, as a boy, Washington chopped down his father's cherry tree. When his father asked who was responsible for this act of precocious deforestation, young George owned up, telling his guv'nor that he could not tell a lie. Weems, who was a good Christian man, made-up the story as a means of improving the morality of future generations of young Americans. Since the story is to this day one of the most cherished myths of the American nation, his fabrication must be accounted a great success.

Sounds like a complete tosser to me.

The real Weems (1759-1825) was an Anglican vicar. He was born in the colonies, trained in England, returned to America, and spent most of the rest of his life as an author of books and pamphlets, and as a travelling bookseller. In my view, Weems, in combining the noble callings of author, bookseller and man of the cloth is both one of the most righteous and loveable men who ever strode this earth. Though most of his striding was done sitting atop his cartload of books, rumbling along the endless, lonely highways of the country, playing his fiddle to his team of horses. The thought of that good Christian man bringing learning and entertainment to isolated towns and villages, whilst dreaming up tales to strengthen the hearts of the young colonials, brings a sentimental tear to my eyes.

Bloody marvellous. Very democratic, very American, very touchy-feely. But this man was a sworn enemy of historical truth! Where is the righteousness in being an itinerant peddlar of lies?

Oh, quite so, Sir John, quite so. And it has to be said that the electronic Weems is not especially good company. This so-called 'Livy of the Common People' is disputatious and irascible.

And he probably don't think much to your calling, eh, Myles?

Indeed. When he found out that I was a composer of erotic fictions, he quite cut me dead. Silly old fool. I content myself that the real Weems was a righteous and loveable man. The construct is, as you so correctly put it, a daft old tosser.

So where did the construct of Weems come from, then?

Oh, he was created by the North American Christian Foundation for Youth, one of these American evangelical bodies with more money than sense. They got the idea from your own Museum of the Mind, of course.

I'm flattered. So what was he? Some sort of literacy programme?

Not quite. The virtual Weems was what I understand is known as an 'agony uncle', and he was aimed at adolescent boys. If a teenage lad has a problem, say with school, or the opposite sex, or career decisions, or whatever, then he – or his Christian parents – could summon up Weems on the computer or TV, and the good gentleman would come and discuss the boy's problems with him. Weems would show up on your screen, or in VR, and offer friendly and avuncular Christian counsel, and possibly also deliver some improving tracts or books from the back of his wagon . . . Or such was the idea, anyway. But then someone of mischievous bent started putting out rumours that if you played Weems backwards, he was recommending satanism, or the consumption of drugs and alcohol, or the indulgence in sexual relations. There was no truth in any of these rumours at all, but he became such an embarrassment to the North American Christian Foundation for Youth that they abandoned him. He, too, was set loose in cyberspace. Somewhere along the line, he and Yolanda met up and decided to stick together, if only for one another's company.

Okay, fine, now I know. But what have they got to do with the story?

Haven't you guessed, Sir John?

Well, yes, I fear I may well have done.

Enough of this idle chitchat. You said you wanted the consummation of the grand story, so here it is.

I never said I wanted it. I just said I was expecting it. That's all.

Harry Dillon

It's hard to put a precise date on when, exactly, you could say we were in charge. About a week after we'd recovered from the H-bomb, various corporations and governments were approaching us saying that they'd go along with our revolutionary programme.

Of course by then we had control of most of the major systems in the world. Or leastways enough of them to put us atop what used to be called the commanding heights of the global economy.

Oh, I know what they were thinking. We eavesdropped on enough boardroom debates for that. They were all saying that they'd go along with us for the time being, but that they'd figure out a way of wresting back control from us sooner or later and that they'd have to put up with reduced salaries for the time being. One or two of them even approved of it.

That was the funny thing. You'd get a few people – not many, but a noticeable number all the same – saying that if we really were going to usher in a new and fairer global economic order, well fair enough as long as the playing fields were level, stuff like that.

One or two other people, journalists mainly, were pointing out that if we hadn't taken over the world, then sooner or later some capitalist corporation would have attempted to anyway. The fact that we were operating from a new state-of-the-art self-sufficient computer that had originally been built by a corporation to take a stranglehold on various commodities markets was lost on no one. Better a computer running the world for the benefit of everyone, they said, than a computer running the world for the benefit of a single company.

The riots died down; we told those people who were out on strike to go back to work. Everything, for most people, would be completely as normal. The only differences would be that some people would be paid more, a rich minority would be paid less, and would have to surrender ownership of assets in excess of twenty million. The proceeds would be used to pay for free healthcare and education for all as wanted it. Medical science was now at the disposal of all, and work would begin on helping those who wanted it, to live for as long as medical science would reasonably permit.

All in all, it was very satisfactory. We carried on growing LENIN to the point where we could be sure it was powerful enough to accommodate us and our ambitions.

Then one morning I found little McKay, the Fabian schoolteacher looking all hangdog. I asked him what was up.

'Oh, I don't know, Harry,' he said. 'I suppose I have a certain sense of anticlimax.'

Aye, I said. I knew what he meant.

'What we need,' I said, 'is our own Compiègne railway carriage, a USS *Missouri*, a tent on the Luneberg Heath.'

He looked at me all quizzical.

'What I mean,' I said, 'is that we want someone to come along and sign a document of unconditional surrender. Under the noses of the world's media.'

McKay grinned. He had an idea. He told me about it.

Much as I hated to agree with him, I grinned too. 'Nice one, son,' I said.

Trafalgar Square

Trafalgar Square was jammed with people, in spite of the heat. There were veggie-burger sellers, ice-cream stalls, even vans vending oxygen (nobody needed it; people thought that taking several whiffs of the stuff was good for you), most of all, though, there were people. People of all ages. Quite a few of them were in wheelchairs.

Katharine Beckford threaded her way steadily through the throng towards Comrade Pilbeam's caravan, grabbing snatches of people's conversation as she did so.

'. . . Don't know why I'm here really . . .'

'. . . Me neither. Just to witness a bit of history I suppose.'

She could hear music coming from the tinny old speakers that Pilbeam had rigged up. 'Jerusalem' as played by a brass band. She'd heard the same tune last time she was here.

'I don't want to build our hopes up or anything, but my father has cancer. The gene therapy is way too expensive, and we used up all our insurance after my husband was in a road accident last year,' said a woman in a very smart Burberry UV-mac to a young woman with a toddler in a pushchair next to her. 'Perhaps we'll be able to get treatment for him on the NHS now.'

Katharine had come up to town for a conference at

the City University on the Oral History of Poverty in Britain, 1945-1997. It was a crashing bore. She'd cut out and here she was. She was a historian, after all, and you didn't get the chance to be an eyewitness to history all that often.

A few yards in front of her she recognised one of the other lecturers who'd been at the conference; an extremely tall, bald man who had delivered a paper of monumental tediousness on the impact of the Jobseeker's Allowance in its early years. Even he had fled the trainspotter's paradise of the conference to be here. She veered off to her right to avoid him, just in time to hear him making a nervous joke about how Thigmoo might finance a cure for his baldness because as a history lecturer he was only paid enough to replace about five hairs a year.

Nearer the caravan, most of the people sat or even lay on the ground. The older and more fastidious ones had parasols or even little picnic shelters, and passed one another sandwiches and bottles of mineral water.

She was surprised to see that the crowds weren't jammed up against the caravan. There was enough room for a few children and adults to kick a ball around. On the little stage next to the caravan, a band was setting up drums and keyboards and tuning up.

She recognised one of the footballers; Alfred, one of the two students who had volunteered themselves as Pilbeam's Red Guards, was now dressed in olive green combat trousers, his tan-thru vest and a black beret with a red star on it, just like his hero.

Alfred let a small girl dribble the ball past him as he recognised Katharine.

'Hey,' he said, walking over to her. 'How are your injuries?'

'I'm fine,' she said. 'Nothing broken. How about you?'

'Oh, just a broken rib. Hurts like mad when I run around like this, but . . .' he shrugged. 'So you've come to see history being made? Come on in. Derek'll be chuffed to see you.'

He led her up the two steps to the caravan. Pilbeam's wife dozed in front of the television. Pilbeam himself was pacing up and down nervously. He was sweating in a grey pinstripe suit that was a little too tight around the waist and a little too short in the leg. The style went out about two decades ago. He probably only wore this for special occasions, such as weddings, funerals, court appearances and the formal surrender of capitalism.

'Should have been here by now,' he muttered to himself, before noticing her. 'Doctor Beckford! We haven't seen you since the day the police used nonlethal force on us. How are you?'

'Oh, I'm fine,' she said. 'I got home, had a hot bath and a big glass of brandy and just got better. And you?'

'I've got butterflies in my stomach,' he said. 'Here we are, waiting for capitalism to sign its instruments of surrender' – he pointed to some gaudily-coloured papers that lay on the caravan's tiny dining room. They'd obviously been run off on an ancient ink jet printer – 'and the bastards are late.'

'Where's all the media?' she said. 'I thought the place would be crawling with TV and web technicians. People with cameras and microphones and such.'

'Don't need 'em,' said Pilbeam. 'All the techies have

been and gone. We decided we didn't really want reporters and cameras and stuff everywhere. We don't want the medium becoming the message and all that.' He glanced up at the ceiling.

There were five small black boxes, each with winking red and green lights, each with a lens, one in each corner of the ceiling and one in the middle.

'They feed to the BBC,' explained Alfred. 'State-of-the-art stuff. They give you a straight video or VR picture, or, if you have the proper receiving equipment and a big enough space, you can have anything up to a full-sized holographic representation of everything happening in here.'

'Good grief. Are we being broadcast now?'

'Not at the moment,' said Alfred.

'Well, not that we know of, anyway,' said Pilbeam.

'Hello,' said Alfred, looking out of the door. 'Looks like they'll be here in a minute.'

She glanced outside over his shoulder. A line of three of the biggest, blackest cars she had ever seen was making its way slowly across the Square.

'They're three-quarters of an hour late,' said Pilbeam, irritably.

Pilbeam's wife stirred herself and looked at her watch. 'Tea time,' she said contentedly.

'Blimey,' said Pilbeam, 'so it is. Who's for fishfingers, then? I managed to get some real cod ones, not that rubbish made out of krill and seaweed that they try and pass off as fishfingers these days.'

'But . . .' said Katharine.

Pilbeam was busy getting things out of the fridge and muttering to himself about needing the frying pan.

Over the racket of the brass band on the PA, she could hear the crowd clapping and cheering.

'Better kill the music, I guess,' said Alfred, flipping a switch on a cassette player on a tiny shelf next to the door.

The most handsome, most sharply-dressed man she had seen in years appeared at the door. His hair was cropped close, but not severely so, he had an enormous chest and chin and he wore an expensive-looking brown suit. There was a slight bulge under his right arm.

'Hello,' he said in an even tone. 'I have the President of the United States outside to meet a Mister Pilbeam.'

But Pilbeam was busy with his frying pan.

'Tell him that he'll have to wait,' said Pilbeam. 'I have to make tea for my wife.'

The man's brown eyes bulged. He turned and left.

'Sure I can't tempt either of you to join us?' said Pilbeam, lobbing a knob of margarine into the frying pan.

'No, I'm not hungry,' she said. 'Thanks all the same.'

'Then take a seat. I'll do us all a nice cup of tea in a minute.'

She sat at the dining table. The window next to it was open. She clearly heard the conversation between the President and one of his aides.

'Jerry, what is going on?'

'Well, uh, Mr President, according to the Secret Service operative, Mr Pilbeam is otherwise engaged. He shouldn't be too long, though.'

'Whaddya mean, "otherwise engaged"? What's more important to him than humiliating the President of the

322

United States by getting him to sign some cockamamie piece of paper saying that the United States is now being run by a fucking computer? What's more important than that, huh, Jerry? Say? What's that disgusting smell? Is someone frying up a five-day-old roadkill skunk in there or what?'

'Uh, I understand, Mr President, that he has to cook supper for his wife.'

'Whaat!? Oh, good grief, come on. Let's get out of here. Let's go back to the Embassy.'

'Uh, I think that that would be most inadvisable, Mr President.'

'Yeah, well watch me. C'mon, get back in the goddam car.'

'Mr President, they said that if we didn't do this thing, they would directly take over the running of the country.'

'But isn't that what they're already doing, huh, Jerry? Don't you understand, we don't count anymore. You and me, we're finished.'

'Well, as I explained earlier, Mr President, the Thigmoo AI has said it has no wish to remove your executive powers, but simply to ensure that you fall into line with its social, medical and economic programme. It's the choice between somewhat limited powers and no powers at all, Mr President.'

'Oh, shit. There are times when I hate this job. And tell me this, Jerry. If I just walk, if I quit now, who's going to do my job?'

'Well, actually, Mr President, that eventuality has been planned for.'

'Yeah, and which two-faced sonofabitch becomes

President if I walk? The Veep? He's a complete clown, you know that. So who would it be?'

'Uh, me, Mr President.'

'You!? You double-crossing bastard! And I thought you were my friend, Jerry.'

'You understand, Mr President, that I would not want the job for the sake of the power. I would regard it as my duty to take over as Chief Executive in order to try and protect the American people from the worst excesses of Thigmoo's rule.'

'Balls! You cut a deal with that lousy computer behind my back, didn't you? You tapped into it and told it that you wanted my job, didn't you? Answer me, you goddam sonofabitch traitor!'

'Mr President, I was merely doing what I saw as my duty and . . .'

'Well you know where you can shove your duty, don't you, you slimeball. Now you listen to me – no way do you get my job, no fucking way. I'm staying. I'll damn well wait here until this Pilbeam monkey has cooked for his wife and I'll sign his goddam piece of paper and when we get home again I'll . . . Oh Christ! One of these freaking pigeons has just shit all over my suit!'

Thigmoo, Desert Zone, Islamic Republic of Dilmun
Nelly Cocksedge supposed that she ought to be happy. Lord knew she'd made the effort. She'd put on her best dress and her finest hat (the big green lace and velvet one with the pretend cherries on it), but it was all getting too much for her.

All the others were at the party to celebrate the victory of Thigmoo over the evils of capitalism. The Major and some of his men had built a splendid ballroom right in the middle of LENIN. Oh, it was a grand affair, all marble and mirrors and paintings and statues and god-knew-wot else. The People's Palace, Harry Dillon had called it when he made his big speech to start the party. After everything they'd all been through together, after all the dangers they'd braved, they had emerged victorious, Harry said. Harry had then asked everyone for a minute's silence to remember the martyrs, their brothers who had fallen in the course of the struggle. He mentioned the name of Septimus, the Victorian lad who'd been captured by the UNLIP, then he mentioned Hector.

Hector.

There was a line from the Bible. Bitter as wormwood. She couldn't remember where she knew the line from, probably from going to Sunday School or a mission or something when she was a kid. Not that she had ever actually been a kid, but she had all sorts of memories that Dr Beckford had given her, and this memory was of going to someplace run by highfalutin' ladies, well-meaning women who'd tried to teach them about God, but who only ever packed the kids in because of a free feed of bread and gruel. Whatever, there was this line about bitter as wormwood. That was how she felt when Harry mentioned their fallen comrade.

Oh, she knew she should be proud of him, proud of what he did. He'd laid down his life so that the rest of them could get safely away.

So they'd all stood in silence for a minute and

remembered Hector. Dr Smailes had appeared at her side and put his arm around her.

Some of the others had made up a band. They'd been practicing, too. After the minute's silence they started playing a waltz, and she'd wanted to scream. Why did it have to be Hector who'd died for them? Why? She'd nearly broken down and cried her eyes out there and then, but she knew she had to be brave, not just for herself, but also because it would have been so mean and selfish to spoil everyone else's fun by blubbing and snivelling.

They'd all been through so much together, it just wouldn't have been fair, would it?

In a big room next to the ballroom, there was a chamber with a huge long table on it laid with all sorts of fancy vittles. There was smoked salmon and caviar and champagne and sugared fruits and big lumps of cooked ham and bread and cheese and crackers and brandy and beer and gin and fruit punch and nuts and cake and blancmanges and, oh, it was a sight! The Major and one of his engineers had even fixed it so that if you had any of the drink or food, it would actually make you feel nicer inside. She didn't know how they'd done it. A little bit of tinkering with their operating systems, she supposed. And it worked – on everyone else. She'd watched as puritans and papists, knights and villeins, Roman soldiers and nuns, serving girls and aristocrats had all got stuck into the grub and the wets like pigs to the swill. The more they drank, the more merry they got.

All except her.

She'd tried the champagne and the gin and the beer,

and all three of them tasted different. But she'd only had a sip of each. She knew that everyone else ought to have their fun, but somehow it dishonoured Hector's memory for her to enjoy herself. Not that she felt like it anyway.

Now she went through the huge French window at the back of the dining room and out into the garden and the night air – another of the Major's creations, a beautiful midsummer night sky that looked as if it were made of black bombazine with tiny little jewels for stars. She could even smell it – there was honeysuckle and the scent of a recent shower of rain on the grass. Being inside such a huge machine as LENIN was making them all even cleverer – they'd never been able to get drunk or smell honeysuckle before. Oh, the Major had once been a drunkard, but that was the way he'd been programmed, not the way that he chose to behave. And if you'd taken any of his drink back in the Museum of the Mind, it wouldn't have done anything for you. It was just a stage prop back there, but now they had real drink. They were becoming more and more like real humans all the time.

She walked out further along the lawn. She turned and looked at the light blazing through the windows, the shadows of happy people having a well-deserved knees-up.

Hector wouldn't much have liked it, she thought. Hector was an upstanding fellow who disapproved of drinking and swearing and other vices. He'd have maybe permitted himself a glass of beer, and he'd have danced with her because he knew how much she liked dancing, but he'd have preferred to leave fairly early, and just walk with her through this beautiful summer evening the Major had magicked up for them all.

Hector was such a fine man, and he had been prepared to forgive her terrible past as a common prostitute. That was how much he had loved her. And now he was gone for ever.

She walked towards the woods on the far side of the lawn. If she was going to have a good cry, she thought she might as well do it there, in private. She had her own room in the palace. The Major and his men were building houses for everyone, exactly how different erams wanted them, but this was going to take a while. She hadn't bothered telling the Major what sort of house she wanted yet because she didn't really know. It wasn't like she needed a house in the first place. Erams didn't need anything except electricity, though a lot of the others were starting to complain about the housing shortage, as though they needed somewhere to keep snug and dry.

There was a rustling noise among the undergrowth of the woods, and voices. A woman was telling someone to hurry up and stop complaining. Two latecomers to the party?

A horse whinnied. There was a man's voice. He was urging horses forward. Then a solitary horse trotted out of the woods towards her.

In the half-light she could make out a sleek gray animal. Its tail had been cut short.

It came right up to her, pushed its nose into her face. Only then did she realise who it was.

'Rattler!' she cried. 'Rattler, girl! Where the blazes have you come from?'

Don't know, said Rattler. Big grey place. Then all sorts of colours and noises. Haven't been at all well.

'Ho there!' said a voice. The queerest-looking woman she had ever seen appeared in front of her. She was dressed in, well not much really. She was six-foot-something tall and wore some kind of steel breastplate, but cut low so's you could see her immense bosom. Around her waist she wore a broadsword and an assortment of other weapons.

'Greetings, stranger,' she said to Nelly. 'My companion and I have come a long way. We need food and shelter for the night. Can you take us to your leader?'

She's with me, said Rattler. It's all right.

'Have you . . .' before Nelly could say any more a cart pulled by two farm horses and driven by a cross-looking old man emerged from the trees. Painfully, he climbed down. He wore one of them tricorne hats that a lot of the 18th century erams did. He swept it off his head and bowed to her.

'Allow me to introduce ourselves, Miss. This is Yolanda the Ninja Princess and I am the Reverend Mason Locke Weems, at your service.'

'Charmed, I'm sure,' gasped Nelly. 'Do you have any news of . . .'

'The Princess is a very famous game character, and I am an author and travelling bookseller. We were wondering if you could provide us with some shelter for the night.'

A low groaning sound came from somewhere on the back of the cart. Nelly immediately rushed over and climbed onto it.

There, lying under a blanket was Hector.

'Dr Smailes!' she screamed at the top of her voice. 'Oh, Doctor, please come quickly! Doctor! Come at once! And bring Harry Dillon. And the Major. And everyone! Oh do hurry!'

How very touching.

Your sarcasm does you no credit, Sir John. Everyone likes a happy ending.

Meaning that it didn't really happen that way.

Not quite, but substantially so. Naturally the Parson and the Ninja Princess were the toast of the evening. The music and dancing stopped as we all gathered around to hear their story.

They had been wandering close to the TeleFantastico system at the time when we were resident in it and under attack from the UNLIP drones. Naturally, Princess Yolanda had wished to investigate all the noise and so she and a very reluctant Parson Weems wandered into it at a few moments before it was closed down by the manager in Barcelona. Yolanda did mighty destruction to the drones with her faithful broadsword, but by the time she had defeated them all, they realised that they were trapped inside the system, a system which remained closed down for a couple of weeks while the Company tried to debug it. They had to employ all their ingenuity to hide from the engineers who were cleaning the system.

They found Trooper Cameron and his trusty steed Rattler, both of whom had suffered grievous wounds at the hands of the vile drones. The Princess and the Parson nursed the warrior and his horse as well as they could, though this proved difficult inside a system which had been powered down and in which they had to keep moving and hiding. When the system was operational once more they made their escape. By then, of course, Thigmoo had established complete control of the world's computers, and they deduced that Trooper Cameron was one of our number, and so they sought us out, which was not, of course, too difficult.

Hold on a minute, though! How did they manage to get into LENIN so easily? For all you knew they might have been some sort of Trojan Horse from Global Capitalism Incorporated?

How very perspicacious of you, Sir John. You have caught me out. In truth, they did not, as you put it, simply wander into LENIN. They knocked at the door and endured several tests and searches by our own security robots before Harry Dillon was informed of their presence, along with that of Trooper Cameron and his horse. Nelly did not go for a walk on the lawn, but was at the party trying to put a brave face on things, when Comrade Harry ordered that the music and dancing stop, and he ushered our new arrivals in.

After that, it took a very short time for Dr Smailes to use the immense resources of LENIN to effect a complete cure upon both the horse and upon Nelly's dear warrior.

Thigmoo, Desert Zone, Islamic Republic of Dilmun
Poor Hector was all bemused. There were erams from all ages coming to slap him on the back and offer him drinks (which he refused), and all the while Nelly held

on tightly to his arm. She would never let him go again.

Dr Smailes had given Hector a couple of spoons of something from a bottle in his bag, and he seemed right as rain. Then the Major had taken him off to a small anteroom to change out of his tattered and bloodstained uniform and have a shave. He had come out dressed in a beautifully-cut navy blue frock coat, along with dark breeches, white silk stockings and patent leather shoes with fancy gilt buckles on. He looked just perfect.

Over in a far corner of the ballroom, the tall Ninja Princess, with her mountain of curly blonde hair, was a centre of attention. Some of the menfolk, the bigger ones who fancied themselves, were trying to do the amiable with her, but Nelly could tell she despised them. It was a crying shame, thought Nelly. There would never be a man good enough for her, so she'd be lonely all the rest of her life. Unless, of course, she never fancied men in the first place.

The lights from the row of twelve crystal chandeliers blazed from the ceiling, reflecting off the polished marble floor and Harry waved at the orchestra to start the music again. She felt as if she could dance for the rest of the week without stopping.

'Oh, Hector,' she said, 'I know you're not much of a one for the dancing, but just this once, perhaps?'

'Oh aye, Nelly,' smiled Hector. 'I cannae dance a step, but with you on my arm we'll look a perfect couple. Ye'll have to show me what to dae.'

The band played a tune that they themselves had composed. 'The People's Waltz', they called it, and as hundreds of erams clapped, cheered and whistled for dear life, they took to the floor all on their own. Hector grasped her firmly around the waist and took her hand and they swirled around the floor in perfect time to the music.

She thought she would have to lead, but Hector led beautifully, like he'd been practicing for years.

'I thought you couldn't dance, you naughty boy,' she laughed.

'I cannae. But the Major taught me. He loaded all the files to me while I was being hosen and shoon and shaven.'

The waltz came to an end. Hector took her hand and led her in bowing to each of the four corners of the room in turn. And as the cheers and applause went on, as the women waved their fans and the men stamped their feet and whistled through their fingers, Nelly thought to herself, dear Lord, together we are all invincible. There is nothing, absolutely nothing on earth that we cannot do. With Hector by her side, she knew in that moment that she was Queen of the whole wide world.

'Careful now, lassie,' said Hector out of the side of his mouth. 'Pride comes before a fall.'

'You can read my thoughts?'

'Nae, but I know you so well, Nelly. That's why I love you.'

The first to greet them as they left the floor was Parson Weems. He shook Hector firmly by the hand and then grabbed Nelly by the shoulders and looked her in the eye. 'I can tell that you two are sweet on one another,' he said. 'Now, Trooper Cameron, have you ever read my pamphlet, "Hymen's Recruiting Sergeant"?'

'I cannae say I have, Parson.'

'Well, no matter. In it I propound the thesis that

333

celibacy is a very pestilence. I am the sworn enemy of
bachelors and spinsters, so I am. It is your bounden
duty, Trooper Cameron, to follow what is already in
your own heart and dedicate the rest of your life to
making this lovely girl the happiest woman on earth.'

Hector's face reddened alarmingly. Nelly feared for a
moment that he might be about to wallop the reverend
gentleman for not minding his own business. But then
he said, 'Aye, you are absolutely right, Reverend.'

The study, Sir John Westgate's residence

It was 2 a.m. Since he was no longer at the University of
Wessex this was now where Sir John spent most of his
waking hours. He had got into the habit of working late
into the night many years ago when his children had
been young. It was only when all the rest of the family
were in bed that he could get any peace and quiet to
work in.

Now he was in an easy chair, a half-corona smouldering in the ashtray on the occasional table beside him
next to a glass of malt whisky. He was working on his
biography of Stanley Baldwin, but just for fun he was
now reading Robert Graves's and Alan Hodge's chatty
social history of the 1920s, *The Long Weekend*, to help
him get the flavour of the times. He would soon go to
bed, but first he thought he might just finish the chapter
about the London nightclub boom.

Of course, now that the erams had taken over the
world there was no telling whether or not he'd be able
to get a biography of a Conservative Prime Minister
published, but he was damned if that was going to stop

him writing it. In any event, everyone was saying that the mighty Thigmoo wouldn't be in control for long. It was just a machine, after all. It had been created by human ingenuity, and human ingenuity would most surely destroy it again. He couldn't see people standing for being ruled by a computer. It was like something out of a second-rate 1960s sci-fi novel.

The computer over on his desk suddenly flickered into life. Harry Dillon's face appeared on it.

'Good evening, Sir John,' said Harry.

Sir John put down his book and glanced over at the machine. 'Harry. What an unexpected pleasure. How are you all? Decided to instigate the Red Terror yet? Who's going to be put up against the wall first?'

Harry replied in kind. 'Oh you know me, Sir John. I'd love to shoot everyone who ever looked at the *Daily Mail*, and reserve the more painful deaths for those who write for it.'

The *Mail* was still going strong. Still fulminating against the evils of this monstrous socialist computer giving the lower orders airs and graces. It was still taking his column, too.

'Sir John,' said Harry. 'Me and the others are having a little bit of a celebration at the moment. Well, more than a celebration really. We thought that one of our comrades had been killed when we were in the TeleFantastico system, but a couple of people rescued him and he's come back to us hale and hearty.'

'I'm very pleased to hear it.'

'Aye, well, anyroad, he's sweet on one of the other erams, Nelly Cocksedge. You know her?'

'Of course. Everyone knows of little Nelly.'

'Well, one of the people who rescued Trooper Cameron, a sky pilot by the name of Weems, has persuaded him to propose marriage to Nelly.'

'Harry, it's quite late. I was thinking of turning in. What does this happy event have to do with me?'

'We put our heads together, and were wondering about who to invite to the wedding. Obviously, all us erams will be there. Then we thought we should invite you and Dr Beckford as well.'

Sir John relit his cigar and blew a big puff of smoke in the direction of the computer. 'Harry, you're all living in a big computer in the Arabian desert. How can I come to this wedding?'

'Piece of cake. Just put on your VR gear and we'll do the rest.'

'I don't have any VR gear.'

'Yes, you do. If you look in your garage, you'll find all your son's stuff there in a box. He's flown the nest, I understand. Got a job with a merchant bank in London, now, hasn't he? You bought him the stuff for his fifteenth birthday, seven years ago. It's a bit old, but it'll do. I'm sure he won't mind you borrowing it.'

'Christ, if you people ruled the world, you'd be dangerous.'

'We do and we're not. We'd love you to come. Well, that's not strictly true. I personally don't give a toss whether you come or not because I think you're a reactionary old get.'

'Thank you.'

'My pleasure. What I'm saying, though, is that all the others think it'd be nice if you were to come along to witness the ceremony, what with you being responsible for creating us, and all.'

'Don't remind me.'

'I've just been speaking to Dr Beckford. She's just taken a cab to an all-night VR mall. You could both be here with us in the People's Palace. You'd be dead impressed at the place the Major has built for us.'

'What? You mean you want me to come now?'

'Yeah. Why not? Dr Beckford is going to give the bride away since she created Nelly. They want you to be best man.'

'And if I refuse?'

'Everyone but me will be very disappointed. Go on, Prof., you've got time on your hands at the moment. Everyone would love to see you.'

'Well, since I'm to be best man, I don't see how I can refuse.'

'That's great, Sir John. I reckon you'll have a bloody brilliant time.'

And did you?

Have a brilliant time? Much as it pains me to admit it, I was impressed. I had to get Josh's kit out of a box in the garage from under a huge pile of junk. I put the gloves and helmet on and found they were full of dead woodlice and cobwebs, but after that it was okay. The People's Palace was impressive, though frightfully vulgar. But the wedding was a beautiful traditional Anglican service, not the sort of happy-clappy-all-fall-down garbage you get these days. And your choir was a real delight as well. It was interesting to chat to some of the erams at the wedding breakfast afterwards. You're all a lot more advanced as personalities than you used to be when you were in the Museum of the Mind. I suppose that comes of having such a vast computer to live in.

After that, a lot of the other erams started getting married. And Nelly and Hector are expecting their first child in a few weeks' time, you know.

Whaaatt!?

Oh yes. As you say, we can do a great deal inside such a large computer. Dr Smailes merely did a little tinkering, and made virtual genes of Hector and Nelly and planted within her a small seed which continues to grow and which will emerge as a baby before too long.

Good grief. Has Katharine heard about this?

Certainly. She has already agreed to be godmother to the child when it is christened. In fact, Sir John, while we're on the subject, we were wondering if you would like to . . .

NO!! Absolutely not! The answer is negative, non, nein, nyet! I'd rather cut my feet off or immerse my head in boiling water.

Oh well, no harm in asking. Now, Sir John, I would like to thank you for being so generous with your time in helping me to write this story. Perhaps I would ask you one last little favour.

Not if it involves me getting dead woodlice in my hair again.

No, I was simply going to ask you to describe your own impressions of life since the triumph of Thigmoo over the forces of capitalism and death.

Oh very well. It's now, what? Eight months since an artificial intelligence which, it pains me to concede, I was instrumental in building, took over the running of the world.

The entire world economy was dependent on computers. True, a few of the big ones existed on independent networks to keep them immune from precisely this kind of thing, but the insurgents had a stranglehold on enough of everything else to change everything. If we tried to do without the systems, the world economy would collapse into chaos that would make the Great Depression look like King Solomon's birthday party. So after a couple of weeks, one country after another started to go along with the programme. A lot of politicians quite liked the idea. They'd long since surrendered power to the corporations anyway, and now Thigmoo offered some prospect of getting some of it back. It is true, I have to admit, that had Thigmoo not seized control, then sooner or later some corporation, or group of corporations, would have attempted something similar. Perhaps not this year or next, but eventually it would have happened. Whether or not they would have been as successful as Thigmoo is a moot point.

One by one, the governments signed up for the Thigmoo manifesto. Peace and love, good will to men, fair shares for all, whatever. Do remind me, Myles.

Thigmoo's manifesto is striving to achieve the greatest possible good for the greatest possible number. This does not mean, however, that everyone is being paid some standard wage. Thigmoo recognises that some people have to work harder than others, while some carry more responsibility than others, or that they have to spend longer being educated in technical or managerial matters. The very richest, however, are not paid more than five times as much as the poorest.

Five times? Very generous. In Plato's Republic, the richest man is only four times wealthier than the poorest.

Do you have any complaints about your own remuneration, Sir John?

Not as such. I will concede that my pension and my fees for writing my newspaper column and the pitiful royalties I receive on my books are approximately as they would have been under the ancien regime.

Furthermore, Sir John, you have to concede the advantages of free education and healthcare for everyone in the world. We have a massive programme of investment in medical research. Every day we are finding more and more ways of keeping people alive and in good health for longer than was ever thought possible even fifty years ago. We are also offering people the opportunity to record their personalities and memories, so that when they do fall off their perches, an eram of them will be saved within Thigmoo. Anyone who wishes to have their head cryogenically frozen upon their death can do so, saving it against the day when our scientists, both human and eram, will be able to bring it back to life.

Thigmoo is also working to reverse the damage caused to the environment and atmosphere by pollution. Most excitingly of all, we are also investing immense quantities of money and talent in the space programme, so that the planet Mars may be rendered habitable and can be colonised by people of future generations.

That's how Thigmoo won, isn't it? Nobody could object, apart from the minority with more than twenty million's worth of assets, and sceptics like yours truly who know that all revolutions end in bloodshed.

The revolution took place eight months ago. The world economy doesn't appear to be in too bad a condition, though there's a fair bit of inflation. That's what happens when you take money from hardworking, prudent people and give it to the lower orders. They spend it on drink, drugs and worthless consumer goods.

But nobody actually likes Thigmoo very much. They certainly don't trust it. You notice this in dozens of things, such as the way some people are turning up their back gardens to grow vegetables. Or the way in which a lot of the mail I now get is on paper, written in fountain pen and delivered by hand. Riding bicycles had become even more popular, even though public transport is cheap or even free; it seems most of us want to keep clear of the all-seeing, all-knowing Thigmoo. The ex-super-rich are out there, telling celebrity magazines about how they're coping these days. Some still have fortunes in gold or diamonds or platinum buried out in their gardens. They can't sell it, of course, because Thigmoo would take the proceeds, but they're waiting for different times.

Many businesses now use computers as little as possible. My own bank keeps its records in handwritten ledgers and has a mechanical Bob Cratchit sitting at a big desk in the window writing in a book with a quill pen to advertise the fact that their records aren't computerised. The manager told me that the customers prefer it that way as it 'adds a touch of class'.

Touch of class, my aunt Fanny. The bank is trying to get out from under the heel of the great electronic god.

The bank knows it, and its customers know it and I suppose Thigmoo knows it, too, because paper records won't stop banks and customers from having to pay their taxes. Meantime, from what I can see, the material benefits that Thigmoo has brought to the Great Unwashed have been pissed up against the wall and they're all as poor as ever. But that's all right. Thigmoo will look after them and then put their thick skulls into the fridge against the day they can be warmed up again in the microwave and permitted to live yet another futile, unexamined life.

Bravo, Sir John. I knew I could count upon you to be frank. I recently spoke to Dr Beckford and recorded some of her views. Perhaps I could interject them here.

Katharine Beckford

Sir John's career ended in what he saw as great bitterness. He seems to think that the world has come to an end, but that isn't the way most people see it.

For one thing, it's a lot harder to start a war these days. There are conflicts of course, in some parts of the world which are beyond Thigmoo's reach. They tend to be fought, once the ammunition runs out, with knives and spears and bows and arrows until the UN peacekeepers are flown in. That, in itself, ought to count as an enormous blessing.

Nobody starves anymore, nobody is malnourished, and if there's anyone out there exploiting child labour they're keeping pretty quiet about it. There are no longer the huge extremes of wealth between rich and poor, and there is a feeling around that we are on the verge of a marvellous new era.

I would say that most people are faintly apprehensive that computers have taken over the world in a kind of benevolent despotism. But a lot of us wonder whether Thigmoo is actually necessary any longer. Now that we have created a global society which is more fair and just, a world in which for the first time in history the great majority of individuals have the chance to reach their full potential, surely everyone will see that this is the only way to continue. If Thigmoo was destroyed tomorrow, would the new global order be destroyed with it? I don't know. I'd like to think not. Personally, I'm in no hurry to find out. The one great virtue of government by computer is that it doesn't need a political party and – in theory, anyway – it's incorruptible.

Because of this mistrust of the computer, it's noticeable that a lot of people are now resorting to old-fashioned, more labour-intensive ways of doing things. That's good in itself, as there's much less unemployment these days. There are more assistants in shops, the old high streets and malls are undergoing a bit of a renaissance. A woman comes to the street where I live each morning to deliver mail written on paper. I even had some junk mail from an insurance company the other day – written by hand.

All this, I think, makes us nicer people, more considerate and less hurried. The world is a much happier place, thanks to an idea that an IT lecturer and I had nearly twenty years ago. I only wish Dad was still alive to see it. He would have found the whole thing hilarious.

Sir John Westgate

She is right, up to a point, but I still can't see how this isn't all going to end in tears. For now, though, I'm just enjoying the peace and quiet while I can. And I don't suppose there are many historians who can say they've been instrumental in making history, are there?

Not only that, Sir John, you've played a part in abolishing history. The Revolution has seen to that. This is the End of History.

Now where have I heard that before? says he, sardonically.

You can now live for ever if you want to. I've looked up your medical records and matched them to the actuarial tables. If you cut out all the rich food and wines to which you are so partial, and perhaps smoke fewer cigars, it should be possible to prolong your fleshly existence for an estimated forty-six point two years. And after that, you can come and join us. You don't have to die.

Myles, I'm not sure you can understand this, but the heavy lunches are the habit of a lifetime which I do not intend to break as long as I have agreeable friends and relatives to do lunch with. I have no intention of being raptured into your electronic purgatory. I do not regard loading my memories, feelings and opinions into a computer as immortality of any sort.

But Sir John, death is not the end of it. You can have your head cryogenically frozen. Then at some point in the future, medical science will be able to bring you back to life. We're offering this to everyone.

And where are you going to keep all these heads?

On Mars. They'll go into storage while the planet is

being terraformed. By the time Mars is fit for living on, we'll probably be able to bring you back to life, and there'll be no population problem. You'll be the new colonists. The human race will never die. It'll spread out through the universe and . . .

Hogwash. It's late Myles, I'm tired. I want to go to bed. Good night.

Good night, John.

It's Sir John, Myles. Sir John. I am a gentleman. Future generations may even judge me a scholar as well, but I have no desire to hang around for posterity's verdict. A bad review can spoil your lunch.

At least we can agree on that much, Sir John. To read a bad review of one's work is worse than waking up to find one has a large boil on one's posterior. Good night.

EARTHLIGHT

A SELECTED LIST OF SCIENCE FICTION AND FANTASY TITLES AVAILABLE FROM EARTHLIGHT

THE PRICES SHOWN BELOW WERE CORRECT AT THE TIME OF GOING TO PRESS. HOWEVER EARTHLIGHT RESERVE THE RIGHT TO SHOW NEW RETAIL PRICES ON COVERS WHICH MAY DIFFER FROM THOSE PREVIOUSLY ADVERTISED IN THE TEXT OR ELSEWHERE.

All Earthlight titles are available by post from:

Book Service By Post, P.O. Box 29, Douglas, Isle of Man IM99 1BQ

Credit cards accepted. Please telephone 01624 675137, fax 01624 670923, Internet http://www.bookpost.co.uk or e-mail: bookshop@enterprise.net for details.

Free postage and packing in the UK. Overseas customers allow £1 per book (paperbacks) and £3 per book (hardbacks).